BRANDYWINE HUNDRED L
1300 FOULK RD.
WILMINGTON, DE 19803

W9-AVR-619

THE
SAVIOR

THE GENERAL SERIES
by David Drake

The Forge with S.M. Stirling

The Hammer with S.M. Stirling

The Anvil with S.M. Stirling

The Steel with S.M. Stirling

The Sword with S.M. Stirling

The Chosen with S.M. Stirling

The Reformer with S.M. Stirling

The Tyrant with Eric Flint

The Heretic with Tony Daniel

The Savior with Tony Daniel

OMNIBUS EDITIONS

Hope Reborn with S.M. Stirling

Hope Rearmed with S.M. Stirling

Hope Renewed with S.M. Stirling

Hope Reformed with S.M. Stirling and Eric Flint

To purchase Baen Book titles in e-book format,
please go to www.baen.com.

THE
SAVIOR

TONY DANIEL &
DAVID DRAKE

THE SAVIOR

A Baen Books Original

Baen Publishing Enterprises
P.O. Box 1403
Riverdale, NY 10471
www.baen.com

ISBN: 978-1-4767-3670-9

Cover art by Kurt Miller

First Baen printing, September 2014

Distributed by Simon & Schuster
1230 Avenue of the Americas
New York, NY 10020

Library of Congress Cataloging-in-Publication Data

Daniel, Tony.
  The savior / Tony Daniel & David Drake.
      pages cm
  ISBN 978-1-4767-3670-9 (hardback)
  1. Life on other planets—Fiction. I. Drake, David, 1945– II. Title.
  PS3554.A558S38 2014
  813'.54—dc23

                                                      2014020259

10   9   8   7   6   5   4   3   2   1

Pages by Joy Freeman (www.pagesbyjoy.com)
Printed in the United States of America

For my father

—T.D.

THE
SAVIOR

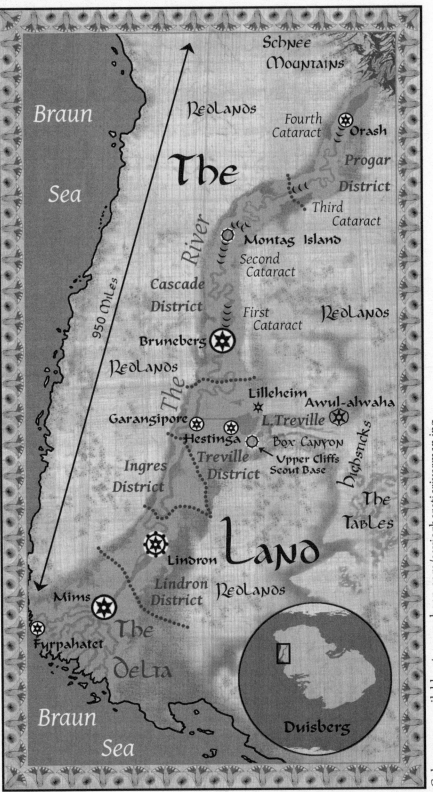

Braun Sea

Schnee Mountains

Redlands

The

Fourth Cataract

Orash

Progar District

Third Cataract

River

Montag Island

Second Cataract

Cascade District

First Cataract

Redlands

Bruneberg

Redlands

The

Lilleheim

Awul-alwaha

Garangipore

L. Treville

Hestinga

Box Canyon

Treville District

Upper Cliffs Scout Base

bigsticks

Ingres District

The Tables

Land

Lindron

Lindron District

Redlands

Mims

The

Fyrpahatet

Delta

Braun Sea

Duisberg

950 Miles

Color map available at: www.baen.com/saviorhereticrivermap.jpg

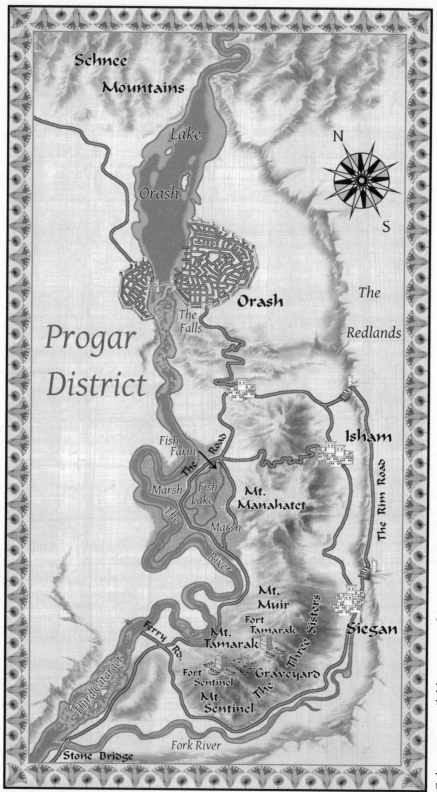

Schnee Mountains

Lake

Orash

Orash

Progar District

The Falls

The Redlands

Isham

Fish Farm

Marsh

Fish Lake

The Road

Mt. Manahatet

Marsh

The River

The Rim Road

Mt. Muir

Fort Tamarak

The Three Sisters

Siegan

Ferry Rd.

Mt. Tamarak

Fort Sentinel

Graveyard

The

Third Cataract

Mt. Sentinel

Stone Bridge

Fork River

N

S

Color map available at: www.baen.com/saviorprogarmap.jpg

Ingres
District

The Road

Von Hoff
Plantation

Entrenchments

Donner's
Landing

The Giants

Tabernacle
of
Zentrum

The River

Lindron

The Road

Lindron
District

Color map available at: www.baen.com/saviorlindronmap.jpg

PART ONE
The Thrust

Eight years after the events of *The Heretic*

1

Ingres District
476 Post Tercium

Three moons hung in the night sky. Churchill, the largest moon, was a quarter-sickle to the east. Mommsen and Levot, much smaller, were chips of fire to the southwest. Both were full. It was, as usual in the Land, a cloudless night.

A bonfire burned in a trampled area in the midst of a near-ripe barley field. Although it was dark, there was enough moonlight for Major Abel Dashian to see as he made his way through the barley and toward the fire to check in with one of the platoons of Friday Company.

The tall barley, a few weeks from harvest, swished against his canvas-wrapped legs, until he got to the edge of the cleared spot where the platoon had camped for the night. When the Guardians of Zentrum were on the march, they used no tents. Each man had a thin sleeping roll laid out on a waxen tarp. Beside each sleeping man was his pack. Each weighed three stones and contained rations, gunpowder in two mountain-dak powderhorns, and wicker containers of percussion caps and papyrus-wrapped minié cartridges. Guardians left their personal effects at home. Abel didn't have many to begin with. The only item that he had any deep attachment to, a lock of his dead mother's hair, he kept in a box in his officer quarters back in the city of Lindron.

The resting Guardians in the barley were spread out around their rifle tripods. Every squad had a wooden rack, and eight

3

musket rifles stood neatly on butt-end in a circle around each rack, their barrels meeting in the crisscross of sticks above the lashing. Each man was only a few steps away from his weapon. There were four squads to the platoon, forming a rough circular pattern around the central cookfire. Two crosshatched paths for walking divided the sleeping men into quarters.

Abel made his way along one of these paths toward the fire.

Friday Company was on the eastern edge of the encampment. There were pickets out a bit farther, but this was the edge of the camp proper. Abel was walking the line, checking vulnerable positions. As executive officer of Third Brigade and aide-de-camp to the colonel that led it, this was his job each evening during the northward march.

He'd been a commanding officer himself in the Regulars just nine months ago: district military commander of Cascade, with the rank of colonel. Then the call had come to assemble all Guardian reserves from the various districts, and he'd returned to his old rank, major. The fact that he served under a man he respected, and for whom he even felt fondness, lessened the sting of relative demotion. Colonel Zachary von Hoff had been his favorite instructor at the Guardian Academy. For the past months, Abel had served as his adjutant and chief of command staff for the Guardian Third Brigade.

It helped that a good many of the lower ranks in the Third were men who had risen through a special selection program Abel had created in Cascade. The chosen men were sent off to the Special Warfare School in Lindron, the noncommissioned version of the Guardian Academy. Abel had been surprised and gratified to find that von Hoff had been on the lookout for his Cascade men and had snatched them up for the Third the moment they finished their Guardian boot camp. There were, then, transplanted Cascade men throughout the Third, men he knew and who knew him.

Although the platoon corpsmen—all men in their teens and early twenties—were bedded down, seven older soldiers remained around the fire. Abel recognized a staff sergeant he knew. He was with the other squad sergeants, and a couple of specialist master sharpshooters attached to the platoon. All of them wore the braided sash and twisted armband of carnadon leather that marked their rank.

The noncoms spoke in low voices, and Abel presumed that they were discussing, as most men did with a day's march behind them, company scuttlebutt, women, pay, the possibilities of loot during the upcoming campaign—and what the hell was going on in the Progar District that was so bad it had caused the Abbot of Lindron to send an army of sixteen thousand troops to deal with it.

Correct. There is talk of the march, and there is also discussion of the relative merits of the various whorehouses of Bruneberg, said a thin, high-pitched voice in Abel's mind.

It was a familiar voice, a voice Abel had heard since he was six years old.

A voice like nightscraper chirps, if they were made of words instead of squeaks, Abel thought. He'd heard more nightscrapers in the past few weeks than he had in years. It was good to be in the field.

These sergeants speculate that there may be a pause near Bruneberg, perhaps an encampment of several days that would be long enough for them to travel into the city proper, conduct experiments in regard to the whorehouses, and compare notes.

The chirping voice belonged to Center, a being who claimed to be an artificial intelligence descended on a traveling capsule from the sky. Center, whom Abel had decided to call "he" long ago, shared a portion of Abel's mind with another ghostly presence: a man named General Raj Whitehall.

The bastards should hope to march on past or the town will drain them of every barter chit they possess, said Raj in a voice so deep it was almost a growl. **If all goes well, on the trip home they'll have a rucksack full of spoils to spend on a proper leave.**

Raj was a rougher being than Center, foul-mouthed on occasion, and most definitely male. He claimed to have once been a conquering general on a planet called Bellevue several hundred years ago and multiple millions of leagues away. Now he was a voice in Abel's mind, an artificial intelligence construct, the same as Center. As forceful as Raj's presence was even now—at times threatening to overwhelm Abel's own will—Abel could only wonder what it would have been like to meet the living general in person.

Abel emerged silently from the barley, surprising the hell out of one of the sergeants who saw a fully armed form materialize from the darkness. Abel might be a commanding officer, but on night duty he carried a rifle himself, slung around onto his back, where it was held by a strap, its bayonet unfixed and strapped in its holder on the underside of the stock. He was also armed with his own dragon, a flare-muzzled blunderbuss pistol held under his belt strap. He carried it on the left side, handle reversed, for drawing. A sword in a scabbard of carnadon leather hung at his left side as well. The sword was a mark of rank, and was generally useless in battle. But it was Abel's concession to tradition, a family heirloom, given to him by his father when Abel had made captain of scouts in the Regulars.

It had not been entirely useless, either: Abel had killed men with the sword. And so had his ancestors.

"Evening, Major Dashian," said the startled staff sergeant, recovering himself and saluting.

Abel returned it.

"Evening, Staff Sergeant," he replied. He knew the man. He came from the Guardian capital garrison and not from the reserve call-ups. What was his name?

Silverstein.

Abel took a knee by the fire. One of the other noncoms offered him a clay cup of steaming hard cider. Abel took it with a nod of thanks. The cider had a burnt taste and was very hot. He held the cup on his upright knee to let the cider cool, and glanced around the fire.

Silverstein was a short man of River Delta stock. The staff sergeant's jaw moved in a regular motion. He was chewing gum. Delta men substituted such gum for the tobaccolike nesh that Abel had grown up around in Treville District. He did not dip or chew himself, but he did smoke a pipe of nesh weed occasionally.

Abel remembered Silverstein because not many of the enlisted from the Delta ever made corporal, much less moved up to a higher rank. He'd inquired and found that Silverstein had made his mark by fighting in a bloody engagement against the Flanagans, the wild tribe of barbarians who inhabited the coast to the east of where the River spilled into the Braun Sea.

"So, Staff Sergeant, how did we do on the march today?" asked Abel. "Do you think we can get another eight leagues out of them tomorrow?"

Silverstein looked up at Abel with a faint smile on his face. "I think they'll do all right, Major," he said. "We have some tired feet and broken sandals, but it's nothing that a good night's rest and a bit of stitching in the morning won't fix."

"Glad to hear it, Sergeant," Abel replied. "Because I think we're going to try for ten tomorrow."

This caused a low groan from the others gathered around the fire, but Silverstein nodded. "We'll soon be in Treville District, where the roads are broad and tended, not to mention much safer, what with your father in charge of the Black and Tans there, sir."

"Yes, should be no need for these whole company pickets in Treville."

Which meant that there *was* a need for such large units standing watch here in Ingres, the less populated district that lay between the districts of Lindron and Treville. Redlander barbarians who wouldn't set foot in Treville, at least in the past eight years after their total defeat at the Battle of the Canal, had shifted their raiding to Ingres.

"Of course, anybody who'd take on an army of Goldies would have to be crazy in any district," another of the sergeants put in. Goldies was the familiar term for the Guardian Corps, whose colors were gold and tan.

"Or desperate," Abel said. He took another sip of the cider and discovered that it had cooled enough to drink. He tipped the cup back and drained it. It was a bit burnt from sitting over the fire too long, but had a familiar and welcome taste from his days as a Treville Scout.

One of the other sergeants looked up and held a dipper full of cider from the pot that was boiling over the fire. "Refill, Major?" he asked.

Swiiiish.

A movement that was not wind through the barley. It came from somewhere off to the side of them.

Silverstein grunted in pain, and dropped the ladle, the cider hissing as it hit the fire.

A crossbow bolt protruded from his neck.

Crackle of barley. Someone out there in the darkness. More than one.

Multiple hostiles at thirty paces north-northeast, reported Center.

Get down, lad! Raj shouted in Abel's mind.

The instincts of his dozen years as a Scout kicked in, and Abel dove for the ground. He immediately went into a roll to pull his musket around to the front, and ended the movement lying prone, his face staring into the darkness beyond the fire ring. He could see nothing, nothing at all.

Dust take it, I've been staring into the thrice-damned fire and lost my night vision.

Whiiiisk!

He might not be able to see, but he knew that sound. Arrowflight.

Whiiisk! Whiiisk!

The unmistakable thunk of more arrows hitting human flesh. No, not normal arrows. Too high-pitched.

You were correct before in your assessment, said Center. **They are crossbow bolts.**

Cries of pain from two other men at the campfire. Abel glanced back over his shoulder, again compromising his night vision. Silverstein was down, grasping at his neck. One of the other sergeants rose up and pawed at his face for a moment, then his arms went limp and he pitched forward into the fire. The other hopped around clutching at his leg. It was too dark to see exactly what was going on, but Abel figured there was a bolt lodged there in his thigh.

With a cry of anger, Silverstein yanked the bolt from his neck. "Bloody hell!" he cried, and ran for the nearest stack of rifles. Before he could get there, three more bolts caught him in the chest and legs. Silverstein collapsed in front of the musket stand, his legs twitching.

Where are they? Abel thought-spoke. *Give me a direction!*

As stated, to the north-northeast, Center replied calmly.

Thrice-damn it, Abel thought. *How am I supposed to know which way is east in this black field?*

Churchill's to your rear, man, and she's in the west, said Raj's deep voice. **You're facing east. Angle to your left.**

The others of the platoon had heard the sergeant's cry. Several started up from their bedrolls and stood—and a couple got crossbow bolts in the back for their trouble. There was moaning and cursing all around.

The fallen sergeant had rolled out of the fire, and it cast its light once again.

"Sentries!" Abel called out to the edge of the darkness. "Keep your back to the flames!"

He wondered if there was anyone out there to hear him. The ambushers may have taken the sentries out first. Or they may not have known about them. Abel found one of the wider paths leading away from the fire and crawled down it as fast as he could. After reaching the edge of camp, he turned to the platoon and called back. "Stay down and get your rifles."

He crawled several more paces into the waving barley. It was only then that he stood up, looked around quickly for any sight of the company sentries, and ducked back down. He crawled another few paces, then popped up again.

There! The silhouette of a man not ten paces away. Could be an ambusher. Abel made his way toward the form as silently as possible. As he approached, he saw the man was facing out and staring into the darkness, moonlight silvering his shoulders. One of the armed sentries, then. Abel let out a low whistle, and the man turned.

"Goldie approaching!" Abel called out in a low but clear voice.

"W-who is it?"

"Dashian," Abel answered. The last thing he wanted to do was announce his rank to the darkness. He crawled closer.

"P-password?" asked the frightened sentry.

Abel had assigned the night's password himself.

"Carnadon Man," he said in a rasping whisper. He didn't want to give the call sign to the ambushers. Then he spoke louder. "Get down. You're making yourself a target."

"Where are they?" the sentry said, and looked around wildly.

"They'll find you if you keep talking!" Abel said more loudly. "Get down, corpsman!"

The sentry came to his senses quickly—he was a Guardian, after all. He sank to a knee beside Abel. And, despite his shakiness, the sentry did not fail to notice the command sash slung over Abel's shoulder, although he couldn't count the knots in the darkness.

"What's the plan, Colonel?"

There's an experienced soldier. He knows when in doubt to use the highest feasible rank.

"Major," Abel said. "First of all, don't look back at the fire. Keep your night eyes. I'll lead us to those bastards, but we need to get in the other pickets if we can."

"There's a rally plan," said the sentry. "But Staff Sergeant usually gives the order."

"Staff Sergeant is down," said Abel. "Call those pickets to us."

"Yes, sir."

The sentry stood up, put a thumb and forefinger together and placed them both in his mouth. He took a breath and blew hard and long. A piercing whistle erupted from the man, as loud as any sound Abel had heard coming from a human before. The sentry followed the long whistle with two shorter bursts. Then he quickly sank back down into the barley beside Abel.

"They'll know it's me and where to look, sir," he said. "I'm standing east quadrant."

Within moments, the other sentries were with them. Abel ordered them all down.

A crunching noise coming from camp. Abel turned, trying to shield his eyes from the firelight. He needn't have bothered. Human silhouettes blocked the light. Several of the men behind had found their weapons and were walking toward them through the barley.

"Stay down, you dickless daks!" Abel shouted back at them. "That's an order! Stay down until we—"

Whiiisk!

Another round of crossbow bolts.

Thunk. Thunk. Thunk. Bolts met flesh. Flesh gave way.

Screams in the night. A muffled cry of anguish. Then the rest of the approaching men quickly dropped on their own accord.

They're down, but they'll still have itchy trigger fingers, Raj said. ***Gold on gold fire waiting to happen, and muzzle flash to blind everyone.***

"Mind your caps," Abel shouted to them all. "Hammers down."

He turned back to the northeast and scouted the terrain ahead.

Sonic spectrum separation complete, Center said. **Running steps discernible. The ambushing group is moving away rapidly toward the rise in the direction you are facing.**

Abel gazed over the tops of the barley plants. There. A low hill. He'd seen it in the daylight and had briefly pondered why it was so much higher than the surrounding terrain—he'd deliberately kept his thoughts from Center in order not to receive a geology lesson. It was a pile of rocks about a fieldmarch high. He figured the stones had been cleared from this barley land over hundreds of years and piled up in a central midden.

He stood up and spoke to the sentries. "It's all right now. Get up. That low hill to the right of Levot—that'll be their fallback point."

"Yes, sir," answered the sentry who had whistled. "Do you hear them, sir?"

Abel turned to him. He couldn't resist. "Don't you? They might as well be a herd of daks," said Abel.

"Uh...no, sir."

Don't tease the lad, Abel. There is nothing for him to hear.

Abel put a hand to the sentry's shoulder.

"It's just my Scout's ear," he said, giving the guy a smile to put him at ease. He turned to the other sentries. "We'll double-time for that hill. Echelon right, keep your sightlines. No verbal unless necessary." He turned to one of the other sentries. "You, what's your name?" He couldn't see faces in the darkness except for brief flashes of the eyes, but the Guardian was sitting in a relaxed position and seemed less rattled than the others.

"Corporal Messerschmidt, sir," the sentry replied.

A Cascader. Son of a Bruneberg tanner, if he had the right man.

Correct. He was sent south from the Bruneberg selection program two years ago.

"Messerschmidt, go back and get the platoon in order. You may be the closest thing we have to a working sergeant. Bring them up behind us."

"Yes, sir," Messerschmidt replied. "I'll see they behave like Goldies." Without another word, the corporal made his way through the barley back toward camp.

"Let's go," said Abel. "I'll take point since I know where we're going."

The three sentries got into position quickly.

"Move out."

Abel swung his rifle back around his shoulder and drew his blunderbuss pistol. He trotted forward, the sentries trailing after him. This would also leave a trampled path in the barley as a path for the remainder of the platoon.

Analysis of aerodynamic sonic signatures indicates an attacking group of six to eight armed men, said Center.

They concentrated their fire, too, Raj put in. **Shows organization. There'll be command among them.**

Concur, Center said. **Behavior indicates a trained unit.**

They'll mow us down if we try to take them head-on. Better to flank them, Abel thought.

Aye, agreed Raj.

Incoming. Center broke in without inflection of alarm—or any emotion at all.

"Down!" Abel called to the sentry nearest himself in a harsh whisper. The sentry passed the word along and then complied with the order.

But the invisible clouds of bolts were not aimed at them.

Another flurry passed over their heads. Mercifully, there was no round of screams to follow it.

Wildfire at shadows. They can't be that *well trained,* Abel thought. *But we are. And Messerschmidt must have the platoon advancing low to the ground. Good.*

Abel waited a moment more to be sure that there was no second wave of fire intended for suckers, then rose up and moved forward another hundred paces. They were nearing the base of the small rise. He signaled to the man behind him to break to the left. They cut diagonally toward the side of the rocky hillock and trotted another hundred paces.

Grouped fire to the right, Center announced. **Well away from our position, however.**

They hear the platoon out there. They don't know we're close, Abel thought.

The ground sloped upward and the barley thinned. The soil underfoot became rocky.

There is a natural alluvial rise beneath the rocky exterior in this place. The hillock is otherwise of human origin from field clearing, Center put in. **Differential soil composition and weathering patterns puts the rise at approximately 10,250 Duisberg years old.**

Okay, Abel thought. *Thanks for that. I don't know how you figured it out but—*

I am able to make use of the contrast ratio between the cones and the rods in your eyes—light receptors—to make analytical calculations for the chemical compositions of the pebbles underfoot. It is a process similar to x-ray spectrum analysis used in physical chemistry—

—but we have no time for this now, Abel thought. The one emotion, the one seemingly not entirely rational drive that Center possessed was an eagerness to share any and all information he had at any given moment. Abel supposed he couldn't blame Center. Information was, after all, Center's primary function and—if he

could believe what he'd been told—Center's very being. To expect Center to know when to shut up was like expecting a carnadon to know when it had eaten enough dakflesh.

They came out of the barley and walked on loose stone. Abel moved his extended palm up and down in a wigwag signal for those behind him to tread as quietly as possible. The sentry behind him passed the order back. They climbed the hill for about twenty paces, and then Abel cut diagonally to his right. He called a halt and motioned for a weapons check. On more than one occasion in the Scouts, he had failed to put in a priming cap, or even to load his weapon, and might have gone into a firefight essentially unarmed had it not been for his captain reminding him to double-check. He thumbed back the hammer on his own pistol and was reassured to see the gleam of the cap on its fire nipple.

He made a quick check and saw from moonlight glint that all the rifles had their bayonets fixed.

"Hammers back. But quiet," he whispered.

Abel cocked the hammer slowly. The others did likewise with their rifles. Rifled barrels or no, these were single shot muzzle-loaded muskets. The first shots had to count. Even for Goldies, with their legendary thirty-blink reloads, getting off a second shot during a charge was unlikely.

That was what the bayonets were for.

Abel led the sentries forward at a trot.

They came upon the group of ambushers from slightly behind the position of the attackers on the hill. When his group was ten or fifteen paces away, Abel signaled a halt. He motioned the sentries to move out of their staggered line and form up beside him. When the sentries had come up, the four of them stood and watched for a moment. The moonlight outlined the shapes of the attackers nicely. Several of the men were cranking their crossbows back. Another of them was standing slightly behind the group, his hands on his hips.

There's the captain, Raj said.

Abel raised his pistol and drew a bead on the man. He knew when he fired he would be temporarily blinded by the flash. He might try closing his eyes, of course, but these weapons were hard enough to aim in daylight with eyes wide open and a steady hand. He would have to count on the flash having the same effect on his enemies as it did on his men and himself.

"Fire!" This time it was not a harsh whisper, but a shouted command. Abel pulled the trigger on his pistol. Its bang was followed by the crackle of the other three muskets.

The man with his hands on his hips crumpled to the ground. Two of the other silhouetted attackers did so as well. This was all he could make out until his pupils widened again.

Three out of four shots on target, Abel thought. *Not bad.* But his men were Guardians, after all. You had to be able to shoot straight just to gain admittance.

Abel tucked his pistol, still hot in the barrel, back into his belt. He momentarily considered swinging his rifle around and taking another shot, but instead drew his sword.

"Ready," he said.

The sentries lowered their rifles to hip height, bayonets thrust forward and gleaming in the moonlight.

"Charge!"

With Abel in the lead, they rushed upon the remaining attackers at a downhill trot.

Abel detected a moonlit glint to his left. It was a line of muskets leaning against man-sized stone upslope from him.

They piled their rifles to the side while they got the crossbows ready. Too much equipment at one time would slow them down. And where are their donts?

Hidden around the back of the hill, Center said.

Abel quickly placed himself between the attackers and their muskets. The sentries rushed in. The nearest attacker turned at the sound of crunching sandals on gravel—and took a bayonet to the stomach.

A man without a crossbow saw the onrushing sentries and cried out. "Arbalests right! No, to the right, thrice-damn you!" Abel thought he detected a Progar accent. The attempted re-aiming move was too quick. The bowmen were confused. Bow met bow with a clink, and some of the attackers dropped their weapons or got them tangled up with another's.

Metallic clinks instead of the clatter of wooden stocks.

The moonlight played upon the weapons.

Bronze and iron, Abel thought. *They're made of metal, except for the stock.* Which meant the crossbows were outlawed by edict. They were nishterlaub, material used in a heretical manner as set down by the Law of Zentrum.

Metal crossbows may as well have been blasphemy.

Even though he understood what Zentrum truly was—an A.I. akin to Center—and knew that the Laws and Edicts of the Land were meant to suppress innovation and maintain an everlasting stasis, Abel couldn't help feeling the crawling sensation in his gut that the sight of nishterlaub evoked.

It had been pounded into him in a thousand Thursday school lessons, after all. Except for permitted weapons, it was forbidden to use metals in combination or for purposes beyond cook pots and knives. To do so was horrible. It was wrong. All technological artifacts must be used in a downgraded manner.

"Nay, nay, forget it, forget it. To the donts," called out the one who had before given the order to turn. "Fall back, you chunks of puke, fall back!"

Definitely Progar—and rural at that.

The attackers turned to run. There were perhaps ten of them still standing. And behind them—

The rest of the Friday Company platoon rose up out of the barley. The click of fifteen muskets cocking froze the attackers in their tracks. Before they could think or move, Abel rushed forward. He grabbed the man who had called out orders and clotted him with the exposed hilt of his sword. The attacker fell to his knees, blood streaming down his face.

"Surrender," Abel called out. "Or die where you stand!"

Slowly, the other men lowered their crossbows. There was something like a collective sigh of resignation that passed among them.

Defeat.

"Mercy," said the man at Abel's feet. "For the love of Zentrum, mercy."

He spoke with the thick accent of a man of Progar.

Abel shook his head grimly. Mercy? That was the last thing the man was going to get.

2

He'd been right. The prisoners spoke in an extreme patois beyond even the normal Progar dialect. With concentration, it was comprehensible to a speaker of Landish, but never easy. Yet it was close enough to the Scoutish patois in which Abel was fluent that Abel could understand the captured men fully. Plus, he always had Center to fill in the gaps with his accurate grammatical extrapolation.

Abel would rather have missed watching the excruciation of the prisoners, but since no one else in Third Brigade headquarters spoke Scoutish, he must be present as an interpreter during the interrogation.

Also there was the fact that his best friend was the Third Brigade's chief interrogator, and he wanted Abel there.

As with all things having to do with the Guardian Corps, there was specialization and professionalism in the ranks, including specialist interrogation squads. The Third Brigade interpreters were led by Timon Athanaskew. Timon had started out as Abel's great rival at the Academy.

Law and Land, we hated one another.

Timon was First Family on both sides, and he didn't see anything wrong with using that fact to get his way when he could. Abel was only First Family on his mother's side of the family, the Klopsaddles. His father was the highest military official in Treville District, but this didn't obscure the fact that Joab Dashian came from a second-tier clan. Such a taint of common blood was enough to mark Abel as lower in status to one such as Timon Athanaskew.

As Abel later came to know, Timon was not to blame for his attitude. Or at least not *wholly* to blame. He had been suckled on the idea that the blood of the ruling class ran in his veins. His brother, Reis, as stuck-up a prig as Abel had ever met, was a priest serving in the Tabernacle inner circle. Reis Athanaskew was a favorite of Abbot Goldfrank, the ruling cleric himself, it was said. The brothers had long planned to be High Priest of Zentrum and Commander of the Guardian Corps, respectively, one day. They considered themselves steward princes of the Land, answerable only to Zentrum.

No matter how high he might rise, Abel would always be only a soldier to the Athanaskew brothers, answerable to the priesthood and high command. In other words, answerable to *them*.

Abel had, at first, believed Timon just another First Family brat raised on privilege and useless when needed most. This was accentuated by Timon's appearance. He was groomed down to the finest hair and always immaculately turned out in his uniform. Yet if he'd stopped to consider back then, Abel knew he would have realized this was impressive in itself considering that no servants were allowed to students at the Academy, no matter what status the students held in the outside world.

Timon had a first-rate mind—Abel soon saw as much in class—but despite both of them being the cream of the crop, the two hardly spoke to one another their first year. It seemed the dislike was mutual.

Then, during the second year at the Academy, Abel ran up against a cabal of cadets—his fellow students—who ran a secret game of carnadon baiting and fighting in the Tabernacle pools at night. They'd made a small fortune in barter chits taking bets on the action from locals.

Abel admired carnadons for what they were: ferocious creatures, never sated, born predators that would kill a man as easily as they could a grazing riverdak. Even so, he hated to see them suffer. The cadets doped the pool water with a scent gland cut from a carnadon female in mating state. Confined in a small enclosure and exposed to such a stimulus, the carnadon males were sure to tear one another apart.

The ring of cadets had tried to draw Abel in, offering him a piece of the action if he kept his mouth shut, but he let it be known he was opposed to what was going on with the carnadons. He gave them a week to end their stupid games or he'd turn them in.

Timon was also against the fights, but on religious grounds. The carnadon was the symbol of the priesthood, of power in the Land. They were Zentrum's beasts, not man's.

In the end, the cabal was outed not by Abel or Timon, but a stupid mistake of their own making. They shorted the pay of the black-market purveyor of female scent glands. He'd sent a goon squad to get the barter chits from them. The cadets had made short work of the goons, killing two of them—the cadets *were* Guardians in training, after all—but the bodies had to be explained. Under interrogation, one of the leaders broke and spilled the whole sorry operation. He was allowed to leave the Academy and return to the Regulars. The other leaders of the gambling cabal were ejected from the Academy in disgrace.

The remainder of the ring couldn't believe one of their own had ratted on them. Instead, they decided that Abel and Timon had betrayed them all. In an attempt to frighten and intimidate Abel and Timon, the remaining members of the carnadon ring had announced the fact that they would take revenge out of Timon and Abel's hides.

Bad idea to announce your intentions beforehand.

The gang caught Abel and Timon on watch duty at the lower pools one day, and attacked. Timon's First Family upbringing included years of martial training, and he'd served as a Regular officer in Lindron's border force. Abel had been the captain of the Treville Scouts. Both were prepared and on the lookout.

It hadn't been much of a fight.

When it was done, four attachés were injured, two with broken limbs, and one had fallen into a pool and been torn to shreds by the Tabernacle carnadons—a fitting fate if ever there was one. After an official inquiry, Timon and Abel had been not only let off the hook for the death but also commended for trying to save the man at their own risk.

From that day on, Abel and Timon had one another's backs. Grudgingly, slowly, their trust grew into real friendship over the next two years.

What Abel had taken for aloofness in Timon was actually a

devotion to justice that Timon took to extremes. Though he was quite religious, Timon also hated dishonesty and the lies of the hypocritical faithful as much as he did slacking off when it came to the Laws and Edicts of Zentrum. Abel had to admit Timon walked the walk better than anyone he'd ever met. Yet Timon's coldness was a fact of his personality.

Abel had not been surprised when Timon chose interrogation as his specialization during fourth year at the Guardian Academy. Being an Athanaskew, he'd gotten the assignment he wanted. Since then Timon had risen to second in command of the secretive Tabernacle Security Service, a special Guardian-priest joint force. He'd been serving there when he'd heard about the coming Progar campaign. Timon had pulled every string he could to get assigned to a fighting unit somewhere. Being an Athanaskew, his request had been granted.

Which was good for us, Abel thought.

He had recommended Timon for the position, and von Hoff, who remembered Timon from his days at the Academy, had backed Abel's choice.

Abel had himself been ordered to a position on Guardian planning staff in the Tabernacle. It was a plum assignment, he had to admit. He'd served for a year before being appointed district military commander of Cascade upon the recommendation of his boss at planning, Colonel Zachary von Hoff. "There are a dozen senior men, but none of them have orchestrated the destruction of five thousand Blaskoye mounted riders," he'd said. "Now go clean that place up."

Timon, for the most part, conducted his dark business bloodlessly. Much of the pain that was his stock-in-trade was brought about by pulling bodies into unnatural positions with hemp ropes and woodblock pulleys. Abel had seen Timon use other methods, however: thin obsidian knives to jam under fingernails and toenails, and smoking hardwood sticks with red coals at the end for the puncturing of eyes.

All the stakes, ropes and pulleys, and other accouterments of the Corps interrogators had always seemed overly elaborate to Abel.

Sadistic, Raj said. ***But effective to a degree.***

Decadent coercion is a common end product of utilitarian social structures within autocracies, Center put in. **Coercion is**

meant to be employed in an impersonal manner for societal purposes only. Yet individuals cannot intentionally give pain to others without personal motivation and personal cost. As the psyche is scarred, evil easily becomes an end in itself. That such practices asymptotically culminate in acts of cruelty is readily apparent within the Seldonian calculus for any who care to make the computations. These involve the integration of a Series A longitudinal for *n* equals any numerated inter-ethical valuation units with a latitude of Series B—

I'm sure you're right, Center, but please let me just take your word on the math.

Timon and Abel had maintained their friendship after graduation, and taken an interest in one another's careers—so much so that Timon had gotten special permission for Abel to accompany him on what he said was an "interesting" interrogation of an accused murderer.

That time, it was the fire coal stick that led to a confession and the location of the murder weapon—a reaping sickle that had been used to take off the head of a lover of the accused man's wife.

"The stick is for show," Timon explained to Abel. Timon and Abel stood by a brazier of coals some distance from the accused. Timon was reheating his coal stick for a final round of questions after waving it closely before the eye of the accused. He glanced back over his shoulder at the sweaty little man tied to the interrogation chair. "Mostly for show."

"Have you ever actually gone through with it? Put one in an eye?"

"Yes," Timon replied, after a pause. "Putting out an eye is one of the initiation requirements for first-year men in the Security Service. We pay the ones we do it to in barter chits. Pay them very well, I might add. Truth is, we have to turn volunteers away."

Timon and his men used a spot near Abel's own bedroll in the command area to conduct the interrogation. There was an irrigation ditch nearby filled with quickly flowing water. It served as both a threat for dunking and drowning, and as a source of white noise to mask screams. The Progar men were lying on the ground. Each was bound hand and foot to two stakes of about a fist's thickness, one an elb from the head, one a similar distance below the feet. The stakes had been deeply planted in the soil by Timon's enlisted team, who had metal-bladed posthole diggers for the task. The use

of metal posthole diggers by the military had ancient sanction. They
had been declared a weapon by Edict of Zentrum.

The stakes were outfitted with wooden pulleys through which
ran ropes tied to the subject's bound wrists and ankles. The
apparatus was obviously constructed by the book, and Timon's
squad went about their task with a ruthless efficiency.

The pulleys had a ratchet action, and the ropes on the Progar
men had been drawn tight enough to suspend them a finger's
width off the ground. It looked terribly painful to Abel. Bones
and cartilage would begin to separate as the ropes grew taut.

**When properly erected, the device is quite capable of pull-
ing a man bodily apart**, Center intoned. **Joints separate before
their containing tissue entirely gives, so it is possible to stretch
without breaking—**

That's really all I need to know right now, thank you, Center.

A younger man with black hair and a sunburned face was the
first to capitulate. He turned out to be the son of the commander
Abel had shot dead. The young man—he was eighteen—was as
angry at being captured as he was swimming in pain.

Timon noticed, and seized on this immediately.

"Your father sold you cheap," he said to the young man. Abel
translated into the Northern patois. These men were from a section
of Progar called Hurth, and the patois was known as Hurthish.
"You know that, don't you?"

Abel translated.

When the man didn't answer, Timon signaled his assistants,
all specialist noncoms. The rope tension was smoothly taken up
a notch.

The young man cried out, bit his lip in an attempt to control
himself, but there was no standing this kind of pain.

Timon leaned down and abruptly shouted into the young man's
ear. "I said, you know that, don't you?"

Abel mechanically translated his words.

"Yair," the man croaked out, his speech slurring into the
Hurthish for "yes."

"Your old man was a fool, wasn't he? Wasn't he?"

Timon didn't wait for a translation, but signaled that the ropes
be pulled tighter.

A moment of hesitation from the Hurthman, and then the
words tumbled out. "Yair and curse his thrice-damned bones!"

"You have a family back home." Timon framed it as a statement.

"Yair. Dar left Mar and the girls, and brung us down here. Now he's got himself killed." Tears welled in the man's eyes, not merely from the physical pain. "What is Mar to do?"

Timon turned to Abel. Abel gave him the gist of what had been said.

Timon nodded. "And you did it for this." He threw a sack to the ground beside the Hurthman. The bag had been found in the saddlebag of one of the donts. Inside were clay promissory notes. These were finger-length clay tablets etched with debt tallies and promises to pay, then the etched glyphs hardened by fire. Barter chits. The money of the Land.

Timon upended the bag and let one of the chits fall into his palm, and another onto the ground. He held the chit before the young man's pain-widened eyes. "For this, your father made your mother a widow. I don't blame you for cursing his name."

As Abel translated, Timon slowly squeezed his hand into a fist. The barter chit in his grasp shattered. This was quite a feat of strength. Barter chits were almost as hard as stone. Timon opened his hand and scattered the shards that remained onto the ground.

The Progar man burst into a shower of curses.

After he had cursed himself hoarse, Timon smiled, emptied the purse, and stomped the remaining chits to smithereens.

"Well, now all that is done." Timon leaned down close once again. "I'm going to ask you some questions. For each one you answer truthfully, I'll have my men let out a notch on the ropes. But I warn you, I'll know if you lie. And when you do, they'll pull those ropes all the tighter."

Timon sat down casually beside the stretched man and tossed the empty bag aside.

"Do you understand?" he said.

Abel left this untranslated. He figured the Hurthman got the idea of what was being said.

"Yair," the young man answered.

"Good," said Timon. He nodded to his men, and took the smallest amount of pressure off the ropes.

The Hurthman began talking in harsh gasps, but spilling out information. Abel translated as rapidly as he could.

The ambushers were a mercenary militia unit from Progar. They had been sent south by one of the oligarchs of Orash, Progar's

capital city. It only took a bit more stretching at the rack before
Timon had extracted the oligarch's name: Bigelow. The Progar
District military commander had long since lost control of most
militia units, if he had ever had it to begin with, and that control
had gone to the local strongmen who ran the district. Bigelow
was one of these men.

Even in Progar there had been news of the Guardian Corps's
muster. Many in Progar had been anticipating a police action.
Nishterlaub materials and methods had long been a staple of
life in Progar, so far was it from Lindron. Lately there had been
experiments done even with weapons. For years, most of Progar
had lived in the knowledge that it might be smited—it was only
a matter of when. Now that time had evidently come.

The attackers had been paid to travel south and find out all
they could. The mercenary group was to observe—and to harass
and slow the Guardians if the chance presented itself—if, and only
if, they could get away without being caught. They had placed
their faith of a sure escape in the accuracy and range of their
metal crossbows, and it had cost them.

A crossbow made entirely of metal except for the stock—a
nishterlaub item, forbidden by Zentrum. A crossbow could be
made of wood; when there was an alternative to metal or technological change, it must be used.

After the fight was over on the rise in the barley and the prisoners were secure, Abel had had trouble getting anyone to pick
up the vile things from where they'd been stacked on the ground.
He finally allowed his men to tie the crossbows on one of the
Hurthish men's dont and lead it into camp, minimizing the time
any must be in contact with the nishterlaub metal of the bows.

So the Hurthmen made their night attack silently with iron
crossbows and then retreated to the hill as a rallying point for flight.
From the looks of their underfed mounts, they had come down
along the grass-bare Escarpment, avoiding settlements and fields.

Center's voice cut into the vision in Abel's mind. **It is highly
likely that the route took them through the Redlands itself.
Observe:**

Sunburnt face, sunburnt body previously pale from Northern
climes. The young Hurthman had a name. It had been woven
into his dont's saddle to mark it as his property.

Center had, of course, noticed and recorded.

That name was Bara. Bara was also the Hurthish word for a type of small and harmless cliff-dwelling flitterdak.

Bara had always hated his name.

His own father had given it to him. To call your only son after a weak and easily frightened nothing of a cliff-hanging creature was low and mean. This may have been the first thing, but it wasn't the last thing his father had done to humiliate him—that was thrice-damned sure.

On the way south, they'd climbed up the Escarpment trail it seemed forever, breathing their own dust and that their donts and pack animals kicked up. Bara rode in the front, just behind his father.

The band was made up of men who lived on the lower portion of the Escarpment in the village of Hurth from which the region took its name. The Hurth clans made part of their living by gathering the eggs of flitterdaks and their carnivorous cousins, the flitterdons, which nested among the Escarpment crags.

The Hurthmen made the other part of their living by engaging in forbidden trading with the Redland barbarians.

This was the reason Bigelow had used them. He needed men who could travel unmolested down Redland paths to spy on the Guardians, and yet who would not look and act like barbarians once they came back into the Valley. So he'd hired a Hurthman militia.

Now they were almost at the Valley Rim. Bara rode behind his father in the line of donts climbing the secret and dangerous paths.

Dar always with his back to me, and expecting me to trot right along, my nose to his ass, curse him. I'm eighteen; I'm my own man, thrice-damn him. I should never have come. I should've put my foot down.

Should've. Hadn't.

But when they returned to Hurth, things were going to be different.

Bara wasn't sure how he would accomplish this, but he was determined to strike out on his own, find some other way to make a living. Maybe he would make the frightening decision to move to the provincial capital of Orash itself, find some kind of work there. Or find another trade in Hurth itself. It was a town, wasn't it, even if only a small one?

They had crested the Rim and ridden a short ways into the Redlands when, seemingly out of nowhere, a force of Redlanders appeared. They were at least fifty strong, warriors of the Miskowski tribe led by a Blaskoye noble from the look of it. The Miskowski wore russet robes, practically the same color as the surrounding Redland terrain. The leader, however, wore white robes edged with blue, the garment of the Blaskoye sheiks. Nowadays no tribe traveled or traded without its Blaskoye overseer sent by the Council of Law-givers and its new chief—a Blaskoye named Kerensky.

I'm my own man. I can turn around now. I don't have to get involved in this.

His father smiled that crooked smile of his and stretched out a hand as one of those Blaskoye rode up. The Blaskoye leader grasped his father's arm in greeting.

They would have a royal escort through the Redlands.

I'm still on the Rim. I can turn around now, go back to Mar and tell her I'll have no more to do with Dar and his heresies. Him treating me like the Blaskoye treat them Miskowski, like slaves.

Then his father motioned Bara and the others forward with a flick of his hand.

Curse him. I can go back now. I will!

But he didn't.

Because he was more afraid of his onrushing choices than he was of the Redland wastes. He may be a Valleyman, but he knew the way of living in the Redlands well enough, knew how to act. The Redlanders treated the Hurthish traders with at least some measure of respect. Here he could be sure of not being taken for a rube, as he might be in Orash. Or as the new village idiot, as he might be in Hurth.

Here in the band of his father, Bara felt safe.

Wretchedly unhappy, but safe.

Safe from the unknown future.

Interpolation complete.

Accurate to the ninety-five point six percentile, Center intoned. Abel snapped out of his vision of the Hurthman's progress. It had lasted, in real time, only the blink of an eye.

"If he's the son of the leader, his name is probably Bara. And I can tell he's been in the Redlands," Abel said to Timon. "The Blaskoye led them down and put them on our flanks."

Timon looked up toward Abel. "What? How do you know that?"

"I was in the Scouts, remember? I've spent time in the cursed place," Abel replied. "Anyway, Bara's a common Hurthish name. It means something like 'Junior.' Ask him."

Timon gave Abel an inquisitive look, but turned back to the young man. He motioned for his squad to crank the ropes up a notch. Timon leaned over, turned the Hurthman's head, and looked the young man straight in the eyes.

"Speak," Timon said. "Speak, Bara of Hurth."

Cursing himself and his father, Bara began to spill all that he knew. Abel translated. After this, Timon sent a runner to notify the regimental commander that the interrogation had reached a critical point. The first of the prisoners had broken.

Colonel Zachary von Hoff had been an instructor at the Guardian Academy, and then Abel's commanding officer for his year in the planning division. Timon may have chosen his specialty after graduating the Academy, but Abel had his chosen for him—by von Hoff.

"Do you think the man who orchestrated the destruction of the Blaskoye horde at the Battle of the Canal is going to get a regular company command? Think again, Dashian."

"My father led the Battle of the Canal."

"And his son understood the use of the nishterlaub breechloaders, drafted the battle plan, and led the Scout charge that broke the final Blaskoye resistance," von Hoff had replied. "I know this because your father told me as much in a written response to my inquiries. You see, I am writing the record of that battle for the Tabernacle archives."

"My father exaggerates."

"I think not," said von Hoff. "In any case, you came into the Academy already a captain. Tradition dictates you leave a rank higher. To give you a company would be akin to military heresy. Not quite a breach of the Laws and Edicts, but close enough in our world. No, your specialty will be planning with an eye toward eventual brigade or district military command."

So, whether Abel liked it or not, von Hoff had appointed himself Abel's mentor. And when the Progar Campaign was announced, the Academy martial instructors had taken their primary posts: as brigade commanders. This was the Goldie way.

Usually brigade-sized units within the Guardians were demobilized for much of the year. Most of the Corps's day-to-day activity was garrisoning the capital and policing the Lindron District in company-sized troops. Brigade-size maneuvers occurred only in the yearly war games and practice drills.

An appointment as a tenured military scholar at the Academy was also an appointment to brigade command staff or higher. It was Goldie tradition that teachers must also be fighters.

As soon as von Hoff had taken up his brigade duties, he'd requested Abel as his executive officer for the campaign. Abel's long and fairly content stint as Cascade District military commander had come to an end, as he'd known it would.

Center had predicted the call up nearly a year before it happened.

Von Hoff is no fool. He knows a good thing when he sees it, Raj had commented when the messenger delivered Abel's new orders.

To accept the commission is a necessary strategic move, Center put in. **Abel will now be in a position to affect long-range outcomes through individual initiative—with proper guidance.**

But you're not going to like this excursion up north, lad, said Raj. *The Goldies are not being sent to Progar to police it or even merely to conquer it. They are going to make an example of the place. You haven't seen that kind of slaughter yet.*

How is that not policing?

If I were in Zentrum's place, with his goals, I would burn the place to the ground and salt the earth with the ashes of the people.

There had been the Progar water heresy, which had been going on for decades. The people of Progar had developed ways to harness the abundance of water and the power of the quickly running streams in their mountainous region. Plus, there were rumors of experiments with metal and weapons even beyond the crossbows of the Hurthmen. There was some sort of modification of the musket underway. Modifying the rifle, as Zentrum had shown in Treville by burning the chief priestsmith, Golitsin, was utter nishterlaub. An unforgivable breach of the Edicts.

It was time to put a stop to it.

When they reached the interrogation site, Timon saluted von Hoff with a hand across the breast.

"Which one?" von Hoff asked, nodding toward the prisoners.

Timon pointed out Bara. "That one, sir."

Von Hoff strode forward and knelt beside Bara. He scowled, but spoke to the Hurthman in a low, friendly tone. Abel had gotten in position to translate, but, to Abel's surprise, his colonel spoke the Hurthish patois tolerably well.

"What I want to know," said the colonel, "is how many other militia bands like yours are there?"

"Want my mar," said the youth, gasping between his words. "Want to go home."

Instead of answering, von Hoff reached out with a hand and placed it on the rope above the young man's head.

"I won't lie to you. Your chances of going home are not good." Von Hoff leaned over and casually applied pressure to the rope. "Now, how many other bands are there? Where are they heading?"

"I don't...know, sir," Bara gasped.

Von Hoff shifted his weight, pressing down harder on the rope.

One of the Hurthman's elbows seem to disintegrate—the cartilage that held the bones parted—and Bara flopped down to one side, his right elbow bent in the opposite direction from its usual fold.

Bara screamed a rasping, almost silent scream, like steam escaping from a pot with a tight lid. Abel glanced at von Hoff. He was trembling, deliberately controlling his breathing, a terrible scowl on his face.

The colonel is not enjoying this, Abel thought.

Von Hoff seemed to have had enough with the young Hurthman. He rose, set his jaw firmly, and moved to another of the staked men.

This man was older. The screams of Bara had agitated him—which had perhaps been von Hoff's purpose. The older Hurthman was grunting and feebly struggling against his bonds.

Von Hoff put a hand to the rope that bound his ankles, pressed down. "The youngster won't answer me, and will die in agony for it. So I'll ask you," said the colonel, still in the patois. "How many others?"

This man bit his lip until blood ran, but then something inside him seemed to crumble and he answered in a dry, choking whisper. "Seventeen that I know of, bossman, sir," he said. Von Hoff eased the pressure, but left his hand on the rope.

"Seventeen bands from Hurth?"

"Yes, bossman, sir."

"Go on."

"The seventeen First Families, they were to put in two bands apiece, the way I heard it. Twenty men each. One to fight and one to go scouting." The man closed his eyes and gritted his teeth. Tears welled from his tightly shut eyes. "For the love of the Law, please remove your hand, bossman, sir."

"All right." Von Hoff pulled his hand back and stood up. "But my officers may have other questions." The colonel turned to Abel. "Anything, Major?"

Abel asked the obvious question. "Is there a general agreement between Progar and the Blaskoye? Do all the scouts travel along the Rim?"

Timon took the colonel's place and touched his fingers against the rope that bound the man's wrists. One tap was enough to send a paroxysm of agony across the man's visage.

"Your answer?" said Timon. He took the pressure from the rope.

The Hurthman cried out, gasped to catch his breath.

"Yes. It is known. The eastern paths are open if Kerensky of the Blaskoye has sent guides."

"So other bands such as this one might be lying in wait as we march," von Hoff said. He smiled grimly. "Well, we know what to look for."

The colonel turned to Timon. "Get him out of that contraption, Captain."

"Yes, sir."

Timon motioned to one of his men, who stepped forward with a knife and followed von Hoff's orders. The Hurthmen lay gasping and moaning on the ground. There was no question of any getting up to flee, even if there were a chance at escape. None of them presently had working joints with which to do so.

Colonel von Hoff brushed the dust from his pants. "I think we're finished here," he said.

"Yes, sir," Timon replied. "And what's to be done with them, Colonel?"

Von Hoff shrugged. "Suggestions?"

Timon answered without a moment's hesitation. "Recommend crucifixion, sir."

Von Hoff put a hand to his chin and considered the groaning prisoners. "Yes, that will do, I suppose."

"I'll see to it, sir."

"No, please, master bossman, sir!" one of the Hurthmen called out. The prisoners may have spoken Hurthish, but they understood the word "crucifixion" well enough. It was the same word in Hurthish.

Von Hoff glanced at the group with distaste, then turned back to Timon. "Captain, pierce those Progar tongues with their own nishterlaub crossbow bolts while you're at it," he said. "That should be a display the locals won't forget. Someone of the Land let them pass through the eastern fields without alerting us, after all."

He turned to Abel. "What was the platoon that was attacked, Major?"

"Friday Company, the Second, sir."

"See that these prisoners are staked along the roadside near the Friday Company encampment. They'll want to see justice done."

"Yes, sir."

Abel showed them the way to the roadside and stood by to watch as ordered.

Timon knew his business. When they reached the spot for the crucifixion, dawn was beginning to break. Timon's interrogation baggage train carried three wagonloads of stakes for crucifixion.

Of course they do. Stout riveroak is scare anywhere north of the Delta.

The stakes were lashed to daks. Likewise, the prisoners had been slung over daks and tied in place as well. Once at the roadside site, the riveroak was quickly drilled and beaten together to form crosses. The interrogation detail used wooden dowels made of heartwood maple from the Delta as fasteners.

By the time they arrived, some of the prisoners had recovered enough to stand upright. These were made to dig holes by the roadside. They were then ordered to strip naked and place their remaining clothes—only a loincloth at this point—and sandals in a pile.

A group of four of Timon's soldiers laid each Hurthman upon his cross. This was done gently, not out of pity, but to ensure proper alignment for the nails that would be driven through wrists and feet.

When his turn came, Bara struggled momentarily, broke free, and tried to crawl away, but Timon kicked him hard, professionally, and the Hurthman stopped moving. This time, Bara's arms were bound to the crosspiece to hold him in place.

Timon's squad worked as a well-honed unit. The backs of the wrists and feet were aligned with perpendicular grooves previously drilled in the crosspieces. Then maple stakes were driven through wrists and through the bone cluster on the top of the feet, out the back, and into the grooves. The result was a neat tongue-and-groove bond that was tighter than mere nails driven into wood might have been.

The prisoners writhed and groaned at first. They were soon made silent when their tongues were pulled out with tongs and a crossbow bolt driven through each tongue's flesh.

Some tried to rip the metal rod through their tongue by pressing it against the inside of the lip in order to rip the bolt out. None succeeded.

Tongues are made of some tough meat, Abel thought grimly.

Upon Timon's order, the crosses were lifted up, along with the men hammered to them. Each cross was dropped into its hole. Stones were piled at their bases to hold them upright. The staked men were perhaps two elbs from the ground, but the distance might as well have been a hundred leagues. Their feet would never touch the earth again while they lived.

Timon had placed them on the western side of the road, facing east. Dawn brightened to day. The sun rose over the Rim, and the crucified men closed their eyes against the sudden brightness.

Abel considered for a moment whether or not to order them blinded in order to avoid the slow torture of the rising sun in their eyes. It went beyond his colonel's orders, and he wasn't sure Timon would do it in any case.

Best not, lad. The sun in their eyes is the least of their worries, said Raj. ***Besides, you still have the dead to bury, don't you?***

Yes, I do, Abel thought. The Friday Company funeral. He'd almost forgotten.

3

Staff Sergeant Silverstein and the three others who had been killed lay wrapped in their own wax tarps. Temporary sergeants had been appointed, and the platoon had eaten breakfast and packed while a detail dug a hole in the middle of the trampled barley field.

Presiding was the squad sergeant who had given Abel the hard cider the night before. He was platoon staff sergeant now, in charge of the entire twenty-five men of the second platoon. Abel learned his name was Grimmett. He had a calf wound, which was treated and bound, but blood still seeped into the bandage and formed a red splotch on the side of his leg. Grimmett had tied his sandal straps over the wound and was going to make the day's march with his men.

Derek Ogilvy, the company captain, was present. They'd been waiting for brigade command staff to arrive. The staff sergeant called his men to attention.

Abel straightened himself as well. Coming to attention was a relief. He had been hunched and tight from watching the interrogation and then the crucifixion, his muscles tensing vicariously with each pulled joint and hammered stake. He raised his right arm diagonally across his breast in the Guardian salute.

"Would the major say a few words?" Ogilvy asked him. This was ceremonial, *de rigeur*. The highest ranking officer present must speak the eulogy.

After a moment of silence by the open grave, Abel spoke the words he'd learned his first year at the Academy in Marching Order and Protocols.

"We are but wheat in the fields of the Law. We are grain in the hands of Zentrum. Let these who have served the Edicts and the Stasis faithfully be commended to the ground."

Abel turned to the assembled men.

"Repeat after me," he said. "We are the harvest."

"We are the harvest."

"We are the Land and the Land is us."

"We are the Land and the Land is us."

And the codes, spoken by Abel alone: "To serve Zentrum is to serve the Land. To serve the Laws of Zentrum is to serve the Land."

Abel made the circled pyramid sign of Zentrum over each of the bodies with his right hand.

"As it is now, it always was, and ever shall be, Stasis without end." He looked up, faced the men. "Alaha Zentrum."

"Alaha Zentrum," they returned. And it was done.

The burial detail dragged each of the dead men by their tarps and, with a yank, dumped them into the hole. The detail carefully folded the tarps and packed them away. A good wax tarp was not an item to part with.

The detail went to work with a will and filled the grave quickly, while the remainder of the platoon looked on until the task was complete. The men of the burial detail then took their place back in formation.

"Shoulder arms!" called the sergeant.

With a clank of metal and wood, the assembled men raised their musket to marching position.

"Right face!"

The men turned.

"By the left, double-march!"

With two abreast, the staff sergeant marched them over the fresh grave in the barley three times, each time stamping the earth down more. No one would disturb these bones, for there would be only a flat bit of bare ground in a field after they were through, soon overgrown with grain. The bodies of the dead would feed the Land. The dead would serve Zentrum's divine purpose even in decay.

Then the sergeant marched them to the road, careful to join it south of the spot where the Hurthmen hung crucified.

When the platoon passed the crucified prisoners, the Guardian troops barely glanced aside. None stopped to gape or gloat. Abel wondered if even his Treville Scouts would show such restraint. He doubted it.

Zentrum's finest.

The same did not apply to the crucified men. Although they could make only grunts and groans, their agonized eyes followed Abel as he moved past them. Bara, the youth, hung crookedly, like a shield that had been carelessly placed on a peg, his tendonless elbow distended on his right arm.

Abel could feel the young man's eyes lingering on his back. He had never so badly wanted to go against the utilitarian path his head told him he must follow.

The boy's agony, his desire to see his mother again, tugged at Abel's heart.

He's like me. He never will.

He glanced back.

I could break his legs; I could cut his throat quickly, Abel thought.

Not advised, said Center. **Observe:**

No matter how carefully Abel did it, there was a witness. He was seen and reported. He'd given the Hurthman an easy way out. He'd disobeyed orders.

The following day, he was brought up on charges. Flanked by two Guardians, Abel found his sword removed, his weapons stowed.

Then Abel was forced to gaze into the suffering eyes of von Hoff as the colonel pronounced judgment on his protégé. There was nothing von Hoff could do. Orders were orders.

Abel's sword was brought forward. Von Hoff laid it next to a stone and broke it with a quick kick to the flat of the blade.

Abel was turned over to Timon for punishment. Friend or not, Timon did not shirk when delivering the one hundred lashes. He could not.

Then, with his back torn to ribbons, Abel was forced to complete the day's march. He was put in ranks and did as his sergeant bid him. He was a private now.

And when the Progar campaign was done, he was nothing at all. For then Abel lay on the field of battle, a minié slug in his brain.

Projection sixty-eight point four percent accuracy, with a seventy-five percent accuracy on similar variations.

A private. So what? Abel thought. *So I'm busted to ranks? And there's a thirty-six percent chance I won't be killed.*

Even so, any chance of your death greater than fifty percent is unacceptable, said Center dryly.

To hell with our present purpose! Abel thought. *Our purpose has always meant Center's purpose, anyway.* He did not preverbalize the thought, the way he did mind-speech that was directed at Center and Raj.

There was a place within Abel's mind that he believed Center and Raj could not reach. It was a quiet, preverbal way of thinking. He'd tested them several times on it, and he was fairly sure he'd succeeded at keeping his secrets. He'd thought things he knew would always get a reaction from either Raj or Center, but not brought those thoughts to the edge of speech. No reaction. Abel called this place within himself the "Hideout."

Still, he could never be sure that pretending not to "overhear" Abel's innermost thoughts while in the Hideout was part of a long game by Center. Yet he believed this was not the case.

When he spoke directly to them, the words were always as if on the tip of his tongue. Not now. Despite his affection for his inner voices, he had spent years perfecting his ability to keep his thoughts from the presences in his mind. The truth was, in the past few years, and after all he'd been exposed to in the capital, they had begun to sound a bit old-fashioned to Abel. A relic of his childhood. As unreal as the Carnadon Man.

In his better moments, he knew this not to be the case, but there were times he couldn't help pondering the possibilities.

This was *definitely* a train of thought Abel didn't preverbalize. Raj and Center possessed the key to motor control of his muscles, both voluntary and involuntary, even if they did not subjugate his will. They could shut Abel down if they deemed it necessary.

Yet—

Center took me inside the mind of Bara. Now I know a person is dying in agony, not just an enemy.

Of course he doubted if Bara would give a damn in cold hell if their places were reversed and it were Abel nailed to the cross.

But that wasn't the point, was it?

Will you stop me if I do it? Abel thought-spoke, this time aloud to the presences.

A man become a brute won't be of much use to us, said Raj.

Abel realized he was speaking to Center, giving Abel the benefit of hearing their reasoning together, which must normally take place in the millionth part of an eyeblink. *After all, human instincts have to be part of the plan, or we're no better than that benighted computer in Lindron.*

A moment's pause. A long moment.

Center had once told him: **I am a fifth-generation artificial intelligence running on a one hundred gigacubit quantum superimposition engine. I complete more calculations per one of your eyeblinks than all the computers of the first millennium of the Information Age could produce together if all of them ran at full power for each of those thousand years. It would be best if you took my projections seriously.**

For Center, a long moment was practically an eternity.

To disregard Center was to open the future. Since he was six years old, he'd lived with Center's plan and his own destiny within it. To step away from that plan . . . was it madness?

Of course it was.

In the usual future of the Land, all roads led to Stasis. Freedom was an illusion. Zentrum shaped all.

But to do this one thing on his own, to do it because it was right and not because it was a means toward an end . . .

Couldn't he have that chance as a man? Shouldn't he?

Finally, Center spoke. **No. I will not stop you**, Abel.

Good then.

Abel quickly left ranks, spun around, and trotted back down the road south. They'd already marched a half a league, and it was a long way back.

All of the Hurthmen were still alive when he got there. Bara's head was two elbs above Abel. The sun was risen fully now, and Bara was attempting to squeeze his eyes shut against it.

Too far to reach if I want to make a clean cut with a knife.

As Abel stood and considered, he could tell the passing ranks of Guardians were noticing him from the corners of their eyes, considering what this major might be up to.

There is no doubt whatsoever that that is what they are doing, said Center.

Abel looked back at the youth. Bara opened his eyes, saw Abel for the first time. He tried to say something, perhaps deliver a curse, but the crossbow bolt in his tongue prevented it.

In case you are wondering, Raj said, **the best method is a bayonet strike through the stomach and into the heart.**

Abel unslung his rifle from the strap on his shoulder. He let his pack drop to the ground in the same motion. With practiced speed, he removed the bayonet from its stowage under the barrel, pushed it into its socket, and twisted the stop pin into the slot on the locking ring.

Fixed.

He looked at Bara. The man was watching him now. Abel considered speaking, maybe attempting to explain, but there was really nothing to say.

He either gets it, or he'll die confused. Either way, the suffering will be over.

Abel put a hand behind the butt of his rifle, and with a hard thrust did exactly as Raj had suggested.

Slicing into the stomach was not difficult, but the bayonet lodged in the thicker muscle of the diaphragm. The crucified man attempted to writhe away from the penetrating blade, but it was no use.

Abel gave another strong push. After the blade cut through the tough muscle, the going became easier. Abel pushed through, no doubt, a lung—and into the heart. A gasp from the stabbed man, nothing more. Abel withdrew the blade. It was followed by a gush of bright arterial blood flowing from the stomach wound, and Abel knew he'd struck home.

When he looked back up, Bara's eyes were fixed in death.

It was a terrible sight. He'd seen many terrible sights in war and skirmishes. Yet this was one that Abel knew would join the personal, hellish collection that contained the special moments of horror that he could not forget.

I knew his name, Abel thought. *I don't know the others of these Hurthmen. But, curse it, now I've got to do the same to them.*

He didn't fool himself into believing any of them would be grateful.

He moved down the line and one by one pierced the crucified men. Only one gave him any struggle, and that was easily dealt with by a wicked twist, then rocking his weight back and forth on the rifle handle.

Soon they were all dead. Abel stood breathing hard. He'd moved quickly, and he was winded. Exhausted.

He had not slept in over a day.

A shadow fell across his back.

Abel turned.

On a large dont with a huge crest of feathers sat Colonel Zachary von Hoff.

Von Hoff held his mount, which the men called Big Green, still, and, with a hand to his own chin, considered Abel.

"I could have you flogged, Major, and sent to ranks," he said. "I expect you know that."

Abel nodded.

"I would even be within my rights to have you executed."

Abel knew military law as well as anyone. What the colonel said was true. "Yes, sir, you could."

Again von Hoff was silent. He shook his head. "But could I do without the man who won the Battle of the Canal? That is the question."

"That was my father, sir."

"That's not the way Joab Dashian tells it," said von Hoff. "No, I think for my own purposes, I can't you spare you, Major. Don't be fooled. It is a selfish decision on my part."

"Yes, sir."

"Now clean yourself off as best you can and go find a mount in the train. You look like you're ready to collapse in that bloody dirt."

"Yes, Colonel."

"Then you will join me at the vanguard," he said. "I'll require your counsel in the days to come, and any example you make by personally marching with the men is now complete."

"Yes, sir."

"We have more killing to do shortly, Dashian. Some in battle, but most of it is going to be pure murder." Von Hoff glanced over at the crucified, now hanging heart-stabbed and dead. "It looks as if you've got a start at that."

After another long look at Abel, the colonel spurred his dont and turned to the north.

Abel stood for a moment until his breathing was under control. He took the bayonet off his rifle, wiped it as clean as he could on one of the dead men's thighs, and slid it back into stowed position. His tunic sleeves were bloody, but it would dry and flake away. He daubed it with a moistened handkerchief.

A thirty-six percent eventuality, said Center. **Remarkable**.

We roll the bones, take our chances, Raj put in with a low rumble of laughter.

Abel pulled on his pack and slung the rifle back over his shoulder.

Corpsmen marched by in their eights. More and more.

When Abel turned for a last glance at the line of crucified men, the blood on the ground and on their torsos and legs was already covered by a layer of dust kicked up by the sandals and boots of the passing Guardians.

PART TWO

The Penance

Six years previously

1

Treville District
The Village of Lilleheim
470 Post Tercium

Mahaut DeArmanville Jacobson had come to love Lilleheim. Ten years ago, she would never have predicted this would happen in a thousand lifetimes. Yet the little village three quarters of the way up the Escarpment had become her home. At first, she'd thought there was nothing that changed here, the same day just like the next. She'd come from Hestinga, which could at least call itself a town, maybe even a small city. Worse, she'd stepped, of her own free will—even if it had been the will of a rather naïve nineteen-year-old girl—into a marriage of epic awfulness.

For months she pined for Hestinga and her family's little cottage of stuccoed wattle. She'd been raised in a mid-level military officer's home, which meant, in Mahaut's case, lots of love, lots of off-the-cuff training in weapons and tussling (especially with her brother, who was two years younger than she), but not very much prosperity. Yet, in so many ways, living in the town made up for this.

Hestinga had riches of its own: merchants, inns, a large temple, and a military garrison. Lilleheim had none of that. It was a farming center, a place to collect olives and olive oil, wine—and grain. Lilleheim owed its very existence to the enormous Jacobson granaries at its center.

Here there were hardly any tradesmen. Yes, there was a cobbler, old Tomy Biteberg, a bakery run by the family Krakauer

43

with its twelve children. People bought their lamp oil from the olive farm run by Jurgen Danziger, the son of Horst Danziger, a man who'd been killed by the Blaskoye when they'd sacked Lilleheim two years ago.

And that was it. There was no store. For that, you had to travel to Hestinga, over a league and a half away. And of course, everyone in Lilleheim, everyone in Hestinga, and people throughout the Land, bought their grain from the Jacobsons. This was now Mahaut's clan.

The Jacobsons were ancient First Family blood. They had settled the village and had ruled it for generations. A Jacobson ran the mill. A Jacobson owned the gargantuan granaries and silos. Her father-in-law, Benjamin Jacobson, held the land around the village for fifty leagues and more. Anyone who farmed it worked for Jacobson as a sharecropper. Anyone who owned their own plot and produced something beyond enough to feed a family had to deal with the Jacobson mill and granary.

Mahaut was married to Benjamin Jacobson's second-oldest son, Edgar. Now she was a Jacobson herself, a land-heiress, as the title went, to be addressed by "your grace."

She'd found that Lilleheim did change. There was the season of blossoms: figs, dates, pricklebrush, sage, columbines, and hyssop. There was the growing season with green grain yellowing to ripeness. And then the brown season after harvest, when the Escarpment had its own variations in color and texture when she finally took the time to look.

There were variations among the people, too. There was the surge of the children into the fields during harvest and planting, back to the Thursday schools each week, back into the village when not required at home, the more well-to-do into the school, the poor children learning a trade, or—more often—running wild through the village lanes.

Before, she'd made a weekly, sometimes daily, trip to Hestinga, where she'd led the Women's Auxiliary to the Treville Militia. She had been a natural selection, growing up as she did in a military family, and also being First Family now by marriage. This had been her excuse to get away from Lilleheim, and she'd blazed a path like few women before her. She'd transformed those mothers, sisters, and wives into a true auxiliary that had done well in the Battle of the Canal. More than just well. They had used rocketry to trap the Blaskoye horde and push them into annihilation of breechloader rate of fire.

She'd kept her position and captain's rank, but in the past few years had slowly allowed the leadership to pass on to others. She'd done this willingly. They were her lieutenants. They would do a fair job, and not let the Auxiliary fall back into its former sewing-circle ways. The Blaskoye raiders were still about, after all, even if they dared not show their faces in Treville.

Truth to tell, she had grown tired of the trek into Hestinga. As Edgar was more and more horrible to her, the other Jacobsons had rallied around her. Old Benjamin, who was a widower, and Edgar's sisters, had come to depend on her first as the de facto mistress of the house, and now as one of the managers of the vast network of grain shipping and trading concerns throughout the land run by House Jacobson. To her surprise, she'd discovered a talent for the task. It was like commanding the Women's Auxiliary, but on a vastly grander scale.

Otherwise, her future was limited. A musket ball had torn into her womb during the Blaskoye siege. She could not have children. But she adored her nieces and nephews, and there were plenty of them tearing around the Jacobson compound. At first, it had surprised her when they came to her with their hopes, their dreams—and their problems. Not any longer.

So she was not taken off guard when Loreilei Jacobson and Frel Weldletter came with the expectant look of those seeking advice into the Jacobson compound's inner garden one afternoon.

Normally no one used the courtyard this time of day. Mahaut knew this well, which was the reason that this was when she usually got in her archery and knife-throwing practice. She liked to do this within the compound so that she could walk the two blocks from her office and be sure to get practice in daily. Her target practice with musket pistol and derringer she conducted a short distance from the village within a dry hammock. Sometimes she did not get to her range for a whole month at a time, although usually she did so weekly.

Within the Jacobson compound, she'd set a target up across the courtyard and was notching the arrow when Loreilei and Frel came bursting through a side door.

The two were trailed by a servant who was trying to stop them—and simultaneously to announce them—perhaps afraid the young people might step in front of a flying arrow. There was no chance of that. She had placed the target cattycorner to the side door, and there was no line of flight that would catch someone near an entranceway. She would have been able to hold up in any case. Now she removed her notched arrow, set the bow down on a bench, and went to greet her niece.

Loreilei and Frel were each a little over fifteen years old now. They were two years away from a terrible ordeal that had almost thrown them into slavery for life. Both had been rescued from the heart of the Blaskoye sheikdom in the Redlands oasis called Awul-alwaha. Loreilei and Frel both bore the scars of their captivity. On each of their faces, cut across their foreheads, was a ragged scar. This was the mark of slavery among the Blaskoye clans.

Loreilei had been abducted from Lilleheim. Frel came from a very different place. He'd been born in the Redlands, the son of the chief of the Remlap clan. It was a clan that had not given in to the Blaskoye when all other tribes were capitulating. They'd taken the chief's son and nearly destroyed his small clan as punishment. That same headman had died in the rescue of Frel. The boy had watched his father's throat being slit before his eyes.

The rescue party had been made up of Scouts of Treville led by Abel Dashian. Among Abel's men was a cartographer named Josiah Weldletter. He had befriended the old headman, named Gaspar, as much as anyone could, and had taken in the boy after his father's death. Weldletter had kept his word, and raised Frel in his house. Weldletter and his wife had not been able to have a child, and over the past year, the couple's pity for the orphan boy had turned to love of someone they now considered a son.

It hadn't surprised Mahaut when Loreilei and Frel had been drawn together once again. After their ordeal in the desert, though, they'd been hurt in ways that only the other might understand. But now here they were together holding hands as they approached her across the courtyard.

Mahaut smiled at them both, but she felt foreboding in her heart.

This is going to be trouble, she thought. *Of course they love each other.*

"It's wonderful to see you both," she said to them as they approached. They both laughed, as if this were funny. She considered, removed the bow from the bench, and sat down herself. The two walked up and stood before her.

"You look very well, Aunt," Loreilei replied.

"'Aunt,' is it?" Mahaut said. "You only call me that when you want something from me, Loreilei. And how are you, Frel?"

"Very well, Land-heiress," the boy replied, using her formal First Family title. "Your grace, we come to ask you for some advice."

"'Your grace' from you, Frel. Alaha Zentrum. All right, then," said Mahaut.

Suddenly Loreilei reached out and took Mahaut's hands in hers. "Oh, Mahaut, Frel and I are in love. We want to get married. He's asked me."

Mahaut didn't say anything for a moment. "I see," she finally said. "I would have thought he might ask your father and mother first."

"You know what my father would have done if we had talked to him, especially if Frel had gone alone to see him."

"But I want to, your grace," said Frel earnestly. "That's why we've come to see you. Could you put in a word?"

"Pave the way, you mean?"

"Yes, Land-heiress. Please."

Loreilei's father was Edgar's brother, Hammond. He was the youngest of the Jacobson sons. He'd traveled all the way to Lindron to find a wife from a First Family, which he had in Loreilei's mother, Adele, and to receive Zentrum's blessing on the match. This was how things were supposed to be done among the Firsts. Mahaut had always considered that it was the fact that, as third brother, he would inherit very little that made Hammond such a stickler for society protocol. Position was his greatest possession. Yet she knew the marriage between Hammond and Adele had turned out to be a happy one, and Hammond, for all his stuffiness, had a good heart—unlike his brother, her own husband, Edgar. Edgar might seem to be a good-natured man, or at least an entertaining man, on the outside, but anyone who knew him well would soon conclude that there was little more than a void of petulance and malice on the interior.

"No, we couldn't do it, Auntie," Loreilei replied. "We talked about it, and we couldn't do it."

"Loreilei, child, have you even considered what this would do to your status?" Mahaut said.

"I don't care about that," Loreilei answered defiantly.

"Well, you ought to," she said. "For Frel's sake."

"You married in from a military family, Aunt."

If only you knew how much I regretted that moment of bad judgment, she thought.

"That's true," she said. "But there's a difference. Do I have to tell you?"

"Because you were a woman marrying a Jacobson man?"

"Yes, Loreilei, that's what I mean," she said. "But it isn't just that."

"She means that I'm a barbarian, I suppose," Frel said, his face reddening in a blush—all except the scar upon his forehead, which now stood out lily white.

"No," Mahaut replied. "Josiah Weldletter has formally adopted you, hasn't he?"

"He has," Frel said. "And I adopted him," he added defiantly. "I've made him an honorary Remlap."

Mahaut smiled. "And you did him an honor. He knows what that means to you."

"Then why can't we—"

"Because you're both fifteen," Mahaut said.

"I could get married at twelve!" said Loreilei.

"But you can't receive a dowry until you're sixteen," Mahaut said patiently. "It's right there in the Edicts for First Families."

Perhaps you should listen better in Thursday school, niece. What else is there to do there? It's not as if you can decide not to attend.

"Do you think my father wouldn't—"

"Child, he can't," she said. She rose and reached out to take both their hands in hers. "I know how it feels. It seems like you'll die if you have to wait, that you'll explode like a rocket. You've probably been together by now?"

Loreilei's skin coloring was too dark to show a blush, but her quick intake of breath told Mahaut all she needed to know. "Lots," she said weakly.

"And you're being careful?"

"Of course," Frel said, a trace of indignation in his voice. "I get the best riverdak skins from the Delta. The apothecary in Hestinga stocks them special."

"Perhaps more than I needed to know," Mahaut continued.

"Yes, your grace."

"But a marriage isn't sleeping together. Bones and Blood, sometimes it doesn't have anything to do with that. You have to look out for each other. And you have to be *able* to look out for each other. Look, you love each other, don't you?"

"Yes, very much, Aunt."

"Then it won't hurt to wait. Give it a year. Turn sixteen, both of you. Loreilei will be able to legally receive her dowry. What are you thinking of doing, Frel?"

"I don't know," the boy answered sheepishly. "I like civil engineering. My father's friend Reidel might give me a start."

"I'm familiar with Reidel," Mahaut said. "And Colonel Dashian, who ought to know, says he's the best."

"So you see, we could make do if—"

"Frel, engineering is all about glyphs and numbers. You can't do that kind of work without finishing school."

Neither replied for a moment, and Mahaut was beginning to think she'd won her point.

Then Loreilei spoke up in a disappointed tone. "We thought you'd be on our side, Mahaut."

"But I am, child. You know that."

"You won't breathe a word of this to Father or Mother?"

Do you know what you are asking me? Do you know how much such a promise might cost me? Of course not. You're both fifteen.

"You have my word."

"Good."

"Loreilei, please don't be angry."

"I'm not," said the girl. "Never at you." She pulled Frel's hand away from Mahaut's. "Come on, let's let my aunt get back to her archery practice. Thank you, Aunt."

"Your Gracious Excellency, Land-heiress Jacobson," Frel said with a formal bow. It was all Mahaut could do to keep from giggling at his seriousness.

The two of them took a few steps down the pathway through the courtyard flower garden. Loreilei turned among the desert sunflowers, still in bloom though it was late summer. She caught Mahaut's eye and spoke in a firm and measured voice.

"I was a slave, you know," she said. "Look at me. Look at this, Aunt." She ran a finger along her scar. "I can never forget."

Mahaut stood silent. She blinked a tear from her eye that had suddenly welled up.

Your being taken a slave was my fault, she thought. *I will never forget, either.*

"It made me...different inside," she said. "I won't be told what to do. Not ever again. Because if I let anybody tell me what to do, it will all come back. I know it will. I can feel it."

Mahaut took a step forward. "Loreilei, as long as I breathe, I will do everything I can to see that you are free."

"We'll be together," her niece said. "You'll see."

She spun quickly, and the two left the courtyard.

Mahaut stood thinking a long time after they were gone. Then she turned and picked up her bow and arrow once again.

Everything could end badly, she thought. *Best to be prepared.*

She picked up her bow and took the arrow from the quiver. These were Scout arrows she had brought in from Hestinga. She ran her thumb along the arrow's fletching. Two notches.

Shorter range. More damage in the barbed metal point.

She nocked the arrow, pulled the string back with a practiced strength, took aim.

She let the arrow fly.

It entered the straw bale somewhere to the left of the bull's-eye. Close enough to pierce a lung if not the heart.

2

Benjamin Jacobson didn't fool himself. He might love his son, but he knew full well that he and his wife had given birth to a monster. Yet what Benjamin remembered, what he clung to, was that little boy of four or five who had seemed like any other child.

Benjamin had doted on him, made Edgar his heart's darling, even, he had to admit, above his younger brother, Hammond, who suffered the misfortune of coming along in Edgar's wake. Edgar's older brother, Solon, Benjamin had to be harder on. Solon would be the inheritor of the Family's interest. Benjamin could afford to pamper a second child, and he did. When Edgar began to have his fits of rage, Benjamin, at first, considered them amusing.

Then servants began to be hurt. A string of teaching masters began to resign. Then came Edgar's teenage years, and Edgar discovered that he was rich and the world would indulge him in just about anything he cared to do. He began to look upon this indulgence as a right, and not, as Benjamin did, as earned by the hard work of keeping the grain flowing in a hungry land. But monster or not, Edgar was a Jacobson, and for Benjamin that was more important.

About the only thing Edgar had ever done to his credit was to marry the DeArmanville girl. She had proved herself time and again an asset to the family. She had an eye for figures, and she had become the manager of the household just by demonstrating her sheer competence at juggling tradesmen, servants, and family members. He had to admit she did so as well as his deceased wife ever had, probably better. The servants respected Mahaut. The grandchildren adored her. And even though she had the odd hobby of organizing that cursed women's auxiliary in Hestinga, it usually only took her away from Lilleheim two or three days of the month. Lately, there had even been signs that she was giving up on this nonsense, in any case.

After she'd gotten the house in order, he'd discovered her eye for business. *His* business—the getting and selling of grain. Now she managed the household from an office at the granary. It was a secondary occupation that she seemed to handle with ease. At the granary, she'd moved from bookkeeper to advisor to decision maker. He'd put her in charge of House Jacobson Shipping. When it came to shipment sizes, the juggling of current and future orders against supply, timing when to sell, when to hold, Mahaut made the call.

He was beginning to suspect that she was not only better than his dear wife at running the house, she might be better than *him* at running the conglomerate of businesses up and down the River that was House Jacobson. He might have resented her if she were not so loyal.

In any case, she was an asset he had come to depend on.

There was one thing about Mahaut that greatly disappointed Benjamin, however. It was not that she had fallen in love with another man, the Dashian boy. Who could possibly blame her? It was not even that she had slept with the other man, and done so repeatedly. After her terrible wound, having children was out of the question. There would be no little Jacobson who did not look at all like his father.

What he could not forgive Mahaut for was that, with all her skills and cleverness, she had not taken Edgar in hand. She had not brought him around and made him behave as he should toward her and toward all of the family. More than anything else, he had approved the match in the hopes that she would do just that. She was a Regular, an army lieutenant's daughter, after all. She'd grown up whacking at people with swords. Surely she ought to be able to bend a man like Edgar, essentially weak in spirit, to her will. Even put some backbone into him.

But she had not. Oh, once he beat her, she had made sure that the next time he tried that he would have to get the servants to hold her down or else she would kill him. Edgar had believed her. Benjamin had hoped that this might be the beginning of his son's taming. But that was not to be.

Whatever love, whatever regard Mahaut had felt for Edgar had died early. She'd come to an unspoken agreement with her husband. He would be allowed to do as he wished, to live the life that he lived before he met her—it would be a good life on Jacobson barter chits. Now Edgar spent most of his time in the whorehouses of Garangipore, or gambling with the other First Family boys—most of that crowd now ten years younger than him—in the taverns of Hestinga.

All that Mahaut wanted in exchange was to be able to write love letters. That's all she could do. The other man, the son of the district military commander, had taken himself to Lindron, to the Guardian Academy. Benjamin had to further admit that, even when Mahaut and her lover had been together, Mahaut had been discreet. She had looked after the Jacobson name.

But every time he saw a servant go out with a letter to deliver to the couriers of Hestinga, every time he saw a similar papyrus scroll come in and be delivered to Mahaut, it dug a little into his—well, not his soul. He'd long since given up believing in that foolishness.

His pride.

He knew that Edgar didn't have any pride, but he, Benjamin, did.

If only she would take Edgar in hand, he thought as he walked home from his office at the granary. *If only she would this time.*

He'd heard that Edgar was back. Edgar had tried to come in unobserved, traveling off-road on his dont and coming down the uninhabited northeastern hill outside of the village. Uninhabited, but not unworked. There were bones to be scattered there—bones that could be made into soap. The fact that they were the bones of Redlanders made no difference. The Blaskoye were animals, not men. Nef the Soapman had been out collecting, and had seen Edgar descending the hill. Nef had reported this at the granary, as he should.

Nothing that happened in Lilleheim escaped Benjamin Jacobson's attention. Nothing that mattered.

3

"He'll be here in a moment, my dear," said Benjamin to Mahaut. "I don't know what he has got himself into this time, but he appears to be injured, at least that's the reports I've heard."

Benjamin sighed and handed his dust jacket, the covering he wore when inspecting the silos, to a servant. He went to sit down in a chair in the large common room of the compound. Another servant emerged from the alcoves and began to fan him with a reed frond.

Mahaut poured a cup of wine out of the clay decanter on a nearby table and brought it over to Benjamin. He accepted it gratefully and took a sip.

Mahaut hated to see her father-in-law like this. She was so used to him being in command, so used to his stern but usually fair judgment. To see him sad and at wit's end pained her heart.

"Whatever it is we will get it tended to, Pater," she replied. She poured herself a stiff cup of wine as well. She was going to need it.

Four servants brought Edgar in on a flat board. He was conscious, and he smiled weakly as he was brought before his father. "I seem to have had a small hunting accident," he said.

Mahaut shook her head in exasperation. Edgar had probably practiced this line over and over again to tell to his father as a kind of joke. Knowing him, the thought of his father's annoyed reaction to those lame words was probably what had sustained him on the long ride to Lilleheim.

"You don't hunt," said Benjamin.

"Yes, I do, and in this kind of hunting my prey fired back at me," Edgar said. He attempted a chuckle, but it only came out as a gagging sound.

It seemed that the two facetious statements he'd managed to get out had exhausted all of the man's reserves. He fell unconscious on the wooden plank that served as a stretcher.

"We found him out in the yard fallen off his animal," said the stableman, Bronson, who looked after the family's personal donts and oversaw a breeding program. "He was lying on his back with one foot still caught in a stirrup. He was holding that arm and moaning."

Mahaut looked down at her husband. Someone had wrapped a linen bandage around the upper part of Edgar's left arm. The bandage was now soaked through with blood and hung partially open. A portion of the arm just below the shoulder showed through. It was torn and bloody. The arm looked as if a large chunk of muscle had been blasted off. Mahaut had seen bullet wounds before, and that's what this clearly was.

"Take him to our rooms," Mahaut said. "Don't touch the wound. I will gather some things and come to tend him in a moment."

The servants carried Edgar away. Benjamin caught Mahaut's eye. "You will take care of him, won't you, my dear?"

"Of course, Pater," she said.

"Will you use the new technique that the soldier taught to you? I was very skeptical of it at first, but it worked. I like anything that works. And since you've been treating the servants' cuts and bruises, we have much fewer sick days."

"I think whoever bound Edgar's wound before knew nothing of infection, but we will clean the wound, sterilize what we can, and maybe that will be enough for him to keep the arm."

Benjamin blanched at this statement from Mahaut. She didn't fully understand why pain for Edgar caused pain in Benjamin, but she admired that in her father-in-law. It was too bad Edgar didn't merit it.

She went to the room with boiled bandages, and her own hands thoroughly cleaned. She had the servants take off Edgar's jacket and shirt, telling them to be careful not to touch the wound in the process. Then she knelt next to him and got to work.

Edgar had passed out exhausted, and even when she picked

through the wound, searching for any stray fragments of lead or shattered bone, his only response was a grunt. She cleaned the surface around the wound as carefully as she could with lye soap. Then she took out her boiled needle and thread and began to stitch the wound back together. This did awaken Edgar, and he attempted to twist away, but Mahaut had beforehand instructed the servants to hold him down. They did so, and Edgar was too weak to resist. She continued with her stitches until she closed the wound as well as she could with what skin and muscle she could catch for an edge. She bandaged her work with sterilized cloth.

The servants let Edgar go. He sat up quickly and took a swing at Mahaut with his good hand. She had expected something like this and easily blocked it.

Never again, she thought. *You lay a hand on me, you pay.*

She reached down and put her fingers around his neck. She pressed. Hard.

For a moment. Edgar stared up at her in terror. Was she going to choke him to death now? Mahaut smiled and said, "Not yet, my husband." She lowered her hands to his shoulders and pulled him up. "Get some pillows behind him," she said to the servants. "Prop him up."

He would be combating dehydration and the loss of a great deal of blood. She made him drink several cups of tea before she allowed him to lie back down. Within moments, he had passed out again.

"The fever will set in now," she said. She turned to Wolfe, the senior-most of the servants in the room. "You'll need to prepare some cloths to bathe him. We'll soak them with cold water to keep the heat down, so we must use water from the deep well for that." She considered. "And I'll want a bathtub always standing by. He'll also get chills. Have some blankets ready in case I need them. Boil more cloth for bandages. Lots of it. We're going to keep this wound as clean as possible for several days."

"What will *you* do, Land-heiress?" asked Wolfe.

"I'll stay here with my husband, of course," Mahaut replied.

Wolfe nodded and glanced away, but not before Mahaut saw the disapproval in his eyes.

"Please do not exhaust yourself on his account, your grace."

"It will break Pater Benjamin's heart if we lose him," she said. "So I will consider it tending to the Pater as well as to my husband."

"Very good, mistress. As will we."

4

As she'd predicted, the fever struck Edgar hard. She bathed him frequently to bring the temperature down and made sure that he did not yank the bandage off his arm, which he tried to do several times in his delirium. After two days, the fever broke. Edgar drank a prodigious amount of tea, and she had to order the servants not to bring him wine because he wanted a bottle of that, as well.

"So you stayed with me through all of this?" Edgar said to her. "I suppose I ought to thank you."

"I was doing my duty to the house," Mahaut replied.

"Yes, the house. Meaning the old man of the house."

"And to you."

Edgar smiled, closed his eyes, and nodded. "Damn right you were." He chuckled. "Do you want me to tell you what happened?"

"If it will make you feel better to go into it," Mahaut said.

Edgar snorted in contempt at her, but apparently his need to talk overcame his petulance, and he began to speak.

It was, as Mahaut had suspected, a dueling wound. He'd fought in Garangipore at the dueling grounds the First Family bravos preferred down by the Canal. The weapons had been blunderbuss pistols. The other had gotten his shot off first, at least according to Edgar. He'd scored the hit in Edgar's arm, but the shot had not brought Edgar down. To the contrary, it had only made him angrier. Edgar had then taken his time lining up his weapon.

"The bugger stood in place, as a gentleman should, do you believe it?" Edgar said, shaking his head.

Edgar had shot the other straight through the heart.

"I don't consider myself a crack shot or anything," Edgar said. "But at twenty paces, I'm rather proud of myself for that one."

"You killed him?"

"Dead before he hit the ground."

"And who was this?"

Edgar winced. "I'm afraid that's the problem. He wasn't a nobody, and he wasn't just anybody."

"Just tell me who it was, Edgar."

Another wince from Edgar.

This really is going to be bad news.

"It was Walter Eisenach," Edgar replied in a pained whisper.

"Walter Eisenach of House Eisenach? The firstborn son of the gunpowder baron of Bruneberg?"

"I see you've been paying attention to your First Family genealogy lessons."

Did he think she would not know House Eisenach when she was competing against them every day for shipping space on the barges?

"Curse it, Edgar, do you know what this might mean to House Jacobson?"

"Since when did you start caring so much what becomes of the sons of House Jacobson?"

"Edgar, this is not good."

"I know that, you idiot," he said. "He had it coming, though. The bastard challenged me to meet him. I would've gotten away, but my exit plan from the town ran into a snag, I'm afraid, and I was forced to confront him. It's his own fault he's dead."

"Do you imagine that's the way his father will look at it?" Mahaut asked.

"I suppose not."

"Are you going to tell me what the duel was over? Was it over a gambling debt?"

"Oh, now you want to know the details. No, not gambling," he said. "Go on, guess some more."

"It was over a woman."

"Not exactly," said Edgar with a philosophical sigh.

"Don't tell me that you killed him because he made some insulting remark? Even you are not that stupid, Edgar."

Edgar looked up at her with flaring eyes and snorted from an angry intake of breath. But he was too weak to sustain it, and fell back onto his bed. "Like I told you, he's the one that called me out. And it wasn't because I insulted him to his face or anything."

"Are you going to tell me, or shall we wait for Benjamin to drag it out of you?"

Edgar considered her for a long moment. Then he smiled. Not a good sign. When Edgar smiled like this it meant he was up to no good. "I suppose I could tell you. You're not going to like it. Are you sure you want to hear about it?"

"I think I must."

"He believed that I had gotten a woman pregnant. He believed that I had insulted the honor of his house."

"Who did you get pregnant?" Mahaut didn't really want to hear the answer, but she knew she needed to if she had any hope to contain the damage.

"It wasn't even his little bastard! The bugger claimed that I gotten his sister with child. She's married to his best friend from childhood. Can you imagine that? What if your brother Xavier had forced you to marry me, instead of your choosing to do it of your own free will? What if he'd forced you to have sex with me, instead of your liking it so much you begged for more."

"Let's not go down that road, Edgar." Mahaut shook her head. She would not let him get to her, not ever again. "And did you get her pregnant?"

"Perhaps. Who knows? Somebody did, and I have a feeling it wasn't her husband, since he was away on business in Lindron for the past five months."

"I won't ask why you did it," Mahaut said. "But I do wonder why *her*, of all women?"

"You may find this hard to believe, wife, but many women find me difficult to resist. In fact, I had turned the poor thing away several times, but she kept showing up on my doorstep."

"You know how to avoid making a woman pregnant."

"Yes. Marry a woman who gets her womb torn to pieces by a bullet while fighting in a battle that she had no business being involved in in the first place." He finished off the statement with a disgusted smile. "Betta Eisenach is pure First Family. Maybe I didn't use the sheath on purpose. Maybe I wanted to plant my seed in a whole woman of the finest stock."

Mahaut sighed. Edgar's insults were like insectoid chirping to her now. "Edgar, this could be a disaster. Do you know what it means when First Families feud? You didn't *die*. They'll want a price in blood for Walter Eisenach. They may even come after your brother."

"Oh, my brother can take care of himself," Edgar replied. "Or at least Father will."

Mahaut considered him, then leaned back in her chair. She had moved it to be by his bedside and had stayed in it constantly for the last three days.

"It's time to change your bandages again," she finally said. "We'll take a good look at the wound when we do." She allowed herself to smile wickedly. "There's still a chance that arm will have to come off."

5

Mahaut left Edgar's bedside the next day and did not return. He was past the crisis point, and now would only require several weeks of recovery. She was not looking forward to having him around the Lilleheim compound. His official appointment was as House Jacobson factor in Garangipore, although it was understood that a staunch family retainer named Mahler did the actual work of grain transshipment from the Canal to the barges traveling up and down the river.

Edgar had spent the last two years living permanently in Garangipore, with the agreement that Mahaut would visit him occasionally to keep up appearances but would remain in Lilleheim most of the time. There was a large family block of buildings in the town, and Edgar had a palatial apartment within them. He was more often to be found in the area brothels and gaming houses than at home, as Mahaut knew from several sources that she cultivated to keep her informed of the business matters at Garangipore.

And now, apparently in the bedrooms of First Family matrons.

Mahaut was beyond being shocked by Edgar's behavior. The trouble now was how to contain the damage. A war between families would do no one any good, especially if those families were as powerful as the Eisenachs and the Jacobsons.

She called one of those sources of information to her, a grizzled, nondescript man named Jeptha Marone. For over a decade, he'd been a traveling trader for House Jacobson. He'd started out as a wagon driver, and worked his way up as Benjamin Jacobson, and now Mahaut, had discovered that he had that rare combination of trustworthiness and wiliness that was most needed when there was business that had to be conducted quietly. He had also done a stint in the Regulars and was handy with gun, knife, and fists.

Marone stepped into Mahaut's anteroom and bowed. As always, he looked very nervous to be anywhere near a land-heiress's quarters. At least officially. He'd done enough snooping in them to be quite calm when the visit was unofficial—and unannounced.

"Trader Marone, we need something done, and we need it done with the utmost discretion. Will you take some wine?"

"No, Land-heiress, thank you," he replied. His voice was surprisingly high-pitched for one with such gruff looks. "How may I be of service?"

"There's a child. At least, we think there is a child. First, I want to find out if this child exists, or if it is the product of Edgar's imagination."

"Establish if there is a child," Marone said. He liked to restate his instructions carefully, and he wasn't afraid to ask for clarification. "What child is this I am to find or not find, Land-heiress?"

"It is the child of Betta Eisenach of House Eisenach. She is married to the first cousin of the Family pater. She'll either be in Garangipore, or perhaps she's gone to Lindron. I gather that's where she's from. She would go there especially if there is a child and she needs to enter into confinement. I do not think they will want this child known to the world, so it is not going to be the easiest thing to find out what it is or where it is."

"If it exists at all?"

"Yes."

"Very well, Land-heiress, I am to find the child's location."

"And sex."

"I am to find if the child is boy or girl."

"Yes, Marone. Most important of all, however, is this. I want you to find out what House Eisenach intends to do with that child. I want to know if they plan to keep it, kill it, or give it away. This will be the difficult thing to ascertain. I'm going to place substantial funds at your disposal for use in obtaining this information, however."

"Find out ultimate plans for disposition of the child," Marone said. "This is a matter of importance, and expenditure of the necessary funds needed to obtain the information is preapproved by the Family."

"You have it, Marone. Do you think you can do it?"

Marone bit his lower lip and shuffled a bit, considering. "It may prove difficult, Land-heiress. Especially since House Eisenach does not want any of this to come to light. But I think it is not impossible. And whom do I report this to when I've completed the assignment, your grace?"

"To me," Mahaut said. "I will deliver the gist of it to Pater Benjamin."

"As you say, Land-heiress Jacobson," said Marone with another bow. "It's my pleasure to serve the House, as always."

"You do us honor," Mahaut replied.

And you grow richer in the process, she thought.

Which wasn't such a bad thing, considering that Jeptha Marone had six mouths to feed back home, and a seventh on the way, if the gossip around town were true. Tana Marone had been seen at the Lilleheim baker's with quite the bulge showing under her linens—a bulge that hadn't been there two months before.

Marone took another bow and made his way out.

"And what are you going to do about this child?" said Benjamin Jacobson, stepping into the antechamber.

Mahaut started out of her thoughts. "Pardon me, Pater. I didn't know you were there."

"The question stands."

She rubbed her eyes and checked her fingertips to be sure a smudge of kohl had not come off. "It isn't up to me. It's up to you."

"No, this one I am leaving to you. We will go with your decision."

"Then I don't know," Mahaut replied. "I will try to do whatever is best for the house as I see fit, but that will depend on the circumstances. If you wish me to handle this, you'll have to trust me, Pater."

"I have nothing but trust in you, daughter-in-law," Benjamin replied. He shook his head and sat down in the chair that Marone had refused. "But this situation that Edgar has put us into is dangerous. I saw a feud among Firsts when I was younger. It was between House Dupree and House Freemont. So much blood. Three friends of mine dead and floating in the Canal as carnadon fodder. The only thing they ever did to deserve it was to be born in the wrong place and time."

✧   ✧   ✧

A month later, Edgar was back on his feet and stalking around the compound like a pent-up wolverdon. He wore a sling around the injured arm and complained when he wasn't permitted a dont to take out riding. Benjamin had forbidden the stablehands from giving him a mount, but this didn't stop Edgar from railing at them and striking a stable boy viciously with a hand whip.

Mahaut tended the boy's wound, which was ugly but not too severe—although the whip's lash had only missed the boy's eye by a finger's width.

Oh, yes, Edgar Jacobson is back, she thought.

PART THREE
The Load

Six years later

The Present

1

Approaching Garangipore
476 Post Tercium

Abel chose a large female dont from the train to ride. The gunny sergeant in charge said her name was Nettle. Abel began his acquaintance, as he always did with a new dont, by feeding her tender, newly grown rushweeds he'd found near an irrigation ditch on his march to the rear. Normally, he would spend at least a halfwatch getting to know a new dont mount. Today, he had only a few moments, but he did his best to woo her with soft words and more rushweeds.

Then he put on the saddle the supply sergeant had issued him, and carefully girthed it on the dont's inhale. He mounted up and headed back up the line he'd just marched down, setting Nettle to a brisk trot.

It was just past midday and the enormous, self-made dust cloud that engulfed an army on the march had billowed into being. The Guardians marched eight abreast, in four columns of two with a larger space down the middle of varying width— built-in room for give while maneuvering around objects. They stretched across the Road, and, when necessary, marched in the ditches and fields that lined it. Where the road narrowed severely, columns merged, moving through without missing a step or slowing down.

Like the flowing of the River, Abel thought. Or the slithering of a legless cliff viper.

Villagers gathered along the sides of the road to watch the procession, but stayed many paces back. There was awe on their faces, and a certain amount of worry. When a child reached up to wave, or jumped up and down in excitement, parents or relatives would pull the child away and place it behind them. As with a viper in a wicker cage, you did not want to tap too much and make the deadly beast notice you. It might find a way out.

But one could observe from an appropriate distance.

There had not been a march of the entire Corps such as this in over a hundred years. One hundred ten years, to be exact. Abel knew; he'd spent the last four years practically living and breathing military history scrolls. On that previous campaign, the Guardians had been sent to correct a problem in the Delta. The locals had taken to sailing out to blue water ocean. They'd developed a new kind of triangular sail, larger ships, and were even venturing out to harpoon the near-legendary grendels and collect their oil. Grendels were the largest beasts ever seen in the Braun Sea—the size, it was rumored, of over a hundred daks.

According to the scrolls, these sailing folk were of a different stock than the short, mostly dark-complexioned Deltamen who now lived in the area. They had been fair, freckled, and some were said to have flaming red hair.

Abel knew that complexion. He'd seen it before, in the Redlands. Red hair and freckles was the mark of a Flanagan. They inhabited the wastelands to the east of the River Delta and existed in a state of squalor. The Blaskoye looked upon them as subhuman and treated them as animals when they caught one, even occasionally hunting them. The Flanagan tribe subsisted mostly on clams and mussels they gathered along the seashore and cracked open with rocks.

As Abel read the old scroll, it dawned on him where the Flanagans had come from. The people of the Delta, First Family and commoner alike, had been rounded up by the Guardians in a surprise attack. The scrolls were remarkably frank on what happened next. Most had been killed outright, or imprisoned inside enclosures and hastily dug pits. They'd been left to starve to death. Others had been driven into the sea at the point of bayonets. Most of the children who remained had been sold as slaves to a Redlander barbarian tribe of the time.

The very few who escaped had fled east with their families—and these must have become the beach-grubbing, primitive Flanagans.

The day's marching pace was relentless. The Guardian Corps had started out from Lindron four days previously and in that time had covered nearly fifty-five leagues on foot. Three brigades, each composed of four one-thousand-man battalions, plus mounted forces, specialist platoons, and a quartermaster's corps. Sixteen thousand men.

A drop in the sea compared with armies of yore, Center had commented.

You work with the army you have, Raj replied.

Abel could hardly believe it was possible to move a force this large so far and so quickly, but the proof was before his eyes. And they did it all with rifles and three-stone packs on their backs.

The air was hot and sticky. They'd left Lindron, worked their way through the badlands known as the Giants, and arrived in Ingres just four days ago. Now they were headed out the flat flax and wheat fields of Ingres, nearing its border with Treville District. This brought the road close to the River, and the humidity rose with each watch spent marching. The dust cloud glowed a luminous, sun-drenched yellow around the marching men. Fine brown alluvial dust stuck to sweating skin. It got into men's eyes and scratched its way down their craws so that every swallow was dry and every breath ragged.

Even on a dont, the heat of late ripening time in the land was relentless.

The sun seemed not to move for whole watches at a time, although Abel knew it was progressing west little by little. Center was able to tell him the precise time of day if he wanted, but Abel usually refrained from inquiring. To ask Center the time was to risk hearing a history of galactic timekeeping.

Abel knew enough about how the universe truly worked to feel a stranger in his own world. No one in the Land, nor any of the barbarians in the Redlands, had a notion of the central fact of their own existence: that they were all on a planet that was rotating around its own axis, and traveling around its local star, which was what they called the sun, once per year.

The planet's name was Duisberg. It had three moons which revolved around it, as the planet itself did around the sun. Some of the stars, the steady-burning ones, were other planets of the Duisberg system. Most were not.

Most of the stars in the night sky were distant suns.

There were other worlds, other men, out there.

Humanity had come from those stars over three thousand years ago. They had arrived in ships descending from the sky and had built a great civilization in the Valley of the River, which was the only easily habitable portion of Duisberg. It was a civilization that, compared to Abel's own, had been magical and godlike. It was a place where every man, woman, and child had powers as great as those of Zentrum.

But men were not gods. And that shining civilization had collapsed. The fall had been total and galaxy-wide, the transportation gates slammed shut. Not even Center knew the full cause of the Collapse.

Center had been but a military computer on a planet called Bellevue. The only computational devices that survived the Collapse were those that had been hardened against infiltration by programming viruses or nanotechnological attack on the hardware. Usually this meant a military artificial intelligence.

After the Collapse, star travel ceased. Humanity, scattered across the galaxy, was thrown into a new Dark Age. Generations were born and died in the ruins, and on many worlds there was only a dim memory of a past now translated into myth.

In some places, such as Duisberg, all knowledge of the origins of humanity had vanished.

There was no memory of the time when people had not been inhabitants of the Land. Zentrum had seen to that. The Land was all, and all belonged to the Land. The Land was where civilized people had always dwelled. And then there were the surrounding Redlands, hellish places inhabited by terrible nomads. Devils. Barbarians. Worshippers of the dust with a god named after dust itself, *Taub* in their tongue.

And down the middle of the Land, feeding the irrigation ditches, flooding the rice paddies, and watering the sugar cane, wheat, flax, and barley fields, was—the River. It was the only river humans on this planet had ever known.

The River was life. It was death. The River was the blood of the Land, and everything depended on it.

And that was the way it had been for three thousand years.

Stasis.

Unending cycles of harvest and planting, threshing and grinding, eating, then planting once again. There was Zentrum's Law to enforce the Stasis, and Edict upon Edict to guide behavior. These Laws and Edicts were what every child studied in Thursday school.

Certain actions must be always and forever interdict. There were lists to memorize. Only technology which Zentrum approved of was allowed to flourish. A ceramic dish that, Abel knew, had once graced a sophisticated electronic transmission facility and gathered messages from the stars might be used as a cook pot over a simple fire in the hearth of a villager, or as a slop bucket for daks intended for slaughter. Metal of every kind was forbidden but for the great exception: weaponry.

The list of allowed metal objects included the steel action and barrel of a musket or pistol, the lead of a minié slug, and the iron of a bayonet or knife.

All else was forbidden, on pain of punishment and even death.

With minor exceptions, all else was nishterlaub. Even to possess it was prohibited to any except for a priest. Most Landsmen believed in the depths of their beings that to merely touch nishterlaub was poisonous and deadly.

It was into this world that Abel Dashian had been born. And he might have remained as ignorant and unaware as the rest of the population had his curiosity not taken him one day into a warehouse within a priestly compound in his home district of Treville.

He'd been six years old when he first encountered Raj and Center, arrived two hundred years before as programs written into a capsule that fell from space. Since that day in the nishterlaub warehouse, the computer and the general named Raj had been constant voices, constant presences, in his mind.

Friends. Guides.

Whether he wanted them or not.

They had chosen him.

Their purpose in coming was to lift humanity from the doomed plans of Zentrum.

The three moons of Duisberg, two of them captured, near-miss asteroids, spoke of the danger. Abel now knew that the planet rotated in the opposite direction of the other five planets in the system. Something had reversed the planet's spin. Something had raised the enormous lava plains that covered most of the surface.

That something was a system full of rocky debris.

This was the great flaw in Zentrum's plan. A terrestrial computer, Zentrum thought in terrestrial terms. He must be sure that the dark age following the Collapse did not return. His purpose was to provide civil protection. Men may die in their thousands, but all was justified if dynamic equilibrium was maintained.

Nothing could ever, ever change. Any change would inevitably lead to another Collapse.

Yet those star travellers upon entering the system had immediately seen the flaw in Zentrum's plan.

Disaster would return from the sky, like clockwork. The outer portion of the Duisberg system, its Oort cloud, was an asteroid-laden nightmare. Center had detected this on his approach, and barely made it through undamaged. Perturbations could send storms of asteroids inbound toward the sun. It had happened over and over again in increments of single-digit thousands, sometimes only hundreds, of years. Much of the surface of Duisberg was a cratered ruin.

The asteroids would strike. All humanity would be wiped from the planet one day if they didn't develop proper defenses—advanced defenses. It was only a matter of time and the roll of the universal dice.

The only hope was a return to science-based civilization.

The only hope for *that* came from the voices in Abel's head.

Voices he still wasn't sure were real. He'd spent years pondering the impossible dilemma of knowing for certain. Center and Raj seemed real. They could, if they wanted, control his body, even kill him.

That didn't mean they weren't his own mental creations.

What if it's all me? What if they're all me. What if I'm as benighted as any village beggar, babbling to some nonexistent phantom?

Who was to say that even his perceptions were his own? Maybe the voices let him see only what they wanted him to see. He could be quite insane and not know it.

He'd learned much about the history of the Land. It was unarguable that Zentrum's plans had provided stability for many periods of relative peace. The price humanity paid was eruptions of barbarity and slaughter from the Redland tribes.

At those times, the tribes swept in and the old aristocrats

were replaced with new overlords. These changes were called the Blood Winds.

Yet even after the Blood Winds blew, the system remained intact. The Land had a way of taming even those who arrived in conquest.

Even in his moments of greatest doubt, there was one fact that kept Abel from wholly dismissing Center and Raj as voices.

His mother.

Her death when he was five.

Five.

The idiocy of her dying from a toothache. A cavity. Practically nothing. A tooth out, and then a week later, she was gone.

Center and Raj had told him—taught him—that there was a way for this sort of death to never happen again.

Whatever exasperation the familiar drone inside his mind might produce, however much he might wish to adopt the more sophisticated approach of the Academy, Center and Raj offered him one thing that the Academy never had: the chance to avenge his mother's needless death. A chance to punish the being who had kept the means of her salvation out of the world as a matter of misguided principle.

2

Toward evening, the column crossed the boundary into the Treville District. Abel was now in familiar country and began to make out landmarks he knew well. They would not be passing through his hometown, Hestinga, where his father had his headquarters as district military commander. Hestinga was seven leagues to the east at the end of the great Canal, which fed into Lake Treville. This was the widest portion of the Valley.

They would pass Garangipore, however.

For Abel, Garangipore would always evoke the odor of hyacinth.

It was the perfume of the woman he loved, Mahaut DeArmanville Jacobson. So many meetings here in Garangipore, over the past few years, him down from Bruneberg, her up from Lindron.

She was a woman wedded to a job she loved, a job that gave her meaning. She'd found her calling.

He would never deny her that.

They were doomed.

The vanguard of the column reached Garangipore on the second day of the march through Treville. The town was a large grain repository, a transshipment center, with barges traveling down the River and heavily laden carts heading up the River Road to the northeast. It was also the place where the Canal left the River and headed for Lake Treville. Since the River Road ran along the eastern side of the River here, the Canal cut it off. The Corps would have to board ferries to cross.

Third Brigade had been chosen to handle transport of the entire Corps. Von Hoff, knowing the ability and experience of his engineering company, had volunteered.

Which meant that, as executive officer for Third Brigade, it was Abel's job to work with his engineers to be sure this happened securely and on schedule. Fortunately, this was a task that pleased Abel. The chief of the Third Brigade Engineers was also Abel's friend, the third part of the triumvirate at the Guardian Academy that had included Abel and Timon Athanaskew.

Landry Hoster was his name. Like Abel, he was a Guardian reserve officer, until recently stationed in the Regulars. For the past six years, that posting was serving as Abel's right-hand man and chief of combat engineering of the Bruneberg Black and Tans. In his maintenance shop a new type of bullet was being manufactured. It was a bullet based on the work of the heretic priest Golitsin. While Law had condemned Golitsin to burn at the stake because he invented breechloaders—nothing was said regarding the cartridges they used. These were bullets with the percussion cap, gunpowder, and slug held together by a stiff cylinder of papyrus.

In many ways, Landry was the complete opposite of Timon. About the only thing they had in common was a fanatical devotion to duty. Timon did it because he was a believer. Landry did it because, as he'd once told Abel, *he was having so much fun*.

"Tell me we have boats, Landry."

"We have boats, Major," the engineer answered, "and a lot of them. The engineering advance team got here five days ago. We hired or requisitioned damned near every vessel in the province."

Landry was a heavyset man, almost a head shorter than Abel. He wasn't fat exactly, but he had a pudginess that never quite melted away and seemed almost a part of his character. Landry was thirty, two years older than Abel, and had risen through the ranks in the Delta District Regulars before being accepted into the Academy. In the swamps and bogs of the Delta, an engineer had to know his stuff.

Landry was a shy man at heart pushed into leadership. Abel figured he'd probably been bullied a lot and scapegoated when he was younger. If so, Landry had gotten past that by the time he got to the Academy. There was a quiet competence about him, and he always seemed happy, or at least amused, even in the middle of the hardest tasks. Abel had learned not to under-estimate Landry's core military skills, either. He was a magician when it came to math, siege weapons, the layout of battlements and forts—anything having to do with numbers, angles, and the use of space.

Sometimes, when an idea struck him, he had a tendency to overdo it, however. Abel surveyed the huge gathering of River boats along the Canal's southern bank.

"Looks like a bit of overkill to me."

"Hey, we'll end up glad we have them, sir," Landry said, but cracked his usual smile. "I kind of had an idea about lashing them side-by-side and planking them over to make, well, sort of a bridge, but when I brought it up, our wonderful brigade chaplain nixed my idea. Said he'd hate to see me burn at the stake the way that priest did. You knew him, didn't you?"

"I knew him."

"Breechloading rifles," said Landry, shaking his head in wonder. "Insanity. No wonder they set fire to the man." Landry gazed across the water and mused. "Wonder how he handled the back-blow. I'd of liked to see how one of those things worked before they burned them all up."

"I know you would," said Abel. "Let's get those boats loaded and moving, Captain."

Landry straightened and saluted. "Yes, sir."

Abel spent the day directing traffic. Landry's men handled most of the launches, but Abel found he was needed in five places at once to solve small but potentially march-slowing logjams. Most of all, he made sure no boat was overcrowded. He told the loaders to remind the men at least three times what capsizing would mean.

This close to the River, the Canal was crawling with carna-dons. An overturned boat full of men and donts would bring on a feeding frenzy of horrific proportions.

Besides, almost none of the men could swim.

His own captains knew Abel and Landry well, and gave Abel no trouble. However, some of the company captains from the First and Second Brigades were complete and cursed assholes about the whole thing. They didn't like the way Abel was running the operation. They took exception to the warnings in his standard lecture—a speech that was designed to be sure the men knew what might happen if they dangled their hands in the water. They rolled their eyes and made fun of his hardcore attitude, as if they knew better.

Let them think what they want so long as they do what I say, Abel thought. *What difference does it make if they know or don't know that I'm saving their cursed lives?*

Abel had been near two men when carnadons tore them limb from limb. Neither experience was one he wanted to relive.

But the truth was he was too busy to care what was said behind his back. In the end, with the help of Landry Hoster's extremely efficient engineering company, he managed to cajole and bully the entire Corps over—men, donts, wagons, and all. The trailing pack train of the Quartermasters Corps was waiting to cross behind them. They would use Landry's boats, but they had their own officers to oversee the specialized transfer.

Abel wished them luck.

It was after sundown, but before nightfall. The cloud of dust kicked up by sixteen thousand men making camp for the evening glowed a dusky, golden hue. The murmur of a thousand rough conversations filled the air, along with a few shouts at donts and daks to get out of the way or get a move on. The Corps was spread up and down the northern banks of the Canal, since it was a readymade water source, and in spite of the fact it was carnadon infested.

He noticed that men were going in details to dip pails of water, and their companions were armed and vigilant.

Good.

Maybe he'd put the fear of Zentrum's wrath in a few of them after all.

Abel unsaddled his dont and released her into a corral near the command area. Groelsh, the command master sergeant, who made the staff camp arrangements, had chosen a good spot on a rise that overlooked the troops in either direction along the Canal. Abel stowed his saddle beside the others on the makeshift corral railing. His pack and weapons he carried a short distance away. He put his rifle into the command staff rack, but kept the pistol in his waistband. He stowed his pack against the trunk of a small willow tree nearby. He slapped the pack to clear the sandy buildup on the canvas, but succeeded only in raising a cloud to further thicken the dust already hanging in the air. Ever-present insectoids buzzed around his head, but he ignored them.

He turned and looked down the rise at the Third Brigade encampment.

The flower-shaped sleeping circles of men were easy to see from this perspective. There were dozens of them—enough to fill the north side of the Canal as far as Abel could see from his position.

Then, something odd.

Farther along the Canal, there was a long line of men stripped down to bare chests. At the head of the line, a man stepped into a spray of water that came from an uplifted section of pipe supported on a wooden framework. He'd seen many such sod pipes before. They bent to a certain extent without breaking and were a staple of the irrigation system in the Valley.

Someone's redirected the irrigation ram from downstream, Abel thought. After a moment, it came to him what was going on.

They've set up a shower for bathing.

The line was moving through at a steady clip, with one man standing under the falling water for a moment, then giving way to the next.

Not a bad idea, Raj said. **This might be the last chance to get the stink off them until Progar.**

Yeah, with muddy irrigation water, Abel thought. But it did look cool, at least.

Suddenly, around the pipe a cordon formed, a circle of men standing almost shoulder to shoulder. Some had bayonets detached from their rifles. Some had their bows notched, with arrows pointing down but at the ready.

What the cold hell were they up to?

Was there about to be a fight?

Another group of soldiers approached. There were about ten men, and they were trying to bypass the line and get directly in the water. Abel couldn't hear it, of course, but one of their number stopped and spoke to a soldier in the cordoning circle. The other began waving his arms, then appeared to be shouting. After a moment, the man he was shouting at turned away from the cordon, his hands thrown up in disgust, and went back in the direction from which he'd come. The other line-jumpers followed.

Abel walked down the rise to the shower—slowly, he was in no hurry, and had a halfwatch to spare before the colonel would want him again—and found the soldier who had done the talking. Abel recognized him at once. He was the Monday Company first sergeant.

"Evening, Major."

"First Sergeant, what was that about?" Abel asked.

"What was what about, sir?"

"That talk you just had with the soldier who turned around and left."

"Oh, that? He was a First Brigade sergeant, sir. Didn't you see his triple knots?"

"What did he want?"

"To take a bath."

"To take a bath?"

"Yes, sir."

"And this is the Third Brigade sod pipe?"

"Yes, sir. A field-ready high-quality bathing facility."

"I see. What did you tell him exactly, First Sergeant?"

"I told him to get his stinking carcass and the rest of his trash back to their own camp or we'd gut the lot of them where they stood. I told him I'd see every thrice-damned Third Brigade soldier I'm fighting and dying with through this water before I let a drop of it touch a shitkicker from the First or Second. Sir."

Somewhere in Abel's mind, Raj Whitehall was laughing.

"All right, carry on, First Sergeant."

"Yes, sir."

Abel strode back up the rise to the command area. When he got there, von Hoff was standing gazing down in the same spot Abel had occupied before.

"What was that about?" he asked.

Abel told him.

The slightest smile crossed the colonel's face. "I see," he said. Then the smile became a scowl. "We have a very dirty task to perform, Major. I wish it was going to be that easy to wash ourselves clean."

Von Hoff turned away without waiting for an answer, and went back to the small lean-to he slept under. Having a tarp roof over his head was the only concession von Hoff allowed to his rank.

Abel sat on the rise for a long time and looked over the Canal as dusk became the dark of night. Soon he could see the lights of Garangipore across the water.

She might conceivably be there.

The Jacobsons had a villa in town, and Mahaut sometimes came up River from Lindron to oversee a particularly valuable shipment.

When she did, he'd often found a reason to come down and meet her. They got away from the compound to one of her maids' apartments near the River's edge.

Smooth stucco walls. A scuffed wooden floor with a carpet thrown across it. Fine linen sheets. The odor of hyacinth and lavender.

He would see her on his return. He had to.

He'd almost joyfully given over Cascade to his second and traveled back to Lindron when the reserve call-up had come.

But with her duties and his, they'd only managed to see each other every Mommsen moon or so. But that nine-month taste of being near her had been exhilarating. Only now, instead of cooling with distance, his desire for Mahaut had turned into a constant longing that was always in the back of his mind like the sounds of the night.

Blood and Bones! He should have killed Edgar Jacobson when he'd had the chance back in Treville, saved Mahaut the years of putting up with him. But blowing Edgar Jacobson's brains out was not the way to Mahaut. He didn't know the way. Maybe there wasn't one. But if he couldn't find it, he would carve the path himself.

Abel wasn't particularly trying to keep his thoughts private at the moment or to remain in his Hideout. Nevertheless, Center and Raj maintained a diplomatic silence.

3

The morning brought more marching. And after a day and a half they left Treville behind and entered Cascade district.

Almost the moment they crossed the border they were attacked. This time it was not crossbows at night. The raiding party was mounted on donts, and they rode down upon the column about its midpoint. Abel was riding with von Hoff to the front, and the pop of firearms behind them alerted them to the attack. Von Hoff ordered an immediate cavalry charge, and he and Abel joined in. In front of them, puffs of black-powder smoke were rising, but before they arrived, the raiders had fled. Abel took reports. The attackers had fired salvos from carbines, reloaded while they were riding, fired again, and then switched to bow and arrow. Progar—whatever oligarchy was in charge—was serious about their harassment raids.

The attack left behind sixteen casualties, with ten dead.

There might have been many more, but instead of disarray, the attacked portion of the line fell out in good order and took positions behind a low hedge on the Road's eastern side. They lay down mass fire, aiming for the legs of the donts. This had brought down a good third of the attackers. The cloud of gun smoke Abel had seen had come from the rifles of Guardians. There were perhaps one hundred raiders in all. More of the column came up, and instead of standing around gawking, joined in the fray, giving the front lines time to reload. The Guardians' counterattack moved steadily forward like carnadons drawn to a kill.

Finally the raiders had had enough. They'd broken off and fled back toward the Escarpment. Several officers started to give chase on foot, but von Hoff called them back. Instead, he sent a company of cavalry after them.

That night, the cavalry brought the heads of twenty raiders into the camp staked on the end of banner poles. These raiders they had ambushed and killed. The others had made it to the Rim by the skin of their teeth.

You tangled with Goldies at your own peril.

General Josiah Saxe, who commanded the entirety of the Guardian Corps, did the wise thing and marched the corps off the Road, overland, and around the sprawling city of Bruneberg, staying a respectful two leagues distant. Even Abel cast a long look or two toward it.

This was his domain. His command until a short time ago. He was the one who had taken on the corruption, the decadent idiocy of the ruling class.

Taken it on and beaten it with terrible cost.

Of course, there was a memory that lay lighter in his mind: he'd also once gone into that city a virgin, but hadn't left one.

They circled back to the Road near the top of the First Cataract, the system of shoals and rapids that lay near Bruneberg on the River. Then it was northeast again. After a bewildering series of twists and turns, they arrived at the base of the Second Cataract. By afternoon that day, they were in sight of the great fortress of Montag Island.

Fort Montag was garrisoned by Cascade District Regulars. Their commanding officer was the extremely competent Eugen Metzler, whom Abel had promoted and appointed himself. Metzler rode out to meet Saxe, and offered the Corps the hospitality of the place. The fort was not large enough to hold sixteen thousand troops, but the island was, and the men bedded down around the stone walls and down to the River shore. The island sat at the midpoint of the Second Cataract, but this did not mean the swiftly flowing rapids had no carnadons in them.

That night, Second Brigade lost a man to prove it.

As per Abel's instructions to Metzler before he left, Saxe and all the command staffs were invited inside the fort. Saxe had lined them up to enter through the gate, but Metzler led them south along the eastern wall. As Abel knew, and Saxe discovered to his amazement, the wall ended. There wasn't a wall, and only the sparest of battlements, to the direct south. About a fieldmarch away, Abel saw the wall on the western side pick up again. There was a large gap separating it from the eastern wall.

"I guess the idea is to guard against Redlander attack from both Rims," von Hoff said.

"But they're wide open for an attack moving up- or down-River."

"Well, the only ones moving in the Valley would be us friendly forces, wouldn't it, Major?" von Hoff answered. "Still, you can't count on that. It is an odd arrangement."

Created under Edict of Zentrum, said Raj. *All modification forbidden.*

Like a window for the Blood Winds to blow through, Abel thought.

Precisely, said Center.

They stayed under a roof for the first time in nine days. The garrison Regulars had been turned out of their barracks for the evening to join the Guardians outside, and their bunks given to Corps staff officers. Abel didn't complain. Each bunk had a mattress filled with cane-silk.

Metzler had given von Hoff a captain's quarters, a double-roomed affair of mud wattle, with its own privy hanging over the ditch of river water that flowed northeast to southwest and bisected the interior of the fort. Abel had at least ordered Metzler to see to it that the fort took its water from a point above the row of cabins that lined it. The previous Cascade DMC and his fort commander had not bothered.

The barracks were for enlisted and had no luxury at all. There was a common outhouse shared by every two buildings—outhouses that had to be mucked out daily.

Abel knew that on the north end of the island near its point was a giant pile of nightsoil waiting for the spring floods to finally carry it away.

Von Hoff invited the command staff in to cook on the hearth in the cabin. Here there were cookpots and spits, and in a larder closet Abel discovered a smoked hank of dak shoulder. Everyone reasoned that the owner of the cabin wouldn't have left it there if he didn't mean for them to have it.

They sat at a real table, in real chairs, and fell to their meal with gusto. Someone else found a half keg of beer, and clay mugs from the crockery closet were passed around. After eating, the nesh chewers went outside to chew and spit, and the smokers took out their pipes and lit up around the table. Abel brought his out for the first time in a very long while and joined them.

Von Hoff was convivial but subdued through the evening, yet he seemed happy to have company. Several candle lanterns hung on wall pegs burned, casting a warm hue on everything in the cabin. Their wicks were guttering before everyone had gotten up and made his way to the barracks and his bedroll.

Abel himself sat on a bench on the porch of the cabin after the others left. He gazed up at Churchill, which was three-quarters full now. In the distance was the low roar of the Second Cataract rapids. Abel shivered even though it was late ripening time; the evening was as chilly as a winter's night in Lindron would have been. They were getting farther north.

In the sky burned the stars. Constellations he knew: the Dragon. The Bridle. The Scythe. Reitz the Water Carrier and his bucket full of clustered stars.

Those stars of the bucket are very close together in actuality, Center said. **They are a nebular cluster burning blue and hot. They have only lately emerged from a gas cloud and are quite young, at least on a galactic time scale.**

Where is Bellevue's star? Abel asked. This was the system that Center and Raj came from.

It is too faint to observe in the Duisberg sky, Center replied.

How do I know it exists at all?

You can never know unless you go there. As with many things, all you can do is infer its existence.

Or take your word for it.

Yes.

Does it ever rain there?

A lot more than here, Raj replied.

What about Earth?

It is said to rain there all the time, said Center. **But the truth of the matter has been lost.**

Just then, Abel heard the sound of a chair scraping inside the cabin. He'd thought the colonel had gone to bed. Maybe von Hoff was up rummaging for another mug of beer or cup of water. Then a light came through the door cracks.

He's lit a new candle off the hearth coals, Abel thought.

Another scrape of the chair. Abel was on the verge of knocking to see if he was needed, but thought better of it. Then he heard a sound he could not mistake.

The cocking of a pistol.

Abel opened the door and came inside.

Von Hoff was sitting with his back to the door. He did not turn at the sound of Abel entering.

Von Hoff was light in complexion. He'd probably been blond when he was young. He was well-proportioned and compact. He'd created a complicated set of exercises that Abel had seen him perform religiously each morning. Evidently they worked. His arms and neck were textured like tightly coiled rope.

"Go away, Dashian," he said.

Abel considered. This didn't sound like an order to him. It sounded like a desperate request. He ignored it, closed the door, and took a seat on the end of the table, facing the colonel in profile.

In a wall niche, the new candle was burning, putting out more smoke than light. Von Hoff's blunderbuss lay on the table.

"What are you thinking about doing here, Colonel?"

Von Hoff did not turn to face Abel. He stared at the pistol.

"None of your thrice-damned business."

"Colonel, I believe it may be. Colonel, you seem . . . Are you all right?"

"In what way all right?"

"You seem . . . agitated."

"Agitated?" von Hoff said. He let out a strained chuckle. "Agitated. Yes."

"Colonel, what is it? If it's something personal, I'll butt out."

Von Hoff's mouth ticked into the approximation of a smile. "Oh, it's personal," he said. "A personal weakness, you might call it."

"I don't understand, sir."

"Do you realize what our orders say, Dashian?"

"No, sir, they're secret as of now, and you haven't made me aware of their contents."

"Have you made a guess?"

"I suspect we are supposed to wipe out the private militias

that have sprung up in Progar, probably kill every last one of the officers, maybe even the men, and drag the oligarchs who hired them back to Lindron in chains, where they'll be executed by crucifixion or burning."

"That would be acceptable," said von Hoff. "Harsh, but acceptable."

"Then what?"

"We're going to sell them to the Redlanders."

"All the private militia men?"

"No. They die. You were right about that."

"Then who."

"The others. Orash."

"I don't understand, sir."

"Every living person in the capital city. Men. Women. Children. To be either killed or sold as slaves. To wipe out this water heresy, you see."

"There are...there must be many thousands of people in Orash."

"There were sixty thousand in the last census."

"How would we do it, even if we tried?"

"A pretty problem. I suppose we will have to do it systematically, create some sort of slaughter facility. That problem the Abbot of Lindron graciously left up to the commanders of the Corps," said von Hoff. "If we can't sell them, we have to kill them. No exceptions."

Abel nodded. He didn't need Center and Raj to explain to him the inexorable logic of Zentrum in this matter. Wipe out whatever heresy had sprung up in Progar and open the door for a slow Redland invasion. Or, as he knew Zentrum thought of it, reap and burn the blighted crop, and reseed the field.

He might be horrified, but he was not surprised.

"You don't agree with these orders, Colonel?"

"That is completely beside the point," said von Hoff. "As long as I live, I'm bound to carry them out. There can be only one Law in the land, and that is the Law of Zentrum. This is what makes us...civilized."

Abel glanced at the blunderbuss pistol.

"Are you thinking of taking your own life, sir?"

"What makes you say that, Major?"

"The loaded pistol on this table, for one thing."

Von Hoff's eyes went back to the gun. "Do you know why I became a Guardian, Dashian?"

All Abel knew was that von Hoff was originally from Ingres.

His instructor, and now commanding officer, had hardly ever spoken of his younger days, except for an occasional comment about his tour in the Regulars and his promotion to the Goldies. He had been very proud of that.

"No, sir, I don't."

"To get the cold hell away from my father's plantation, that's why."

"Where was that?"

"Was? Is. It's still there. Ingres. In the middle of the province. Best land. They grow wheat and flax. There are whole villages of people who work for my father. People who will always work for my family. Serfdom. That's the way it's done in Ingres."

"I know about the plantations."

"From scrolls? From passing through on your way to better things? No, you don't know anything!" Von Hoff slapped a hand down on the table. The pistol jumped and rattled back down.

"Why don't you tell me, Colonel?"

Von Hoff was silent for a long moment. Then he brought his hand back up, kneaded his forehead, and finally spoke. "They say we have no slavery in the Land. That's one way we are different from those cursed dust-worshipping Redlanders. They take slaves, but for us civilized people, slavery is counter to the Laws and Edicts of Zentrum." Again, the faint smile crossed von Hoff's face. "I've seen slavery. It's alive and well in Ingres. And my family have been slave masters for three hundred years."

"So you joined up to get away from all that?"

"So I wouldn't have to become a slave master myself."

"And now—"

"I'm about to make my kin look like children playing at what they do."

"Unless you put a minié ball through your skull?" said Abel. "And how is this going to help those people in Progar?"

"Nothing can help them." He smiled, still looking at the gun. "But it doesn't have to be me who does it."

The colonel's conclusion does not follow, Center said in his impersonal voice. **He makes a utilitarian argument for his inability to effect change, but from that argument it would follow that it is better if he is in charge of the extermination to minimize pain and suffering.**

The man's wrestling with his soul, said Raj quietly. *He's run up against the trouble with that sort of thinking.*

Utilitarian philosophy is normally sound. It is that which is often deemed practical, with end justifying means.

It's that kind of thinking from Zentrum that's left this world wallowing in Stasis, with children dying from the measles and mumps, and men with ideas kicked to the stones. It isn't cowardly to want to escape from doing evil.

I was not accusing the colonel of moral weakness. I was merely pointing out the logical contradiction in his argument to justify self-slaughter.

Abel found himself wanting something he'd never desired before. For a moment, he wanted to share Center. To show the colonel what a future would look like with no Zachary von Hoff.

Can I? Is it possible?

No, Center replied. **You were conditioned during your proximity to the capsule which brought us to this world. Your mind was tuned on a quantum level, beyond mere rearrangement of neurotransmitters. Raj and I are with you in a very real way. We could not be with the colonel in such a manner unless he were to come within several paces of the capsule.**

Show me, then.

Acceptable. Observe:

Cold.

It's a cold he's never felt before. Beyond the cool of a winter evening in the Land. Breathtaking cold. And there is snow. He's never seen snow before, has known of its existence only from scrolls. Now he understands it at a bone-deep level.

And it is hard to breathe. Almost as if the air has given out. He is not walking particularly quickly, but every step is a struggle.

He looks behind and sees a line of men following. What was supposed to be a flanking attack has instead turned into a death march to escape the weather and an enemy in pursuit.

Abel looks down at his hands, uncovered, growing blue, and doesn't recognize them. They are a brown color, many shades darker than his natural hue even with a full tan. He turns over his palms. Lighter skin there. He is a black man.

You are Captain Leonard Fowlett of Third Battalion Wednesday Company. The men following you are the remains of your entire unit.

I haven't counted them, but there can't be more than thirty or forty left of a hundred, Fowlett/Abel thought.

Chambers Pass. This is what it had come to, where they had come to. The headwaters of the River when it wasn't a frozen hell of snow and ice as it was at present.

Fowlett knew it was a fool's errand going in. The company was not equipped for snow. But it was the natural element of the enemy.

Brilliant. Fucking brilliant.

Colonel Vallancourt, now a general. Promoted from the rock-fucking First. Always sure he's the smartest guy in any room. Always certain he's right.

Well, this time he wasn't right. It was only the latest of a series of stupid blunders on this bloody, benighted campaign. Oh, the Corps would win, all right. That was apparent from the start. But to pay this kind of price, when it should have been relatively easy. *To lose so many of my men.*

To die in this cold hell.

Chambers fucking Pass.

A man comes huffing toward him, plowing through the snow. It is the young lieutenant, the trustworthy one with the platoon taking up the rear guard.

Breathless, he arrives, stands before the captain. Tries to speak, but cannot.

"Easy, man," says Fowlett. "It takes time to catch your breath in this thin air."

The young lieutenant nods, takes a moment to get his breath under control.

"They've caught up with us, sir," he gasped. "We couldn't hold them. They're using... I don't know what to call them. Things that slide over this white horror we're wading through."

"Skis," Fowlett said. He'd read about them, somewhere. In some impossible children's tale of the frozen north. He turned his gaze back down the snowy valley which they had been heading up in their attempt to escape.

Hunted.

There, not far away, perhaps a few hundred paces. Brown and black dots, moving impossibly fast. Men walking—no, men sliding—on the *top* of the snow.

"Form ranks!" he called out. His weary men moved to obey.

Even after all this, the stupid losses in an insane charge on the walls of Orash. The repulse. The counterattack. After all this, Wednesday men had fight left in them. But it was so cold.

The flight. The cold.

A night of hell. Men dying standing in their own tracks. Dying of cold.

Yet the ones who remained pulled together into a ragged line, their sergeants' shrill voices goading them once more into battle formation, two deep.

Across the valley floor from him, the black and brown dots grew larger. No longer dots, but forms with arms and legs. Men. Gliding over the snow like magical beasts.

"Tell them to hold fire!" he called to his first sergeant. "Wait until those cursed rockfuckers are in range."

We can't waste the little ammunition we still have.

The enemy drew closer. Closer.

Then stopped.

They stopped well out of range.

What the cold hell . . .

Someone was forming them into a line. They raised their rifles.

They're out of range. Don't they know the chance of hitting us is one in a thousand?

But the rifles weren't aimed at Wednesday Company. They were aimed at the sides of the valley, the steep slopes packed with snow.

The enemy fired. It was ragged fire, no discipline there. And they were shooting into snow.

For a moment, he laughed. Blood and Bones, was this some sort of joke?

He couldn't understand why they did it, but he didn't need to. The enemy would have to reload. His entire unit was armed and ready. He would charge. Even bounding through snow, they would come into range.

He would rout those rockfuckers after all!

That was when he heard the rumble. It sounded like distant thunder, but Fowlett didn't recognize it. He'd only seen his first rain six days ago. This—was outside his knowledge.

The rumble grew louder. Where was it coming from? What was it?

He looked wildly around.

The walls of the little valley—were they shifting? Was the snow itself on the move?

It was.

Then the rumble became a roar, and he understood.

The enemy would not have to shoot them. No, the snow would take care of that.

He watched the avalanche approach. Some of the men turned to run. But the other side of the valley was avalanching as well. There was nowhere to run.

He tried to brace himself. Tried to be ready. But the snow hit him like the punch of a giant. So cold. Flung, churned. Nothing but white, white, white in his vision. Pulled in opposite directions.

He felt his right leg break at the thigh.

Pulled, yanked, turned.

Finally he came to rest. His eyes were still open. Darkness. Wet when he blinked. He couldn't get his hands free to wipe them, couldn't move at all. He struggled, but it was no use. Was he upside down? Right side up? How deeply was he buried? There was no way to tell.

He knew he was freezing to death, because the cold didn't seem to bother him anymore.

But then Fowlett realized he wasn't going to die from the cold after all.

No, it would be suffocation.

There was no air here, except what he brought with him in his lungs. He couldn't breathe. He couldn't move and he couldn't breathe.

Cold hell. He'd sworn by it a thousand times, not realizing it was real.

And now he was there.

Cold hell was Chambers Pass.

"No, you can't help them, and you can't help yourself out of obeying these orders. But it's the Goldies who'll suffer if you leave us, Colonel. Third Brigade in particular."

"You can't know that," answered von Hoff with a shrug. "I'm just a man. Men are interchangeable. By the will of Zentrum, that's how the system is designed."

"Colonel, don't ask me how it is I come by this, but I know for a fact that they will give the Third Brigade command to Colonel Vallancourt."

Von Hoff looked away from the pistol, turned to Abel and laughed, as if Abel had made an absurd joke. "No, I don't think so."

Abel met the colonel's gaze, slowly shook his head. "It's true. It will be Vallancourt. I know this. It's practically a done deal."

"Absurd. How do you know it?"

"I can't tell you, but it's from a source I completely trust."

For a very long time, von Hoff held Abel's gaze. "Who are you?" he said. "No one your age at the time could have won the Battle of the Canal. What do you see? What are you?"

"A man, like you," Abel answered. "But sometimes I know things. The way I knew how to use the breechloaders Golitsin made. This is another one of those times."

Von Hoff looked into Abel's eyes a little longer. Then he dropped his gaze and reached for the pistol. He carefully removed the firing cap and lowered the cocked hammer. Then he pushed the gun abruptly away. It skittered across the table, but did not fall off.

"I can't," he whispered. "I can't visit a plague like Vallancourt on the men. I just can't." He looked back to Abel. "And you're sure?"

"Almost certainly matters are going to align in such a way that he'll get the command if you're gone."

The crooked smile slowly returned to the colonel's face.

"Back when Vallancourt and I were both in the Academy, I looked at that First Family dolt and said to myself, 'Someday, Zachary, your life is going to depend on him, on something he does or does not do. What will you do then? Will you accept that fate can be that cruel?' I even thought about killing him at one point."

"Is that true, sir?"

"I always figured he would be the death of me, through one or another of his incredible fuck-ups. It would be justified self-defense."

Von Hoff took up the pistol, pushed back from the table, and slid the dragon back into his waistband.

"Damn Vallancourt to cold hell," he said—but with resignation, not anger, and with the same crooked smile on his face. "Now he's gone and saved my life."

PART FOUR
The Toll

Six years previously

1

Lilleheim
Treville District
470 Post Tercium

There had been no report from Jephta Marone in over a month. This was not good news, as far as Mahaut was concerned. It probably meant he had found out something and was following up on it.

Meanwhile, grain promises-to-buy were wildly shifting. The trend was falling for Lindron-bound mixed grain and rising for Bruneberg-bound wheat and Delta rice, but that changed almost daily when the runner came in with the previous day's numbers from Garangipore. Mahaut didn't need a special investigator to tell her what was happening.

The Guardians were at their war games in Lindron. Sixteen thousand men, a town's worth, were on the move. Anyone who knew exactly where the Guardians would be could make a tidy sum off the information. This was because the grain promissory notes were guesses at what offers to buy in a certain location would be. Cascade-bound grain, meanwhile, was in freefall. Unusually good harvests—from the fields of Progar, no less—had flooded the markets of Bruneberg with grain. A few years ago, Progar was a meat supplier. Its grain production was mainly confined to barley, and not much at that. Now it seemed they'd shifted over to more water-hungry wheat.

If it weren't for the large carrying distance from Progar to

95

Lindron, and the fact that all shipments would have to be landed and ported around three sets of cataracts, she might fear for House Jacobson prospects in Lindron itself.

Anyway, thank Zentrum for the Guardians and their war games.

Mahaut, Solon, and Benjamin were bent over a scroll comparing the Garangipore House offers with what they knew were in the Lilleheim silos when the messenger from Hestinga arrived.

He was carrying a reed basket on his back. It was held on by two dakleather straps over his shoulders. Mahaut recognized him as one of the warehousemen from town. He dealt in imports, mostly from up-River, and specialized in the cheaper, lesser quality pottery from Cascade.

The fine stuff, the expensive stuff, was made by the artisans in Lindron, of course. Yet Bruneberg had street after street of kilns many times larger than all of the one-man shops of Lindron combined. The Lindron porcelain was for Firsts and those who emulated them. The Bruneberg potteries, which were controlled by a House Dupree, House Ziman, and House Weatherby cartel, turned out cups, pots, and pitchers for everyone else.

The front clerk had brought the warehouseman back to the granary offices. He was a known and trusted merchant—and one who usually had a lot of good-natured bluster to his attitude, if Mahaut remembered rightly. Now something was wrong. Instead of confidently striding through the door, the man hung back. Benjamin look up, considered him.

"Come in, Master Knopf. Don't stand there like a post. You know you're welcome here."

The warehouseman shuffled across the threshold.

"Why don't you lay your burden down and sit? Have some wine. Daughter, can you pour him a cup?"

Mahaut moved toward the pitcher, but Knopf held up a hand. "No, please, Land-heiress. Not now." He gulped. "I have something to . . . show you."

"Well, what is it?" Solon said briskly. "We are a bit busy at the moment."

"I'm very sorry to interrupt, but I thought . . . you would want . . ."

He took the basket from his shoulders and set it down in front of him. He unclasped the latch and, with a resigned sigh, opened it up.

"We received a shipment from Lindron yesterday."

"Lindron? I thought you only dealt Bruneberg pots, Master Knopf."

"Business has been good, so we've been branching out, me and the missus. She's been after me for years to deal in the fine stuff. Thinks it'll sell in Hestinga as well as anywhere. Well, we took the chance, and she was right, she was. We started off with those porcelain half-elb cookpots, and damn me to cold hell if they haven't been going out as fast as we can get them in."

"Interesting, but what does this have to do with House Jacobson?" said Benjamin. "You know I don't care who a man trades with as long as he gives me a fair deal."

"I know, I know, Pater Jacobson," Knopf replied. He paused, as if to gather his wits. "Yesterday, Pater, we got in an order of more of them half-elb cookpots, about a thousand this time, and some plates in there, too." He coughed, cleared his throat. "Anyway, in the middle of the cookpots, packed in there with the straw and such, the boys in the warehouse found something. Something in place of a pot, if you know what I mean—" Knopf pulled a canvas sack from the open basket. "This," he said.

"What is that?" Solon asked. "A rotten Delta melon? Is it some kind of practical joke or something, Knopf?"

"I wish it were, Land-heir, sir. I wish it were. No, there was a scroll attached." Knopf patted his tunic, pulled a small roll of papyrus from an inner pocket. "Here it is."

Mahaut took it from him.

"Read it, Daughter," Benjamin said. He was staring at the sack, and his eyes had grown cold. Mahaut unrolled the scroll.

> *On pain of your own life, deliver this to Pater Benjamin Jacobson, House Jacobson, Lilleheim. Say it is in payment for killing a son. Tell him that cold hell awaits him and his house.*

"Open it," said Benjamin.

"I...I don't like to," said Knopf. "It's just...I don't want to be the one..."

"Oh, for pity's sake," Mahaut said. She took the bag from him. It was heavier than it looked. She put a hand under the bottom and pulled back the top—

And almost dropped the contents in shock.

It was a head. A human head. A man's head.

The skin was desiccated. The hair was stringy and filled with a dandruff of flaking chips of dried blood.

She'd grasped the bottom with the neck stump to one side. Now she took it by the neck stump, so she could hold it upright.

The eyes were closed. The mouth was sewn shut.

Benjamin Jacobson let out a cry of anguish.

"What is it, Father?" Solon asked.

"My friend," said Benjamin, moaning. "It's my friend."

"Who? Who is that, Father?"

"Abram." Benjamin began to sob. "My friend. My old friend."

It was Abram Karas. He had been the Jacobson House Factor in Lindron. Benjamin Jacobson's best friend from childhood, and long-time chief of staff in Lilleheim until Solon had reached maturity.

After that, Karas had been given the important posting at Lindron, where the largest share of Jacobson grain was sold, where deals were made, and he was also the overseer of a large portfolio of House Jacobson loans to Lindron merchants and investments in Lindron real estate.

This was the severed head of Abram Karas.

It's either retribution from House Eisenach, Mahaut's shocked mind told her, *or someone willing to go to any length to provoke a Family war.*

Her father-in-law recovered himself sufficiently to look Knopf in the eyes. "This is not your fault, Knopf, and we don't hold it against you. Thank you for your troubles. See Dillard, and he will reimburse you for—"

Then a sob rose in Benjamin's throat again. He shook his head, unable to speak. Knopf, taking the hint, bowed and exited, leaving the basket pack behind. Mahaut carefully covered the head again with the sack and set it down inside the basket.

Solon put a hand on his father's shoulder. Benjamin stood silent, staring at the basket pack. His jaw was clenched so hard his face trembled.

"This will have to be done carefully. Thoroughly. And without mercy."

"What, Father?" said Solon.

"He's talking about revenge," Mahaut said.

Benjamin Jacobson turned to her. "Yes," he said, catching her eye. There was impersonal malice in her father-in-law's face. The expression of a carnadon waiting on the banks for one false move from its prey. "I'm going to need you, Mahaut."

"Me, Pater?"

"Yes. Will you help me do this?"

Mahaut nodded. "Of course I will."

"Cold hell, Father, I'll help, too!" Solon said. "Curse them. Curse them all."

Benjamin held out an arm. "No. That would make you the next sure target. I cannot have that."

"But Father—"

"I said no!" Benjamin lowered his hand. He was still gazing at Mahaut. "What do you say, daughter?"

Mahaut nodded. "Yes."

"You owe this house nothing. If anything, we owe you."

"That's not the way I see it, Pater."

Benjamin nodded. "Then it's done." He looked back down at the basket, suppressed another sob. "I have to go for a walk. A long walk. I won't be back today. I won't be—"

Benjamin could say no more. He strode past the basket pack and out the door.

Mahaut and Solon stood silently for a moment.

"Land and Law, I'm not meant for this," Solon finally said. "I want to sell grain. I want to sell grain, then go home to Mary and the children in the evening. And that's all."

"I know, Solon."

"What are we going to do?"

Mahaut knelt beside the basket pack, pulled it up, and put one strap over her shoulder.

"First, we'll bury this," she said. "Then you leave it to me."

2

She began to take her archery practice as seriously as she had when she was in operational command of the women's auxiliary. She rose early and worked with knife and gun with a former soldier who was on staff as a guard. The skills came back to her fairly quickly. In the afternoon she tried to put into practice what she had learned in the morning, although, as always, she avoided firing her pistol inside the compound.

She studiously avoided Edgar, and it seemed he was doing the same with her. He was much better now and began to take rides in the countryside. She had figured it would not be long until he strayed around the southern lake shore and wandered the league and a half into Hestinga. This was the longest time she'd ever seen Edgar go without visiting a tavern or whorehouse.

Plenty of people made the journey both ways every day. The children who were learning to read and do arithmetic rode donts or were trundled to and fro inside dak wagons to the private school in Hestinga where the better-off families had hired tutors, often moonlighting Regular officers or priests, to teach their children what they would need to know to maintain their status in society.

One of these students was Loreilei, of course. Mahaut knew that Loreilei was using her trips into town to visit with Frel, who now was apprenticing afternoons with Reidel, the civil engineer, while he finished his studies. They seemed to have taken her advice to heart, at least the part about not running off to be married so early. She hoped that Loreilei was being careful in other ways as well.

Frel had to come to Lilleheim occasionally on business from his master. Reidel was trusting him more and more with the layout of irrigation systems, especially the simple ones that fed off of a central ditch leading from the lake. Often Frel stayed the night in Lilleheim with a couple who were friends with his father. Mahaut was not surprised on those nights to wander by Loreilei's bed and notice that the sleeping form under the covers looked suspiciously like a pile of pillows.

She'd received word from Jeptha Marone, both in coded scrolls sent along the trader network and from the more expensive flitterdak winged messengers used for important matters. Marone had discovered that there was a child, but he had few other details, and was following up on the matter. The woman had moved back to her parents in Lindron, while her husband remained in Garangipore as the Eisenach factor. Mahaut had considered having the man assassinated, but he was well-guarded and his death would not serve as just revenge, in any case. He was a wronged party in this matter, and if anyone had a legitimate grievance against Edgar, it was him.

Besides, mere assassination wouldn't be enough.

In the meantime, there was grain to grow, harvests to get in, and contracts to fulfill. Together with her weapons practice, her days were completely filled. She had to arrange beforehand for moments of necessary rest, or those moments would never come.

Firing guns on the range was exhilarating, and the archery was calming in its way. She'd been shooting with a bow and arrow almost before she could walk. She hardly needed to think during practice, only draw the bow and listen to the arrow sing on its way to her targets. Sometimes her mind wandered, and when it did, usually she was thinking about the man, Abel Dashian.

With all that was going on here, and with Abel's studies in Lindron, they hadn't arranged to get together in over ten months.

Ten months, eighteen days and counting, she thought. *Too long.*

She liked to imagine him sitting still after lovemaking, the way he did. He would hardly move a muscle, listening with that slightly puzzled look to what he called his "inner voices." She didn't know who or what these voices were, but she imagined they were just part of himself that he'd attached personalities to, as a lonely child might invent an imaginary friend. Whatever they were, she understood they were important to Abel, and she never made light of him in these moments of communion.

Abel always acted calmly and decisively after such a spell, but it was in that quiet moment before taking action that he was most like a child overcome with wonder. It was as if he were seeing a world vastly larger than everyone else, vastly more complex and more beautiful. It made Abel himself seem otherworldly, filled with an inner light. And it was the vulnerability he showed when concentrating on those thoughts, those voices, the intensity he put into making a decision, that she most loved.

That she longed for.

Mahaut let go the arrow and it flew into the target, striking a thumb's length from the bull's-eye. This was the long-range arrow, the white-fletched one with the less damaging tip. She needed to practice with both versions, and next she pulled a black-fletched arrow with its double-notched feathers from her quiver. This was the mankiller. It had a shorter range than the white-fletched arrows, but its strike was meant to tear a jagged hole in a man when it struck, and take him down quickly.

She had notched the arrows on her bowstring when a beaded curtain over a doorway in the courtyard rattled and was pushed aside. She took the arrow off the bow and set the bow down, not putting the arrow back in the quiver. Maybe this would be a short interruption and she could quickly get back to shooting.

It was Loreilei. And she was not walking toward Mahaut, she was running. As she drew closer, Mahaut saw that tears were running down her cheeks. Her face was flushed.

"Aunt!" She called out. "Auntie Mahaut!"

"What is it, niece?"

"You have to come," gasped Loreilei as she charged up to Mahaut. "He's going to kill Frel!"

"What are you talking about? Who is going to kill Frel?"

"My uncle, that's who," said Loreilei, now shouting into Mahaut's face. "You have to stop him."

Edgar. Up to his old tricks.

Mahaut took the girl's hand, gave it a quick squeeze. "Yes, of course I'll come. But where are we to go?"

"The entranceway chapel. He caught us in there, Frel and me. We were only talking. Just talking. He said Frel was insulting the Family and he was going to make him pay."

"What?" said Mahaut. "Frel never insulted this Family. He's a good kid."

"Uncle Edgar said he'd insulted it by being with me. Because he is the son of a Redlander barbarian, and he's with me."

"How does he even know about that?"

"He was in Hestinga yesterday. He saw us together. He saw us kiss. Come!"

Mahaut quickly followed the distraught girl out of the courtyard and through the maze of passageways that led to the family chapel. It was a large empty room used for Thursday school gatherings and other religious ceremonies. It was also a place for reflection and meditation. Almost nobody used it for that, of course, so Mahaut suspected Loreilei wasn't telling the whole truth. It was the perfect place for clandestine meetings between lovers. The chapel was empty but for one thing: there was a room-size pyramid at the front built as a replica of the great step pyramid of Lindron, where the spirit of Zentrum was said to dwell.

Frel was lying at the bottom of the altar with Edgar standing over him. When they drew near they saw that Frel's face was badly bruised and scraped up. His lip and nose were bleeding, and one eye was swollen.

"Edgar!"

Edgar turned to Mahaut. "What? Oh, curse it all, what is it now?"

"Stop this."

"This? Why should I? Do you know what this piece of trash was trying to do?" Edgar raised a hand. In it was a pistol. Mahaut stopped in her tracks. "He and dear niece there were going at it behind the altar. Going at it like rutting donts, they were. And when I kicked him off her, she told me that they were going to run away together. How very sweet." He aimed the pistol at Frel's prostrate form. "But I don't think that's going to happen."

"Please don't shoot him!" Loreilei whimpered. She rushed forward, but Edgar cocked the pistol, and she, too, stopped.

"It would be better if you stay where you are, niece," Edgar said.

"Haven't you done enough to the boy, Edgar?" Mahaut said gently. "You've shown him his mistake."

"I don't think it's quite enough. And I think Father would agree."

"He wouldn't."

"What the cold hell do you know about it!" Edgar screamed at the top of his lungs. "Who are you to have an opinion on my father? He would not want that...thing inside his granddaughter, that I can promise you."

"Maybe not, Edgar, but Benjamin wouldn't want you to permanently hurt the boy. I'm sure of that," Mahaut said.

She tried to shuffle forward without Edgar noticing, but her feet made a noise against the stone floor and Edgar shouted, "Stay where you are, woman!"

"All right."

"What do you think you're going to do with that arrow, anyway?" he said. "Toss it at me like a spear?"

Mahaut looked down. She was still clutching the black-fletched arrow. "No, I was practicing with it when Loreilei came to get me."

Frel groaned and tried to sit up. The effort was too much. His arms shook, came out from under him, and he collapsed.

"Please, Edgar. Let him go," Mahaut said. "You've taught him his lesson."

Edgar shook his head. "He'll come back. His kind always do. Look at you, for example."

"As I remember, you came after me," Mahaut said quietly.

"You didn't mind. You loved it."

"I didn't know any better. And I was seventeen. I'd just discovered sex. It wasn't you in particular, Edgar."

"He needs to be dealt with," Edgar said. "My contribution to the Family."

"Not this way."

Edgar spun, pointed the gun at Mahaut.

"Shut up!" he said. Mahaut gasped, took a step back. "Just shut up." He turned back around to Frel, steadied his aim.

"No!" Loreilei shouted. Whatever fear had been holding her in place melted and she rushed forward. Edgar backed away from her, but she wasn't going for him or the gun. She placed herself between Edgar and Frel. "No, uncle," she said.

Brave, thought Mahaut. *And foolish.*

"You were a slave once, weren't you?" Edgar said. "Weren't you, niece?"

Loreilei slowly nodded.

"It seems the filth did not quite wear off of you. You are still a slut, I fear."

"You will not shoot him."

Edgar lowered the gun. He took a step toward Loreilei. "Of

course not," he said. As he did so, he turned the pistol around in his hand, now gripping the top of the barrel.

Mahaut shouted a warning, but it was too late.

With a vicious snarl, Edgar swung the pistol butt at Loreilei's head. The crack of the wood handle against skin and bone was audible. Loreilei dropped like a rock through water and hit the stone floor. Her head was spurting blood from a gash from her temple to her ear. She did not move.

"Stupid little slave whore," Edgar muttered.

Mahaut was wearing a simple tunic belted over women's leggings. She transferred the black-fletched arrow to her left hand, and her right hand went to the back of her belt.

Edgar lined up on Frel.

Mahaut's hand emerged from behind her back with a throwing knife. She turned the action of drawing the knife into an overhand cast, as hard as any she'd ever made. The knife flew across the five paces separating her from Edgar. It sunk into his left shoulder, the wounded shoulder. His arm jerked at the pain.

The pistol fired.

For a moment, Mahaut feared she'd been too late. But there was a puff of rock beside the altar, beside Frel, where the minié ball struck the pyramid altar.

Then, in the same eyeblink, there was the sickening sound of a ricochet.

Loreilei cried out. She clutched her side. Blood began to pour from a wound that could be nothing else but the bullet Edgar had fired.

It was a terrible wound.

Loreilei is not going to get up from that one.

"What did I do?" he said, looking down at the girl. It wasn't said with pity, Mahaut knew. It was anger that the unjust world treated Edgar Jacobson so shabbily.

Edgar dropped the pistol. With a yell of defiance, he took the knife in his arm by the hilt and pulled it free with his left hand. "I'll kill you for this, Mahaut!" he said. "This time, I'll kill you."

He spun around, Mahaut's knife in his hand and raised to strike.

With a quick, sharp, and strong shove, Mahaut sunk the black-fletched arrow into Edgar's chest. It scraped against a breastbone but found a way through, between. She pushed harder. She pushed until the arrowhead tore through Edgar's shirt in the back and emerged on his other side.

"You bitch," Edgar gasped.

"Husband," said Mahaut, "you never said a truer word."

Mahaut backed away, and Edgar stumbled backward, clutching the arrow shaft. He struggled feebly, and Mahaut realized he was trying to pull it out.

Good luck with that, she thought. The black-fetched arrows were made with a curving barbed arrowhead to make such an attempt futile.

The Scouts called them mankillers for a reason.

After a moment he either gave up the struggle or lost strength. He stumbled toward her. She took a step back.

And Edgar Jacobson toppled over and fell face-first at Mahaut's feet. This drove the arrow the rest of the way through until the better part of the shaft was sticking out his back.

Edgar's leg spasmed once. Twice. And then he ceased to move at all.

"No, no!" It was Frel. He'd pulled up his pants and found the strength to crawl over to Loreilei and examine her. "No, no, no." He took her limp form into his arms, cradled her.

Mahaut stepped over Edgar's body and came to kneel beside the two lovers.

"She can't be, she can't be gone," moaned Frel. "It's not fair. She was rescued. She was saved. Nothing bad should ever happen to her again. Nothing, nothing, nothing."

He truly does love her.

Mahaut did not reply. She let Frel hold Loreilei for a moment, rocking her, stroking her hair. Loreilei's head lolled to the side.

Mahaut touched the boy's shoulder. "You have to let her go now, Frel," she said.

Slowly, Frel lowered Loreilei's body to the floor. Mahaut looked down at the wound that had killed her. On her right side was a hole oozing blood.

When the shot woman's head touched the stone floor, Loreilei gasped suddenly. Her eyes sprung open, then rolled up in her and head and closed again.

"Blood and Bones!" Mahaut leaned over, felt Loreilei's neck for a pulse.

There. Faint, but there.

"She's alive, Frel," Mahaut said. Another gasping breath from Loreilei.

The girl was a fighter.

Her niece tried to speak, but only a bloody bubble emerged from her lips. Mahaut leaned over and brought her lips to Loreilei's. She pinched her niece's nose closed, then blew air into the mouth. Down to the lungs.

Loreilei's chest rose. Then, with a primal heaving sound, Loreilei threw up. The bile ran onto the floor, mingling with her blood. But after that, the girl breathed more easily.

"You stay with her," she said to Frel. "I'll go and get help. Can you do that?"

Frel nodded.

"Good." Mahaut rose. The hem of her tunic and the knees of her leggings were now soaked with Loreilei's blood. And that of her husband. She turned and stepped over Edgar's prone body.

Then she spun back around. The arrow, point first, was still sticking up from Edgar's back.

No need to let that go to waste. I might need it again soon.

Mahaut reached down. She got a good grip on the shaft. With a yank, she pulled it the rest of the way through.

Then, putting the arrow, slick with blood, into the quiver that hung at her side, Mahaut went to find enough servants to transport her niece to Mahaut's own quarters.

She did not send for a doctor. Instead, she settled down in a chair beside the bed. She had a cot brought in to sleep on.

It would start all over again. The picking through the wound for ball shrapnel, the boiled bandages. The long wait to see if any of it had worked.

She was nursing Loreilei when Edgar was buried in the Family yard on a small rise outside of Bruneberg. No one insisted she go. No one came to get her. She might have made the effort, despite it all, but Loreilei needed her. The living needed her.

Mahaut didn't make it to Edgar Jacobson's funeral.

3

Loreilei Jacobson did not heal easily. The shot had hit her lower rib and broken it. Mahaut suspected that it had then been deflected into her small intestines and done damage there. There was no exit wound. Controlling the bleeding was very difficult. The wound was large—the ball seemed to have entered at an angle—and she had to apply bandages and pressure to a large area until the servants came with a board made into a stretcher.

It's the same board they used to carry Edgar in, she reflected.

It had been scrubbed, but there were still bloodstains within the willow-wood grain. Getting Loreilei onto the board had provided its own difficulty. Mahaut was determined not to move her very much, and she'd had to make the servants understand this and not jostle her.

Meanwhile poor Frel sat nearby looking on worriedly with his one unswollen eye. He was hurt, and maybe hurt badly, but someone else would have to tend to him. Later she learned that the someone else was Bronson, the stable master, and his wife. Frel had recovered for a day in the feedloft while the couple attended him between their duties. A day later, Josiah Weldletter had come to take his son home in a padded wagon bed.

By the time Loreilei was in a bed, shock had set in. There was little Mahaut could do but keep the girl in clean bandages and alternately warm or cool her as her body shuddered with fever and chills. She did not regain consciousness for three days. During that time, she had occasionally stopped breathing, and Mahaut had pushed her own breath into the girl's lungs to keep her alive.

Always Loreilei's breath came back within moments. Her niece was tough.

Deep sepsis had set in, and with it great pain. Mahaut allowed Loreilei to eat and drink only broth of wheat, strained dak soup, and water for many days. She was afraid that whatever healing might be going on in Loreilei's gut would be undone by food passing through it. The wound healed slowly, but within a month new skin and scar tissue had covered it.

It's a very pretty little scar in comparison to mine, Mahaut reflected. *Of course, she'll never think so. If she lives.*

Yet slowly the girl recovered. After three weeks, Mahaut believed her niece fit enough to leave her side for several hours to take exercise and weapons practice. Loreilei's parents and uncles and aunts came by frequently after Mahaut permitted them in her rooms.

Never Benjamin.

Even in the early evening, when she went through the main sitting room to get to the latrine, she did not find him in his usual spot in the large chair he adored.

"Has he left the house?" she asked one of the servants coming by on his rounds.

"No, Land-heiress, he is still sleeping here. But he takes his meals alone and comes and goes like a ghost."

After two weeks had passed, Frel and his stepfather, Josiah Weldletter, had appeared at the door one afternoon. They would never have been allowed to come unless Benjamin had known of it and approved. Loreilei had immediately brightened. The two sat and talked while Weldletter, who was a captain in the Regulars and a cartographer working full time in the office of the district military command, told Mahaut what news there was of the wider world.

After the first visit, Frel came often. It seemed that Benjamin had resigned himself to the match. He'd spoken before of marrying Loreilei to a powerful First Family in Lindron who had expressed interest in establishing a connection to House Jacobson. Solon had four daughters, however, and Loreilei had a sister who was now a toddler. Benjamin might get his wish for the union of alliance sooner or later without Loreilei. He usually did.

Finally, after ten rises of the three-day moon, Levot, Loreilei was well enough to walk, gingerly, to her own quarters and begin her life anew. Mahaut doubted she would ever be able to run and gambol again. Any jarring movement brought her pain. Being alive at all would have to be consolation.

4

Mahaut took a long ride down to the lake and did not return until well after dark. She'd ridden past the family graveyard, but hadn't felt the slightest interest in going to see Edgar's grave. The next day she got up and went in to work. Benjamin would have to be confronted one way or another. But she sent word ahead that she was coming.

Benjamin looked at her without betraying an emotion when she entered the office. Solon found something that needed doing outside. They went to the corner desk where Benjamin liked to work. As usual, it was piled with scrolls. Benjamin's absolute control of his surroundings did not extend to the desk. Mahaut took the visitor chair. Benjamin pushed a scroll aside and leaned on his desk, looking down at her. He gazed at her a long time, then allowed himself the faintest of smiles.

"We've missed you here," he said.

Mahaut nodded, but said nothing.

A sob rose in Benjamin's throat. Mahaut could see him choke it back. "You killed my son."

"He was coming at me with a knife, Pater."

Benjamin held her gaze for a moment, then said, "I know."

"I'm sorry. I never wanted to hurt Edgar. I did love him once. Briefly."

"We have that in common, don't we? Only I find that I love him still, despite what he became."

Again, Mahaut did not reply.

"But it hurts me to see you," Benjamin said. "I think it will for a long time."

Mahaut let out a nervous breath close to a whimper. She'd been expecting this moment, but still it was a like a pain shooting through her heart.

So this was it. She was being thrown out of the family. Benjamin wouldn't put it that way, but that's what it would be. Where would she go? To her parents, she supposed. Or maybe her brother, Xavier, and his wife would take her in. She would still have the Treville Women's Auxiliary to keep her busy. But after the heady days of working with a trading house that stretched up and down the Land, this option seemed to her . . . smaller. Or was it that her world had gotten larger?

No, maybe going back to the auxiliary was not a good idea. She'd put new leadership in place herself. To demote them would do a lot of damage to morale she'd spent years to build. So she'd have nothing. Maybe when Xavier's children came along, she'd at least be able to help Helga raise them.

"I'll leave in the morning for Hestinga, Pater," she said.

Benjamin shook his head. "No. I have another idea in mind, if you'll hear me out."

"Yes, of course."

"It occurs to me that we have an opening in Lindron."

Benjamin scooted himself up on his desk and sat with his elbow on a knee and his hand on his chin. A wave of nostalgia washed over her for a moment. She'd seen him in this posture so often when he was working out a problem or thinking through a possibility.

So, she was to be shipped off to clerk somewhere far away. It wasn't the worst thing.

"Are you sure whoever you've put in Abram Karas's spot will want to work with a woman? The men who don't mind are rare. You know that."

Benjamin smiled slyly. "Daughter, I want to put you in charge in Lindron."

"In charge? You mean factor?" She could hardly believe this.

"We can't call you the factor. We'd call it chief consort to the House. We'll send someone along, someone who will know his place, to take on the factor title. But he'll answer to you. I'll make that clear. Dillard might suit."

For a moment, Mahaut allowed her heart to leap. But the feeling was quickly replaced by uncertainty. Could she do the job? So far, she'd been a second to Benjamin and Solon, a manager, certainly. But not in charge. Not ultimately responsible. Not like the factor of a large trading house in the biggest city in the world.

"Dillard would be fine."

"So you accept?"

"I would have conditions."

Benjamin took his hand from his knee, sat back on the desk. "Oh?"

"Freedom to invest fluid assets where I see fit."

"Of course. That's part of the job description."

"Perhaps not for a woman, though?"

"I said you'd be in charge. You will."

Mahaut nodded. "Good."

"What else?" asked Benjamin.

Mahaut took a deep breath, let it out. "I want freedom to avenge Abram Karas. In my own time, and how I see fit. I want to use the full resources of the House to do this if I have to."

Benjamin smiled. "A license to kill, eh?"

"Assassination would be easy enough. But maybe I can arrange something worse."

Now Benjamin did allow himself a full smile.

"You are free to do as you want in this matter, and the House resources will be at your disposal in Lindron and at all Jacobson Houses," he said. "But there is something else. I want your advice."

"Yes?"

"Loreilei and this boy," he said. "Edgar was right in a way. It probably isn't a good idea. A land-heiress's place is to serve her house. In return, she has the house's protection, its wealth and power. Of course, Loreilei will not be poor when she marries. We'll always see to that. But she'll miss out on her chance to make a mark. A son is like chits that can be spent a little at a time. A daughter—"

"—can only be sold once, and had better bring a good price?" Mahaut said. "And the price is alliance."

"Or a truce. Or a spy. You get something."

"She was a slave to the Blaskoye. I'm pretty sure she doesn't ever want anybody telling her what to do again."

"But she trusts you," said Benjamin. "She loves you."

"I love her. Most of all, I feel responsible for what happened to her. You know that."

"Then take her to Lindron with you." He said it as if Mahaut had already accepted the position, as if he had heard it in her voice. Maybe he had. "Take her for a year or so. I won't forbid her attachment to the boy. I know where that would get me."

"Yes."

"But you think a year apart would break it?"

"I don't know," he said. "But she's very young, and we owe it to her to test it, don't you think?"

"I agree with that."

"I'll talk to the boy to make sure they don't try something idiotic, like running away together. I'll put it to him as a way of proving himself. In a way it will be."

Mahaut nodded. "I think that's a good plan, Pater. I believe I can convince her. I'll try, at least."

"So it's decided? You'll do this?"

She took a moment, looked down, rubbed her forehead. "And what will I call myself? Not the position, I mean. What will be my name now?" she asked in a low voice.

Benjamin smiled crookedly. She recognized that smile. He wore it when a deal of his had gone particularly well.

"Why, Her Gracious Excellency, Land-heiress, the widow Jacobson, of course."

This will be my life for years to come. To say good-bye to the family here. To say good-bye to my parents and brother. No more rest day trips to Hestinga to see Mamma and Pappa. To be really, truly, for the first time, my own woman.

Then she realized that this is what she'd been waiting for all along.

"Thank you for the opportunity, Pater," she said. "Yes, I'll take Lindron."

5

Her desk was made of imported Delta hardwood, and large enough to lay a body on. But when she rolled out the ledger scrolls for House Jacobson Lindron, they covered the whole surface. In this way, she could see it all in a glance. The accounts, the connections, the flow of grain, goods, and barter chits. The liabilities. The possibilities.

Karas had done a good job, as far as it went. He was conservative with Jacobson funds, as was she. But it was clear from the outlays that he had been more concerned with keeping peace among the First Families of the capital city than with making a profit. And look where that plan had gotten him.

That's not fair, she thought. *No one could pay his way out of a House disaster such as Edgar Jacobson's duel had been. No, that took blood. It may take more.*

Karas was also cutting deals with the Blaskoye raiders from the southern border of Lindron. They were deals to trade the goods that they'd robbed from elsewhere in the Land. She supposed Karas would view this as a necessity of doing business. Perhaps. But maybe something could be done to stop the blackmail once and for all.

She'd hired a tutor for Loreilei and was bringing her along on her rounds of house visits to the capital First Family matrons—a necessary social duty—and on evening functions and get-togethers. She'd even allowed Loreilei in on some business meetings. She supposed she was trying to train Loreilei in the things of the world that she, Mahaut, had learned the hard way. It wasn't so long ago that she herself was headstrong Mahaut DeArmanville of Hestinga, invincible, young, ready to take on the world—and hopelessly naïve.

She'd been beaten down, wounded, betrayed—but she'd fought back. Now she was chief consort of the House of Jacobson in Lindron. Factor. Here in Lindron there were so many things to consider. And most days she felt up to the task.

"Master Marone to see you," said Dillard, who worked in the outer office.

"Send him in."

"Very good, Land-heiress."

Marone looked even more grizzled than usual. There were several bulges under his jacket that would be weapons, and she noticed that the knuckles on his right hand were scraped red. She motioned for him to sit, and he lowered himself into the chair with a delicate grace for such a big man. He sat ramrod straight.

"What do you have for me, Marone?"

"It took a bit of doing and more than a bit of spending, but I believe I've found the child."

"Submit your expenses to Dillard," she said. She leaned forward. "Tell me."

"The Eisenach woman came to term and delivered a boy," he said. "Then it was carried away quickly, out of Eisenach House here in Lindron. I have this from the nurse. She gave the child to a man she didn't recognize. I spent more than a few day tracing this person, but I finally found him. I questioned him thoroughly."

Mahaut glanced down and noticed Marone's skinned knuckles.

"His name is Dubin, but that's no matter. He's an orphan monger. He takes them and sells them, Mistress. He'll take a fee and place them as shop apprentices, fieldhands, sweeps, whores in training—and other things too vile to mention."

"I understand, Master Marone," she said. "Go on. What happened to the child?"

"He was sold to the orphanage near the Lindron gunpowder works. It's run by priests. Sort of a monastery."

"That doesn't sound so bad, considering. At least he'll be near the family trade."

"It is bad, Land-heiress." Marone shook his head ruefully. "It's the workhouse that the Silent Brothers are drawn from."

"Those wretches who work at the gunpowder factory?"

"Yeah, those ones, Land-heiress."

The Silent Brothers were the priestly worker caste who made gunpowder. Making gunpowder was a prerogative of the priest-smiths only. The recipe, or magic, that went into creating it must be kept a secret at all costs. One of those costs was to develop a priest caste of men to carry the secret knowledge of gunpowder's making. The Silent Brothers were castrated at a young age, and their tongues were cut out. Abel had dealt with them. He'd told her that they had a complicated sign language among themselves, but otherwise they communicated with no one. They went about their jobs in the gunpowder yard, they ate and slept there, and never left except as a cadaver—an event which usually came at a young age. Those who worked with the materials that went into gunpowder tended to have short lifespans.

"When is the . . . when does the operation on the children take place?"

"The tongue at age three. The other at around seven years old, I believe, your grace."

"So they haven't . . . done him yet. Cut off his little balls, I mean. The tongue's no matter."

Marone started at Mahaut's graphic language. "That's right, Land-heiress."

Mahaut was quiet for a moment, then cleared her throat and spoke. "I want this child. I want him here."

"Here?"

"In this house. In House Jacobson. He is a Jacobson, after all."

"A bastard urchin."

Mahaut bristled. "Don't ever let me hear you say that again, Marone. If I do, I'll have you turned into one of those Silent Brothers."

Marone hastily nodded. "No offense intended, your grace."

"Can you arrange to take the child? Steal it, I mean?"

"Might take some doing, but I think I can handle it with a good purse of chits."

"Whatever it takes," Mahaut said. "No price is too high."

Marone allowed himself a smile. "It won't take that much, considering the kind of folks I'll be dealing with. Nothing that will break the House, that's for sure."

"Like I said, do whatever it takes. Understand, Marone?"

"I do, your grace."

"The sooner the better. I want those scissors as far away from the little thing's testicles as possible."

"Yes, Land-heiress," the trader replied.

"We have to keep this as quiet as possible. I think one of the maids has a sister who has recently delivered. I'll make arrangements for her as a wet nurse."

Marone nodded. He shuffled his feet a bit, started to speak then stopped himself.

"What is it, Marone?"

"I was just thinking, your grace..." He hesitated, then seemed to start over and spoke again. "You know I have young 'uns of my own, Land-heiress. I know that every day I miss 'em something awful, and I think they miss me. So does the wife. Miss me, I mean to say. But what I'm saying is, the boy should have someone to look after him like that. Like they would a son."

"He will," Mahaut said. "He'll be a son of Jacobson House. He'll get plenty of affection."

"Very good then, your grace."

"Get going, Marone. The sooner the better. Keep those cutters away from the boy, and I mean it. See Dillard for whatever funds you'll need."

"Yes, Land-heiress Jacobson."

The trader rose, bowed awkwardly, then turned and left.

She was alone again. At her very large desk. In her very own office.

For a moment, Mahaut allowed herself to enjoy this, all of it. Then she turned to the ledger scroll on her desk and got back to work.

PART FIVE

The Command

Two years later

1

Lindron
472 Post Tercium

After Abel's years at the Academy, he'd gotten used to the Tabernacle of Zentrum and even begun to think of the Tabernacle complex, which included the military academy and the administration offices for the priesthood and army, as familiar ground. His ground. There were other adjuncts: the secret-service prison, cut into the rock below, a barracks for academy students, and a row of housing for the prelates and instructors.

Then, of course, there were the carnadon pools surrounding the Tabernacle pyramid itself and, terraced down the bluff to the River, four fieldmarches below the outcrop of quartz-veined sandstone on which the compound was built.

He'd first seen the carnadon pools as a kid, and been suitably impressed and terrified. Now he had a history with them. He had stood up to the carnadon gambling ring at school when they'd come for him. He even knew some of the carnadons on sight.

Several of them had been named after the more annoying Academy instructors. He liked watching the beasts churn and swirl after the sacrificial meat, cleaned from the outer temple, was tossed in at feeding time. This was the main purpose for keeping the carnadons, after all.

Yet Abel didn't for a moment believe that his regard for them was mutual. During his sojourn at the Academy, people had lost hands and whole arms. Two Academy cadets had been torn to pieces. Of course, that was mainly their own fault.

121

Even the town people, who should have known better, were not immune to foolishness. A year ago, a teenage boy trying to impress his friends by walking along an edge of the enclosures had misjudged just how high a carnadon could leap into the air chasing prey. He was gone before anyone could cry for help. Abel had served as honor guard for the priest who was sent to inform the parents. If the dead boy had not been a First Family scion, he doubted the parents would have even been notified by the Tabernacle, much less received a personal messenger.

But the royal treatment didn't make the boy any less dead. Whether you were First Family or a Delta farmhand, it did not pay to mess with carnadons.

In the midst of the pools, the step pyramid rose. It was double the height of any other building in Lindron. It seemed to be made of impregnable crystal. Each stone was a slightly different hue, and from within the structure of the stones themselves, lights shone. The effect was muted during the day, but at night the pyramid glowed. What was more, the lights alternated on and off, and blinked in changing patterns. It was said that they represented the thoughts of Zentrum, and any who stared into the lights long enough would either become a saint—or go mad.

A portico opened on the pyramid's side. A hall led past ceremonial chambers, a guard station, and Abbot Goldfrank's personal chapel. It terminated in the Inner Sanctum, the place that housed The Eye of Zentrum. Most assumed that Zentrum somehow lived in the Inner Sanctum, perhaps as a spirit. But Center had set Abel right on that score: Zentrum's programming was contained in the structure of the entire pyramid. The colored lights were, in a literal sense, his mind at work.

The Inner Sanctum was an interface device keyed to human neurological patterns. In the Inner Sanctum, you didn't need the communication wafer used by provincial prelates. Zentrum could impress himself upon your mind directly.

Abel bowed, walked inside, and performed the First Chamber oblation. As a full Guardian, he was expected to sacrifice something of himself whenever he visited Zentrum. He'd consulted with a former instructor, who had told him a lock of hair was the customary offering.

No doubt for DNA analysis and confirmation of identity, Center commented.

Zentrum is nothing if not careful, Raj put in.

But he can't read my thoughts yet?

Zentrum has a limited range over which he can engage quantum induction. He will be able to project thought before he can access yours.

Not like you.

I have considerably more advanced features. The AZ12-ill-e Mark XV is an early model A.I. It was used primarily for planet-based military activity, almost exclusively terrestrial, Center said. **It is an anomaly that this one was hardened against the nanotech plague that brought down the empire. In fact, it would be very interesting to learn** *how* **that came to happen.**

Irisobrian, Abel thought. *Zentrum's mother. Could she have been one of those . . . tenders of the computers? Maybe she did it.*

That is a most interesting idea. It is obvious now that you state it clearly.

What's obvious?

Iris O'Brian. A name handed down verbally over many generations.

Raj laughed. *All those billions and billions of quantum computing whatnots and you didn't see that? I had it figured out years ago.*

Why did you say nothing?

Didn't seem important. Besides, I thought it was apparent.

I am good at math. I was not designed for word play.

Evidently.

Can we just pay attention to where we are? This is the most dangerous spot on the planet to all three of us, after all.

Abel had left his weapons outside in the first guard station. There was a sacrificing knife on the dais, however, and he used it to cut off a hank of hair. This he laid on the table, and the knife alongside it.

The dais began to glow. Then it changed colors repeatedly for a few blinks of the eye. When it was done, the hank of hair was gone.

There is a small trapdoor opening on the dais concealing an analysis mechanism beneath, Center said. **The trapdoor appears to be nanotech-activated and returns to being part of the stone itself when not in use.**

Abel continued down the central passage. He passed several side chapels and priests' stations along the way: the Tabernacle pyramid was huge. The passageway began sloping downward, and its walls spread out. Two Guardians stood in the hallway in front of a side doorway. Each man stood at attention and spoke no word when Abel arrived, although he recognized Sutherlin, a former classmate, serving as the right-hand sentinel.

This was the Abbot's Station, although Abbot Goldfrank was not always present there, by any means. It was, however, manned by a high-ranking priest day and night. Today Goldfrank was performing the ceremonial duties, and he emerged from his post. Abel bowed, and Goldfrank nodded. With another nod, he beckoned Abel to follow him farther down the hallway. Goldfrank moved at a stately pace, his orange priest's robe trailing on the sandstone floor behind him and making a tiny scratching sound in the general silence.

The passageway sloped farther down. After what seemed a walk of another fifty paces, it terminated at a doorway. The Abbot stood to one side.

"Behold the Beating Heart of the Land," he said. "Behold the All-seeing Eye."

"Do I have permission to enter the Inner Sanctum, Law-heir?"

Goldfrank made a slight bow. "I find you at one with Law and Edict. Go forward."

Abel stepped past Goldfrank and through the doorway. He entered a large room. It was three-sided, pyramid-shaped, and the apex must have been twenty elbs above. Two of the walls were stone. The third wall, the one directly across from the entrance, seemed to be one enormous crystal. It pulsed with dancing lights of changing colors.

The air was cold. Abel could see his own breath.

Air-conditioning for the language-processing electronics. Primitive by Empire standards. This planet was truly a backwater: Zentrum was likely purchased used. The entire pyramid itself serves the secondary function of heat dispersal from nano-generation.

There was a throbbing sound that filled the chamber. Abel realized his heart was beating along to this rhythm.

Are you sure this is going to work?

Chances are high that it will succeed.

Which meant that there was also a chance that it would not. They were planning to temporarily remake a human mind, after all. There was nothing to do but to go forward.

Enter my presence, Major Abel Dashian.

The voice seemed to come from both within and without. It resonated within him in both high and low levels, as if he were a set of chimes through which a strong wind had passed.

Abel walked to the center of the chamber and hesitated.

Approach. Lay your hands upon the Eye.

He crossed over to the blinking crystalline wall.

Here goes.

He touched his palms to the crystal. It was quite warm. The flashing lights gathered around his points of contact.

Analysis proceeding. Please do not disengage.

He remained still.

Analysis complete. DNA records retrieved. Identity confirmed.

Abel realized he'd been holding his breath. He let it out, took a deep breath.

"I await your bidding, Lord Zentrum," he said, repeating the litany he'd been drilled with from his first Thursday school class onward. "It is my honor to do your will."

Very good. The general staff with the consent of the Abbot has recommended your appointment as district military commander for the Cascade region.

"Yes, Lord."

You are quite young to be considered for such a position of responsibility.

"There have been others younger than me. Pliny in the Delta, in 235 P.C., von Stubbe in Cascade itself in 193. According to the scrolls, each served with distinction."

Yes, I remember them well.

"Should you find me worthy, I will walk in their footsteps to maintain the Stasis."

This is pleasing to me. Now it is time for your examination. It will go easier if you open your mind to me, Abel Dashian. Hold nothing back, for I must and will seek into all corners, and if I must pry open a door held shut in your mind, it will cause damage, great or small, to your psyche. Some have gone mad.

"I will strive to do as you bid, Lord Zentrum."

Then the examination will commence.

Center's voice immediately cut in following the throbbing pronouncement of Zentrum.

I am initiating the consciousness sequestration routine. Expect

to lose ninety percent of sensory awareness until modifications are in place. Center sounded thin, less powerful than the booming presence of Lord Zentrum.

Abel had the sensation of falling, although he did not move. His field of vision became a line, then a circle the size of Levot, and then the circle closed down to a dot. He felt as if he were standing in a deep well looking upward—a well from which there was no hope of escape without aid.

Where was this place within him? It was not the Hideout. There were portions of himself he could cut off from Center and Raj—at least he believed he could. Clearly there were portions of his mind that they had cordoned off from his personal awareness, as well.

Of course they have their panic rooms, their secret caches within me.

He had realized even when he was a child that he was as much a construct as Center and Raj. When they entered his mind in the nishterlaub warehouse so long ago, they had rewritten his mental makeup. Raj had told him as much—out of respect—and Center had afterwards confirmed this basic fact of Abel's existence.

Suddenly he felt himself rising out of the well and toward the light. There was a tingling in his body, as if he were being dragged through a thicket of particularly sharp Redland pricklebrush. Portions of him were being scraped away and left behind.

Memory sequestration complete. Implanted engrams activated, said a voice. At least Abel thought it was a voice.

Not one he recognized. Maybe it was Zentrum.

Suddenly his senses returned.

Returned from where? What had happened? The last thing he remembered was touching the Eye of Zentrum. He was amazed and deeply ashamed of himself. How could he have doubted for a moment? Who was he to question the Creator himself?

Zentrum was Lord. Zentrum was God.

Abel could not move, but if he could have, he would have fallen to his knees in worship.

He viewed his life as if it were a story playing out in shadow form, in flickering firelight before his eyes.

Confess your shortcomings.

He would confess all.

I believe myself more intelligent than most of the people I meet. In fact, showing appropriate respect to those I consider mentally inferior is often an irritation.

This is understandable. Show me more. Show me all, Abel Dashian.

My father is one I respect above all others. He has taught me that only the Land matters. That is where my loyalty will always lie.

I have not understood that to be dedicated to the Land is to be dedicated to you, Lord. Now I do.

That is well. The reason for your nomination is your excellent performance at the Academy, your skilled completion of your duties at command planning, and, most of all, your leadership of the Treville Scouts during the battle with the Blaskoye incursion of Treville that occurred five years ago. Yet there was heresy at the heart of this defense.

Yes, Lord. I understand that now.

These nishterlaub weapons you employed—do you understand how they threaten the Stasis?

Yes, Lord.

Explain.

Victory is not worth the price of blasphemy. All means must lead to the end of balance. Your Laws and Edicts are just and right, and there is no other truth that need be revealed to man.

And heresy?

Heresy upsets the balance. It's a striving of individual men to be like God.

And what must be done with the heretic, Abel Dashian?

"He should burn," Abel said aloud.

You were close to the heretic priest.

There was no point in denying this to a being who knew all. "Yes, Lord."

You accepted the breaking guns.

"I made myself believe all was well. They came from a priest, the chief priestsmith of Treville. I should have questioned this extraordinary development, but I was eager to destroy the Blaskoye."

And you did.

Yes. We did.

Now, considering all that has come afterward, what do you have to say of your actions?

Abel agonized. Before this moment, before he knew the reality of Zentrum's existence, he might have answered differently. In his heart of hearts, he had wanted to win, and would do anything to achieve victory for the Land and his father. Now everything was different.

"Better that I die before I break the Edicts of Zentrum. To put myself before your Law is to exile myself from the Land itself. Your will sustains the people and Land. Nothing else is of consequence."

Very good. I can see the faith burning brightly within you, Abel Dashian. This is why a greater revelation will be yours. Behold:

He was soaring over the River, flying like a flitterdak, moving up-River. And as he traveled, the Land changed. Wheat, barley, rice gave way to barren terrain. Clumps of men clinging to existence in tiny enclaves. So little to eat. So short and bloody each single life. The world fallen to ruin. Humanity brought so low that all hope was gone.

A dark age that might last a thousand years. Perhaps a hundred thousand.

Then he was down among these people. He was one of them. Behold the past:

He is a young man leading children, the oldest survivor after disease has taken his parents. Five brothers and two sisters. Starving. Desperate. The others dependent on him.

They wander endlessly among the ruined hills. His baby sister is crying constantly. She cannot stop no matter how he rocks her. His youngest sister's stomach is distended terribly. She has not eaten for eight days, and then only a few swallows of rotten meat he himself has shared with her.

I have not eaten in eight days. The thought echoes, repeats itself in his mind like a taunt, a prophesy of doom.

Ahead, he sees an overturned cart. He and the children hurry to it. It is a handcart, empty. Beside it a man lies on the ground. Someone has ambushed and robbed him.

He looks around wildly to be sure the attackers are no longer here. The only sound is the wind blowing over the broken stones of the ravaged world.

The man is alive, barely. A leg has been smashed and a portion of bone juts from the skin. The man looks up at Abel.

"Water," he croaks. "Please."

Abel, the boy, considers for a moment. He might pass by. He might lead his desperate little band onward.

But he is so very, very hungry.

With a growl, Abel lifts a nearby stone. It is not a particularly large stone, but almost more than he can handle in his feeble state.

The man sees what he is doing, cries out, and tries to twist out of the way.

Too late.

The stone crashes down upon his skull. Abel hits the man again to be sure.

He looks up. His brothers and sisters have gathered around him and the man. They stand in a circle, silent, anticipating.

Abel tosses the rock aside. He looks down at the man's ruined head. He can't help himself. He is unable to think of this as a man he has murdered.

All he sees is food.

With a ragged roar, he scoops his hands into the skull cavity, pulls out the bloody matter, and begins to eat.

As if on signal, his siblings run to the corpse and follow their brother's lead.

Behold the Past before the Past:

He is soaring again, farther up the River, to it source. Buildings as tall as mountains. Men dwelling in them, walking among them. Strange animals whizzing to and fro. No, these are the machines of men. Men who are convinced they are at the apex of civilization. Nishterlaub, nishterlaub everywhere.

Pride.

Arrogance.

Imbalance.

They deserved what they got.

Collapse. Ruin.

He can hear the screams as the buildings fall down around them, as all they knew crumbles to ruin in ten blinks of the eye.

From this egotistical height of technological wonder to eating manflesh in one generation. This is the state from which I raised you humans. All of you. Do you see what heresy breeds?

Yes, Lord.

The desires of men are like the River at flood. They must be regulated and contained. At times the Land must burn so that civilization can be renewed. Do you understand, Abel Dashian?

Yes, Lord. The Blood Winds. They are a part of your will, as are all things.

Better that thousands die than civilization fall into the hungry darkness again.

Yes, Lord.

There are more important things than winning a battle—or even a war.

"I repent of all I have done contrary to your will, Lord Zentrum. You have raised me from nothing. All praise is yours. I should never have touched the breechloaders. I should have killed the priest with my own hands. From this day forward, I will accept defeat before heresy."

You have learned, Abel Dashian. That is well.

"You have shown me. I never knew. I never knew." He felt tears welling in his eyes. His whole being resounded with anguish at his shortcomings, with ardor for his newfound convictions. "May your will be done now and forever. Alaha Zentrum!"

He stumbled back as he was released from the crystalline wall and his bond with Zentrum.

You are acceptable in my sight, Abel Dashian. You may go now.

"Thank you, Lord."

A low bow.

Then—

Something inside him is quivering, something being born. What is this?

What's happening to me?

I am—

Not me.

Not this quivering, frightened me. No!

I am—

Someone else.

Something else.

The new man. The second coming of knowledge.

Welcome back, lad, Raj said. **Give it a moment and the rest will flow into you.**

But I . . . but the Lord Zentrum . . .

Zentrum is not God, Abel.

You dare . . . you dare . . .

And then he really was back, reconstituted. He was standing at the doorway, breathing hard.

I . . . believed. You made me totally believe all of it, all the bullshit. It was so . . .

Demeaning.

Yes.

Dehumanizing.

Yes, that, too.

Nasty.

What Raj said was true. But moments before he had completely believed every word from Zentrum.

How can I know you are not lying to me, too? Maybe you're all lying, and the truth is something entirely different.

You've asked the question before, and we've given you the only answer we have.

Choose the truth that will most help the people of my world survive.

That's right. It's the only answer we can give you. Kind of refreshing after listening to all that nonsense from a Mark XV computer that thinks it's God, no?

I guess.

There is one thing Zentrum is right about, though. War is a means, never an end in itself. Forget that, and you're doomed to repeat the cycle of destruction over and over again.

Wonderful. Can we get the cold hell out of here, General?

Aye, we can. And welcome to high command. You're about to be the DMC of Cascade.

2

One year later

Cascade District
473 Post Tercium

The stockade stank of sweat tinged with the iron tang of blood. The Cascade Scouts looked fearful in their guise as Blaskoye. Some of the Firsts were still convinced that they were the captives of Redlanders. The more perceptive knew this was a lie, but, Abel hoped, had not yet discerned what it was he and the Scouts intended to do with them.

Good. They'll be more pliable that way.

It was night, but Abel knew the real Blaskoye were gathering to the west. To the east, in uneasy alliance with the Redlanders, the Cascade militia was camped. All told he figured he faced a thousand warriors, including the women and children the Blaskoye sometimes brought to war as auxiliaries, and sometimes as fighters when needed.

The Cascade Regulars were nowhere to be found. They would stand back until the matter was decided one way or another. Abel might curse them for their fickleness—they were supposed to be under *his* command, after all—but he was glad not to be facing their numbers, all the same. He assumed they'd taken themselves across the River until the fighting was over. Abel swore that after this was over, he would make it his solemn mission to

132

turn them into a real fighting force. At present they were little more than a lackadaisical police force or worse—an armed gang of protection racketeers.

So he had his Cascade Scouts, about three hundred of them, against the district militia—rabble bought and paid for by the oligarchs—and against a thousand Blaskoye. Even though the militia was better armed than the Redlanders, he was much more worried about the Blaskoye.

Deal with them, and the militia will scatter like flitterdaks.

The attack came near dawn. It was far from concerted. The Blaskoye attacked in their customary waves. The militia marched up in tattered columns and fired uselessly into the stockade wood-work. Did they hope to clatter him to death with banging minié balls? What was more, except for a few units, they had fired en masse. Now they were all simultaneously reloading.

Abel sent his fifty or so mounted Scouts charging out at them. This worked exactly as he expected. A general panic spread down the militia lines. Behind his cavalry, he sent out a handpicked one hundred in lines twelve abreast and three deep.

They attacked in a spreading arc. At least a hundred militia men fell dead or wounded before the first of Abel's Scouts took a bullet. Within a quarter watch, the Cascade militia, at least five hundred of them, were in headlong retreat toward the River.

Let the carnadons take them. He had other worries.

To the east, the fighting was more intense and even-sided. After the Blaskoye first wave was repulsed, not without Scout loss of life, they drove in behind their own dead donts and used them for cover to dismount and proceed forward on foot. They were not exactly in a battle line, but they did fire in salvos divided by clan, with others firing while those with spent rifles reloaded.

The stockade—really only an ammunition dump on the outskirts of Bruneberg—was not built to withstand a siege. They could hold out for a while, but already the musket shots were chipping away at the thick wooden planks that protected those within.

But it wasn't only himself and the Scouts pinned down in the stockade. Unbeknownst to their attackers, some of the best men of Bruneberg were in this sty.

First Family oligarchs. Their chief retainers. A handful of gang leaders who didn't claim aristocratic blood, and some who did.

He'd had his Scouts snatch them from their homes, their places of business, their whorehouse stalls, the day before, when he'd gotten word of the impending attack. It was a grand kidnapping. And if this gamble didn't pay off, they would see to it that he died slowly and horribly in payment for it.

Eisenach, the leader of the First Families of Bruneberg, was a man with whom Abel had dealt before. He ran the Bruneberg Powderworks like a merchant prince. Although gunpowder was considered sacred, and deliverable to the priestsmiths and the armorers of Lindron at no cost, House Eisenach set the market price for all others—and, having a monopoly—set it at what they wanted. When Abel took over, one of his first acts was to remove Eisenach from his temporary military appointment as commandant of the powderworks. Eisenach had responded as if Abel were joking. He hadn't gone anywhere, and had kept his base of operations in the powderwork offices as always.

From that action to the situation in which he found himself at the moment there was a direct line of causation. Fuck with House Eisenach's cash flow and a horde of inhabitants of the Redlands would descend on you with massacre on their minds.

For much of the morning, it seemed as if that was exactly what was about to happen. Massacre. Eisenach, though tied to a post by hand and foot, was exultant.

"You're going to scream, Dashian," he called out. "They'll ram a stake up your ass and out your throat, strip your skin, and put you out for the carrion eaters. They know how to make the stake miss all of your organs. Keep you alive so you can die slowly. And I'll be there the whole time, laughing in your fucking ear."

Abel shook his head. "Seems unlikely, Eliot."

"You'd better keep me alive," he called out. "You'll beg me to call them off soon."

The man is not a coward, Abel thought.

He may or may not be in truth. This talk is pure nonsense, calculated to rattle you.

No shit.

He believes he has your number. Does he?

We'll find out soon enough, won't we?

Aye.

Perversely, the more Blaskoye they shot, the closer the remaining warriors crept, using the bodies of their fallen comrades for cover. The corral itself had a low stone wall surrounding it. When they reached that, they could set up behind it and take potshots at the Scouts to their hearts' content.

In the distance, there was the rattle of gunfire. Concentrated. Precisely timed. Definitely not Blaskoye.

The Treville Regulars were coming—Abel's father's force. They'd infiltrated Cascade District as merchants and traders. Distrusting both Road and River traffic—the Firsts were in total control of area transport—Abel had communicated with his father by flitterdak scroll and requested the reinforcements. Since the exchange of messages had been, of necessity, hit-and-miss, he hadn't known for sure he would receive support today.

Treville was a very different place, politically, than Cascade. The district military commander and the chief prelate worked in concert. The Firsts, men like Benjamin Jacobson, were powerful there, but they kept to their place. Those that didn't were apt to receive a lesson from Joab Dashian. Unlike the oligarchs of Bruneberg, those of Hestinga and Garangipore usually got the message and backed off.

It was Abel's goal to bring the ways of Treville to Cascade.

This was the right thing to do, first of all. And second, it advanced the cause of progress, although he was perhaps the only man living on this world who appreciated that fact.

His worries were resolved. The Treville Regulars hit the Blaskoye from behind. The attack was completely unexpected and devastating. Abel didn't wait.

"Over those walls and at them, boys!" he called to his Scouts. To their credit, the tired Scouts didn't hesitate for an instant. The front line of the Blaskoye, seeing a pack of screaming men brandishing rifles charging their positions behind the piles of dont bodies, wavered, and then leaped up and ran.

If it had only been one glorious charge, his Scouts would have run out of steam quickly and been exposed to a counterattack that would have obliterated them. Instead, the assault was the hammer to Joab's Trevillian anvil. Abel charged along with his men. He fired first his rifle, then a pistol, and finally he was reduced to cutting a Blaskoye's neck with the old cavalry sword his father had bequeathed him.

Through the smoke and fury, Abel could look over the heads of the fleeing Blaskoye and see the approaching dust cloud of marching Treville Regulars. The Blaskoye ran into its deadly volley full tilt, and fully exposed. Men, boys, women dropped—such close-range fire was indiscriminately horrific. Some fell crying out in pain and anguish, many threw down their weapons and begged for mercy, sheik and commoner alike. Some were silent, to move no more. Those that could streamed to the north and south and scattered across the wheat fields of eastern Cascade. They would find their way back to the Redlands, but not as a cohesive fighting unit.

By mid-afternoon, Abel's Scouts linked up with the Treville Regulars.

He had won.

Five Blaskoye sheiks had either surrendered or been unseated from their mounts and roughly taken prisoner. Abel knew them from the double blue line hem to their otherwise white robes. He had these brought to the stockade's main room.

From the rafters of the stockade's barnlike interior, several bodies were hanging, ropes about their necks. These were older men, fatter men—men who were past their prime for physical labor.

The others were huddled into a clump in the center of the enclosure.

Staring up at the hanging men, the Blaskoye sheiks perhaps believed they were about to die as those others. They had begun to chant their death songs.

Abel had reed mats laid out for them.

"Please, sit," he said to them. "We will bring refreshment." True to his word, he personally doled out cups of wine and beer.

The Blaskoye stopped chanting and accepted the drinks—they were so thirsty after hours of fighting that anything would do, even Landish wine. They sat down warily, some prodded by the tip of a Scout bayonet.

Abel had his Scouts pull a First oligarch out of the clump of still surviving captives from town.

"Gentle sheiks," he said, startling them by speaking in their own tongue. "What am I offered for this one? He will make a fine hand at cleaning stalls, I think. Or perhaps he can work the sulfur mines in your Table Lands?"

After an astonished moment, they realized what Abel was saying. The Blaskoye began to bid.

The remaining oligarchs and headmen were auctioned, one by one.

There was whining, begging, offers of immense wealth. Threats of eternal blood feud and retribution.

Abel just smiled his grim smile and sold another.

Eliot Eisenach was the last. He stood wearily, resigned to his fate, but seemingly determined to give Abel no satisfaction by flinching or begging.

By this time the Blaskoye sheiks were quite drunk, and the bidding had gotten sloppy and out of hand. They were beyond the meager chits they'd brought with them. There were solemn promises of donts and dak herds, mounds of Table Lands sulfur, and sacks of dates and figs from the gardens of the Great Oasis itself.

The woman entered the stockade.

As if a signal had been given, the drunken palaver died to silence. She was lovely. She was dressed in a diaphanous robe of fine linen, and the kohl around her eyes glistened black. She was accompanied by a retinue of four large men—men who looked quite dangerous. When she came to stand beside Abel, they took up positions around her that would cover attack from any quarter of the room.

"Good evening, your grace."

"Commander."

"I would like to ask for your advice in a matter now before us."

"I'll be happy to be of service if I can."

"This one," Abel said, motioning to Eisenach, "tried to have me assassinated. Several times this year. When that didn't work, he instigated armed insurrection. Got all those unfortunates involved." He gestured toward the clump of former oligarchs, now bound together in a Blaskoye slave transport line. "He deserves to die. Do you agree?"

"Undoubtedly, if all you say is true."

"It is."

"Then yes."

"Can there be any mercy?"

Mahaut turned and gazed at Eisenach. He glared hatred back at her.

"Well, you might end his line yet spare his life and sell him," she finally said. Mahaut shrugged. "I know this is better than he deserves, but you did ask me what would be merciful."

"Thank you, your grace. Your advice will become my command," Abel said. He turned to the captain of the Cascade

Scouts. "Castrate him," he said. "Then throw him in with the other Blaskoye chattel as a bonus."

Eisenach had begun to violently tremble. After a moment, his legs gave way and he dropped to his knees. He glared up at Mahaut.

She regarded him for a moment, then stepped close to him. He tried to strike out at her, bite her, but a Scout guarding him caught the movement and savagely yanked him back by the rope about his neck.

Mahaut bent low and whispered in Eisenach's ear. Abel couldn't make out all that she said, but Center reported her words: "This is for Abram Karas."

When Eisenach heard her words, he cried out, gnashed his teeth, and beat his head against the stockade floor. It was soft dirt, however, so he wasn't able to dash his brains out, if that had been his intention.

Abel turned to Mahaut. "Satisfied?" he asked.

"As soon as I send word to my pater."

"I'll see you tonight?"

"Of course."

Mahaut smiled, bowed, and made her way out.

After sending the amazed Blaskoye on their way east with their new acquisitions (and an armed escort back to the Rim), Abel wearily took up the task of burying his dead.

Cascade District was his now, but it was they who had paid the price in blood.

PART SIX

The Clash

The Present

1

Approaching Progar District
476 Post Tercium

Once they were above the Second Cataract, the road climbed steadily. Rocks jutted more often from the soil of the Valley, and the Rim grew closer and closer. Soon the Valley was barely a league across from West Rim to East Rim. Finally, they were walking on broken stone rather than dirt. The scree was smooth enough for passage of the wagons, but crunched with every step.

What bothered Abel, and was clearly bothering von Hoff, was that the cliffs on either side were now at the edges of the Road. They were marching through a constricted passage, perfect for an enemy sniper or bowman. It troubled von Hoff enough to send Abel to General Saxe and request that he be permitted to send skirmishers up the rocks to take care of any threat from above.

Abel picked his way forward to find Saxe. He heard a rumble at first Then from ahead came a thundering roar. Rocks? Had the enemy launched an avalanche? Then Abel rounded a bend and saw what created the noise.

A secondary river was pouring into the River. Abel had seen it on a map, but had assumed it would be another stream to cross, similar to the Canal.

This was something else again. This river was called the Fork on the maps. Ahead of Abel, it descended through high canyon walls that stretched to the east. It was huge and torrential. Abel had seen streams, but had never seen a large tributary to the

River. That was because this was the only one. It originated in the high plateaus of the Progar Escarpment, draining the northeastern Schnee for hundreds of leagues. There was no way a boat could cross the Fork, much less the hundreds of boats that would be needed to ferry an army.

Abel rode closer. He could feel the pounding power of the water in his body. He looked above. There, shrouded in mist, was a way over. It was a bridge made of cut rocks, a bridge as singular in the Land as the Fork. A trail switchbacked up to its southern entrance, and then the bridge itself arched over the torrential Fork.

The Stone Bridge. It marked the exact border of Cascade and Progar, one of the great wonders of the Land. He'd learned of it as a child. The Stone Bridge of Progar, the Tabernacle of Zentrum, the lighthouse at Fyrpahatet, Lake Treville—these were all on the list.

Abel rode up and joined the stream of soldiers crossing over. On the other side of the bridge, where the Road widened out, he found the general and his staff.

Saxe was a man made to sit on a mount and look commanding. Even Abel, who had learned not to judge the skill of the military man by his appearance, couldn't help thinking so. He had a graying beard so closely trimmed that he must shape it with a steel blade rather than obsidian. He was bronze-skinned, with deep-set eyes and a raptor's nose. He was also one of those men whose torso was a good deal larger than his legs. This caused Saxe to appear enormous when he sat in the saddle. Abel had been in his geography class at the Academy, and knew Saxe was shorter than he was when standing. Now, sitting on a large male dont, Saxe gazed down at Abel while Abel delivered von Hoff's request.

The general had moved over to one side with his staff in order to review the troops as they marched. The officers were passing around a wineskin and squeezing a short stream into their mouths. Saxe himself did not partake, but worked a cud of nesh with his jaw while watching the troops.

After Abel was done talking, the general spat out a stream of nesh juice onto the dusty road, somehow avoiding getting any on his beard. He turned to Abel and laughed genially, then denied the request. He sent Abel back to tell von Hoff that the cliffs were so steep he doubted any man could climb them, and they had to take their chances.

Von Hoff calmly nodded when Abel delivered Saxe's reply. "It's my job to worry, and his to sort his priorities," he murmured. "Still, let's have all sharpshooters to the middle of the column. That'll give them a better field of fire if they have to take the enemy off those cliffs."

Abel sent out couriers with the order. On they marched, and soon the Road became so steep and narrow that the donts couldn't handle it with men on their backs. Abel had the command staff dismount and lead their rides upward. He was, as he'd started the journey, back to the steady drumbeat of a double-time march.

No attack came from above, and the path widened a bit. Abel discovered that there was a louder and more powerful roar than the Fork entering the River. From ahead came the pounding thunder of the Third Cataract. Here there was a far steeper and more constricted passage than even that of the Second Cataract where it flowed around Montag Island. Soon they were marching alongside the River as it raged down the Valley. The Road became more level, and the brigade staff was able to mount up again. But the sound of the roaring River kept the donts skittish, and Abel had to give Nettle a reassuring stream of gentle words now and then to keep her calm.

Others were not having as much luck, and one of the brigade cartographers fell off the side of a veering dont and landed on his arm. Abel, not far away, heard the sickening crack of bone, and the man stood up wailing in pain. Von Hoff was too far ahead to have noticed, and Abel decided not to trouble him with the situation. He had the man set to the side with a medic to tend him.

They rode on.

After what seemed an endless series of rapids, they reached the top of the cataract. The River widened, and a descending wagon path crossed over the Road and down to a ferry landing at the water's edge. No carting boat was in sight. Abel looked across the River and saw a boat pulled up on the other side and turned over, as if it had been stowed—except for the fact that its underside had been stove to white wooden splinters.

To Abel's right, the cliffs of the Rim turned directly east, while ahead of him stood the first true mountain he'd seen with his own eyes.

Somewhere in the back of his mind, Raj was chuckling. *You'll see higher still. Much higher.*

He'd climbed plenty of hills and rocky towers in the Redlands, and gazed up canyon walls, but he'd never seen anything like this, not in person. Center had created images of mountainous terrain for him that was impossible to tell from the real thing—he'd believed. But there was something about the hugeness of this actual mass of earth and rocks that made a physical impression on Abel's senses.

At the crossroads, the wagon path headed to the northeast and disappeared into some low-lying trees. According to the maps, it ran northeast between the mountain before them and the Rim cliffs to its south. The main Road still headed north, hugging the River as ever, and worked its way around the western side of the mountain and out of sight.

"What's its name, that mountain?" Abel asked Wolfe, another of the mapmakers.

"Sentinel," Wolfe answered. "And there's more behind it that we can't see. There's three peaks, one after the other, with a low ridge connecting them. Sentinel, Tamarak, and Meyer. River flows to the west of all of them, and the Road follows it."

"What about that path?" Abel said, nodding toward the wagon track leading away from the ferry.

"It's called the Ferry Road on the maps, even though you can see it's two ruts cut in the ground, and not much else. It circles around the three peaks on their eastern flank, hugs the Escarpment. The two roads meet back up in the Plains of Orash. At least that's what the maps say."

"Do we have any men of Progar in the Brigade who can confirm your maps?"

"I don't know, sir. Not that I'm aware of."

"Find out."

The Guardian column crossed the wagon track and continued up the Road. It seemed that they were headed straight for Sentinel for a long time, but then the Road veered to the left, which placed the mountain on Abel's right. They'd gotten far enough away from the River to lose sight of it, but now the Road crossed a rise and angled down into bottomlands, and the River reappeared in front of them.

As they neared it, the ground underfoot became softer and muddier. Abel first noticed it when Nettle couldn't pull a foot out of some sucking mud quickly enough. She stumbled and barely recovered. Another moment, and he might very well have had a thirty-stone beast wallowing on his body, crushing muscles and bones.

Marsh, said Raj. *Poor ground for a fight. Or perfect, depending on your position. You know what use we made of marshy land before.*

How could he forget? The Battle of the Canal. The priests had opened the headgates and allowed water to flow through the Canal levee and into the rice paddies of Treville. The Blaskoye horde, those excellent riders who seemed to live on their donts, had charged into it—and become mired.

The Treville Black and Tan Regulars, though outnumbered, had breechloading rifles that gave them a three to one rate of fire advantage over their enemies. The wallowing, disorganized Blaskoye had been cut to pieces, a horde of ten thousand reduced to piles of slain donts and men. Those bones still lined the top of the Canal levee on the road to Hestinga.

But the soggy ground was also the first spot wide enough to accommodate a mass of men. Saxe, near the vanguard of the column, called a halt to allow the others to assemble. There were already several thousand men who'd crossed the rise and descended to the marshland. These spread out, mostly toward the River, and many of the men took the chance to curl up next to their packs and grab some rest.

They've been marching for fifteen days and covered over two hundred leagues, Abel thought. *These men deserve a thrice-damned breather.*

What men deserve and what men get are two different things, growled Raj. *Look up and to the east!*

Abel's gaze trailed up the slope of Sentinel Mountain. Its flanks were bare of anything but grassy vegetation and shrub...that is, except on the top, where there was a darker band of what must have been trees or dense brush. About halfway up, a rocky crag jutted out, granite gray against the green slope. From the top of that crag, a white puff of smoke rose, as if the crag were a chimney venting a fire down below.

We're in musket range of those cliffs, Abel thought.

Then something he'd never seen before. Something dark flying through the sky. Not alive. Jagged. Like—

A rock. A very large rock.

It crashed among the Guardian columns, ploughing lengthwise down the Road, crushing men and tossing others to the side like blown chaff.

From the side of the rock projectile, from a hole in its surface, smoke rose.

White smoke that Abel was all too familiar with.

Gunpowder.

"Dive!" he screamed. It was useless. He could barely hear himself in the confusion.

The rock exploded.

Fragments flew in all directions, killing more men, taking off limbs, a head.

Abel looked up. Another black spot in the sky, descending in an arc.

"Incoming!"

This time the Guardian troops threw themselves on the ground. The projectile landed and exploded. Several more men were killed by the impact, but none by the explosion.

From nearby came the commanding voice of Colonel von Hoff.

"Forward! Get beyond the range of those arbalests!"

The troops rose and milled about in confusion. Abel snapped the reins of his dont and set her into motion toward the troops.

"Up!" he yelled. "Up and forward, you pukes!"

He burst among the ranks that had been hit, Nettle neatly dodging both the living and the dead.

"Forward," he yelled. "Double-time! Forward!"

Almost miraculously, the men responded.

"Look above!" shouted one man.

Abel looked up. Another huge stone had been launched from the revetments above.

"Move it," Abel shouted.

The ranks surged forward.

The rock landed, but the range was off and it fell too far on the other side of the Road and half buried itself in the mud.

"Major, hold there!"

Abel spun to see von Hoff, who had caught up with him.

"Let's you and I get to the front and locate Saxe or one of his couriers. We'll all get out of range of these thrice-damned stones if we can keep the boys moving."

Now that the troops had started, the march seemed to continue under its own power. When another stone came and found its mark to the east side of the Road, men dove for the ground, then hopped back up and continued marching once the danger had passed.

Abel and von Hoff worked their way through the marching soldiers, Abel riding in front to clear a way, calling "Colonel coming through! Make way!"

From ahead, a cry of alarm. An officer came charging down the side of the Road toward them, his dont's forelegs raised in the air and the dont running on two legs, as the animals did at full speed. When he got to von Hoff, the rider pulled up, the dont crashed down on all fours, and the officer breathlessly delivered his message.

"Men down ahead. Rifle volley from up the Road and rifle volley from above."

"We'll pull back," said von Hoff. "Thrice-damn the rocks. Let's get these men off the Road and out of rifle range."

Then the air was filled with the crackle of muskets, which Abel could hear even over the shouts of the men.

The messenger cried out and grasped his back. His eyes rolled up in their sockets, and he slowly fell from his dont onto the ground. He landed on his back. In his stomach a hole the size of a green fig had been blasted.

Exit wound, thought Abel. *Got him from behind.* He'd seen enough of such wounds to know.

The remainder of the couriers and brigade staff caught up with Abel and the colonel. Von Hoff glanced down at the dead man, then looked up, a resolute expression on his face, and shouted to his gathered staff. "Take them to the west side of the Road out of range of muskets and those falling stones. Find cover wherever we can. This rifle fire may only be a minor nuisance. We need to see what we're dealing with." The others stared at the colonel as if nothing he'd said was comprehensible.

They're dumbfounded from the march. Get them moving, man. Give them something to do.

"You heard the colonel," Abel screamed out. "Get those orders to companies and stop hanging around here like a bunch of flitterdonts looking for dead meat!"

He began shouting precise assignment.

The couriers and command staff seemed to start back into the present with Abel's words. They had trained for this. They knew their stuff.

They'd better, thought Abel. *We went over and over this in drills the past couple of months.*

Those who were messengers reined their donts to attention, kicked them to speed with their heels, and rode away to their assigned companies at once.

Master Sergeant Groelsh, dismounted nearby beside his dont, nodded up to Abel. "That's the way to tell them, Major. I'll tend to the lines hereabouts."

The men began to line up by company and march off the Road toward the River, several fieldmarches to the west. Another round of shots smashed into the ground nearby, not striking any men, but kicking up stones.

"Better move ourselves," von Hoff said. Abel issued the order for the remaining staff to move west a fieldmarch. He was happy to see they did this in good order. No one was panicking yet.

The company commanders formed their men into ranks, and turned them west. Within a few steps from the raised bed which held the Road—a dirt causeway through the marsh—there quickly was no ground, only bog. It grew deeper and wetter the closer they moved to the River. The men began to sink in up to their knees in the mire.

Another massive exploding rock fell, but the troops were out of range. It caused no casualties, only noise and spectacle.

His couriers returned and Abel fired off more directives. "Move to the north, through the muck. Tell them to stay out of range!"

He and von Hoff did the same, They kept their donts on the road, but on the far side, away from the mountain. After a few harrowing moments, they were outside of musket range, or at least shot ceased raining down near to them.

When they reached position that seemed safe, von Hoff turned and stared up at the mountain. "Did you notice the way that fusillade came in all at once, Dashian, like a slap across the face?"

"Yes, sir, I did."

"And those rocks. Ballistas, arbalests. Powerful ones, to get that kind of range. Using nishterlaub methods, I'll wager."

"Must have about the same range as their muskets."

"I'm not so sure those are all muskets, either. Who the cold hell can get off volleys that well timed? It's sure not any of those shabby militiamen we've been picking off along the way."

"If they have those nishterlaub extreme-range catapults, there could be other new weapons, sir," Abel said. "These people are known heretics. They're liable to try anything."

Von Hoff nodded. "Yes, we need reconnaissance. Saxe will see that. The cavalry can work their way up that hill from the side, come in on their flank or even above them. They probably don't even have to engage. We need information and then—"

Abel was listening, but he was staring up the hillside as well. "I don't think that's going to happen, Colonel."

"What the cold hell do you mean, Dashian?"

"Look up ahead. The mounteds are charging. Looks like half the regiment."

"Curse it! No, they can't be—"

But then von Hoff saw what Abel was pointing to. Donts streamed up the hill, looking like small nutterdaks at this distance, leaving a cloud of dust behind them. Yet the attack was no more than three or four fieldmarches away, and the mountainside was sparsely vegetated. Abel and von Hoff had a good view of the action.

"What are they thinking?" von Hoff shouted plaintively. "What cursed idiot sent them?"

Abel knew when a commanding officer was asking a rhetorical question.

He did not reply.

Up the hill the donts charged. Although the donts the mounted regiments rode were of good stock—all Guardian animals were the cream of the crop—this was not the terrain they'd been bred for, and it showed.

The movement upward started as a two-legged sprint, with forehooves in the air, sharp end out and held at about the height of a man's head. This was the classic mounted charge, terrifying to an infantryman. But as they struggled up the mountain, the leading wedge dropped to four hooves, and then the mass behind them dropped in droves. Soon the donts were trudging up the hill little faster than a man could walk. Another massive volley from the stronghold above reaped men from saddles and felled donts, but the bulk of cavalry continued upward, upward.

"Brave," said von Hoff matter-of-factly. "So brave and stupid."

But suddenly, as if they'd emerged from the mountain itself, a line of men with rifles rose up. They were halfway down the slope from the craggy stronghold, and stood between it and the charging cavalry in a line that ringed the mountain as far as Abel could see.

There must be five hundred men up there, Abel thought.

Plus or minus fifty by immediate estimate, Center said. **I am, of course, extrapolating how many may lie around the curve of the mountain at either end of their line.**

The cavalry was at nearly point-blank range.

Those five hundred Progar men took aim. The sun flashed off their barrels.

The Guardian cavalry continued its charge. Some brought carbines and dragons to bear on the newly revealed enemy. But there wasn't time.

A crackle of ragged fire down the line of Progar militia. Those in front, leading the charge, went down as if mown by an obsidian-bladed scythe. The line of men in the fortress—for it was a fortress, had to be—stepped back and began frantically reloading, while behind them another line stepped forward with rifles already at ready.

Now several of the mounted got off shots, and a few of the Progar men fell. But not many. Not enough.

The Progar line fired again. Far from perfectly together, but they didn't have to be. They were firing into a mass of men and donts. Another swath of mounted troops crashed down, dont and man screaming, entangled, crushing one another, dying together.

"By the Bones and Blood," von Hoff said softly. "It's pure murder."

A horn blew in a low, loud blast that reverberated off the mountain. A huge group of mounted separated from the mass of men on marshy Valley floor north of Abel's position and tore up the mountain to reinforce.

"Blood and Bones! Kanagawa's thrown his reserve in," von Hoff said. "It may be enough to carry those trenches."

Abel realized the trenches he was referring to must be where the men had been hiding before they'd risen up and blazed away with their muskets. They'd seemed to come from nowhere.

Wave after wave of mounted attacked, fell to the ground or were driven back. Yet they attacked again, struggling up the mountainside yet another time. The musketry from the trenches might not have been enough to stop the charge, but the rain of fire from the craggy stronghold above the trenches added to the cavalry's misery, falling down on them from positions almost directly over their heads.

Then, from the north, another hue and cry. Men shouted. Horns blew. Donts screamed and honked. The crackle of gunfire, only a few pops at first, grew.

Von Hoff surveyed his men deployed into the marsh. "This won't work," he said. "We'll be forever getting up to fight. We'll have to take to the Road again." He considered a moment. "Order them back to the Road, Major. In enemy range or not, we have no choice."

"Yes, sir."

Your colonel has made the correct decision, given the circumstances, said Center. **The Road in this area is an artificially created raised causeway through these wetlands. The only higher ground is the mountain slope presently occupied by the enemy.**

The colonel may be right, but your general has walked right into this one, Raj said darkly. *What happens next won't be pretty, either.*

This time Abel didn't need to send riders. He instructed Groelsh to set his specialist signalmen to their wigwag, directing the most northerly companies back onto the Road first, then the others, line by line.

Abel could imagine what the troopers were thinking:

First the thrice-damned Lieuts tell you to run. Then, when you're winded, he orders you back to get slaughtered. If I were a grunt, I'd believe command had lost its mind, Abel thought.

But Guardian discipline showed, and fighting lines were quickly formed as men streamed back to the Road, most within range of the muskets above. Much of the musket fire was still directed at the charging mounted forces, however. Nevertheless, every few moments another catapulted rock fell on the Road and took out another few men.

Exposure couldn't be helped or avoided. They must move forward. And they did, muskets at the ready, in four-deep, shuffle-stepping lines, exactly as they'd been drilled.

"May I suggest we split the lines into squads instead of companies, Major?" said Groelsh. "We'll move faster and present less of a target. We must look like a line of insectoids from up there, just waiting to be crushed."

Abel nodded. "Yes, Master Sergeant, do it the best way you

can. Get the wigwag going." Abel nodded down the Road. "I
think the battle's underway up there."

"We'll get them up double-quick, sir," said Groelsh. "These are
Goldies, after all." He turned and barked at a signalman, and the
directions went out in a flash of flags.

Abel rode up and down the line and watched his men form
fighting ranks. He tidied up their edges here and there, but for
the most part, they were in good order.

Amazing, considering they were withstanding barrage after barrage of musket fire, not to mention giant boulders raining from
the sky. Although the musket men in the trench were engaged
with the mounted attack, the guns on the crag above had now
been turned on the Third. Most of the fire flew over their heads
or impacted on the ground to the side of the road. But a few
fusillades found their mark—some of it arriving in almost perfect
sequences, perhaps eight or ten shots at a time.

Suddenly a portion of the ranks would find themselves hit
and a group of men would go down at the same time, clutching
shoulder wounds, neck wounds, legs shot out from under them.
And some suffered the worse wound of all, a minié ball that tore
into the side or gut, that hit the rib cage or pelvis and bounced
through the organs in a ragged path of destruction. Their fel-
lows lifted the lightly wounded, in some cases throwing them
into shoulder carriers. The dead and seriously wounded were left
behind for the time being.

Despite this, the ranks held.

Von Hoff, who had gone up front to get a better view of the
situation, came charging back on his huge dont—Big Green.

He picked out Abel and rode up to him. "We're going to be
here a while. It's chaos up there. Let's have ranks return fire at
that thrice-damned sentinel fortress while we wait." He spun
Big Green around, spotted Groelsh. "Think you can pirouette us
without shooting ourselves, Master Sergeant?"

"Absolutely, Colonel, you just watch us!"

Groelsh shouted the movement order down the line, and his
other sergeants took up the cry. When all was ready, he turned
to Abel. "Major, would you like to give the signal now, please?"

"Yes, Sergeant." Abel raised a hand, lowered it. The ranks, four
thousand men in all, spread up and down the Road, turned on
his command.

"Front line up!" screamed the master sergeant. The cry was passed down the line. While the line was aiming, another flight of bullets took down several of them. The ones that remained standing did not flinch.

"Fire!" shouted Groelsh.

An ear-rattling din of firing cap pop then musket boom as each gun went off and sent its missile flying toward the crags above.

"Line back, second up!" shouted Groelsh. "Fire!"

This time Abel watched where the shots were hitting. He could barely make out several of the puffs of rock dust in the stone just above the flat spot on the crag—the place he assumed the attackers occupied.

"Third up!"

"Bring it down three or four elbs, Master Sergeant," Abel called out.

"Yes, sir," answered Groelsh, and shouted the instruction.

This time the Goldie fusillade was rewarded with a man rising from behind what must have been a barrier atop the crag, grabbing his stomach, and pitching forward to fall twenty elbs onto the rocks below.

Got one, at least.

I imagine you've given the others something to think about, Raj said.

But what the cold hell weapon are they firing?

Analysis in process, but estimate to seventy percent plus or minus three is that they possess volley guns in the upper portion of the fortress.

Volley guns?

Multiple musket barrels probably secured to a wood base with removable breech pieces and a common charge. Crude but effective.

And nishterlaub, Abel thought. *Absolute heresy to make something like that. How many do they have?*

Enough to keep up a near-continuous fire on a good portion of your line, even while the muskets are taking on the mounted charge, Raj said. **Those fusillades have come in groups of eight, so these are most likely eight-barreled weapons.**

My estimate is that there are a total of one hundred and five guns with seven that have gone out of commission, judging by the decrease in the rate of fire. The operators are firing in three

stages, so there are no more than forty volley guns brought to bear at a time. But volley guns have inherent limitations, most obviously the need to reload each barrel separately. That indicates at least two or three hundred men on that crag above the trenches.

I'm amazed it can hold them all.

They are most likely dug back into the mountainside, or perhaps they are making use of a cavern. This is a formidable redoubt they have constructed.

Almost impossible to take in a head-on charge, even with Guardians, said Raj. *Look at those fields of fire it covers! It's designed to make this Road a slaughterhouse.*

So we don't take it from below, Abel thought.

That's right, man. What we need is to find the back door.

2

A courier charged up from the front of the marching line and reported to von Hoff.

"The First has fought their way onto some harder ground," he reported. He had to speak loudly to be heard over the huffing and chuffing of his dont, which was breathing hard through its blowhole and expelling acidic snot. "General's forming a line."

"What the cold hell are we facing?" von Hoff shouted at the man, his agitation showing.

"Progar riffraff, sir," replied the man. His shoulder sash marked him as a captain on the corps command staff. "But lots of them. Looks like the whole province has turned out to greet us."

"Why in Law and the Land didn't the cavalry make first contact and hold them off while we formed up?" von Hoff said. "That's what they're for."

The courier captain shrugged and nodded toward the fighting on the mountain. "You saw it, sir. The general sent them up to take out that position."

"*Saxe* sent them, by cold hell? I thought this was Kanagawa's doing," von Hoff said, shaking his head. "General Saxe sent up the entire mounted regiment—"

"Yes, sir, he did. And then the reinforcements Colonel Kanagawa had held back."

Von Hoff shook his head, as if to clear it. He looked at the captain. "On with you, then, and back. Tell Colonel Muir and the Second that we're moving out and to be ready to follow us."

The Second Brigade was behind them in the order of march today. "Yes, sir," said the courier captain. He yanked his dont around with the reins and charged away south, cutting down the extreme side of the road, since the middle of the road itself was filled with stalled men who wanted to fight but couldn't get up to the front to do so.

Groelsh turned the regiment again to the north, and von Hoff ordered the march. The company commanders knew what to do from here on out. When they reached the fighting, they would deploy to either side, spreading out in four-abreast company lines, shoring up the men already engaged wherever they found themselves. After that was accomplished, and if he received orders, von Hoff would see about positioning them offensively.

As they grew near, there was far too much smoke in the air for Abel to do anything more than catch a glimpse of the enemy ahead. All he saw was the flash of teeth and the glint of gun here and there.

Center, I want to understand what's happening.

Interpolating. Interpolation complete. Observe:

Abel was flying. He was standing on the impulse flyer he'd flown once before in his vision—the vision where he'd first met Center and Raj. Up and over the fighting he soared. A turn here, a twist there—he found he could change his position minutely—and the overview was perfect. Inertial dampers and force fields kept him steady, even though he was standing on what amounted to a small ledge many hundreds of feet in the air.

Of course none of it was happening. Or rather, all of it was happening within his mind. He understood that. But he didn't feel it. He felt like he was flying. And it was great!

With a twist of his hips and a shift of his weight forward, Abel rolled the flyer to the side into a banking curve, the wind of his passage screaming in his ears.

Please settle down and remember the purpose of this projection, Abel.

All right, all right.

He righted himself, slowed.

He looked down.

The valley floor in front of the Guardians was filled with

Progar militia. The Guardians were fighting only the front edge of this mass. The militia stretched far up the valley, thousand upon thousand of them.

And yet Abel couldn't see much organization to them. In fact, it looked far more like a huge rabble or mob than an army.

Yet there were so many of them.

The fort on Sentinel Mountain is the first of three such installations on the western flanks of those two sister mountains to Sentinel's east-northeast, the other two being Tamarak and Meyer.

On the western sides of the mountains lies the River Valley which is, in this region, a series of marshlands, as you have experienced. These wetlands continue for several leagues up the Road.

Great, thought Abel. *More pushing through hip-deep mud if we get off the Road.*

The high ground upon which General Saxe is taking on the Progar militia is not a large enough piece of land to accommodate the whole Corps. This was intentional. At most, your brigade will be able to deploy to join with the First. The Second Brigade, behind you today, must remain there in a logjam of too many men on too little ground.

So that gives us ten thousand troops. We should be able to deal with the Progar militia with that.

Yes, but at great cost. That is the idea. They don't expect to win here. They want to bleed you. These other forts on the mountains possess not merely volley guns, but rock-throwing ballistas and, in all probability, crude cannons. The mountain forts will keep Saxe from maneuvering along the hillside to flank the Progar militia. The marshland will bog him down as he goes up the center of the Valley. And, of course, the River itself cuts him off to the west.

What a pretty little trap your general has marched right into, said Raj. *He's even done the Progarmen the favor of pulling back his mounted regiment and sending them up the mountain, so his men could stumble on the enemy entirely unaware and unprepared.*

Well, what can we do, then? What can I do?

Fight it out, man. Fight it out. Seek an opening or some leverage. We'll help.

Abel took another look at the forces massed below him.

What's on the other side of those mountains? he asked.

A narrow valley lies between them and the eastern Rim, Center replied. **It widens into the Manahatet Valley farther north past the Three Sisters. At the northern end, where the Manahatet and the River Valley converge, lies Orash, the capital city of Progar District.**

So what if we turn around, take the ferry road east, and go up the other valley instead?

You observed the wagon track. It is too narrow to concentrate a Corps-sized force until you reach the plains below the city of Orash. Also, the Sentinel fort, and the forts on the two peaks to the north of Sentinel, are manned on the eastern sides of those mountains as well as the west. They command the valley from above.

Take me across the River, Abel said.

He turned the flyer and leaned forward to put on speed. Soon he reached the River's edge and zoomed across. Below was a different landscape than on the eastern side. Here was rolling hills and plain, with some belts of trees, but mostly grasslands. Enormous herds of daks were scattered everywhere grazing.

Why not come up the western side? Abel asked.

Difficult. The River makes a great turn and constricts this plain up against the western Escarpment several leagues to the north. There lies the settlement of Tomes. It would be a near impossible pass to fight through, and could be bottled up.

Duisberg's Thermopylae, said Raj.

It could be held with a small force almost indefinitely.

Then the east it is, I suppose, said Abel. It was time to leave the vision, but he didn't want to. Instead, he angled the impulse flyer upward and climbed higher, higher. A wispy cloud lay ahead, and he passed right through it. It left a cool condensation on his arms and face. He looked back down.

Very high now. The whole of Progar stretched out below him. The mighty Schnee Mountains to the extreme north. At the base of one of the tallest of the Schnee was a huge lake. This collected the snow from the melting glaciers of the Schnee and from that lake flowed the several streams that made up the headwaters of the River. The body of water was Lake Orash, and on its southern end lay the city it was named for.

Orash. Capital of Progar.

So many rocks, mountains, hills in this land. And wet. Water everywhere. So different from anywhere else he'd been.

We are coming here to destroy it. Wipe the population and their heresy away as if they never existed.

Take me back to the battle, Abel said.

Instantly the vision fled and he was in the real world of dust, guns, and blood.

3

The Third Brigade plunged into the melee with the Progar militia on the northern Road, and for a long while Abel was busy processing all the incoming reports from commanders for von Hoff, and sending off von Hoff's orders and queries in the most efficient manner he could, whether that was by mounted courier, mirror signal, or flag wigwag.

Now that the field was smoky, the quicker methods became less effective, and after a while mounted or running courier was the only thing that would do.

The Guardians were hacking away at the Progar militia as if they were nasty vines overgrowing a garden, but for every man they cut down, another was there to take his place.

The Progarmen fought like madmen. Apparently everyone in the district realized what fate had in store for them if they didn't stop the Guardian advance.

Abel visited the front lines only once, when von Hoff briskly ordered him forward to see about a reported enemy breakthrough. On the way, he grabbed a platoon from the rear, eager to get into the fray, and led them forward toward the hole in the lines. The platoon's young lieutenant was visibly trembling, but trying to put on a brave face. Abel didn't blame him. He'd felt the same way himself before.

It seems so long ago now.

He'd been in his first firefight when he was fourteen.

"Don't worry," he said to the man in a low voice. "Just stand tall and do what your staff sergeant tells you."

And then they were among men falling back and shooting, then falling back again. "Get in there!" Abel shouted to the platoon.

They charged forward into the breach with bayonets fixed and guns blazing. Abel drew his dragon from his waistband—he'd left his rifle stacked back in the command zone—and trotted along with the platoon for a moment. He wanted to charge forward. Everything in him told him to do it.

But von Hoff has specifically ordered me not to, thrice-damn him.

Reluctantly, Abel slowed himself and watched the others disappear into a haze of smoke lit by flashes of fire. It was as if they plunged into one of the thunderstorms of Valley legend. He himself had never seen rain.

He stayed long enough to be sure that the line was holding. Those who had fallen back began working their way forward again. For a moment the smoke parted and there was the platoon Abel had led forward. Many of them lay dead on the ground. He tried to see if one of the dead men was the young lieutenant, but couldn't make him out in the scrum.

Then Abel turned and worked his way back to the rear and von Hoff.

When he arrived, at first he couldn't find his colonel. He began to fear that von Hoff had gone down, but then he spotted the colonel kneeling beside a tarp laid out on the ground. Several other older men stood around, also staring down.

On the waxen tarp lay General Josiah Saxe. Around him was a hovering cloud of commanders and staff officers.

Saxe was alive, but blood was flowing from a wound under his right arm, spurting out with each beat of his heart. A rough tourniquet had been tied at the shoulder, but the wound was too far toward the shoulder for the tourniquet constriction to do much good. The artery was protected by bone here and couldn't be squeezed shut.

Saxe was trying to say something, and Colonel von Hoff was leaning over, his ear to Saxe's mouth, attempting to listen. But blood bubbles were forming on the general's lips instead of words. Then the general gave one violent shudder from his head to his feet, and lay still.

Von Hoff slowly stood up, still staring down at Saxe and

shaking his head. "Gentlemen, the general has gone to the grain halls of Zentrum, just as we all shall."

The other men Abel recognized now by their shoulder sash insignia: gold and red. Green and red. Yellow and red. And von Hoff's own gold and indigo. The other two were the commanders of the First and Second Brigades, Muir and Deerfield. Kanagawa, captain of the mounted regiment, was also present. The only leader missing was the colonel of the quartermaster corps.

As if on cue, the sun set behind the western Rim. Dusk fell across the Valley. The fighting continued until pitch blackness arrived. It was only when complete darkness arrived that the armies slowly disengaged, and they did so in haphazard fashion. Abel did not know who, if anyone, had taken overall command. He suspected they had been fighting as separate battalions.

For the most part the forces pulled back out of musketry range of one another, and then collapsed where they were. Abel led an attempt by the engineers and medical units to distribute rations and, more importantly, water, to the exhausted troops. The operation lasted late into the night.

Landry Hoster stood by Abel's side the entire time. His engineers had put wooden spigots on the water barrels instead of the usual cork plugs at the bottoms. Spigots were items brushing close to nishterlaub, but Abel figured it was Landry's right to endanger himself if he wanted. In any case, the spigots worked wonderfully as the water wagons trundled along the line, and much water was saved from spilling uselessly onto the ground.

Abel stumbled back to the command camp to find the brigade commanders gathered around a small fire. They were speaking in low voices, but an argument was taking place.

He tried to listen in, but could not make himself concentrate. Then he found himself sitting down next to his pack, and couldn't remember how he got there.

Sleep, man, said Raj. *You're doing no good awake. You'll find out in the morning what they've decided. I expect you'll going to need some rest to act on it, whatever it is.*

Abel dozed for perhaps a halfwatch, then started awake. It was still dark. He stumbled to his feet, looked around for a latrine, and, when he couldn't find one, pissed in a spot he judged was outside of the sleeping area. Even though he still felt tired, the edge of exhaustion was gone from his body. He found a barrel of water, drank a dipperful, and splashed a few drops on his face.

When he looked up, he saw von Hoff sitting on his camp stool gazing into the remains of the little fire from the night before. Von Hoff saw him and, with the wave of an arm, motioned Abel to join him. Abel went to stand by the pile of coals.

"The brigade colonels have elected me as provisional commander of the Corps," von Hoff said. "I'm taking Saxe's place for the duration of this operation."

"Good," said Abel. "That's for the best."

The two sat silently for a moment.

"How old are you, Major?" von Hoff finally asked.

"Thirty, sir."

"I see." He nodded, laughed to himself. "So you wouldn't be the youngest in recorded history."

"Youngest what, sir?"

"There were at least three before you: Vajiravud about a hundred years ago. I think he was twenty-seven. Kulmala, of course. That was under extreme conditions during the Delta campaigns. He went on to lead the Corps. And that other one, I can't remember his name."

"I don't follow, sir."

"The youngest Goldie brigade commander," said von Hoff. "In the military, you don't want to set precedents if you can help it. Brings too much attention. Makes you a target if anything goes wrong."

"I suppose that's true, Colonel."

"So you see, I don't want to do that."

"What . . ." Abel's head was spinning. What was von Hoff talking about? Then it hit him with a certainty as solid as a brick in the face.

"Vallancourt," Abel said. "You're going to give Vallancourt the Third because of seniority."

"Blood and Bones, man, why would you think that?"

"He's safe. He's next in line for promotion to brigade commander. It wouldn't set a precedent." Abel swallowed. His throat felt dry even though he'd just taken a drink of water. "I suppose I could work with him. If it were a direct order from you to do so."

"Why in cold hell would I give it to Vallancourt?" von Hoff said. "He's a complete idiot. No, I'm giving you the Third, Dashian. Starting with a field promotion right now, Colonel."

Abel stood still for a moment, trying to be sure he'd heard correctly.

"Me?"

"That's right."

"But—"

"I've informed the other brigade commanders. It's done."

"Colonel, you should reconsider this decision."

"Why?"

"I'm tired. I could make mistakes."

"Excellent point. Yes, I've changed my mind."

For a moment, Abel thought he'd won the argument. Then he saw the crooked smile on von Hoff's face.

"The colonel is being sarcastic."

"The *general* is being sarcastic," von Hoff said. "The colonel is in need of hot cider."

He's talking about you, Raj said.

"Yes," Abel said. "I'll have some shortly." Abel rubbed his temples.

Something Father said years ago when he'd made lieutenant in the Scouts. How'd the saying go? "If you're going to do it, own it."

He looked up, met von Hoff's gaze. "General von Hoff, now that I've got the Third . . ."

"Yes?"

"I've examined the terrain, and I have an idea for a flanking maneuver that I hope you'll consider."

"I'll consider it," said von Hoff. "How many men do you think it will take?"

"About five thousand."

Von Hoff said nothing for a moment, huffed out a laugh. "Where am I going to get five thousand men?"

"The Third Brigade has approximately five thousand troops in it, although we've taken casualties, of course."

Again von Hoff was silent for a moment. He finally spoke in a low voice. "You want me to divide my army, Dashian? Divide my army in my first act as a general. Is that what you're saying?"

Abel nodded. "I wouldn't suggest it if I didn't think it would work, sir."

4

Rousing the Third before dawn and having them on their way was the hardest part of the morning, but finding the Third was in itself a very difficult task. The battle had devolved into separate pockets of fighting throughout the course of the previous day, with some tiny landmarks—a mound of dirt here, a low embankment there, even a clump of thick swamp grass—becoming focal points, landmarks the men would long remember as places of glory, shame, and terror. Names that would call up memories for the rest of their lives, for those who had more life to live.

Bodies lay strewn about at dawn. No one had yet had the time or strength to move them. The wounded who could, dragged themselves toward the rear. The severely wounded remained, mixed with the dead, especially those within musket range of either side. The only way to tell the two apart was by the faint movement. It was terrible to see the mounds of men that twitched here and there and be able to do nothing about it.

There were some slain donts on the field as well, but most had been lost on the charge up the mountain and they lay there on the slopes. Those that remained had been held in reserve.

Most of the fighting was musket and bow and arrow. In only a few places had the forces gone at one another hand to hand, but those taken down by bayonet wounds were the slowest to die, and many of them moaned and cried out for water, cursed the world, or begged for their mothers, throughout the night.

Many had been dragged to relative safety by a brave foray into the darkness, only to die quickly once they were back behind the line. The huge Escarpment flitterdonts wheeled in the pink-black air above.

Some brave ones were already on the ground feasting. The smell of spent gunpowder and carnage hung in the marshy air. It was only a matter of time before the odor of decay would mingle with it, bringing more.

Groelsh and Abel's company sergeants seemed to have a special sense of direction when it came to their units, and Abel was surprised by how quickly and silently the muster was accomplished. The Third Brigade withdrew in relatively good order, and assembled a dozen fieldmarches behind the front line. Von Hoff had even given Abel the few specialized mounted who possessed donts, and artillery transports. Abel knew how difficult assembling for march was even in ideal circumstances. That the assembly took less than a watch impressed him.

Abel figured he had gotten about four hours of sleep. He sensed himself sagging, and nearly slid off his dont—would have, if Nettle hadn't been a sensitive creature that moved to keep him on. But the sight of the brigade assembling drew him back to full alertness.

His brigade.

His responsibility.

Groelsh and his sergeants banged them into rough company order and had them marching south just as the sun rose over the eastern Rim. Abel ordered them to double-time it past the guns of what everyone was now calling Fort Sentinel, the redoubt on the mountain.

They were spotted and fired upon. But it was as if the enemy had acquired a coldblooded sluggishness in the night, and they managed to get off only a few strafing fusillades from the volley guns, and one badly aimed rock throw, before the entire brigade had made the passage and was out of range.

Abel asked Center to make an interpolated tally of casualties. He learned he'd lost ten so far.

Then it was a matter of threading their way through the pinned-down Second Brigade, which had retreated south along the road until they were just out of musket range from Fort Sentinel. The Second did not want to give an inch of the Road, and there were some minor tussles between Guardians that threatened to turn deadly. Fortunately, tiredness overcame anger, and most decided the easiest course was the course of least resistance. The Second took a look at the beat-up state of the Third and knew that they soon would be ordered forward to join the same fight.

A watch and a half later, the head of Abel's columns arrived at the ferry crossing. Here Abel called his company commanders to him. His newly appointed adjutant and executive officer looked them over with a cold eye.

He'd appointed Timon Athanaskew to the position.

Timon rolled out a map and went over the first part of Abel's plan. "We will divide into company-sized units and head down the Ferry Road, circling east of Sentinel Mountain. We'll run the gauntlet one company at a time at quarter-watch intervals, more or less. These may be divided into units as you see fit—but must be well on the way before the next are sent."

Abel continued, "Each captain will be responsible for getting his company to the rendezvous point: the base of the saddle ridge connecting the two southernmost of the Three Sisters." Abel pointed to the papyrus map. They were gathered around a large flat boulder and Timon had the map laid out over its top, which served as a makeshift table. "Don't want to be too regular about it. Major Athanaskew will keep time."

Abel looked up at his captains. "Do you understand?"

A chorus of "yes, sirs." He hoped they meant it.

"Any questions?"

"What if we come under fire at the assembly point?" asked the Sunday Company commander, Wilton. "There's another fort on the next mountain over, sir, if I'm reading the map correctly."

"There is," Abel answered. "But we demonstrate. In other words, be out of rifle range at the our rally point. When you get there, I want you to make a racket. I want anybody on Tamarak Peak to know we're down there, understand?"

"Yes, sir."

"Any more questions?"

This time there were none.

It was midmorning when they set out, Abel and his command staff on donts, a few auxiliary scouts and skirmishers on animals, and all others, including company captains, on foot with their men. It did not take the eastern lookouts of Fort Sentinel long to spot them, and a rattle of fire began from the fort. The sound was intimidating, but they were still well out of musket range. Let them waste shot and powder.

Yet it appeared they had a near infinite supply.

Abel sent his first company down the Valley at a trot. The musket fire from the fort's lower trenches might be technically in range, but evidently its soldiers couldn't shoot well enough to hit much of anything this far away.

The company—Wilton's Sunday Company—made it past with no men killed, and only two wounded. Thursday Company was next. It made its way carefully up the Ferry Road just as the Sunday men had done, keeping as far to the eastern side of the little Valley as they could.

Suddenly there was a tremendous roar and a rising billow of smoke.

Something—something large—crashed through the midst of Thursday Company, cutting down donts, decapitating men, and splintering bones.

Cannon, said Raj. ***But why on this side only?***

Not wheeled, probably impossible to aim. Barely classifiable as a cannon at all. It is a welded-seam device, Center replied. **Inaccurate and inherently dangerous.**

Inaccurate? It just cut a swath through my men!

A random shot. The probability of a strike was fairly low, but the probability of mortal injury once the projectile did strike was very high.

No shit, said Abel. *Does that thing fire the clumps you were telling me cannons used to shoot out?*

Grapeshot? said Raj. ***I don't see why it couldn't. But grapeshot's for close range. They'll stick to cannon balls if they want to touch you.***

Another *WHUMP*, and yet another ball flew by, this one crashing into the brush on the eastern side of the road.

Abel realized he needed to lead the command staff through next to set an example. He ordered his group forward. They were mounted, and they moved at a steady clip, but by no means as fast as a dont could run. He wanted to save the donts for later. A lot was going to be asked of them today.

The cannon got off two shots as Abel was crossing under it. One struck the road just in front of his flag, kicking up dust and gravel, but harming no one.

The second took off the head of Colquehoun, a captain who had two watches before been promoted from courier to command staff proper. Blood and viscera surged in gouts from the severed neck for a moment, then ceased. Colquehoun's body fell to the side, but a foot remained in a stirrup.

Timon took the reins of Colquehoun's dont and led it forward, while Colquehoun's body dragged along beside it.

And then the command staff was by and out of range.

The next company, Ogilvy's Friday, began its run. Abel looked up the mountainside. He could see tiny stick figures of men swabbing the cannon, getting it ready for the next shot. Then they levered it back down. Aimed.

A boom louder than any before. Abel was focused on Friday Company, so he did not see at first what happened above. A miss. They were coming through unscathed, thank the Lady. Distant shouts. Then he looked up the mountain.

Fire had broken out in the fort. Pieces of burning timber were everywhere, strewn down the side of the mountain. The cannon was hanging over the edge of the fort's wall. For a moment, Abel didn't recognize it. It was burst and splayed outward. It looked like a metallic chrysalis, opened by an insectoid rebirth.

Not unexpected. As I noted, cannons made with welded seams are prone to bursting, Center said. **The manufacture of true cannons requires casting technology.**

Abel could hear the sound of men screaming above. It seemed burst metal cannons made their own deadly shrapnel.

The remainder of his companies passed without incident. But now that the enemy knew they were headed up the Manahatet Valley, he had to hurry. He knew there must be wigwag between Sentinel and Tamarak. The other fort would be on the lookout for them, training their guns down into the narrow valley. Which is what he wanted.

Abel had no intention of continuing along the valley floor to make a target for them, but he needed a diversion to occupy the other fort's attention.

"Timon, get Landry over here."

"I first heard about it from an old Scout," Landry Hoster told Abel. "They found it out when they were making those nishterlaub lucifers they love to carry around with them in the Redlands."

Abel's hand strayed down to the pack of lucifers in his tunic pocket. Old Scout habits never died.

"Then, as you know, the damn thing nearly got me kicked out of the Academy."

Abel remembered: the entire level of student quarters had been enveloped that day by thick smoke streaming from Cadet Hoster's rooms.

"I was worried they were going to hang you for heresy," Abel said.

"Nah, but the priests tried to expel me. Got called up to the Tabernacle review court, all that mess."

"And yet you walked out of there a free man, and whistling that annoying Delta jig you like."

"'Veronica's Barrel.' Twice-damn right I was." Landry stood a moment as if remembering the song, then spoke. "They found me innocent of incitement to immorality. Case closed."

"You were guilty by every Thursday school lesson I've ever sat through."

Landry nodded. "It was Goldfrank."

"The Abbot?"

"The very same," Landry replied, shaking his head in disbelief still.

This was something Abel had not known.

"The Chief Priest of Zentrum? He let you off?"

"He said no particular part of what I'd done involved nishterlaub. The fact that I'd made a stink and a spectacle wasn't the matter at hand. He said it was up to him to decide if what my ingredients made when I put them together *was* nishterlaub. That was the only call the court could make." Landry nodded. "And the guy let me off."

"On a technicality."

"Hey, I was glad to take what I could get." Landry unconsciously fingered his unhung neck and shuffled to a more comfortable position in his saddle. "Anyway, I saved up my barter chits and made an even bigger one. Then you and I and Timon took it out to those wastelands you like to wander around in."

"The Giants."

"Hate that place. Creepy. But good for the purpose."

It was a region north of Lindron of enormous stone blocks cut through with a crazed grid of gullies, and rock lying on rock.

The largest original settlement on Duisberg. A city of five hundred thousand people in its day, Center had told Abel. **Transformed by the nano-plague of the Collapse into solid rock. The towers, no longer supported by concretized steel, toppled over, giving the area the appearance of an enormous battlefield filled with fallen warriors, each a colossus. This is likely where the name originated.**

The perfect place to conduct a secret pyrotechnic experiment and not get caught.

"Timon said he was coming along to make sure we kept Edict, but I know he wanted to see something go boom."

"Yes. He was disappointed it didn't make more sound."

"This one's going to be bigger." Landry's grin became a smile of happiness. "This will be the biggest ever."

The wagon floor was layered with percussion caps. Over this, Landry's engineers sprinkled soda ash, a product otherwise brought along for gun cleaning. Then another layer of caps was laid down, each soldier in the brigade contributing half of the caps from his own cartridge box. This would, of course, cut in half the number of shots available for each soldier on the campaign. Couldn't be helped.

Over this material, Lowry sprinkled several sacks of granulated Delta cane sugar. It was precious stuff, and the few nonengineer soldiers whom Landry ordered to help were agog at the seeming waste. Landry's engineers, however, knew exactly what they were doing, and they poured the sugar with a cheerfully unconcerned attitude.

A final layer of soda about a thumb's-length deep was poured over the second layer of caps. Then, from openings he'd carefully drilled in the bottom of the wagon, Landry ignited his "infernal device," as he called it. He took sticks as small as kindling wood from a prepared fire and slowly worked them into the bottom of the wagon through his access points. He'd laid a layer of ground moss on the very bottom to elevate the lower layer of caps enough to have some—but not much—air flow under them. The kindling ignited the moss, which smoldered rather than burned. The kindling coals and smoldering moss slowly heated the caps, setting off a slow burn in the powder inside them. They expanded, crackled open, spewing their innards into the soda ash. The tiny, slow fires in each cap produced smoke that must travel upward and escape. As it did so, the vapors combined with the soda ash and grew many times thicker. The vapors finally emerged on the top of the layers as a dense gray smoke, and lots of it.

Potassium chloride, bicarbonate of soda, sucrose. The recipe for an effective smoke maker, Center said.

"Get on!" said Landry to the team of daks harnessed to the wagon. They leaned into their traces, snorted dak snot from their blowholes, and lumbered forward, pulling the smoking wagon north along the Ferry Road. He and his command staff sergeant rode the seatboard and, if all went well, would be the only ones fully exposed to enemy fire.

Abel gazed up at the fortifications of Tamarak on the peak behind Sentinel. He detected the glint of two large guns, brighter even than the gleam from the assembled musketry.

More cannons?

Yes.

This will be interesting.

The smoke from the wagon was pleasingly thick—thicker than any River fog Abel had ever seen. The contraption trundled along at the speed of the lumbering daks. The company sergeants ordered their troops up and, company by company, the Third made a quick march behind the smoke wagon.

The wind was light. The wagon's smoke hung over the roadbed. There should be no way anyone above would be able to see through it to locate individual men or even bunched units.

It didn't take the commanders at Fort Tamarak long to realize this. The only choice was indiscriminate fire. This they laid down in volley after volley. The smoke wagon continued down the road.

Now the cannons above—there appeared to be two—were levered downward, lined up with where the Road would usually be had it not been covered by smoke, and fired. Ball after ball smashed into the roadway. Some balls were hollowed out, filled with gunpowder, and had fuses set within them. When these exploded, they might take out dozens of men at a time if they landed in an unlucky spot.

Fortunately, every spot was lucky, for there were no men in the smoke. For the Third was marching into the miasma, and then, after the distance of a fieldmarch, they moved off the road and sat tight. Rank after rank marched in—and sat down.

Farther along the road, minié balls, cannons, and fused balls flew into the smoke like a swarm of biting insectoids. Explosion after explosion lit up the thick billows with flashes of fire. But the explosions did not disperse it.

And they did not reveal that the enemy was shooting at absolutely nothing.

Under the smoke, the road was empty.

Tamarak, of course, took potshots at the smoke wagon. One lucky shot passed over the smoke wagon and almost hit Landry's staff sergeant, but the man happened to be bending down to recover a dropped rein at the time, and it flew past.

While Landry was preparing his device, Abel had sent his mounted scouts—about ten in all—up the flank of the ridge that connected Sentinel with Tamarak peak, and now they'd returned.

He and Rigga, his Scout commander, conferred on the road at the base of the ridge as the last of the Third disappeared into the smoke.

"You were right, Colonel," said Rigga—he was another of the Cascade reserve Goldies serving in the Third. Rigga was gasping from the hard-riding dash up the hill and back again. His dont, too, was wheezing through its breathing hole. Abel stayed far enough back to avoid the mucus. Dont snot was acidic and could burn flesh—not badly, but enough to hurt. Rigga gathered his breath and continued.

"There's a good path along the ridge top, all right. Wide enough for two wagons. It connects the two forts."

"Good," said Abel. "Anything else?"

"Well, the whole place is a graveyard."

"Say again."

"All along the ridge saddle, and up the two slopes it connects, pretty far up. Gravestones. Hundreds of them, all facing south, I guess toward Zentrum. Some high as a man. Maybe thousands of them, now that I consider it. Looks like the whole of Progar gets themselves buried there."

"Interesting," Abel said. He turned to Timon. "Major Athanaskew, get the men roused and moving up the ridge. And let them know they're to take cover when they get to the top."

"Take cover where, Colonel?" said Timon.

"You deliver the message and I'll provide the cover," Abel answered.

A sea of gravestones, some high as a man. Perfect.

5

Abel and the Third Brigade worked their way up to the saddle between Sentinel Mountain and Tamarak Peak. They were well shielded from Fort Sentinel in this position, but in view of anyone peering over the revetments of Tamarak. But it seemed the men there were too intent on blowing the cold hell out of the troops they supposed were within the smoke to keep a sharp lookout to their southeast.

It looked like they'd gotten over three thousand men onto the ridge top, although some were still arriving. And Rigga had been right about there being thousands of gravestones. There was easily a stone for every man to lay low behind.

He had position and he had cover for attack.

When he reached the ridgeline, Abel had planned to cut south and attack the fort on Sentinel. But now it became obvious that Tamarak should be dealt with first. It was closer, for one thing, no more than ten fieldmarches above them along the ridge. Abel could easily make out its walls from where he stood, and the gate set in them. The communication track between the forts went up the ridge meandering like a stream around clumps of graves. The ridge itself was sparsely populated by trees, and there were many stumps.

Likely the dwellers of the fort don't like to go far for firewood, Raj said.

So the way to Tamarak was clear enough. But how to get over or through that wall? The only siege weapons he had were willow-wand grappling hooks, one carried per platoon. If they couldn't scale the walls with those, they wouldn't get over.

The slope upward to the Tamarak position was gentler than the climb in the opposite direction to Sentinel—although it was steep enough. The graves were not uniformly spread, but occurred in clumps, as if they'd grown that way.

Family and clan units, Center said.

The track wound through them. A charge, when it came, would have to be straighter, on the wagon track when possible, but off and through the graves when necessary. The mounts wouldn't be of use at this incline, and Abel ordered all riders down.

It would be a charge by all.

They could begin from where they were. The men were already spread out by company. The leaders could easily form them up.

When?

No time like the present, man, growled Raj. *Your captain's smoke was a marvel, but somebody up there is going to notice you sooner or later.*

Abel pointed up the mountain. "Timon, let's get them up there and see what we find. In lines, by company."

"Yes, sir."

"And Major," said Abel. "Let's be as quiet as we can. We don't want to wake the dead."

"Will do, sir." Timon turned to his runners, and they headed out with the orders.

Within moments, rough lines were formed.

Abel pulled out his saber from its scabbard. It was useless against muskets and artillery. Not useless when leading a charge, however.

He raised the blade, held it aloft for a long moment, giving the men plenty of time to turn eyes to him.

With a downward slice, he lowered the sword, its tip pointing up the ridgeline.

Eerily, quietly, the Goldies began their uphill charge through the graves.

Commanders and their officers charged upward, and their men followed. Abel waited until several companies had moved ahead of his position, then put himself and his staff into the mix.

The vanguard of the charge was at the wall of the fort before the enemy on Tamarak saw them coming. The leading wave let off a rattling volley before they were able to stop and aim, but, being Goldies, some of the balls found their marks even so, and two sentries topped from the breastworks. The remaining lookouts called out in alarm to the fort. Then they turned and fired down into the charging mass.

When Abel grew closer he saw something that left him dumb-founded. The wall that had looked so formidable from below was no more than a man's height from base to top.

There was no need for grappling or climbing. Men could simply be given a leg up. In fact, some were practically launched and thrown over.

The fort was not designed to defend against an attack from the ridge. The ramparts were a joke.

In the end, the swarming Third could not be held back. They boiled over the gateway of the outer ramparts, taking down the sentries by sheer force of weight.

The gateway opened. It was wide enough to take a cart through, easily wide enough for five men shoulder-to-shoulder.

Once they were inside, things got harder.

Show me what I'm up against, thought Abel.

Interpolating. Observe:

A desperate resistance had formed among the enemy. Also a well-armed one. There was a standing firefight between pistols and muskets at no more than five paces. But there were a thousand men behind each Guardian who went down, and far fewer to replace the fallen Progarmen.

A rush with bayonets sent the enemy running, but it lost momentum for a moment as the Goldies in the front, stepping over bodies, slipped on the blood-swathed floor. Several fell. It might have been funny, had the blood not been partly that of their platoon mates.

Some were trampled from behind, but most picked themselves up or were yanked up, and the surge continued.

Then, rounding a corner, the Goldies came face-to-face with something they'd never experienced before, had not been allowed to experience.

A cannon had been wrenched around on its iron base and pointed down the corridor in which the charge was coming on.

Those in the lead faltered for a moment, more in bewilderment than dismay, then continued screaming toward the cannon. When they were mere paces away, the cannon fired. It was loaded with the scattering shot Abel had heard of from Center, and the men in front were shredded, torn apart, and spattered in all directions.

The cannonfire was ultimately a useless gesture, however. There was no time to go through the laborious motions of reloading. The cannon crew knew this, and immediately took to their heels running down the corridor behind them.

Guardians followed, now more careful.

One Progarman with a volley gun attempted a last stand. But he was shaking, and tipped the gun too far upward as he set off the intricate trigger-and-hammer system. The shots rattled off the ceiling, ricocheting down into the ranks, but only taking down one man, and him only injured.

The soldier with the volley gun seemed bewildered and did not run. The Goldies rushed him and bayonetted him like a pincushion in retribution for those killed by the cannon shot.

Interpolation complete.

Abel blinked back to his own reality with the screams of the Progarman echoing in his mind.

There were, at most, three hundred soldiers manning the fort. Now, with no defenses facing the right direction and a breakdown of command, they didn't stand a chance against the weight of nearly five thousand.

Within what seemed like a handful of eyeblinks, Abel had the place, its former inhabitants captured or killed. The dead lay in contorted ruin against walls, slumped over powder kegs and provisions or piled in stacks three men deep to get them out of the way.

The fort smelled of spent powder and blood.

Then Abel had to contain the victory itself. He quickly had Groelsh send a squad of his hardest men to cut off a move to throw the enemy survivors over the sides.

"We need to interrogate them," he said. This was the only excuse he thought the men might listen to.

He had captured Tamarak, and it was not yet noon.

6

Abel climbed up a flight of stairs to a signal-flag platform. From this high point, he made out Sentinel and its fort on the adjacent mountain. The task of taking it did not look easy.

The way up from the saddle was steeper and longer. Attacking straight up the ridge would be far more difficult. Tamarak's summit was broad and flat. Sentinel rose to a point.

The walls of Fort Sentinel are higher and the gateway there will be stronger and better guarded.

Aye, that's about right from the looks of this place.

How do you know from that?

The architecture of this fort marks it as a former storehouse and ammunition dump for the larger fort on Sentinel Mountain, Center said. **Tamarak was never meant for defense. The works here have been hastily constructed, and, as you saw, there are points of fatal weakness in the design.**

The ridge wall and gate.

Precisely. The Sentinel structure, however, is built for strength. It will have a smaller constricting ridge gateway that can be closed tightly, or opened and used as a grinder of the men sent through it. Furthermore, the walls appear to be too high to assault by grapples.

Then we'll have to do it another way.

You have a plan in mind?

Yes. Landry Hoster.

✧   ✧   ✧

"Hmm. We do have these two cannons," Landry said.

Abel had found Landry on the parapet where the cannons were mounted, as he'd expected to.

"We saw them blown to pieces," Abel said. "They're not to be counted on."

"Ah, yes," Landry replied. "I have a couple of ideas about that. It's the seams that split. That's what I've been doing here—checking out the way they've rolled this metal together."

The very statement of the process brought the feeling of revulsion, of contact with nishterlaub, into Abel's mind. Even after all these years of knowing better, the Thursday school lessons of childhood still had an emotional grip on him down deep. But he ignored the feeling.

I've also had Center in my mind for twenty-two years to tell me it's all nonsense.

"See how they used other metal to form the seam? Now, I know a few priestsmiths, and they tell me one rifle barrel isn't always as good as another."

"They're not supposed to tell you anything, on pain of death," Abel mused.

"There's ways, and then there's ways, to talk to a priest, if you know what I mean," Landry said. "And I expect you do, since you've done you're share of talking to them. If you ask the right questions, there's lots a man can tinker around with in his mind and figure out for himself."

"Right."

Landry nodded with a wry smile. "What it comes down to is that you can overheat a weld. I reckon the same applies to these cannons. There's ways to tell what's sound and what's not. Now, I looked at a couple of barrel pieces of the one that exploded up here, and sure enough, the seams were deformed."

Landry picked up a heavy piece of metal from the floor with a grunt. If he had ever had any nishterlaub aversion, he was long over it. Landry also was a lot stronger than he looked. Underneath that perpetual pudge lay some muscle.

The metal piece was smooth and curved, with a seam of rougher looking material running along it in a line.

"See how that line isn't quite true?" Landry asked. He held the barrel piece in one hand and drew a finger along the seam to illustrate.

"Yes," Abel said. "But it's fairly straight."

"Not straight enough. Somebody overheated the bronze when he was forming the weld, and it left the seam too wide and out of true in places. One of those places, probably where it was too wide and out of whack, decided to give, and: boom!" Landry spread his hands wide to show an explosion. "That little spot out of true is the difference between whether it'll blow up in your face or not."

"Good to know."

"Sure is." Landry dropped the piece. It fell on the rocky floor with a clang. He turned to the cannon. "Now, I had a look at the seams on these two. That one over there"—he pointed down the rampart wall to the second cannon—"is an accident waiting to happen." He patted the cannon near him as he might a pet donderdak. "This one, she's sound."

"She?"

"Why not?" Landry said. "And look at the size of her. Half an elb bore! She can fling a quarter-stone ball out of that maw of hers."

"And you're sure you trust it?"

"I guess I'm sure enough to bet my life on it," Landry replied.

It was the work of twenty big men and a half a watch to get the cannon out the gateway. The movers alternated between pushing it and putting rounded poles taken from the wagon stays beneath the cannon to let it roll farther. Another twenty ferried powder and balls outside.

Abel ordered an intermittent fire of muskets, kept up to avoid alerting the fort on the other end of the ridge that their sister fort was taken.

The hardest part was hefting the behemoth cannon onto a wagon bed. Landry's solution was to have the men lift, fill in the gap with smaller stones, and slowly build a support pile under the cannon. When this pile grew even with the wagon bed, ten men pushing and pulling slid the big gun into the cart. The wood creaked, but Landry had ordered the strongest cart they had brought up, and the riveroak bed held. He secured the cannon with stout ropes so it wouldn't slide out once the trek up the opposite slope became steep.

The wagon was hitched to a four-dak team. Landry and his newly assembled team climbed on board, and the skinner touched his whip to the daks and they moved forward. It was not fast, but the daks' strength was enough to pull the wagon. Behind the gun wagon came another one loaded with powder and shot.

The daks grunted up the slope, and the men proceeded at the same pace, Wednesday Company ahead, and the other six companies to the rear of the wagon.

Soon his skirmishers reported in to Abel. There were guards on the wall over the gateway. At least fifty men.

"I'm pretty sure they know we're coming, sir," said Tanner in a broad Cascadian accent. Yet another reservist. He was an older man with a wide scar running diagonally across his face. Abel had known him now for years and didn't think he'd ever seen Tanner smile.

They trundled along as the path wound through the scattered gravestones. There seemed to be even more of them on this slope of the saddle than the other side.

They are bunched toward the south to be closer to Zentrum.

So we have no surprise, Abel thought. *Well, maybe one.*

They halted out of musket range, and Wednesday Company deployed in a rough line along the flanks of the slope. They were led by Fowlett, the black-skinned commander from Abel's vision of Chambers Pass.

I've been inside his head, Abel thought. Center's interpolations were very precise.

This very real Fowlett was on familiar ground now, and extremely competent. On both sides, the ridgeline quickly gave way to cliffs. There was no way to maneuver around and attack another point on the fortress. It was the gateway or nothing.

Behind the front lines, Landry led the dak team drawing the wagon around in a circle, and now the back end of the wagon—and the muzzle of the cannon—pointed upslope.

Abel gathered his captains to the wagon.

"Tell them how it works, Captain Hoster," he said to Landry.

When Landry was finished, the officers looked skeptical. By appearances, they were already feeling very uneasy around such a piece of nishterlaub technology.

On the other hand, their brother Goldies were fighting and dying below in the valley, and this fort was raking their flanks and pinning them forward.

The fort had to go.

"We line it up with the gateway and blow a hole in the wall with it."

"But the wall's made of stone!" one of the captains objected. Landry snickered—he had a boyish habit of laughing at the wrong moments, a habit that had annoyed the hell out of some of the other cadets at the Guardian Academy, and that clearly annoyed this captain as well. "A cannon ball will punch a hole twelve feet deep through that stone. It's merely stacked and not mortared, if it's anything like the one at Tamarak."

"But what good will a hole the size of a ball be to us? A man can't fit through it."

"That wall is a pile of rocks. Look at it!" Landry pointed. "And I think all of you gentlemen know what happens when you take a stone out of the bottom of a rock pile." Once again Landry illustrated with exaggerated hand motions. "It falls! A couple of shots, and I expect a gap to open up you can fit your company through at one go."

Even Abel was skeptical it would come off this well. He had little choice but to try. Abel issued his instructions for attack if—when—the walls came down. Landry and his team busied themselves working to prime and fuse the behemoth cannon. Then the ball was dropped in and stuffed down the barrel.

Abel turned back to look at the Sentinel fort. Could this possibly work?

Center and Raj were notably quiet on the matter. Were they, too, in quantum computer fashion, holding their breath?

From this distance, two musket-shot lengths away, he could see that the fort was well-designed and strong. From the number of sentries and the rain of fire off the other side, he reasoned that it had to house a far greater number of men than had Tamarak.

The level of manpower now evident indicates that this fort is built on a pre-Collapse structure, Center said, breaking the silence. **There are warrens of tunnels carved into the mountain rock to house them. There is no way such extensive earth-moving could be accomplished with present technology.**

So it was made by . . . the nanotechnology you've told me about?

Evidently some protective process kept it safe from the nano-plague virus that was the signature of the Collapse, Center answered. **If not, the structure would have immediately**

decomposed and collapsed, as did the great dams that now form the three Cataracts of the River.

Is there any nano still there? Abel thought.

Not active. Standard retaining nano required periodic recharging from a separate power source. These nuclear and antimatter generators were destroyed in the Collapse.

Then how is it still holding the tunnels you predict to be there in place?

It is designed to freeze in place. Remember, the molecular bonds of the structures of pre-Collapse civilization were destroyed by an active nanovirus. The viral nano machinery did not lose its charge until its work was entirely done. There would be a great many more ruins remaining, even three thousand years later, were that not so.

Now what do you make of that thing sitting up there at the high point? Looks to be on stilts, doesn't it? Raj put in.

Abel considered the structure, which he'd been looking at or otherwise Raj wouldn't have observed it.

It definitely had a strange silhouette against the clear sky. Something on poles, with the poles supporting a large barrel-shaped structure atop themselves.

A water tank, said Center. **This will be the method they use to crank their catapults.**

How do you know that?

Such stands to reason. The reported water-powered methods with flues and wheels is the heresy the Guardian Corps has ostensibly been sent north to stamp out.

So that thing is full of water, like a giant barrel?

Yes.

Abel stepped down from his vantage point on the wagon seatboard and turned to Landry. "Captain Hoster?"

"Yes, sir?"

"I have a target for your first shot."

7

Standing this close, the roar of the cannon going off was as loud as anything Abel had ever heard. Fire shot from the muzzle, smoke puffed out, and the wagon rattled as if shaken by an earthquake.

The first ball completely missed the water tower.

Landry let out a curse, but immediately ordered his men to reset the cannon's elevation.

He and a sergeant swabbed the inside residue from the barrel with a stick they'd found near the cannons at the other fort. Landry had immediately grasped its purpose.

Then something odd: Landry was trying to spark the fuse with a flint and steel. Abel strode over to his engineer.

"That looks difficult, Captain," he said.

Landry smiled sheepishly. "That shot threw me on my ass," he said. "Wouldn't you know it, I lost my cursed punk stick when I fell." Landry pointed to the rest of his team. "None of these other fools thought to bring one, either. Of course, who is the greater fool not to have ordered it? Me."

Abel reached into his inner pocket and pulled out his box of lucifers.

"I assume you know how to use these Scout sticks?" he asked Landry, handing him the box.

The engineer smiled with boyish glee. "Oh, yes, I do."

✧   ✧   ✧

184

The second shot burst into the water tower container, practically in the center.

The tank exploded in a burst of water and wood. One moment it was sitting atop its support pilings, the next it had disintegrated.

I would have thought a nice big hole, but that *I didn't expect.*

Water is essentially incompressible under normal conditions. The entire kinetic force of the cannon ball was transferred to the liquid, which caused the tank to quickly and completely rupture, said Center. **This is basic physics.**

And impressive physics, at that, put in Raj.

A third shot went through the scaffolding legs and brought down the remainder of the structure.

Meanwhile, the guards on the ramparts kept up a sporadic fire to remind the Guardian front line of their range.

"Should we try for the gate?" Abel asked Landry.

Landry took a look, thought for a moment. "Frankly, sir, now that we've shot her off, I think I'd like to be closer," the engineer replied.

"Closer and we'll be in range of their guns." Abel cocked his head, considered. "We need to make you less of a target."

"Not much chance of camouflage or fooling them. What trees there are up here are scraggly affairs, and we'd be advancing over a clear field of fire. Couldn't find any thick enough to stand in for a cannon, either, if we wanted to try some trickery and make them think we have more such guns."

"I was thinking of something more radical," Abel replied. He turned to call Timon, but found his friend waiting patiently by his side. Abel started at the sight of him so close.

Had he himself been that anonymous, yet present, when he was von Hoff's exec? Must've given the colonel a fright now and then.

"Major Athanaskew, here's what I want the men in the rear to do." Abel detailed his plan. "Now get those orders out immediately."

It took almost a watch to ready the attack. The men were strong, and the platoons had a scattering of entrenching tools, mostly maplewood shovels, but the gravestones were very reluctant to be uprooted.

"It's almost like the dead are hanging on to them stones down below," Abel heard one soldier say.

But the stones were thin—as thin as a hand held sideways.

In the end, most of the men resorted to giving the tops of the gravestones a running kick. This was usually all it took to break them off near the base. Toward the end, it had become a competition to see who could snap them off faster.

The next step was to lift the stones up to carry to the front lines. Most were light enough for a single man to carry. But quite a few were much heavier. These were usually the headstones of First Family members. They were carved with names and the symbol of a Progar first: an octagon shape with a diagonal stripe through it. Some of these First symbols were elaborately decorated, but they always remained recognizable. The First stones required two or three men.

The ranks gathered with their stones a few paces behind Wednesday Company on the front line. They were roughly ordered in lines four deep with a gap between them, opened up. Each man had his hands on a gravestone, his muskets slung behind his back.

Abel stepped in front of the front company and raised his saber. He looked up and down the line. Wednesday was nervous, ready. Behind them, the lines of men were grinning. Some were laughing. After Tamarak, they were in a good mood.

Bones and Blood, they're relishing this, he thought. *They're looking forward to it even though they'll be moving forward without being able to fire a shot.*

He noticed that most of the rifles slung over the backs of the men had bayonets fixed.

Abel brought down his saber, and the front line surged around him. Wednesday, at least, was going into the charge with their rifles ready. Their orders were simple. Lay down enough fire to keep the men on the walls distracted from the unarmed targets coming up behind.

When they were a fieldmarch away, the peppering from the parapet abruptly ceased.

They're close enough for the fort to see the gravestones, Abel thought. *They know what they are now. We've flabbergasted them to silence.*

It was as if a collective shock had passed through the Progarmen. After what they were observing had sunk it, they returned to firing with a fury.

Slowly, and remaining well behind the advancing men with

stones, Abel and Landry turned the daks around and followed with the cannon wagon.

The fire from the fort began to take its toll. Men crumbled, their headstones falling with them. Some may even have had their skulls crushed as they dropped, even if they were only wounded when they started the fall.

The cannon wagon was soon well within range of the fort's muskets, yet only a few stray shots came their way. One of those hit a dak in the team pulling the wagon. Abel rushed forward and cut it loose from the leather harness with his saber.

Abel called on Landry's detail, and they and the command staff moved the dead dak to the side with several great heaves. The other three daks strained. For a moment, Abel believed he was going to have bring up one of the spare daks, which were following at some distance behind them. But then the wagon moved forward. The daks plodded on, more slowly than before, but elb by elb, the wagon rolled closer.

Abel glanced up at the parapets. The men were not only shooting down at those carrying headstones, they were shouting at them. He couldn't quite make out what they were saying, but he was pretty sure they were cursing the Goldies to cold hell for sacrilege.

"Here is good," Landry called out. He jumped from the wagon and grabbed the bridle of the lead dak himself, walking the animals around in a half circle. The cannon now faced the walls of the fort.

The first cannon shot struck partway down the walls. Shards flew, and the wall seemed to tremble.

A second shot struck, below and a few elbs to the right of the first.

At that, a large chunk of the upper ramparts crumbled, just as Landry had predicted it would. The wall simply collapsed. It looked like fat in a cook pot, melting over a flame.

Building stone and man fell together. Those not killed in the tumble were soon cut down by the muskets of Wednesday Company.

Landry and his team swabbed and carefully repacked the cannon. This time Landry took longer to aim. He fussed at the elevation of the base, putting in a small stone on one side of the base, trying to put its match in size on the other.

"Thrice-damn it!" Landry said. "I have the height, but I can't find leveling stones to get rid of the tilt."

Landry looked around in frustration. Nearby were the shattered remains of one of the headstones. Abel saw the engineer consider for a moment, then picked up two pieces. While his men levered the cannon up, he pushed the gravestone chunks under the base, flat side down.

"All right, lower her, boys!"

Landry stepped back, held up a thumb to gauge. A musket ball struck the ground near his feet and threw up a cloud of dust, but Landry ignored it.

"That's it!" he said.

After he was done with the cannon, he turned to look at the gate distance one more time.

Another shot struck near the engineer, this one close enough to cause Landry to dance a skip-step. He hurriedly climbed back into the wagon and moved to the base of the cannon.

Abel's lucifer struck. The cannon fuse lit and sizzled.

The cannon blasted.

Abel snapped his gaze downrange just as the gateway door blew to pieces.

The attack plan was more orderly this time. The company commanders had learned their lessons at Tamarak. Rather than swarm en masse, skirmishers moved forward first. A few of the men who had been on the parapet when it collapsed were still alive in the rubble. One pulled himself from the rubble, raised a rifle to shoot.

A skirmisher bayonetted him.

The men, led by Fowlett's company, followed the skirmishers at a trot. They were organized into squads, and the sergeants made sure each went forward with a gap between them and the squad in front of them.

Curiously, the remaining Progarmen on the section of wall that had not fallen ceased to fire. In fact, there was a general silence from the fort. Even those around the side of the mountain firing down into the valley at the Corps seemed to have stopped shooting.

What the cold hell is going on?

With just bayonets opposing them, it only took a couple of company's worth of men to overcome the opposition. Soon one of Abel's attack force stepped outside. He hesitated for a moment, fiddling with something tied around his waist. It appeared to be a linen belt of some sort. With the help of another he got it off. The two men stretched it out, and the first man began to wave it back and forth.

It was the gold and indigo banner of the Third Battalion.

With the cannon to prepare the way, the upper fort was taken.

As Abel had requested to enter, Timon came to him from inside the fortress. Timon, brave as always, had entered with the vanguard. Abel had let him.

"This place is immense, Colonel," he said. "There are passageways that look like they go down to the base of the mountain, and shafts a man might fall into that seem bottomless. A lot of those hallways are filled with stores. I'd suggest sending a party down to take care of any Progarmen who have taken refuge there."

"Good idea," Abel said. "See to it, will you?"

"We have all the prisoners under guard in two of those tunnels. I haven't done a count yet, but we must have a thousand men in there," Timon continued.

"Very good, Major."

"And another thing, sir," said Timon. "You may have noticed that the enemy fire broke off after a time."

"I did," Abel said. "And a good thing for us."

"When my men were securing arms and cartridge boxes from our prisoners, we saw that all of the cartridge boxes were empty, or nearly so."

"Empty? I thought you said this place was filled with stores."

"It is, and it has a mighty ammunition magazine," Timon said. "But they kept it near the exterior here in a huge storeroom at the end of a short tunnel that slopes down into the mountain." Timon tried to suppress a smile, but couldn't help himself. The resulting grin was rather gruesome. "At least it used to be a storeroom. Now it's a lake."

"The water tower," Abel said. "It soaked the gunpowder."

"Right over the magazine," replied Timon. "When it came down, it flooded the storeroom. It appears the Progar militia used up what ammunition they had, but there were no replacement cartridges that weren't wet and useless."

"So that's why their muskets fell silent."

"Yes, sir. It would seem so, sir."

Abel laughed. "Two shots," he said. "Two shots by Landry, and he takes out the fort's supplies. Everything else we did was cleanup."

"I would say that is a plausible interpretation of the situation, sir."

But the fort was not taken. Not entirely.

There were still the riflemen in the redoubt fifty elbs below the fort proper to deal with. These were the men who had risen seemingly from nowhere and surprised and dismayed Kanagawa's cavalry charge.

There was a switchbacked corridor at least ten elbs wide that led from the upper fort down to the redoubt. Without his commanding it, a large group of men, mostly Wednesday Company, charged down the corridor. Within minutes they had overrun the redoubt. Unfortunately, most of them had not paused to reload. When they found their muskets wouldn't fire, they resorted to bayonets. Abel hurried below, but not in time to stop the general carnage. Gutted bodies lay strewn everywhere. There was not a single Progar militia man left alive in the redoubt.

Within half a watch, Fort Sentinel was his. He turned to Timon—coolly hovering nearby—and ordered him to personally strike the Progar colors and run up the gold and indigo.

This brought the first smile to Timon's face that Abel had seen in some time. "Yes, Colonel," he replied. "My pleasure."

Once the flag was flying, an audible cry rose up from the Valley.

A good two-thirds of the Second Brigade had been held back due to lack of firm ground at the battlefield. Then the fire from the Sentinel redoubt had forced them farther back still, effectively keeping them from forming a reserve. They could only run the gauntlet of fire a few men at a time. Now, with no harassing fire, the whole force was freed up.

What a vantage point I have!

Abel watched the battle unfold below. With two battalions surging forward, the ragged line of the enemy wavered.

Still, it managed to hold.

"Major Hoster, come here and examine the seams on these guns!" Abel called out. "We aren't yet done for the day!"

They turned the fort's three cannons to the north. The Progar army might be out of musket range, but they were not beyond the reach of cannonballs.

Landry found two of the cannons welded to his satisfaction. After a mighty effort, he brought them to the west side of the fort. With powder ferried from Tamarack, he and his artillerymen rained hell down on Progar for a watch and a half.

Abel was watching when the Progar militia broke.

It pulled back fighting until it ran into the marshy ground that its leaders had used so effectively to stymie the Goldies. A battling retreat continued, but there was no room on the Road, and the militia rearguard had no time to stop and reload. Those men were soon overrun by Goldies. But the action had given the main army enough time to run without taking a musket ball in the back.

There was nowhere for the Progarmen to go but back north along the Road. Von Hoff set off in quick pursuit, but it was already dusk. He called his exhausted men to a halt. It was time to feed the living and bury the dead.

For the moment, the Progar militia had slipped away.

PART SEVEN

The Tinder

One year previously

1

Usually, Abel came to Mahaut when she was visiting Bruneberg. Partly, this was because of logistics. His quarters at the garrison were spacious enough—he was district military commander, after all—but getting into the compound was a complicated process, for which Abel was partly to blame. He'd instituted constant guard duty, complete with a change of personnel each watch, bolted gates, and rotating passwords. At first, the Regulars had thought this was a joke. Then irritation had set in. Finally, they'd come to not only accept the new rigors, but to appreciate them. A strong perimeter was a sign of serious purpose. And as Abel's other changes trickled through ranks, they saw the fear and contempt the townspeople had formerly held for them turn to respect, and often into full admiration.

"Just following orders, sir," they could now truthfully answer when challenged at the gates. When you could refer to real regulations, you didn't get personally blamed when you turned away a local grandee looking to curry favor and arrange for the kind of special treatment that had greased the wheels of Bruneberg mercantilism for decades.

So it wouldn't do to make the land-heiress and chief consort of House Jacobson in Lindron an exception to this rule. Much better for Abel to walk to the River, and to the Jacobson compound that was built on a wharf overhanging the bank. Plus,

195

Mahaut was usually busy as well. Her visits to Bruneberg, or Garangipore, where he occasionally also met her, were working trips, and not mere excuses to see him—although they were that, too. It had taken him a while to get used to the idea that her job was as important as his to as many people, although he should have expected this could happen when he'd seen her turn the Treville Regulars Women's Auxiliary into a deadly fighting force all those years ago.

Mahaut's personal quarters were the House Jacobson visitor's suite. They were at the far end of the wharf, most of which was a warehouse. The living quarters had a bay window overlooking the River below with a view of the western reaches of Cascade District. The Bruneberg Riverfront was built out over the River in such a way for many marches up and down the eastern bank. An enormous complex of scaffolding and pier posts extended the buildings over the water as much as a fieldmarch, almost to the main current in some cases, and beyond the usual reach of the River carnadons. So if you happened to fall out a window, you would probably drown before you were eaten.

Although he only saw her a few times a year, he considered the past three years some of the happiest in his life. He'd spent his four years in the Academy seeing Mahaut only six times total. In the meantime, he hadn't slept with anyone else, not even one of the amazingly beautiful whores near the Tabernacle, whose origins and types ran from Redland barbarian women to First Family second and third daughters. It had been a frustrating time.

Now Mahaut travelled to Bruneberg at least once a ninety-day three moon, coming upriver on a towed barge delivering grain, papyrus, and the fine pottery of Lindron, and returning on another transport laden with gunpowder, obsidian, skins from the north, and the everyday clay ware and plain linen that Bruneberg turned out in such prodigious quantities. She usually managed to stay a week, with her niece, Loreilei, in tow to babysit.

In a room nearby was the boy, the one who always travelled with her. She'd named him Abram, after the man who had been the Jacobson factor in Lindron before her. The boy was a toddler, and Loreilei and a wet nurse were attending him in his quarters. *That* hadn't stopped Mahaut from getting up in the middle of the night to check in on him.

Abel liked the boy well enough, and since Mahaut clearly

considered Abram near to an adopted son, he supposed he would learn to love the lad. At the moment, he was glad the child wasn't old enough to come wandering in after a nightmare to crawl into bed between the two of them.

A breeze through the open window fluttered a vermilion colored linen drape. Abel brushed it aside and gazed out over the River. He had awakened before dawn, as he usually did, and was now watching Churchill set. The sky was growing lighter, so the sun must be cresting the eastern horizon, although he couldn't see it, facing west as he was.

Mahaut stirred, sat up in her bed. "What are you looking at?"

"Moonlight on the River," Abel replied. "Nearly done now."

"Let me guess...Levot?" Mahaut didn't know the three moon phases very well. Abel, on the other hand, knew them almost instinctively. He'd spent a good part of his life sleeping outside and planning night attacks, reconnaissance patrols, and ambushes according to the amount of light available.

"Churchill," he said. Abel turned away from the window, stepped back to her bed, and lay down beside her. Both of them were naked, their clothes and weapons a jumbled pile at the foot of the bed.

"Do you have somewhere to be?" she asked.

"Not yet," he replied. "Talbot is handling the morning turnout." Abel had arranged his schedule for the week around Mahaut's visit.

"Good for Talbot," she said. "Yes, I'm thinking of giving him Montag if and when command rotates."

"Work, work, work."

"You're one to talk."

She put a hand on his chest and rolled him onto his back, and in the same motion climbed on top of him. He put his hands on her sides and brushed his fingers along the large scar that covered most of her hip and pelvis on the right side of her body. She had long since ceased to worry that he found it unattractive. Clearly it didn't deter him from seeking what he wanted.

"The scar is how I know you in the dark. That and those breasts," he'd once told her. "I wouldn't have you any other way."

Of course the same bullet that had caused the scar had torn into her womb, leaving her unable to have children—although Center had once said that in a society with more advanced medical technology, such damage would be reparable.

He was sometimes bothered by Center and Raj's presence during times like this, especially when he was unable to shake off the feeling of being watched, yet he knew they would remain silent and never interfere. Still, he'd often considered what it would be like to be with a woman without their presence in his mind.

Abel lifted Mahaut up slightly, and she reached down, found him, and helped him enter her. She straddled him, put her hands on Abel's chest, and moved to the rhythm of his breathing. Often their lovemaking took the form of a battle, complete with advances, retreats, victories, and surrender. But it was nice to wake in the aftermath of the night's twisted sheets and signs of struggle and make use of the indolence of morning.

Mahaut smiled wickedly, and swiped her nails across his chest, hard enough to leave red traces, but not deep enough to draw blood.

That hurt!

She was smiling as if to say, "Oh yes, it did, you complacent bastard."

He growled and turned Mahaut over, pinning her arms in the process, or attempting to. The struggle began again.

When it was over, light through the window signaled the dawn had truly arrived. Abel lay beside her, breathing hard.

"Now I do have to go," he said.

"Yes."

She propped herself up on an arm, looked down on him. "Tell me what a planet is again," she said.

He'd explained to her about his inner voices, even named Center and Raj, a year ago during one of her visits. Center had commented that this would hardly come as a surprise to her at this point.

She is coming to know you quite intimately, inside and out.

She'd wanted to know more, and he found himself spilling all he knew. The planets, the stars, all of it. It was so good to get it out, make it seem more than his own silent delusion.

He sat up, pointed at the window.

"A planet? We're on one right now. The dawn, the sunrise, is not Zentrum's relighting the fire of the world every day," he said. "Zentrum has nothing to do with it. Duisberg rotates. The sun isn't dying and rising again, we are just turning around and around to face away from it then to face it again."

"Because we're sticking to a ball?"

"Yes, a turning ball. A planet named Duisberg."

"And at night the stars are other suns?"

"They are."

"Where do they go during the day?"

"They're still there. The sun drowns them out with its light."

She nodded. "Ridiculous."

He shook his head. "Seems that way to me sometimes."

A moment of silence, then she spoke again, softly. "And Zentrum is not God?"

"No," Abel replied firmly. "Zentrum is a nishterlaub machine."

"Broken."

"Not exactly. Limited."

Mahaut nodded. "This I can see. This I can believe from the world I know."

"You and I understand the world better than him."

"Better than God?"

"Zentrum is not God. Center isn't even sure Zentrum is a conscious being. Not every Mark XV got the upgrade to full self-awareness, especially on outlying planets like Duisberg. Zentrum can simulate a personality well enough—hell, I've had conversations with him, something that I'd rather not repeat—but as to whether Zentrum really knows who he is the way you and I do . . . it could be that he does not."

Mahaut waved a hand in front of her face as if to disperse the cloud of nonsense Abel was spouting.

And it must seem so strange to her, Abel thought. *Mark XV computers. Rotating planets. Recreating a near-magical civilization. After all, why couldn't the sun just as easily be Zentrum's fire? Didn't believing as much make life easier, more simple? Couldn't that be enough?*

No.

Knowing how the universe worked explained so many other things, things of which the Laws and Edicts were silent.

Yet could it really be a fact that he was right, and every other human being in the Land and the Redlands beyond was wrong? It was very hard to keep the truth before his eyes sometimes. The truth was so completely different from the way everyone around him thought.

Everyone except Mahaut. Depending on how you looked at it, he'd either freed her from superstition—or drawn her deep into his own lunacy.

At least somebody is here with me, he thought.

"So tell me this," said Mahaut. "Since you know all this science and history is so, and Zentrum is some kind of sophisticated... thinking irrigation system...then why don't you fix him? You claim to be the one with the godlike knowledge, after all."

Abel sighed, leaned back against the cool stucco wall behind him. He wished he had thought to bring his pipe along. He would really like a puff of pipeweed at the moment.

"Because I don't know how," he said. "Center and Raj believe they do, and I trust them. For the moment, I do what I can. If my father keeps Treville strong and I clean up this cesspool in Bruneberg, maybe we can hold the Blood Winds at bay for another generation. Maybe that will give us time to get the boost we need, the momentum toward change and progress. That's something I understand, at least."

Mahaut chuckled. "Land and Law, if anyone hears us talking like this we'll burn at the stake."

"Just as likely crucified," Abel responded glumly. "Or stoned."

"So what? We revel in our time? Let the future burn?"

"I will not give up," Abel said. He made a fist, tapped it against a bedpost. "I know how to fight."

"That's not all you know how to do," she said to him in a whisper. "Now one more time before breakfast."

She tugged at his arm to pull him down, back into bed.

At least some choices a man must make were perfectly obvious.

2

Awul-alwaha
475 Post Tercium

Ruslan Kerensky had no intention of ending up like his cousin Rostov: slain and left for flitterdon fodder on a losing battlefield in the rice paddies of the Farmers. For one thing, Kerensky considered himself cut from different cloth than Rostov. He was not a warrior. He had long known this about himself. But since the very definition of a man for the Blaskoye was warrior, he'd had to ease his way carefully into a position of power. The solution, he found, was religion.

So Kerensky became a holy man, a speaker for the Blaskoye god Taub.

There was a tradition of holy men within his clan, but such leadership was hereditary, passing from father to son. Kerensky's father was no holy man, and in any case he barely acknowledged his son's existence.

So, as with so many things, Kerensky had carved a place for himself any way he could. The most powerful of holy men belonged to the Blaskoye Council of Law-givers, a group Kerensky knew he must be admitted to if he did not want to end up a powerless monk living in a dirty cave in the Table Lands. Some on the Council had stood in his way.

Several of those same men had found themselves caught in difficult situations with other men or with women who were not one of their wives. These had stepped down in disgrace.

They were the lucky ones. The more stubborn found themselves dead.

Taub was a harsh, demanding god, and Kerensky knew he was Taub's instrument. He'd never wavered in that belief. And because of it, he was permitted many things for which he would have ordered a man stoned.

As Taub's chosen, he considered himself a politician above all, a worker of the god's will, and always tried to put himself in the right place at the right time. While his cousin Rostov had gathered the Redlander tribes into a single army by force of conquest and coerced negotiations that could have but one outcome, Kerensky had been the man behind the scenes who made the new Blaskoye union into a workable system of rule. To be able to turn clan ties and factionalism into a state was a great feat, and Kerensky, along with his now considerable body of acolytes, disciples, and warrior-priests, had done it.

Now he *was* the will of the Council, for all intents and purposes, and he'd made it into a true instrument of Taub's will.

Taub demanded unity.

The Redlander tribes had spent hundreds of years at one another's throats, hating each other more than they hated the Farmers. But now Rostov was gone and Kerensky assumed overall leadership. The Blaskoye union was an inheritance he didn't intend to squander. Besides, someone had to pull the splintering tribes together after the crushing defeat the Blaskoye suffered in the Treville invasion, and Kerensky knew he was the man for the task.

But never during his rise through the ranks of the Blaskoye had Kerensky heard Taub's voice directly. That had recently changed. One day not long after Kerensky consolidated his position, an emissary had arrived with a strange gift. The emissary was a dirty man of questionable clan who grubbed a living by trading with the Farmers of Ingres. He sold them broken slaves and unwanted daughters (allegedly to become serfs or house servants—the hypocritical Farmers denied they kept slaves) in exchange for gunpowder, shot, and Delta wood for making bows.

But it wasn't the emissary, but the emissary's message that mattered.

He presented to Kerensky what he claimed was a means of

communicating directly with Taub. He claimed it was a lost relic that allowed its user to hear Taub's voice.

"I found this in a sacred spring near the Escarpment, Law-giver," said the man. "A hand reached up from the water, and I heard the voice of Taub—it was terrible, like the wind—telling me to bring it to you. He said I was to take it to the holiest of the Blaskoye, and I knew that to be you, Law-giver."

The thing was a small white stone. Flat. It was completely smooth, polished to a dull sheen. He'd found it impossible to scratch even with a metal knife. Yet it was merely the size of a wafer that could be encircled by thumb and forefinger.

So he'd taken it, listened to the emissary's instructions, sup-posedly delivered by Taub. He heard the man's request for com-pensation.

Laughed.

What nonsense!

He'd had the man imprisoned. As he'd suspected, a few fire-coals to the feet had brought forth the whole story.

There had been no sacred spring. No voice of Taub. The disk had been given to the man by a priest at the Ingres border from whom he bought gunpowder. The priest claimed that it had come from Lindron, that it was a stone taken from the tabernacle of Zentrum, and that whoever possessed it would have power over the priests of Zentrum.

He'd offered to sell it to the emissary for a dozen slaves he could trade to an Ingres plantation. When the emissary had balked, the priest came down in his asking price. When the emissary laughed at even this, the priest had made it a condition of his sale of the gunpowder that the emissary take the stone as well. Take it and deliver it to Awul-alwaha. The trader had planned to toss the stone away, of course, but decided to try its magic first. He'd followed instructions, place the stone in his mouth.

His mind had expanded to fill the world. Taub spoke.

At that point, he knew the stone was real, and he knew he had to take it to a true holy man.

The man couldn't explain it further, no matter how hard Kerensky's men beat him.

After the vision, the conviction began to take root that some-thing might be gotten for the wafer stone after all. He'd imagined a gift of daks, or even slaves.

What he hadn't imagined was that the stone would cost him his life. Obviously the man couldn't go walking around with knowledge of a true object of power. When Kerensky thought that he had extracted all the information he could from the man, he ordered him executed.

After that, Kerensky followed the instructions the man had given him.

Why not? The reluctant emissary of Taub had been quite convincing.

Kerensky found that the disk fit easily into the upper portion of his mouth.

He pushed it upward with his thumb into the curve of his upper palate.

There was a moment of paralysis. He couldn't remove the thumb. He could not blink.

Then a flash of light so painful he cried out.

More flashes before his eyes. More pain.

Then, as quickly as they had come, the pain and lights were gone.

So was the paralysis. Kerensky collapsed to the floor of his tent. After some moments regaining his composure, he pulled himself to his feet, shook his head.

It wasn't over.

The lights returned, dancing before his eyes. No matter which way he turned his head, they were still there.

They are in my mind, he reasoned. *They would move if they were actually before me.* This was some sort of hallucination. Perhaps the stone was dusted with some sort of drug.

Then came a voice dry and crisp as sand blown over sandstone, a whisper that was also, somehow, a roar.

Even though he'd never heard it before, Kerensky knew that voice.

Taub spoke.

All doubt vanished.

You and your clan have been chosen among all the peoples to rule the world. I am strong. I will open a path for you. I will give you victory.

I will give you the Valley and its people as your subjects for generation upon generation.

All you must do, Law-giver, is go and take them.

I, Taub, command you: raise the horde!

PART EIGHT

The Campaign

The Present

1

"I've had the cannons destroyed," von Hoff said apologetically. "The chaplaincy prelate told me it had to be done. The man's going to be district high priest after we take this place. You don't argue with a priest of that standing or you'll soon find yourself commanding the lighthouse garrison in Fyrpahatet."

"I understand," Abel said, and he did. Von Hoff was trying to protect him and the Third from any further incrimination in sacrilege for the deliberate use of nishterlaub items. The chaplaincy was only a small unit attached to Corps command, but it wielded great influence. Its priests were all appointed by the Abbot himself, and they were not afraid to use the Abbot's name if they believed heresy was afoot. Enforcing Edict and the will of the Abbot of Lindron was the chaplain's prime duty, not kowtowing to a mere general. The chaplain-prelate had authority to override the Corps commander himself in ecclesiastical matters.

In the Land, everything was an ecclesiastical matter.

Landry would be disappointed that his new toys had been taken away from him, that was for sure. But Abel knew that Landry was working on another idea of his—an idea that had been suggested by a comment from Abel—a comment that Abel had relayed from Center.

207

"You've heard the rumors of what's been going on up here. Nishterlaub methods, nishterlaub weapons. Imagine those captured volley guns bent into a circle. Eight chambers. And maybe not fired all at once and by a single fuse, but one at a time."

"Each chamber with its own firing cap!" Landry had immediately seen the implications. "Or no cap at all, and we finally find a way to combine cartridge and cap together."

"But no nishterlaub use of metal for us," Abel said. "I've already stood next to the fire when one heretic burned. I don't want to smell another."

"Yes, sir," Landry said, frowning—but musing on the problem, working it over in his mind.

They'd moved the Corps headquarters to Fort Tamarak, with its magisterial view of the River Valley for leagues to the north and south. Von Hoff had abided here for nearly two weeks, reshuffling the forces at his command. His main thought was to rebuild his shattered mounted force however he could. He'd sent back to Cascade for more beasts.

They'd lost over half their men and donts. Colonel Kanagawa, the cavalry regiment leader, had somehow survived the charge up Sentinel and remained in command.

"It wasn't Kanagawa that gave the thrice-damned order, anyway," von Hoff said. "Although the fact that he followed it is problematic enough. He knew what would happen." Von Hoff rubbed his eyes and shook his head. "I have no one else ready, however. Kanagawa will have to do."

The one who did order the charge has paid for it with his life, Abel thought.

General Josiah Saxe had been buried on the Sentinel hillside beside the bodies of those who had ridden to their deaths in the charge.

Although the prelate had advised it, von Hoff had refused to order mass executions of the Progar prisoners. Yet, his argument was that if the enemy knew surrender would mean a sentence of death with no appeal, all of Progar would fight till the bitter end. Many more Guardian lives might be lost in such conditions.

"But surrender *does* mean death with no appeal," the prelate had said to von Hoff within Abel's hearing. "That is the purpose of the expedition, after all."

"Let us conquer, and then we will execute them in our own

good time, Prelate," von Hoff answered. "It should be done efficiently, with as little suffering as we can manage."

"Yes, I agree with that."

So the matter was closed for now. The prisoners of war were being held in the dead-end caves of Mount Sentinel, caverns sealed by ancient technology to allow no tunneling, no escape. The only way out was the single opening, which was kept guarded.

Quarter rations were issued to the prisoners daily, and some of the men begrudged them even that. What was the point of feeding them? They were going to die anyway. Abel nipped Third Division grumbling in the bud with a few strategic punishments, but it was rife in the other brigades. He, too, sometimes wondered what the point was. But to kill a man by starving him was a different order of cruelty than a long-drop hanging, even though the ultimate outcome was the same.

The first news from von Hoff's reconstituted cavalry was not good. Kanagawa entered von Hoff's headquarters at Sentinel while Abel was delivering a report.

"We moved up the road a good five leagues, General. Marshy ground, very marshy." Kanagawa's face was doleful in the best of times. At the moment, his scowl made him look devastated. "There's a large lake to the east. The Road runs west of it, between that lake and the River."

The lake is the primary source of protein for the inhabitants on this side of the River, Center said. **Observe:**

Instantly Abel was soaring over the landscape, traversing in an instant the distance that had taken the mounted force a day to travel. The lake appeared as a gash of blue below him.

It's long and not very wide.

Precisely. It is an oxbow lake, a meander of the River that got cut off when the main current changed course. Now it is extensively farmed for fish. At the northern end are man-made rocky structures that I observed while making my survey from orbit.

That was over a hundred and fifty years ago.

Physical characteristics do not often change in the Land, as you know, Center said. **The structures are hatcheries for various gene-modified Earth species of fish, the primary species being trout.**

Earth species? You mean the *Earth? What do they eat?*

The indigenous species of this planet have a compatible protein structure for consumption by Earth vertebrate species. The fish eat insectoids for the most part. How did you think humans have survived on Duisberg? You are, after all, a species from Earth as well.

I see your point.

Look below and see the great meander in the River. This entire peninsula is marsh. But there is solid ground for nearly a half league between the lake, which is known, appropriately, as Fish Lake, and the River. There is also solid ground on its eastern side, although not as much, between the lake and the slopes of Mount Manahatet.

That big bump to the north?

Yes, that big bump to the north, said Center dryly. It is an interesting formation. The mountain is an ancient reef created by a shallow sea approximately sixty-two point seven million years ago. The mountain was not thrust up. It began as a hard spot in a plateau and the Valley has eroded around it. It is composed of compacted limestone and concretized conglomerate and likely has an extensive natural cave system within it, complete with underground lakes and waterfalls.

Not much good for us at the moment.

But good for the pre-Collapse humans of Duisberg. Indications are it was a vacation destination point for settlers in other parts of the Valley, a geological attraction of great beauty. A principal northern settlement was situated atop Manahatet. Although it was almost entirely disassembled by the Gateway virus, ruins along the mountaintop are discernible even now. With the mountains nearby, the economy of what is now presently called Progar in all likelihood revolved around tourism. Perhaps it will again someday, if we are successful.

Maybe not the best part of advanced civilization to bring back, growled Raj. *But it would mean freedom from want, which is not a bad thing.*

We will not bring back anything, of course. That is Zentrum's basic mistake: top-down, hierarchical thinking. Civilization wants to grow, in a manner of speaking. We will simply remove its impediments.

Like taking down God himself.

Zentrum is not God.

Yes, I know. You've told me often enough.

Let us hope it does not take a catastrophic planetary asteroid strike or an unexpected plague to prove it.

Kanagawa was still making his report. "We ran into skirmishers about halfway up the lakeside. We chased them, but then we slammed into their mounted unit. We had a little scrum, and I think we got the better of them, but we had to turn back. I also sent some boys south and around the other side, and they got farther north."

"What did they find, Colonel?" von Hoff asked.

"Looks like every militia in Progar is at the north end. There's a plain of good hard ground north of the River, and that's where they're bivouacked."

"Did we get any estimation of numbers?"

Kanagawa looked down sheepishly. "The boys I sent weren't too good at figuring. My mistake not to send a more seasoned officer. What I did get from them was that the camp went on for about a league or more."

Estimated twenty-five thousand nine hundred militia troops, Center said.

"General von Hoff, I'd put that at twenty-six thousand troops," Abel said briskly.

"Oh, you would, would you, Dashian? And what makes you say that?"

"A quick calculation, sir. Very likely off by a considerable degree."

"I'd say you're pulling that figure out of your ass, young colonel," said Kanagawa.

Abel turned, caught von Hoff's eyes. "Believe me, General."

Von Hoff stared at him for a moment, then he nodded. "I do believe you, Colonel Dashian," he said. He turned back to Kanagawa. "So it appears we're up against about one and a half times our numbers."

"If that's so, it gets worse, General."

"How does it get worse?"

"We saw some smoke to the east, lots of it. Likely a military camp. They may have that little village at the base of the mountain shut up with soldiers."

The village is called Isham. It is capable of housing eight to ten thousand. More, if supply lines are well established.

So we could have over thirty thousand men against us?

It's a militia and mercenary army, said Raj. **That's a different order of beast than the Guardian Corps. I'd call this almost a fair fight.**

"So it looks like we meet them at..." Von Hoff turned to one of his cartographers. "What's that place's name, lieutenant?"

The man gazed down at his scroll. "It's called Fish Pens, sir. No idea why."

"An ugly name for an ugly place, no doubt."

Abel cleared his throat. "If I may, General..."

"What is it, Dashian?"

"That village at the base of the mountain, sir."

"Yes, the possible haven of reinforcements?"

"Exactly, sir. There may be a large force encamped there. If we could neutralize that possibility, you can cut off and kill the main army."

Von Hoff sighed loudly, but he was also smiling. "Dashian, are you about to ask me to split my army again?"

"Yes, sir. Send me up that eastern valley."

Von Hoff put a hand to his forehead, rubbed it.

"All right," he muttered. Then stronger: "All right. Take the Third, Colonel Dashian, and good luck."

2

Three Sisters Valley

Abel had been confident von Hoff would let him have his way, and had already ordered his wagons and animals taken over the saddle to the northern side of Tamarak Peak. After that, it was just a matter of the troops breaking down their camp in the crags and making their way down by squad and company to assemble at the confluence of two rivers. The other river was the Fork, the only true secondary river Abel had ever seen. This was the place where the Fork poured itself into the River. The Fork was the only major tributary the River had for all the hundreds of leagues of the Land. The River only divided again when it reached the Delta country before it ran into the Braun Sea.

There had been a ferry here, but von Hoff's engineers had been busy during the pause. Daring carnadons, of which there were a few even this far north, they had built a wooden bridge across the Fork. It was only a wagon's width wide, but it would serve to bring the Third across without getting the men's feet wet.

Abel's men crossed it at a slow march. Abel wanted no one hurrying up and tottering over the edge and into the water. Carnadons had already gathered under the structure, hoping for a quick meal.

When the brigade was on the other side, instead of going straight along the Road, they turned onto another byway that ran alongside the Fork. Now Abel quick-timed the march. There would be moaning and groaning, and there would certainly be stragglers falling out, but he had a long way to go and very little time if he was to be a help to von Hoff. Comfort would not be a part of this campaign.

The Three Sisters Valley closed in on either side of them, and the Fork poured down it at an amazing speed. The Fork Road turned uphill, and they marched league after league at a steady upward grind. He gave the troops five minutes rest each half-watch, and they were not to sit down.

Late in the day, he had captains reporting to him that their troops were exhausted, stumbling on their feet. They'd left a trail of stragglers behind as well. Some begged for a halt.

Abel shrugged with apparent indifference. "We'll stop when we get there," Abel told each of them. He felt each weary step of his men, but the need to push on was urgent.

"Where is *there*, sir?" they asked. But on this, Abel remained silent. For the moment, he would keep his plans to himself. It was better that way. He didn't want to scare them.

They met their first resistance at the headwaters of the Fork at the confluence of two small streams. There was a covered bridge spanning it in a narrow spot, and on the northern side of the river stood the village of Siegan. A garrison of about forty Progar men was stationed there. When those troops realized that they were facing not just a patrol, but an entire brigade, those that remained alive turned and ran up the valley as fast as their legs would carry them. But they could not run faster than a dont. Abel sent a detail of his few mounted troops after them, and they came back with two of the men tied across the backs of their donts like hunting prizes.

"Rest of them scattered up into the hills and got away, sir," the lieutenant in charge of the squad reported. "They'll take news of us marching up the Manahatet north for sure, sir."

"You let me worry about that, lieutenant," Abel replied. He turned to Timon. "Major Athanaskew, bring me the new captain of interrogation," he said, "but I want you in on it, too."

Timon would be sure to drain these prisoners of what information they had. Every bit might matter.

Most of the men expected to bed down for the night at Siegan—some had already dumped their packs—and were astonished when Abel kept them marching. As they passed through Siegan, the villagers came out to gawk. The road and a small tributary of the Fork River wended northeast. The tributary was no longer the Fork, but was called Manahatet Creek on the maps. It was a fast-flowing, powerful stream—but a stream they could wade at waist height with safety lines. They were now in Manahatet Valley.

Darkness fell. The march went on. It was past midnight when the light of Churchill finally broke over the steep walls of Manahatet Valley. They marched on.

Finally, just before dawn, Abel called a one-watch rest. Most of the men collapsed in their tracks, some not even bothering to take off their packs. He hobbled his dont—he still rode Nettle, the female he'd picked out of the train in Ingres—and sat with his back against a rock.

He dozed. He knew he daydreamed, because when dawn lightened the sky, he started to awareness with an image of Mahaut dissolving in his mind's eye. For a moment, he thought she was there, physically present, smiling down at him as he slept. Then he shook himself awake, and she was three hundred leagues away once more.

He turned to Timon, who was splayed on the ground as if he'd been staked out by Blaskoye raiders. "Get them up, Timon," he said. He had to say it three more times and add a soft kick before he aroused his friend.

Once he was awake, Timon jumped to his feet as if prodded by a firecoal stick. Abel had to smile at the irony. In the past, it was usually Timon who had done the prodding.

"What'd you get from the prisoners?"

"They say this valley is stoppered at the top like a bottle. There are fortifications designed for enfilading fire. It sounds nasty, sir."

"Yes," Abel mused. "Let's avoid those."

"But how? There is no way but up the Manahatet."

Abel nodded. "So it would seem."

Abel allowed a few moments for the troops to shove a mouthful or two of rations down their throats, then got them on the march again. He heard cursing up and down the ranks, mostly in the same breath as his name.

They moved at a quick trot northward. The columns grew ragged, but they hung together, and the men kept on. When he judged they were about halfway up the Manahatet Valley, he slowed the march to a shuffle and sent the mounted troops up the valley ahead of them. He put out a skirmish line trailing behind them. It didn't take long for the skirmishers to come thundering back. The crackle of rifle fire picked up ahead.

"I think we've found a force of them," Abel said to no one in particular. He turned to Timon. "Major Athanaskew, halt the division. Send three companies forward, but hold the rest back. I want to give them a bloody nose they'll remember."

"Very good, sir."

"The orders are to engage the enemy. Use both sides of the creek for lines of movement."

"Yes, sir."

"And tell the captains to be prepared to withdraw at a moment's notice. You have that, Major?"

"Withdraw at a moment's notice, yes, sir." Timon straightened. "Request permission to lead the charge, sir."

Abel considered. He could ill-afford to lose Timon. On the other hand, he knew the kind of fire that burned within Timon. He was going to find a way to thrust himself into the fight one way or another.

"All right, do it, Timon."

It wasn't long before three companies chosen came running forward. Give it to Timon and Sergeant Groelsh: they knew how to move men. Abel stood by the side of the road as his soldiers charged by.

Ahead the musketry crackle became a roar. He pressed forward to catch a glimpse of the battle, but realized it was useless. The valley was too narrow, and he'd packed it full of men.

Show me, Abel thought.

Calculation complete. Observe:

The lines had formed quickly, and the men had spread into the shape of "The Man Who Welcomes with Open Arms," as they called it at the Academy—basically an outward-facing arch. The two flanks were slightly forward so that if the enemy was foolish enough to charge the center, the flanks could lay down fire from either side. Good.

The vegetation had grown thicker in the valley. Scrub trees and grass had given way to forest. Yet the trees were still sparse enough to permit tolerable line-of-sight for most of the troops in the formation.

The enemy, as he had been at the fighting in the marsh, was

a mass with very little organization. What cohesion there was seemed to be in groups of different sizes.

Clans, said Raj. *They'll fight as a family, and they'll die that way, too.*

Still, there were a lot of them. They were massed back up the Manahatet Valley as if waiting in line for the morning's bread at a bakery.

You have pulled them from their position at Isham, said Center.

So you probably know what I'm going to do next.

Lead them down the valley as far as you can, then disappear. It was not a question from Center. Center seldom asked questions.

Yes.

Suddenly, a large group of Progar musket men worked up their courage and leapt into a head-on charge. They couldn't head down the center of the valley, but took to the meadow that lined the creek.

The Guardian rifles were merciless. It was as if the charging men were engulfed in a Redlands sandstorm.

The charge broke. The Progarmen turned and fled from the fury, and when the smoke cleared there were at least one hundred men lying dead or wounded.

They ran right into it. More murder.

No scruples. This is war, not a game. They would gladly kill you from any position, if they could.

"You've got that faraway look in your eyes again." Abel blinked, turned to his right to find Flandry sitting on his dont next to him. "It's a bit alarming to me, because whenever you do that, it seems like you're about to give me a task that can't possibly be accomplished and expect me to have it done yesterday."

"Captain Hoster, all I want from you today is another one of your fine smoke bombs. Do you think you can cook one up for me?"

Landry smiled broadly. "That I did have done yesterday. Got a wagon primed and ready, sir."

"Go alert your team. When I give the word, fire it up."

"Yes, sir," Landry said. He beat his chest in salute, then turned his dont and galloped away.

Abel turned to Captain Caleb Bunch, another of his staff officers, and another Cascadian by birth. Bunch had several times proved himself a good runner, getting through when it seemed impossible. "All right, Captain, it's time to call Major Athanaskew and the men back."

"Sir? Retreat, sir?"

"I want those companies to give me a fighting withdrawal back down the valley," he said. "Tell them to move slowly back, but when they see the smoke, it's time to turn and run."

"Yes, sir," Bunch said uncertainly.

"Do you understand the orders, Captain? Major Athanaskew would."

"Yes, sir."

"Then carry them out."

"Very good, sir."

He stood by the smoking wagon waiting till he heard the sound of the front lines drawing close. He watched as soldiers emerged from the haze in front of him like ghosts, charged past, and disappeared into the brown nothingness to his rear. Finally, it was time to go.

"Come on, Landry, let's get out of here," he said. "I'm afraid you're going to lose this wagon."

"All for a good cause," Landry replied. "One hopes."

"We'll see. Now let's move."

They mounted up and plunged into the mist, with Abel's staff and the rearguard not far behind them.

Abel soon caught up with the main body of his troops. He ordered them into a trot, as close to a run as possible. The men were exhausted.

He pushed them harder.

Speed was essential. He had to lure the enemy as far south as possible, drawing them away from von Hoff with every step. Then the Third must disappear from enemy sight.

Moving downhill, they withdrew over the ground they had covered in half the time it had taken to gain it. Evening fell. They kept up the trot.

It was only when he saw the faint lights of oil lamps at Siegan that he called a halt. There was a wide alluvial flat near the city, more gravel than sand, but smooth enough.

"We'll bivouac here," Abel said to Timon. "They shouldn't catch us in the night, but set up pickets and send out a mounted screen. Find the men who seem at least awake, set them to it. Rotate them all every halfwatch. But get the first watch fed first. Then everyone else. No fires. Hardtack only. We leave at dawn."

"Yes, sir!" answered Timon. He was a hard man, but Abel saw relief in his eyes. "And if the colonel doesn't mind my asking... where are we leaving *for* at dawn?"

Abel shook his head, and smiled a tired smile. He did not answer. This was mostly because he was afraid telling the truth would worry Timon so much he might not be able to sleep.

The Rim could do that to those who had never left the Valley.

After a moment, Abel dismounted, gave his mount over to one of Groelsh's command staff wranglers, and went to find a place to collapse.

3

Abel woke in the chill of dawn. He stumbled around until he found the command provisions, then dug out a jug of water from the wagon bed. He drained it, barely stopping to breathe.

Better.

He took a look around. He had been certain the Progar militia would lag in pursuit, but all the same he was relieved to find that they weren't camped across the field from the Third, massing for a dawn attack. He had slipped away and drawn the enemy far down the valley.

There had to have been a couple of thousand pursuers, Abel thought.

Three thousand one hundred.

That's three thousand men who won't be reinforcing the militia at Fish Pens today, Raj said. ***You did the job, man.***

He couldn't remember the last time Raj had given him direct praise. He felt as if he'd won the Harvest Fair grand prize.

But it wasn't over yet. There was today to get through, for instance.

Abel went to stand over the form of Groelsh, who was sleeping like a baby. He hated to do it, but—

"All right, Staff Master Sergeant, up with you. Get up and let's get them rousted. But do it quietly. No horns."

Abel observed the sky as the troops began to awaken. The day was dry, as any other day in the Land would be. But the sky was beginning to become obscured as clouds drifted over. These weren't the clouds that Abel was used to, either. They hung low in layers, and soon they covered the whole sky. Ominous.

Stratus, said Center. **Common at this latitude and near the mountains. There is far more moisture in the air here than there is in Treville, or Lindron.**

The men rose to the gray day. Abel permitted cook fires to be made and a breakfast of gruel to be cooked up. It was not long after sunrise when they finally set out. Instead of marching back to the west to rejoin von Hoff, as many expected them to do, Abel headed the troops down the Manahatet to Siegan and the confluence of streams that began the Fork. Then they followed the smaller of these. Men looked about quizzically. Where the cold hell was the colonel taking them? They came to where the spring flowed from the side of the Escarpment and still they kept walking. The ground grew steep. The trail narrowed and switched back repeatedly. They were climbing the Escarpment.

"If I didn't know better, I'd say we were going up to the Rim," said Timon. "Are we going up to the Rim, Colonel?" Abel looked over his shoulder at him and smiled.

The maps had the road, now become a trail, climbing up the whole height of the Escarpment. Looking up, anyone could see that this was not possible. Here Abel felt his first doubt. The cliff was too steep and sheer to permit even switchback. Nevertheless, he continued forward. Progar traded with the Redlanders. The Blaskoye raided the Valley. There had to be ways up and down, and this track they followed was very well worn. If the map was wrong, he'd find another way.

Finally, after a series of endless switchbacks, they saw not far ahead the bottom of a high cliff. About three fieldmarches above that was the Rim. The trail went no farther. The cliff was bare.

Except... upon drawing closer, there was something here. Something manmade.

Something that looked as nishterlaub as anything Abel had ever seen.

It was a wooden and metal contraption, very large, with a mechanism that led all the way up the side of the cliff. There were four ropes holding platforms spaced about twenty elbs apart. The platforms were the size of wagons, maybe a little bit bigger. There was something about the construction that said "machine."

And not a simple machine. Abel stared at it as they drew nearer, trying to figure out what it did.

It looks like an oblong water wheel.

Center was quiet.

Finally, Abel sighed and gave in. *Okay, what is it?*

It is an elevator, said Center. **It seems to be designed to carry wagons or wagon-sized loads up the side of this cliff to the Rim. Red staining indicates ferrous material. Iron ore.**

But it's not moving. How does it work?

It is similar in construction to a chain drive.

A what?

Platforms on a rotating, elliptical structure.

Rotating? It's not moving.

No. But it appears to be in good working order.

"Nishterlaub," whispered Bunch, sitting on his puffing dont to Abel's left. Timon, on Abel's right, said nothing, but his scowl told all.

Abel turned to Bunch. "Have Captain Hoster brought up," Abel said. "I have a feeling he'll want to see this."

"Water," said Landry, after he'd stared at the elevator for quite a while. "That's where the power comes from. That's how it's done. See those half barrels attached to the four corners of the platforms? Those will work just as a waterwheel does. Water falls into them and turns the whole thing around. But I don't see where the water comes from. Maybe if we get closer, I could."

"Let's have a look," said Abel. He cast his gaze around. "I think the rest of the staff would rather be as far away from this thing is they can possibly be. Let's you, me, and Timon go."

They had come to a stop on a deep, but dry, gulch. Across it stretched a wooden bridge. Abel led his staff and the troops to one side of the bridge, then motioned the troops to halt. He, Landry, and Timon clopped onto its wooden planking. The middle of the bridge provided a grand view of the elevator.

Abel motioned for them to dismount. They hitched their donts to the bridge railing and left them there, then climbed up a single-file trail that led to the bottom of the apparatus.

"It's not broken, I think," Timon said. He put a hand on one of the huge ropes that held the elevator platforms in place. They were hemp, but as thick as a tree trunk.

Timon may have been a zealot, but his conception of his duties was ethical and spiritual. Unlike many far less religious men, he was not superstitious about touching or handling nishterlaub. It was the concept he abhorred.

"These ropes are fairly new. See? The twist is lefthand lay." He bent closer, examined the strands. "They've been reinforced somehow." He looked closer, teased apart several strands. "Metal," he said. "One of the strands is metal. But to draw out such a long strand—it's impossible. Can't be done."

Progar has mastered the drawing and annealing of steel.

At least someone in Progar has, said Raj.

"It's obviously not impossible." Abel turned to Timon. "We will make use of this."

Landry walked around behind the elevator works as they spoke. There was plenty of room for a man between the suspension ropes and the cliffside.

"Operating lever!" he suddenly shouted. "I've found the way to turn this thing on!" He charged back around to stand beside them. "There are two flues sticking out of the cliff about halfway up. I can see them from back there. They feed right into those buckets. That'll be the water supply for turning. I'd say there's a reservoir up there, cut back in the cliff. I doubt they lifted the water up. Probably fed by an underground stream or spring or something..."

More likely a seep, Center said. **It would appear to be an extrusion of the Redlands plateau water table. Note the mineral buildup approximately halfway up the Escarpment cliff. There are seeps all along the wall in this vicinity. These are, collectively, the source of the Forks River.**

"—dammed up with a headgate that's controlled from down here by a pull rope. They've got it well-secured down here, but nothing I can't undo with a sharp blade. They obviously shut it down temporarily and intended to come back and make use of it again."

"When you undo it, what will happen?"

"Not completely sure, but I suspect the lever controls a headgate or valve on the reservoir up there. Water will pour down both of those flues and empty into those half barrels. It'll weigh them down, and the whole contraption will start to move, to rotate. This front side will move up, and the backside with move down—and all of it powered by those water-heavy half barrels. The half barrels turn round the bottom side here, empty into the sluice here"—he pointed at the ditch leading away from the base of the machine under the bridges and into the gulch—"and the gulch that passes carries the water away to the Forks." Landry gazed up at the elevator in awe. "It's quite something. Elegant. And all done with water power."

Timon had stepped away to do some scouting around, and now returned. "This place was bustling not long ago. Tools seem to have been left where men dropped them. I'll wager the men who work here got called away to the militia. This site is not secure. No one expected us to come this route, I'm certain."

"Not in a thousand years," Abel said. "But here we are. Can you make it work, Landry?"

"You bet I can."

"Caution, Abel," Timon put in. "Consider the effect this will have on the troops."

"Religious effect, Major?"

Timon nodded. "To use such a thing would be in contradiction to all the Combination Edicts. If we had a chaplain along, he would tell you as much. I can see an argument that, since it is already in place, we might make use of it. But that's a thin reed on which to hang the trust of superstitious men."

"Yes, I see what you mean, Timon. What do you suggest?"

"A council of war. We listen to the captains' opinions, make an effort to convince them this is the best course."

"Do *you* think it's the best course?"

"As your adjutant, I would say you are dakshit crazy to consider this. They'll burn you for sure," Timon answered. "As your friend...I still think it's probably a bad idea. But as a soldier..." Timon smiled his icy, carnadonlike smile. "As a soldier, I say we have the opportunity to make our way north along that Rim, bypass every patrol, cavalry recognizance, and skirmisher in the valley below, and pick our moment to descend on the Progar militia like death raining from above. Furthermore, I believe that's what you've been thinking all along."

Abel nodded. "You're right about that."

"So I say let's go and convince those pukes to trust their life and limb to this infernal contraption, Colonel Dashian, sir."

"Let's talk to the captains," Abel said.

He began with what he hoped was his most reasonable tone. "Do you remember the boats that took us across the Canal? These are transports that will take us up that cliff. As you know, General von Hoff is facing a force that is many times the size of ours. Goldies are worth two or three of them, no doubt. But I put it to you that there are three or four of them to each one of us. That is too many. We need a way to even those odds, and this is it."

"What is your plan, Colonel?" said a captain.

Abel smiled. "To disappear from Manahatet Valley, then reappear where the enemy does not expect us. To hit him hard and draw his force off of General von Hoff."

"Whether or not we can get them to climb upon that beast, the men are dead tired, sir," said another captain.

"They'll keep going," Abel said. "We all will."

"You're asking the impossible, and asking us all to become heretics in the bargain, Colonel," said a third company commander.

"I spent half my life traversing the Rim as a Scout, gentlemen. We'll find our way once we're up there. As for heresy—we didn't build this thing, but, thrice-damn it all, we're going to use it. We'll use it for our brothers' sake. And we'll use it because we marched three hundred leagues to win, not to lose. We're not going to go home beaten or get ourselves dead because I left something undone that might have been done."

"Some of the men won't do it," the company commander replied.

Abel turned to Timon. "Captain Athanaskew." Timon had been standing at the edge of the circle of captains, listening carefully, but remaining his usual aloof self. He stepped forward.

"Yes, Colonel?"

Abel stared him in the eyes.

"Will you do it, Captain?"

A moment of hesitation. Then Timon's jaw clenched and a tremor went through him. His answer was low, almost a whisper. "Yes, sir," he said. Then louder: "Yes, sir. After what you did at Tamarak and Sentinel, I believe I'd follow you to cold hell and back. You fight, Colonel. That's why we're here."

"So be it," Abel said. He addressed the others. "Put it to the men the way I have done to you. There'll be no shame if they don't want to go. I'll send those who wish to remain here back to the garrison at Siegan to await orders. But let's show them what they're in for if they come with me." He turned to Landry. "Captain Hoster, go and open that gate."

✧   ✧   ✧

In the end, only a few men refused to board the elevator. They gathered sullenly to the rear, defiance and misery on their faces in equal measure. Two were lieutenants, and Abel put these in charge of the fifty or so men who would be heading back down the Fork.

All of his captains were with him.

Psychological interpolation indicates that most of these officers and men believe they may be endangering their eternal well-being, yet are willing to do so on your say-so, Abel. This is an interesting outlying condition on several Seldonian self-preservation curves.

They want to win, Raj said. **Abel has convinced them that this is the way.**

I could have told you that, Abel thought. *Despite what you've taught me over the years, that thing scares the cold hell out of me, too. If I get on it, it will be because I trust you both. Listen to it turn and grind! And thrice-damn whether or not it's nishterlaub; I'm just as worried about it crashing down and killing us all.*

An inflection point has been achieved, Center said. **Further calculations are necessary, but turning back is no longer an option.**

For the first time Abel could remember, Center seemed... sad.

Abel rode up first with Timon by his side. Landry remained below at the controlling rope. They rose for a good twenty elbs, then lurched to a stop. The ground grew farther away, and the soldiers below gawking up at them smaller and smaller. After a moment, the contraption got going again. Then another, smoother pause, as Landry got the hang of the levering system. Of course each platform would have to be held in place while men and equipment were piled aboard. The ascent would be a slow rise with a lot of stops on the way.

If Abel hadn't known the elevator was powered by scientific principle, he'd have believed in magic. First of all, the thing was huge, its scale beyond the human. Even wagons loaded onto its platforms seemed puny. This was a machine designed to move mountains, to move tons of ore and material. He felt as if he'd been thrust into a new reality when he boarded. So this was what civilization was capable of, what men could do when they put their minds to it. This and much, much more.

With each move upward the sound grew fantastically loud, an enormous rumble, along with a grinding, clacking, squeaking, and squealing amalgam of every noise he'd ever heard hitting his ears all at once. It was impossible to communicate without shouting while the platform was in motion.

And there was a smell. The damp wood, the fresh spray of water in the sloshing buckets that powered everything, the faint scent of smoldering wood. How was this thing lubricated, anyway? Was it just the water that kept the turning ropes from burning in two?

There is a great deal of rendered dak grease involved in the lubrication. Some has dried from recent disuse, but the mechanism is still completely functional.

He was traveling as fast as a dont could trot. Each jolt upward felt inexorable, one platform stop at a time. If a man fell into the mechanism, would it even jam this monster?

The gearing would grind a human to pieces. Please mind the edge.

They rose over the edge, and Abel saw what Landry had told him to look for: a signal lever to tell the operator below to stop the platform so its occupants could get off. He pulled it up as they passed it. The action did nothing more than release two signal flags that popped out on either side of the elevator and hung off the side of the cliff just below the Rim. But Landry had placed one of his men a half fieldmarch away to watch for any sign. He must have wigwagged Landry the information, for the platform suddenly came to a jolting stop, more-or-less at the top.

The two men got off the platform onto a wooden plank scaffolding that extended a little way out from the cliff. It had a walkway that bridged from elevator to Rim. They walked over, and for the first time in five years, Abel was in the Redlands once again.

The highland stretched to the east, north, and south. Its rolling, arid brokenness extended as far as the eye could see. Pricklebushes and onyxwood shrubs dotted the hillsides, which were streaked with lines of eroded minerals. Everywhere, in large rocks and fine-grained sand, was the red sandstone from which the vast domain took its name.

"It is a beautiful place," Timon said. He was gazing out alongside Abel. "You told me how big the sky was, but I could hardly picture it. Now I see that what you said was true, and more."

"Yes," Abel said. "I've missed it." Then he turned to Timon. "But time to go back down and prove to the men that we took the ride up and managed to live through it."

He and Timon walked over to the other side of the bridge, and down a short plank gangway to where the platform they had ridden up stood turned over. They stepped onto what had been its underside. Abel pulled the nearby lever downward and the twin signal flags were raised back to position, upright against the cliff and out of sight from below.

Landry's man signaled the engineer. The platform jolted as water fell once again into the buckets. The remainder was a smooth descent. With only Abel and Timon aboard and his practice accomplished, there was no need for the jolting progress of the ascent.

As they neared the bottom, Abel could see the whole brigade looking up at him and Timon through the woodwork of the elevator. He gave them a chest-thumping salute. This brought out a cheer from below.

Then Abel and Timon reached the bottom and disembarked. Abel nodded to Randolph, the Tuesday Company captain. He stepped on the lowest platform along with his senior staff sergeant and a select group of his men. All the men mounted the platform grimly, tension—even fear—in their faces.

"Hold on to whatever you can grab that's not moving, and try not to piss your pants," he shouted to them. "That's what I did going up." He smiled and gave another salute. Landry raised them up until the next platform emptied its half-barrel buckets into the sluice and moved to the bottom for loading.

After a few of these stop and start maneuvers, Landry gave over the details of the operation to his engineering corps. Two eight-man squads of engineers took control of the headgate rope, oversaw the loading, and kept an eye on the signal flags above, as the men hesitantly but inexorably stepped onto the platforms and were lifted out of the Valley.

In increments, the entire brigade made its way to the Rim. Abel watched them as they loaded, occasionally nodding to a man he knew, and returning all salutes sent his way.

Landry rode back up and ascertained there was a cut-off switch from above, just as there was below. He rode back down to inform Abel; then the two of them, along with their donts, became the last platform up.

When Abel got to the Rim once more, he saw that the platoon sergeants all had their men well in hand. There was no shade to be had, but they were at least sitting. Some were taking the chance to catch a few moments of sleep.

Abel rode Nettle north along the Rim. There was a smooth, well-defined wagon trail that ran not twenty elbs from the precipice. He signaled Timon to come up to him, and gave the order for the march to start again.

The men were oddly silent moving along the Rim trail. Except for a few Scouts assigned to the division, they had lived all their lives within the confines of the Valley. They were always down *in* the Land, with the rising Escarpment to west and east. There were crops, trees along the River, and large irrigation waterways. And always the Valley walls to contain it all. The donts and daks did better. For them, a trail was a trail.

Here there was nothing but sky. This was above. And, for a Valley man, the first emotion "above" awakened was deep anxiety.

Above is unsafe.

Abel understood those feelings. He'd had them himself when he'd first climbed the Rim as a teenage water bearer to the Treville Scouts.

You got over it and learned to love the expanse. At least, he had.

They marched northward one league, two. Abel called breaks as short as he had in the Valley below. It was during the third of these that Burridge, one of the brigade scouts riding picket through the brush beside the Rim Road, came charging back on his dont.

"Clouds of dust to the east, sir." Abel rode a fieldmarch apart from his column, away from the dust it was kicking up itself for better sight. Timon and a guard of six men followed. Abel called a halt and gazed eastward.

Curse it to cold hell. Burridge was right.

There was a cloud. And Abel knew what it was.

"Men traveling," he muttered. "Hundreds."

"Pardon, Colonel?" said Timon.

"It's a Blaskoye horde," Abel said, more loudly. "They are heading south. I hope they haven't seen us. They might drive us off the Rim with a single sweep. Thrice-damn it, I knew this was too easy. We have to prepare for the worst. Get back and order the men down on their stomachs."

"Yes, sir," said Timon. He thundered off through the brush and prickleweed on his dont.

Within moments, the division was hidden among the desert vegetation. Abel didn't deceive himself. Blaskoye scouts were very difficult to fool. This was their home. The Third would likely be seen sooner or later.

At least he could try to make it later.

He looked out at the red cloud of the Blaskoye passing. He'd underestimated. It was an enormous group. The dust cloud stretched away north as far as he could see.

"What do you think, Burridge?" he asked his Scout. "How many?"

Burridge shook his head. "Seem to be like the stars, Colonel."

"Yes. That's what I see, too."

"What do you make of it, if I might ask, sir?"

"There's only one place of military significance north of here. It is Orash," Abel said. "I believe that's where they are coming from. Why they went there, and what they may have done, I don't know." He faced Burridge. "Lieutenant, I want you to take a mounted squad of scouts out there and have a look. I'm going to accompany you, and I want no guff about that, but you'll be in operational command and—"

For a moment, Abel sat on his mount without speaking. Was that? Yes, it was. A section of the dust cloud had split off.

It was headed toward him.

He spun his mount around. "Belay that." He shouted to Timon. "Up! Get them up, Major!"

He charged back to the lines, now getting to their feet, to find Timon amid a conclave of captains. He was relaying the order. Abel rode in among them.

"Listen to me, all of you," he said. "Those Blaskoye have seen us. I don't know how . . . well, I can guess—"

It was the lack of flitterdaks in the air. They skirted the Rim's edge to catch flying insectoids. But the passing Guardians had scared them all away.

"—But that doesn't matter. We have the Rim to our backs. It's a bad position."

"Then what do we do, sir?"

"We run," Abel said. "We make for that northern Escarpment trail and go down to the Valley as fast as we can. Got that, all of you? We have to be fast. Get the men into a jog they can keep up. But as fast as they can."

"For a league and a half, sir?"

"That's right," Abel said. "If they catch us against the Rim, it will be the last league any of us ever run."

The men were set in motion. Abel glanced worriedly eastward.

Oh, yes. Still coming.

He turned and rode up and down the flank of his column, urging the men faster, faster.

And they almost made it.

The line of dust became a wavering flicker of silhouettes of men and donts. Then there was color. Solid shapes. The thunder of Blaskoye dont hoofbeats and the sound of battle horns.

Yet near the front of the column, Abel could see it: the notch in the Rim that might indicate a down trail, maybe a gulley that could be negotiated. The men up front had broken into a run, making for the notch.

The approaching riders were doing the same.

It was a race of man and dont on a short track. The donts were bound to win. The Blaskoye riders got to the notch first. They reined up, turned to face the head of the division.

For a moment, there was confusion, even fear. But these were Goldies. There was little chance that the mere sight of danger would cause them to break.

"Form them up," Abel said. "Company lines, four deep."

"Yes, sir."

"Give me a hollow square to the right to protect the flanks from cavalry charge. We can use the Rim for protection on our left."

It was all done quickly. Now the Blaskoye seemed to waver. What was this great animal made of men and guns here in their own lands?

But the charge was already blown on the bone horns, and on they came, guns blazing.

Guns blazing much too soon and too often. Goldies fell along the line, but they were quickly replaced, stepped over, sometimes stepped on, by the men behind them. The lines closed up. The Blaskoye came on, their fire lessening now.

Two fieldmarches away. One. Half a fieldmarch.

"Fire!" the captains called up and down the line.

The donts charging toward them curled forward, crashed.

Riders were flung from screaming mounts, many never to rise again. Some picked themselves up, stumbled onward.

To meet a sideways rain of musket balls.

Another volley. Another line of faltering dontflesh and men.

A phalanx of riders broke to the side, attempted to circle around for a flank attack. The men squared to the east let them have it with a three-deep volley. It was over in two. The survivors scrambled back toward their line. Those who got too close ran a gauntlet of fire as they moved down the line. More riders fell.

A final charge was repulsed, and they broke, reined back.

"Forward!"

Slowly, inexorably, the Goldies marched, keeping up a riddle of fire as they moved. They were in no hurry now. It was the Blaskoye who began to panic. Their enemy had only one goal in mind: gain that notch and get down. Their task was to hold them and kill them all—a much more difficult undertaking.

In the end it proved too much for the Redlanders. With curses and shots cast over the shoulder, the Blaskoye riders pulled away. The bullets of the Goldies were too thick. Those who pitted bravery against them paid with their lives.

The front of the brigade gained the notch, Abel with them. He looked down.

Blood and Bones.

It was another elevator.

"Captain Hoster up!"

"Landry, can your engineers get it started?"

"If it works the same as the other, I'll send a couple of my best climbers down and have it going in a few eyeblinks. Those boys come from cliff villages, and they're fast."

"Send them. Do it."

True to his word, the engineers descended almost as fast as they might fall. Once down, they quickly got the elevator turning.

"Get the supply wagons down first, but leave me ten of them empty," Abel said. He had to shout to be heard over the musket volleys. The Blaskoye may have given way out of brutal necessity, but they had not given up. Now they were dismounted and approaching as infantry, using every bush and rock for cover. There were so many of the enemies spread out over the desert. It was if the Redlands were crawling with man-sized insects.

They popped up, fired, sank from sight to reload. And slowly the crescent line of the Goldies began to contract.

The supply wagons descended, leaving ten remaining, each with a single dak in harness instead of the customary team of two. Then it was time for the men to go. But the more troops went down, the more vulnerable and outnumbered were those who remained. Nevertheless, Abel motioned furiously for platoon after platoon to get onto the elevator platforms. Their force dwindled. The Blaskoye drew in closer with every squad gone down.

"Now get those wagons we kept up here out front," Abel shouted to the drovers. The wagon drivers looked grimfaced, but responded quickly. Their blood ran with the Gold and Tan as much as that of any infantryman. They drove into a crescent just within the outside line of Goldie riflemen. Some were cut down from their wagon seats, but these were replaced by subordinates who jumped aboard.

When the wagons were in place, the drivers leapt off and cut loose the daks. Most of the beasts charged off into the Redlands—anywhere to escape the smoke and noise. One dak, infuriated by a shot in its flank, turned the wrong way and ran at full speed over the edge of the Rim. It plunged out of sight.

About half of Fowlett's trusty Wednesday Company remained, along with many of Landry's engineers. A platoon-sized contingent moved forward and put shoulders to the wagons. With several heaves, the wagons turned over on their sides. When the cordon was complete, the crescent line dropped back behind their cover. Some climbed the undercarriage of the wagons and fired from the top of the makeshift wall, while others leaned around the spaces between the wagons, fired, and ducked back to cover.

This defense couldn't last long. But it didn't have to. Those who had toppled the wagons were now loading onto the elevator. Wednesday Company was trickling away. All that remained were a dozen or so men who found themselves making up the front line.

I will not leave even them to be overrun and slaughtered, Abel thought.

For you to remain invites ruin. Observe:

The Blaskoye caught him. He'd run, but it was no use. In the end, the riders had roped him like a dont in a corral. They dragged him over the ground back to the main body of riders. When they arrived, he was cut to ribbons. Nevertheless, he discovered he did have strength left in his flayed muscles. They made him stand. A circle of riders formed around him and the few other men who had survived the dragging.

One man stepped forward. He wore the double blue-edged robe of a Blaskoye chieftain, a sheik. In his hand was a scimitar. It gleamed impossibly brightly.

Another piece of chromed metal looted from a desert full of heirlooms of a lost and forgotten civilization.

A civilization that would stay forgotten now.

In the Valley, Abel's troops did not arrive and draw off the reinforcing troops. Von Hoff's worry at his force's nonarrival turned to dismay. The Progarmen hit von Hoff full force. The Goldies were good, but the numbers against them were overwhelming. They broke. And when they broke, they were hunted down the Valley. Only a tiny remnant made it back to Lindron.

Not enough to defend when the Blaskoye horde swept across Ingres and stormed a capital that was defended only by previously beaten men.

The Blood Winds, such invasions had been called in history.

Zentrum's inhuman method of housekeeping. Of beating down change and keeping the Stasis in place.

He'd succeeded again.

Stasis was restored to the Land.

Nothing ever changed again, would ever change. Not until the asteroid came. Then there was nowhere to go, no escape for anyone. There was no notion that the stars were anything other than spangles placed into the sky by Zentrum. Humanity died on Duisberg without ever knowing what hit it.

But Abel died much sooner.

The Blaskoye sheik smiled, motioned to someone outside the ring of men.

"Give them to Taub," he said. Abel cursed the fact that he could speak their language and so knew what was coming.

A detail of Redlanders came through carrying equipment. Spears? Rifles?

Shovels.

Abel's men were made to dig graves.

Then Abel watched as his men were bound and buried alive. One by one. Each buried by the next man in line.

Each pleaded for his life as the sand fell. Pleaded for a final breath, as the dust of the Redlands covered eyes, mouths, heads. Muffled screams. Heaving dirt that could not be shaken off. Then nothing but dirt overlaying and suffocating.

When Abel wouldn't lift a shovel to bury the last man, he was clubbed to his knees with a rifle butt. He was made to watch and listen to the screams.

Finally it was his turn.

He readied himself as best he could.

But they didn't push him in the grave he'd dug. Instead, the leader, the man with the shining weapon of chrome, beat Abel from his knees onto the ground. Again he was trussed. Again he was tied to a Blaskoye dont and dragged across a landscape that was evolved to cut, burn, and hurt.

He was in too much agony to wonder where they were taking him.

When it was over, they stood him up. He stumbled, collapsed. They propped him up again. The man with the chrome sword cut his rope bonds. Abel stood swaying, his mind and body a dull throb of agony.

A stab of pain, sharp. Abel looked down. The chrome scimitar's point was against his breastbone.

He looked up at the Blaskoye.

"Back up, dont shit," the man said in Redlander.

Abel did as he was told. The man pushed the point deeper into his flesh and backed him up farther. Farther.

"Now turn around."

Slowly, his joints rebelling against his every movement, Abel turned himself around.

The edge of the Rim was one step away.

Below him was a five fieldmarch fall.

He should have been ready, but was not. The new sharp agony was a surprise. The scimitar thrust through his back and came out just below his chest. A gout of blood and guts oozed from the exit wound.

He was pushed forward, the blade itself holding him upright.

Pushed to the edge, his toes hanging over.

He tried to turn away, but the blade flat inside him would not let him move.

Then the blade was slowly withdrawn.

"No," he mumbled. "I can't stand if—"

Nothing held him. Nothing at all. All strength was gone. He slid from the end of the gleaming sword and tumbled forward into the abyss. He fell.

Fell.

His throat was ragged and dust-choked. As much as he tried, he could not scream.

I don't care. I won't leave them here.

"We do have one more surprise in store for them," said Landry, who had come to stand beside him and Timon. "We soaked those wagons with lamp oil. We're going to be short the rest of the campaign, but maybe it was worth it."

They were standing near the elevator loading pier, observing the fighting not twenty paces away. He was no longer commander of anything. Nearly three thousand men had made their escape down the elevator, fighting all the time, their number shrinking. All that remained was the absolute rearguard and his handful of engineers. This was the end, and they were here to roll the last set of bones.

"You mean those wagons are—"

"—fire traps," Landry said. "We'll set them ablaze, and that should give us a distraction. Tell me when to do it. I have my men standing by with pitch torches and some of those lucifers you Scouts like so much."

Abel considered. They were down to a dozen or so men. It had to be now.

"Burn the wagons," he said. "Burn them now. Then get yourself and your men onto that elevator. The rest of us will be right behind you."

The torches were lit, and the flames put to the oil-soaked wagons. It took a moment—a few eyeblinks that seemed like days—but once the fire caught, it spread quickly, and the wagons blazed fiercely within moments. On the other side of the barrier, he could hear donts screaming, shying.

Landry's men boarded. The elevator moved up a notch. Another platform was loaded, then another.

Finally there was only Abel and Timon. At his signal, they sprinted for the elevator. It was the nature of the machine to lift them up and over the apex before bringing them down. This exposed them to the rifle fire of the enemy briefly.

But not brief enough. Timon let out a grunt and collapsed to the platform beside him. He gasped, cursed, and held his upper arm as it spilt blood from a gashing wound in his right forearm.

Then they started down. Abel threw off his jacket and tore a strip of cloth from his upper tunic. He used it to bind Timon's arm. The descent took a while, since each platform needed to be unloaded when it reached the base of the cliff. Some enterprising Blaskoye jumped on a platform above them. Abel aimed his musket and concentrated fire on them from below. The platform bottom stopped most bullets, but not all. A couple of Blaskoye toppled from their platform. It was only when they were near the bottom and in range of half the brigade that the rest of the descending Redlanders were cut to pieces by a swarm of minié balls.

When Abel and Timon reached the bottom, Landry stopped the elevator. One of the Scouts, a good climber, managed to scale the cliff up to the reservoir that supplied the falling water. With one slice of a knife, he cut the rope that opened the headgate. The water ceased to run, the wheel stopped turning. Without repairs, the elevator might be scaled by a group of determined men, but it was useless for the large-scale movement of men and donts.

Whatever the vast Blaskoye horde he'd seen was up to, it was definitely not heading in the direction of the battle that must now be raging to the west. It could not bring news of his division's movement any time soon.

He'd done it.

The Progarmen should believe that he was on the run, or at most was lurking in Siegan, planning another attack from the south. But he wasn't there anymore. He was north of them all.

With barely a pause, he set his men to marching for Isham.

4

The most direct route the Third could take would lead to an attack from the northeast, but this would push the militia troops straight west—the exact direction you don't want to push them, said Raj.

So we move north of the city along the bypass track. It joins the western road that passes through the gap between Manahatet and the northern hill country.

Exactly.

Abel sent a holding force of two hundred down the Gap Road that led between the northern side of Manahatet Mountain and the hills beyond. This was to plug a circuitous route that might still be used for reinforcement. The only retreat would be toward Orash. He would have cut that line of retreat off as well if he had another division. But he could be facing up to ten thousand militia in Isham. The road to Orash would remain open.

After days of near constant movement, the men barely complained of the quick-time descent down a rocky, sandal-pounding road. They sensed that a battle was coming, and shook their weariness off one last time to make the final march into position.

As a bonus, his flankers brought in two Progar scouts. Timon quickly had the enemy's disposition out of the men. There was a moment of confusion as all realized there was nowhere to put these Progarmen after they'd been milked for information.

He could have them shot. He could turn every capture into an execution. There was always that way.

But no.

They were hobbled to half strides with their hands bound in front and put to work carrying packs for a couple of weary soldiers. When they slowed, these soldiers hurried them on by bayonet point.

At least it was better than being dead. Probably.

The Third was in position to the west of the village by nightfall.

The attack was almost an anticlimax. Surprise was complete. This was the last place in the Land anyone had expected a division to materialize. The rout began when his front lines charged into the works of Isham at dawn, overwhelming the sleepy watch and catching the men in their tents and bivouacs. The Goldies chased them through the town, but a last-stand defense among the village shops and houses, with a few terrified civilians in the crossfire, reined them in. After a halfwatch of hard fighting, Abel ordered the majority of his troops to bypass the village and its hard nut of defenders. They swarmed past and once again caught the militia unprepared. It had been milling, stunned, with officers attempting to regroup. They achieved some semblance of organization and mounted a rearguard action, which was overrun almost as quickly as it got in place. Now there was nothing against the backs of the retreating Progarmen but Goldie bullets.

They ran like animals trying to escape a fire. There was stumbling, man piling against man, and pandemonium. Again and again the Goldies struck from behind, carving away at the retreating troops.

Then the Progarmen turned and attempted to cut west. Abel's ambush party cut down hundreds of men from where they had dug in along the Gap Road. There was no reply possible from the Progar militia. They were completely exposed, and their harassment came from excellent cover.

So the enemy was herded north, dying in droves along the way. Abel continued the chase until he was certain there was no possibility for them to cut across the hill country and provide help at Fish Pens.

When he got back, he found the holdouts in the town had surrendered, their position hopeless. They sat sullenly under guard along the plank sidewalks. Their weapons and equipment had been stripped from them, and from the looks of them, a great many were wounded.

Can I get a count?

You have one thousand four hundred ninety-two troops in custody, although some will likely expire within the watch from their wounds, Center intoned. **Enemy killed or wounded is close to three thousand, out of a force that I now estimate with high confidence at eleven thousand five hundred total strength.**

And what about my own casualties?

One hundred fifty-seven killed. Two hundred sixty wounded.

Always too many. But we whipped them. We really whipped them.

That is a correct assessment, said Center. **But do not forget the ultimate purpose of this battle: to relieve pressure from the main body of Guardian troops at the Fish Pens.**

Yes, now we reinforce von Hoff.

Concur.

Abel garrisoned the town and called in his ambush party. The men were making sounds of settling down in the brisk chill of the afternoon. Some had picked out women from the civilians of Isham and were about to drag them away. Not today. Abel sent out an order to refill cartridge boxes from the supply wagons and stay ready.

Could he possibly march them again today?

Von Hoff might be desperate for reinforcement. How could he not be? But to arrive bedraggled and useless?

These men are capable of more than you give them credit for, Raj said. *Much more. They arrived in the peak of health in a corps that prides itself on being the best of the best. They have fought long and bravely. But they aren't exhausted. Not by a long shot.*

Well, I feel exhausted.

As long as you feel anything, you can go on.

Thrice-damn you to cold hell, General.

Deep-throated laughter. *What do you think being stranded on this backward planet for nigh on one hundred fifty years is? I've been more than thrice-damned to hell, Abel Dashian. But I have to say there is interesting company here. That compensates for much.*

All right, General. Well, we'll have the moons. Tonight will be a good night to march.

Abel called Timon. His arm was bandaged, but he seemed

otherwise sound. He was also beyond showing surprise at Abel's orders now. In fact, he smiled and anticipated them.

"Shall we depart, sir?"

"Yes. Leave. Go. Everyone at once. Tell them to drop those women softly, though."

"Aye, sir," Timon replied. He signaled the couriers with a quick whistle. They jumped to and soon were approaching weary captains and lieutenants who had thought their day was done.

"Major Athanaskew, do you know what tonight is?"

Timon thought a moment. "Yes, sir. It's three moons night, and Churchill's at the full."

"That it is," Abel replied.

"We'll march at midnight, when Churchill is at its highest."

Timon smiled, shaking his head. "Abel, the men are going to hate you for this. And love you after it's done."

"I'll settle for the hatred if we get there in time to relieve von Hoff."

"Alaha Zentrum."

"Alaha Zentrum, Major Athanaskew."

And you're worth more than an infinite number of Zentrums, my friend.

He turned to gaze over what he could see of the Third.

So are they all.

It took them longer than Abel liked to get moving, but they were on the Gap Road less than a halfwatch after midnight. It was acceptable.

Blood and Bones, it's damn good, considering.

They moved at a steady and deliberate pace. Even with the bright full moon, there was a great deal of stumbling, shuffling into one another, falling down and helping one another up. Fortunately, the Gap Road was well maintained. Unfortunately, it was mostly downhill when travelled from the east, which contributed to the stumbling and falling even more.

The sun rose. They marched on. Stragglers began to fall by the wayside once again, far more than had in the march up the Three Sisters and Manahatet valleys. Center reckoned he had lost over seven hundred that way. But those who still functioned did their job and got the fallen to the side of the road.

There was a great split about league before it reached the River

Road. One wagon trail led north, one south. There was a large meadow here with plenty of water for the donts in a nearby stream. The beasts didn't require much. Unlike humans, they had evolved on this world and needed to drink far less often than a man. Their blood ran with a whitish hemoglobin-hemocyanin mix, and the snot that shot from their blowholes could burn out your eyes if you happened to get too much of it in them. But even donts had their limits, and they were fast approaching them.

One more league to go.

He had Timon form them up in two columns of eight abreast. These were released four at a time, with a wide gap between one thirty-two-man group and the next. This would be their fighting deployment when they arrived. The Isham Gap had been narrow. There was no time to form into a line of attack as they spilled out.

The Gap Road was the rifle barrel pointed at the Progar militia. His men were the bullets careening down it.

When the front line of men reached the enemy, Abel, who was to the rear, saw a tremor run through the men in front of him.

Contact. Observe:

The rest of Third Division poured steadily out of the gap. Two thousand and more men slammed into the side of the Progar militia. The Progarmen were brave, but they had no group discipline. They were herders, miners, tradesmen conscripted by the local warlords.

Yet...

What they did have, ever third or fourth man or so, was a terrible weapon. A weapon he and Landry has speculated about, had dreamed of possessing.

It was real. In the enemy's hands.

It took Abel a moment to understand what was going on. His men had fanned out left and right and attacked the left flank and rear of the militia in an outwardly expanding half circle. But something was halting their progress, and his men were falling at an alarming rate. The rate of enemy fire seemed fantastic.

Even breechloaders could not be fired at this rate. He knew. He'd fought with breechloaders; he'd used them against men armed with musket rifles. The result had been horrific. This was slaughter.

Sonic analysis indicates multichambered weapons. Scattered, but each with the firepower of eight men. Portions of the Progar militia are armed with revolving rifles.

So this was why von Hoff hadn't made short work of the militia. A load of revolvers must have arrived from Orash, or wherever the infernal things were constructed. The Progarmen certainly hadn't had them in the marsh battle.

Aye, they may have them now, but they can't understand how to use them yet, said Raj.

"Major Athanaskew!"

"Sir!"

"We can't let them concentrate those revolvers or they'll wipe us out."

"Those what?"

"Nishterlaub rifles. Like breechloaders, but worse."

"Ah. Agreed."

"We have to keep them on their heels. And we have to turn them toward von Hoff."

"I'm not sure we can, Abel. There are so many of them."

"They're bloodying us, but we have a lot of sunlight left."

A courier charged up with a request from Randolph, the Tuesday Company captain, for support on the southern flank of the deployed Goldies. Abel considered. They had come out of the Gap Road partly to the rear of the enemy, and partly at his flank.

"You tell the captain to hold that position, wherever he is, at all costs. He's going to be our pivot," Abel said. "I'll send help."

The lines to his front had concentrated to counter the revolver fire with massed volleys. But this had squeezed several units out of the line and to the rear. They seemed to be patiently waiting their turn to get back in.

"Major, get those Wednesday men gathered. Send them to help Randolph."

"Yes, sir," said Timon. "Request permission to lead them myself, sir."

Abel shook his head. "No, I need you here. Fowlett can do it. He's good in a pinch, and that voice of his carries like a bone horn."

Timon looked chagrined, but sent a messenger away to Fowlett.

He needed a regiment of cavalry . . . but only had Captain Arondale's mounted skirmishers. They would have to do.

"Tell Arondale to get his cavalry up to the right flank. They'll have the most ground to cover. But he should not stretch farther than the infantry, not today."

"Yes, sir. On it, sir."

Another messenger in from the middle. "Those nishterlaub nightmare guns are killing us, Colonel. The ground's no good. No cover, nothing."

"Tell Randolph to keep them fighting. There's nothing else to do and everything depends on him."

"Yes, sir. We just keep dropping, though. Never seen anything like it."

"Tell Randolph what I said. Now get moving, Lieutenant."

"Yes, sir."

He charged off on his dont to deliver the reply.

A watch passed. The flood of messengers back to Abel began to lessen. Then he found himself slowly moving forward to get a better view. It took him a moment to realize that he needed to do this because his line was advancing. It was advancing at a walking pace, but definitely, inexorably, shuffling forward.

What was more, the massed musket fire to Abel's left had increased perceptibly. Von Hoff was advancing, too.

Now that there was movement, the line began to swing as Abel had wanted. The mounted troops to the north moved faster, carrying the adjacent infantry along with them from sheer momentum.

By the Lady, we might just surround them if this keeps up.

A likelihood of thirty-five percent. More likely their front will break and von Hoff will push them north.

Right through our enfilade.

Exactly.

When the Progar retreat came, it was much more ordered than Abel had expected. The troops he'd routed at Isham must have been green. These soldiers did not cut and run.

But they died like any other man when caught in the middle of two fields of fire. The retreat became more hurried, more desperate. To the north, the mounted units reported that they could go no farther. The Progarmen were erupting past them in a floodtide.

More Progarmen died as they ran Abel's gauntlet.

Toward midafternoon, he caught sight of the Red and Golds advancing from the south. They had already made contact with Tuesday's southern flank. The danger to his left was over. A halfwatch later, the southern advance reached Abel's position.

The shooting did not stop to the north, but a hush fell, as if the advancing troops were a blanket of silence.

The rifles to your front have stopped firing.

There was nothing else to do except let the remainder of the day play out. Abel weaved his way between the troops streaming north, until he found von Hoff. The general was sitting astride his oversized dont. Abel rode up to him and thumped a salute.

"You are a sight for sore eyes, Colonel."

"You, too, sir," said Abel.

"You look as if you've been dragged through a pit of mud and obsidian shards, Dashian."

"Thank you, sir."

"I think they're on the run now. We'll hunt them. We won't give them rest."

"You'll have the moons for it tonight."

"We surely will."

But it did not turn out that way. As the sun set, the exhausted men of the Corps found their limit. No matter how much von Hoff cursed and urged them on, they broke contact with the Progar remnant. They slowed. The Progar militiamen, running for their lives, did not pause. And by midnight, they'd slipped away.

Von Hoff shook his head at the missed chance. But there really was little to complain about. The Progar, for all intents and purposes, were destroyed.

Abel wandered along the mass of the dead for a while. There were many groaning wounded, too. He saw that they were tended. The Guardian medicos used primitive methods, but they were as good as any in the Land.

Then a man stepped out of the field of bodies and ran up to greet Abel.

It was Landry.

"I found one," he yelled. "I found one, Abel."

"Found what, Captain Hoster?"

"This!" He lifted a revolving rifle and pointed it up to the sky. Then he caressed the cylinder fondly, as if it were a beloved pet. "Do you know what this is?"

"Yes," Abel replied. "Very nearly the death of us."

"Yes, yes, really effective. I almost took a shot to the head myself from one of them. Missed me by a hair, I tell you, a hair. Then he pulled the trigger to fire again, but he was out. He had me dead to rights. He was a good twenty paces away, but I knew he had me and he knew it."

"I'm glad you're alive, Landry."

"Oh, me, too. Me, too. I killed that man, too. Blew his brains out. Took his top off like a pot lid. Ugly way to die. But that's neither here nor there."

"I guess it's not. Are you all right, Landry?"

"Yes. I am. A bit agitated. My thoughts running on a bit. Running like the River when she floods." He lowered the rifle in his hands, considered the revolving cylinder once again. "See the grip? That ingenious little bracket? You can't hold the stock. It'll scorch your hand to cinders. So you aim it like this, holding this bracket instead of the stock." Landry demonstrated. "I'm just thinking...I know I could make these. A lot of them." He frowned and shook his head sadly. "Too bad they're nothing but thrice-damned nishterlaub. I would really like to make them. I can see how to do it. You ever had that? Some idea in your mind you can't shake, that won't go away. And you know it's going to task you till the end of your life if you don't do something about it?"

"I'm pretty sure I know exactly how you feel, Captain Hoster," Abel answered.

PART NINE
The Lost

The Present

1

Treville District
476 Post Tercium

Joab Dashian went about the work of his office as he had for a thousand days before. There were military and civilian plans to oversee, provisions to see to, reports to read, threats to ponder. Scrolls came in, he examined them, marked his changes, they went out. His captains reported before going about their duties. Runners from outlying forts and garrisons delivered the daily or weekly dispatches. Joab sent them on their way with new orders.

Then, after a noon lunch, the locals arrived with their plans for approval: all civil works had to be approved and recorded by the District Military Command, including road building, the laying of irrigation ditches, the locating of new mizzen piles for garbage, and a dozen other projects. Joab was himself, via his military engineers, in charge of works and services such as wells, aqueducts, and the military tithe collection of grain or barter chits that paid for it all.

And then of course there was the fact that he was the top soldier in Treville District. Mornings and late afternoons he reviewed the Regulars in the Hestinga garrison, and, though it was not strictly required of him or any on his command staff, he got in sparring, range practice, and exercise with the men at least three days a week. Occasionally, as was his duty, he attended a Friday hanging.

His days of drinking into the night were long past, but he did manage to make it to his favorite tavern one or two nights a week, usually to share a pint of beer with old friends. These were his favorite moments. There was no woman to go home to. Since the death of his wife over thirty years ago, he had never felt the urge to remarry.

This did not mean he had remained celibate during that time. Far from it. There was a trio of widows in the town who sometimes received an evening caller—a caller who frequently wound up staying the night. Joab chose his lovers well, and each was intelligent or at least empathetic enough in her own way to understand that there was not a chance in cold hell of her ever landing the DMC as a husband, however much she might fantasize about the prospect in her heart of hearts. All were too old to have children. Even when, once or twice a year, he called at the whorehouse, it was the proprietress who did him the honors, and she, too, was past childbearing age.

There would be no offspring other than Abel. All of his hopes were wrapped up in the boy—now a man. He had no ambition for himself other than a vague plan to retire some day on a small vineyard or olive orchard on the Escarpment, maybe in a villa that would have a view of the Valley from its portico.

Joab had never been an extremely self-reflective man—he didn't have the time—but there was no place he'd rather be than Treville, and no job he'd rather have than its DMC.

His job-seeking had stopped when he'd been assigned the district, and his main worry in life was that, though some bureaucratic blunder in Lindron, he might one day be promoted. The Regulars had a way of making such mistakes on occasion. This was why he kept up a correspondence with his old brothers in arms, many of whom were Guardians now. The DMC who survived was the DMC who kept his ear to the ground for political shifts in the capital.

So he was surprised, then angry at himself, when he came home late one evening and walked into a trap.

The men who had broken in were good. There was no lamp lit and no door ajar to betray their presence. There were six of them, and as Joab stepped through the door, the two on either side of the doorframe shoved him inside.

He stumbled to a knee on his own reed mat carpet and rose with a pistol cocked in his hand.

"Don't," said a man's voice from the darkness. "Commander Dashian, we are from the Tabernacle Security Service. We wish to talk to you."

"Get out of my house."

"Please do not make this difficult, sir."

"Get the cold hell out of my house, please, before I kill you."

"There are six weapons, two rifles, and a pistol, trained on you at the moment," the voice replied. "I will uncover a lamp and show you."

"It will show me where to shoot," said Joab. "Now get out."

"Very well," said the voice. "Hector!"

A movement to the right of Joab. He turned and fired his pistol at the sound. Before he could drop again and attempt to escape, something hard hit him from behind.

A white sheet of pain in his skull.

Joab awoke to find himself tied to one of his own kitchen chairs. Before he opened his eyes, he collected his wits, remembered where he was, and tested the bonds. They were very tight, cutting into his wrists and ankles.

Someone had lit a lamp on the table, and Joab's captors were revealed.

They were wearing the Gold and Tan of Guardian Corps, with an orange sash that also marked them as priests.

So they really are security service, after all.

Which meant this was more than some idiotic kidnapping attempt.

These men were professional bastards.

"What the cold hell is going on?" Joab said. His head throbbed, but he ignored it. "What do you want?"

A tall, thin man with wispy, thinning hair sat down across from Joab at the table. When he spoke, Joab recognized the voice he'd heard before in the darkness. "Commander, I've been sent to take you into custody and present you for court-martial in Lindron."

"On what charge?" Joab said in outrage.

There's more to this than I'm seeing, he thought. *Calm down and let the man spill as much as possible.*

"I'm afraid I can't answer that," the man replied. "Just be assured my orders come from the highest levels."

"My superior is your superior, unless I'm mistaking those uniforms. That man is General Josiah Saxe," Joab said. "Has the general ordered this?"

"General Saxe is on campaign in Progar," said the wispy-haired man.

"So what right to do you have to barge in like this and assault me?"

"We only assaulted you in self-defense, Commander. You were about to shoot us."

"Damn right I was. You're lucky to be alive."

"This attitude will be taken into account at the tribunal," the man replied with a faint smile. "Commander, I must warn you that anything you say can and will be used in your prosecution."

"Again I ask you, what is the charge?"

"All will be made plain in Lindron."

"I'm not going to Lindron until I find out what this is all about."

The man's smile returned.

The smile of a carnadon about to pounce on a clueless dak, Joab thought.

"Oh, but you are, Commander. In fact we are leaving tonight."

"Blood and Bones, I'm not!" Joab began to shout. "Help! Somebody help me!"

The man shook his head sadly and motioned to one of his compatriots. Another hard clout on the back of the head that left Joab's ears ringing. He didn't pass out this time, but nausea rose in his stomach.

"Please don't try that again, Commander," the man said, "or we'll be forced to take more drastic measures."

"Like kicking the cold hell out of me and tying me to a chair?"

"Like killing your friend, Prelate Hiram Zilkovsky. We have him, you see. Both of you are to stand trial."

"Zilkovsky? The chief prelate of Treville? By what authority do you believe you can do this?"

"Again, I cannot comment on this."

"It had better be Zentrum Almighty himself if you have Zilkovsky."

"Please do not add blasphemy to the charges, Colonel Dashian."

"You should hope that authority is ironclad, because if I don't tear your skin from your bones, you can be sure Zilkovsky will. He's a man you cross at your peril."

"Your rancor is misplaced. I'm doing my duty," the man said. "All of us are. Following orders." He raised a pistol and pointed it at Joab's chest. "Now we're going to untie you, and you will follow me out your back entrance to my wagon."

One of the others, a muscle-bound pallid man who looked as

if he'd spent more time in the practice arena hefting weighted, dummy weapons than on a field of battle in the hot sun, took out a knife and slit the ropes from Joab's legs and then his wrists. "Get up, you rockfucker," he grunted into Joab's ear.

Joab turned and snapped at the pale man's face with his teeth. He was lucky enough to catch a piece of chin, and clamped down.

Dig deep, this may be the only chance you have.

The pallid man screamed in pain, and Joab snatched the pistol from where it was tucked in the man's waist belt.

He let go of the pale man and simultaneously kicked him into the two men standing behind him. With another quick motion, Joab upended his kitchen table and sent it toward the wispy-haired man seated across from him.

That was four engaged. Two more to go. Joab whirled around with the pistol, seeking a target.

There, by the door, the one with a jagged scar across his face. "Stand aside or I'll shoot you down like so much dakmeat," Joab said. Iron tang and goo in his mouth. Joab spat and a glob of skin from the man whose chin he'd chewed landed with a splat on the floor of the kitchen.

The scar-faced man stared at Joab and then stepped to the side.

Where was the other? Maybe in the other room? Maybe in the back standing guard?

Doesn't matter. I have to get out of here.

Joab made for the door that led to his living room. He'd go out the front.

This time the blow to his body felt as if it had been delivered from the inside out. Pain erupted in his back, his left arm—

Joab spun around.

Behind him, the wispy-haired man stood with a pistol aimed at Joab. Its muzzle was smoking. Joab looked down at his side. Blood flowed from his forearm and hip. The ball must have gouged a path through both of them.

Then yet another flash of intense pain, and all was blackness once again.

He awoke trussed hand and foot with something heavy over him. The smell told him it was a blanket of dak wool. There was a rattling sound, and he shook back and forth. Even in total darkness he knew where he was: in the bed of a wagon. He was being carted away to Lindron in the dead of night.

He tried to call out again, but discovered his mouth was stuffed with rags and a rope tied over to keep them in place. Even with this, he could manage a muffled yell, and he did so until his voice gave out. With each jolt of the cart—if that's where he was—a lance of agony travelled through his side where the bullet had gouged its path. After a long time, blood loss and fatigue overcame him.

He awoke to the sun, as his covering was thrown back. He tried to sit up, but it was no use. He was trussed at the knees and elbows as well as wrists and ankles.

He did manage to roll over, however. And on the other side of him lay a man whose eyes were wide with shock and terror.

Joab recognized him immediately. This was the prelate of Treville, Hiram Zilkovsky.

Joab tried to speak, but, of course, he remained gagged. At least now, with the rug removed from on top of him, he did not feel as if he were suffocating while attempting to breathe through his nose.

The cart hit a rut and there was a clatter behind them. Joab looked down the bed of the wagon.

Something odd, as if all of this weren't dreamlike enough. There in the back was a bent-up piece of metal or something beyond either. It had a pyramidal shape and stood perhaps three elbs high and as many wide at its base. Joab recognized it. It was a piece from the Treville nishterlaub warehouse.

He'd heard Abel referred to it offhandedly as "the capsule" several times. A capsule containing *what*, Joab did not know.

Why had they brought this along, of all things?

The cart trundled on, each jolt painful to his wound, his joints aching to move, his tongue jammed into the back of his mouth, his throat desperate to swallow.

What in Zentrum's name was going on?

Joab knew better, but he began to wonder what the charges against him could possibly be, and how he would answer them.

He knew this was a fantasy. There wasn't going to be any real trial. There wasn't going to be any real anything. He was well and truly fucked.

That much he might come to terms with.

But what hurt him the most, what he feared he might never get past if it were true, was his sneaking suspicion that he would never see his beloved Treville again. Or his son.

2

Orash
Progar District

The Guardian Corps buried their dead and burned the Progar-men for two days. And then they marched on Orash.

Abel had been prepared to face a siege, possibly a long one despite the few defenders remaining. Ambush and trickery. Unexpected mountain weather. What he found left him stunned.

Orash was a city of death.

Center, did you know this would happen?

It was always a strong possibility. There was no reason to discuss it until now.

Because you thought I might try to do something about it?

That was one factor.

Fuck you.

Difficult.

The Progar militia was in the city—about fifteen thousand survivors—but any thought of defense had collapsed when they'd marched through the Orash gates after the battle at Fish Pens. Two days later, the Corps arrived and encamped on the Plains of Orash. Almost immediately, the gates of the city opened and a man rode forth on one of the smallish, wiry donts the Progarmen preferred.

He approached over the plains and was in sight for a long spell. He rode slowly, holding aloft a fluttering white cloth fixed to a bayonet.

"What in the name of Zentrum?" said von Hoff after he'd been called to observe the approaching militiaman.

Von Hoff sent Abel and Muir, commander of the Second, out to bring the man in.

His name was Paulus, and he called himself the leader of "Bigelow's Boys," the largest of the Progar militia divisions, he claimed. He all but surrendered in his first breath.

When the general heard this, Abel saw von Hoff noticeably cringe.

Paulus seemed to be in a hurry to give up everything as quickly as possible and return to the city, but von Hoff forced him to stay and negotiate the exact terms.

Throughout the talks, there was a haunted look in Paulus's eyes that did not seem to Abel to come from military defeat alone.

He looks as if someone has reached inside and pulled out his soul, Abel thought.

Von Hoff ended up demanding that the Corps would need *more* time before they entered the city and accepted the formal surrender of arms. Von Hoff was careful to have Paulus repeat the exact timing of the surrender von Hoff offered: two days hence at dawn.

"You understand that things might not go well for you after that," von Hoff told the man. "The Abbot of Lindron does not deal mercifully with heretics. Any we find guilty of heresy, we have orders to kill."

"Yes, I understand," the Progarman said with a distracted air of resignation.

"Do you truly, Captain Paulus? I *will* carry out those orders."

Suddenly a sob shuddered through Paulus's body. He shook his head and stared at the floor. "What does it matter now?" he said, as if to himself. "Many of us are ready to die."

Von Hoff was exasperated. He repeated his previous directive very carefully. "Captain, I'm giving you two days' advance warning. Do you understand me? I'm trying to tell you that your militia must not disband and flee the city. That would make it much more difficult to find and execute the guilty."

Paulus looked at him with a gaze of empty despair.

Von Hoff leaned over the negotiating table, shook Paulus by the shoulders. "Listen to me, Captain. We will have our hands full preparing to administer Orash. *There will be no patrols of the city exits for the next two days.*"

He may as well be shouting: "I want you to get out while you can" at the top of his voice, Abel thought.

"I understand if we flee individually you will not stop us," Paulus said. "I'll pass this along. I don't think it will make much difference. Most of us have lost our wives, our children. Everything. We're prepared to die."

"What do you mean 'lost your wives and children'?"

"You will see."

"Tell me now."

"I cannot...I cannot speak of it. You will see."

Von Hoff sat back, shook his head. "All right then, Captain, you evidently have no intention of allowing a poor general to wash his hands of any of this. Dawn on the day after tomorrow it is. You will open the gates in unconditional surrender, and we will take control of the city. There will be firing squads."

"Yes, sir," Paulus said. He looked over at his dont, staked nearby. "I will be going now."

"Stay, man. Surely we can stand you a drink before you're off," von Hoff said, but Paulus appeared not to hear. He strode numbly over to his mount, climbed into the saddle, and rode back across the plain at the same funereal pace that had brought him to them.

At dawn two days hence, true to his word, von Hoff marched the Corps in through the city's main gate.

What was that awful smell?

The militia were not there to surrender. For a moment, Abel feared ambush.

No. There is no organized resistance in this place.

The Guardian vanguard marched slowly forward. Then they saw that there *were* Progarmen about. Individually, in small groups. Here, sitting on stoops and hanging their heads, there, walking about in twos and threes, each man with empty eyes, were the Progarmen. A few appeared to be scavenging, or desolately looking for something, at least.

And the smell was intense. He'd walked among dead bodies for the past two days, but even that was nothing like this, nothing like—

"Blood and Bones, turn around!" It was the voice of one of von Hoff's command staff. He'd happened to glance around behind to see if all were following correctly, and so was the first to glimpse the bodies.

They hung like peppers from the city walls, clumped in layers five or six people deep. Many had been gutted or shot, but most had been left to choke to death. There were women, women old and women young. There were old men. There did not seem to be any children, however.

That is not a good thing, rumbled Raj.

It looked as if a few of the hanged people had managed to escape their bonds, slip a noose, and scramble down. These lay beheaded at the base of the wall, stacked in separate piles of heads and bodies.

There were dont hoofprints everywhere on the dusty ground.

Now Abel understood the smell. Death seemed to hang visibly in the air. Insectoids rattled, swarming to their meals.

Timon, who stood beside Abel, seemed to crumple like a stone wall that suddenly gives, its mortar undermined by weathering. Until this moment—in fact as long as Abel had known him— Timon had been rock steady in all circumstances. Even when he'd been shot in the arm, he'd barely flinched, and he was enduring the first painful stages of healing stoically. But this was too much for him.

He began to gasp. He tried to catch his breath, but could not. Abel moved to shore him up, and saved his friend from falling to the ground. Instead Timon bent over with his good hand on a knee. He gasped heavily until he finally caught enough of his breath to stand up.

"They aren't here," he said, when he could speak. "The children aren't here."

"I see that."

"They've been taken as slaves. That's where they are, isn't it, Abel?"

"Looks like it."

Timon wiped his eyes, shook his head. "That's what it is," he said.

"Yes, Timon."

"What kind of God lets that happen?"

If only you knew.

Timon didn't wait for an answer. He began to nod, as if a new thought had come to him. His smiled a terrible smile.

"No," he said. "This was the plan all along. The question is: What kind of God *makes* this happen."

"The Blaskoye did this."

"No," Timon said with an angry laugh. "The Blaskoye are a tool."

Abel nodded. "Yes." He put a hand on Timon's shoulders. "Maybe some of them got hidden. Maybe some escaped. Let's go look."

With no one offering to surrender and no challenge, the Guardians streamed into Orash by unit, each ordered to find billets within a ten-block radius of the gate. A few moved to beat up lingering Progarmen, but soon gave up. There was no sport in it. There were many empty dwellings. Von Hoff immediately deployed a detail to take the hanged bodies from the wall and sent workers and wagons to clean up the decapitated corpses. All were taken to an area of dry ravines a half league from the city, and—most importantly—in a position that was lower than the city's water supply. There was some attempt to powder the dead with lime, but there were too many and the supply soon ran out. Most were left in the gulches to rot.

Landry returned from completing this task somber and red-eyed. He spoke only with monotone short replies for several days after.

An inter-brigade security detail was set, and these guards managed to contain the sacking of Orash to petty looting. Pickings were lean, in any case. The Blaskoye had already done a good job of stripping Orash of wealth.

The men of Progar docilely accepted their new masters. When von Hoff ordered them back to their work and took many away in work groups, most of them seemed relieved.

They were still technically under death sentence, but no one, even the chaplains, had the stomach for the task just yet. It could wait. These men weren't going anywhere.

Many of them seemed like sheep waiting for the slaughter, perhaps even longing for it.

After having won so decisively, this did not seem much of a victory.

Timon spent several days searching for survivors—and not in vain. There were some living women, and a handful of children. They emerged from hiding places when the need for food and water drove them out.

Some of the troops looked hungrily at the women, and some did more than look. After a woman was publicly raped in the town square, Timon asked Abel for his old interrogation detail back to serve as a rudimentary police force in the Third's sector. Abel let him have them. He doubted patrolling for rapists would distract Timon from the central problem facing his friend now, however: he was a believer who had lost his faith.

How the Blaskoye got in wasn't difficult to ascertain, either. A breached wall on the eastern side of the city. Gunpowder residue. They'd blasted their way in while the men were gone to fight in the militia.

They'd been ruthless and efficient. In places they had met resistance from the women, and some of the bodies had the battle wounds to prove it.

Some had also had time to flee. These trickled back into the city from caves and hidden villages high in the Schnee Mountains. Orash itself was built upon a foothill in the range.

But signs of a Blaskoye slaving operation were everywhere: slave corrals in the town square, a pricklebush security cordon surrounding it. There was no way to know, but it seemed they'd taken thousands of children, perhaps ten per warrior.

Abel was alone in the warehouse storeroom he'd had converted into brigade command. The day's business was concluded and all now had beds and bunks to go to. A platoon remained on nightwatch outside, covering all entrances to the warehouse, but otherwise the chamber was empty. It had once been used to stockpile pelts for shipment to points south, where they'd be used for ornaments and clothing. He'd ordered the place cleaned out, but there were signs of its former use all around: in the corners, stray down and feathers. These were not the beautiful plumage of donts. They were functional, the oily, horn-thick feathers of mountain creatures native to the Schnee range. The warehouse's wooden floor he'd had covered with the tough hides of northern daks used as rugs. These also hung along the walls, too, and kept the place from becoming an echo chamber.

After a day of firing off orders, making minor, but pressing decisions, listening to appeals from soldiers slated for punishment, and even assigning some punishment himself, sitting in the quiet was calming. For the first time in days, Abel took out his pipe and smoked a bowl of Delta weed. When it was done, he set the pipe down on his desk and rose to go to the map table. There stretched before him was a large representation of Progar on several papyrus scrolls joined together. There were also smaller maps of Orash and the Land itself.

Abel had always liked maps. He'd been taught to read them by one of the best cartographers around, Josiah Weldletter, his father's chief cartographer in Treville. He'd always been good at translating in his mind the lines of a map into a vision of the actual terrain. He believed he would have possessed this ability even without Center's presence in his mind, but he supposed he'd never know.

Abel touched the circled star symbol that indicated Orash on the large map, and stood for a moment pondering.

Why was it so easy?

The Progar oligarchs believed they had a deal with the Blaskoye. They had traded so long with the Redlanders, they'd been lulled into thinking that all things could be arranged with a bit of dealing and barter chits on the side for lubrication.

Not this time.

There is one positive aspect to the situation, Center continued. **The captives have spoken of a Law-giver named Kerensky. It would appear a new element of thinking has arisen among the Blaskoye.**

Abel had finally begun to forgive him for not informing him of the Blaskoye raid. Center had predicted it long before.

What could that possibly be?

The most important aspect of all. The Blaskoye, and Zentrum, who must be controlling the leadership in some manner, expected the Progar militia to win.

You mean Zentrum sent the Guardians up here to get us slaughtered?

Shattered. And then to fatally weaken the resolve of the men of Progar by this total deceit—the destruction of all they believed they were fighting for. I have shown you in visions before how it was all set to begin. The Blood Winds were to start in Progar and sweep south. Now there is no beaten and retreating Guardian army for the Blaskoye to destroy from behind. Invasion from the north is cut off.

Zentrum will not get his invasion down the Valley. You and your brigade tipped the balance. He's sure as hell not going to like this.

So what will he do?

Aye, that is the question, isn't it? He's not done. Not by a long shot.

Probabilities are in rapid fluctuation at this time, Center said. **In fact, they have been since your decision to kill the crucified Hurth boy.**

What? Why?

Unanticipated variable introduced at a crux point in Seldonian calculations.

What does that mean?

It means that once you showed mercy to that boy and beat the odds, all bets were off in a lot of other matters, Raj said with a rueful chuckle. *Center has been winging it since that moment, haven't you?*

It is true that a series of recalculations had to be conducted. They are now complete, however. Long-term adjustments are underway, and given sufficient time to develop should greatly accelerate the downfall of Zentrum. We have only to—

Center's raspy, insectoid voice suddenly ceased.

Have to what?

No answer.

Have to what, Center?

The eerie silence in his mind continued.

Raj?

Center?

No answer.

"Raj!" he shouted. "Center!"

Silence. Silence. Silence.

And then a long, raspy scream. It was like the crack of an avalanche in a Redlands ravine, but a hundred times as loud.

Abel covered his ears, but the sound was not coming from outside himself.

It was resonating inside his mind.

It was Center.

Dying.

The pain of an A.I. stripped of its functionality, its data, its memory translated into sound.

He has found us! He is here!

Who is here? Who is here, Center?

Zentrum.

Then the scream began to fade, to transform from articulation to a sound akin to the passage of wind over broken stones.

But as that wind died away, blew itself out, Abel believed he heard one final word, a blend of the gruff voice of Raj and the precise clatter of Center.

Good-bye.

3

He lay abed for days, his mind a blank. He was unable to act, almost unable to think. Most of all he felt empty—utterly, completely empty.

I've been drawn and quartered. How can I be drawn and quartered and still live?

He lost the capacity for simple movement for hours at a time. Several times he shit himself and lay in the muck until he could summon the mechanical impetus—it was not will, not even close—to clean himself and change his clothing.

Timon tended to him for a time, but realized his presence was useless. Besides, Timon's arm, after healing nicely, was now giving him trouble. He limited his visits to twice a day and kept everyone but a servant from entering.

Abel had no idea what Timon had told his staff. He didn't care.

Sometimes he concentrated on one thought for a watch or more before he had another.

I am sick.

I am not hungry, but should be.

They are gone.

Slowly his perception returned, beginning with hunger. With that sensation came the will to eat. From there, Abel slowly became functional once again.

He knew he would never, ever be whole, however.

After a week, he returned to work, mostly because he could think of nothing better to do.

Then, after the numbness dissipated, the despair set in.

That was how von Hoff found him.

"You helped me once," he said. "I thought I might try to return the favor."

The general had taken Abel out to look at a most curious place a scavenging squad had discovered. Abel had almost demurred, in fact he had at first, but von Hoff insisted.

"One should not die without seeing this."

The location was on the other side of Orash near the north wall where an enormous waterfall roared down out of the mountain.

"This is where the water heresy was born," von Hoff had said. "It's a sight no man should miss, and who knows how long the priests will allow it to exist? No, you must come right now."

They'd taken donts across town, then tied them under an arbor and walked the rest of the way up a steep path to the spot where the huge waterfall from Lake Orash emptied over a cliff a fieldwatch high and many fieldmarches long. It was as if the lake were a giant cup full of liquid and tilting just enough for a steady flow to spill over half the rim.

All along the waterfall were wheels. They were akin to the bucket-powered chain drive of the Escarpment elevators, but most were circular rather than oblong. Each spun around a shaft, and those shafts were connected by an intricate series of power transfer points, each a carved wooden cog, to a large assortment of forges, mills, shops that fabricated who knew what. It was the largest single man-made project Abel had ever laid eyes on. Even the Tabernacle in Lindron was dwarfed by the sheer size and intricacy of the enormous mechanism.

And so they had gone to the edge, felt the spray against their faces, and then von Hoff had led Abel to a nearby destination he'd clearly had in mind to visit. It was a long building with several chimney flues emerging from it in odd spots along its canted roof.

Those chimneys did not vent mere cooking fires.

Inside, Abel found out what they did vent. Coal-fired forges. This was a metalworking shop larger than even the priestsmith's facility in Treville.

It was empty. The men of Progar had abandoned it. They were living on handouts from the army that had defeated them now, debased, without hope. Von Hoff had hung the oligarchs. Bigelow he'd had before a firing squad of his own men. He'd moved their mass execution a little farther into the future.

"What do you think?"

"Nishterlaub hell. The priests won't let this stand for long."

"What else do you think?"

"That this is where they made the revolving rifles."

Von Hoff smiled. "Precisely. I want you and the Third in charge here."

"No, thank you."

"That's an order, Colonel Dashian."

"Then I must respectfully decline to obey, sir."

"Again, I could have you shot."

"Go ahead."

Abel rested a hand against a large anvil. A hammer lay beside it on a work table, as if it had been abandoned and dropped in mid-blow. The anvil surface was cold. The entire forge was cooler than the surrounding air. There was some sort of natural air-conditioning system at work.

Von Hoff stood nearby, his arms crossed over his general's sash, his expression thoughtful.

"Do you really mean that, Dashian?"

"Yes. I don't know. I do not seem to know my own mind at the moment, General."

"You've ... you've lost something, haven't you?"

"Yes."

"It is that certitude you had before. Whatever brought that to you."

"That's right. It's gone. Dead."

"Too bad."

Von Hoff uncrossed his arms and dropped them to his side. "I was serious. You helped me once. I want to help you, Dashian. I truly do."

"This isn't the same problem as yours," Abel said, staring down at the charcoal dust that covered the floor. "You won't understand."

Von Hoff set his jaw, considered Abel for a moment, then spoke. "Do you perhaps feel that a destiny you were certain of has been yanked out from under you?"

Abel lifted his head up, blinked. In his mind he waited. He waited for the dry commentary of Center.

"The general has encapsulated the matter with admirable succinctness."

He waited for Raj's low rumble of a laugh at the folly and glory of humankind.

Neither came.

"General, I know you mean well, but—"

"But you'd much rather be left in your misery than deal with the likes of me?"

Abel chuckled. It was the first time he'd laughed in days. It felt wrong. A denial. Maybe even a betrayal.

"No. Not entirely."

Nearby, at a large fabricating table of some sort, was a line of workmen's stools. Von Hoff stepped over, got two of them, then brought them both back to the anvil where Abel was standing. The back legs of the stools rattled against the uneven mortar chinks in the floor. "Mind if I sit down?"

"It's your forge, General."

"You sit, too, Colonel."

Abel nodded. "All right." He sat down on the other stool.

Von Hoff signaled across the room. An aide was discreetly watching for this. Soon two cups of beer were set before them on the table.

It's good to be the general, Abel thought.

He raised his cup, took a tentative sip. It was cold, far colder than any beer he'd ever tasted. The cold suited this beer, as well. He took a longer swallow.

"Not bad?" said von Hoff.

"It's the best beer I've ever tasted."

Von Hoff nodded enthusiastically. "They sure as cold hell know how to brew the stuff in these parts."

"Probably with nishterlaub methods. It's heretical beer."

Von Hoff snorted at the joke, but then shook his head glumly. "No doubt you're right. Let's not speak of such things, however. This is the beer we have now." He raised his cup in a toast. "Bottoms up."

Abel smiled wanly and touched his cup against von Hoff's. The meeting of the soft clay that made up the vessels produced a muffled clink.

Good beer. Cheap infantry-issue cups. Hard to get everything right at once.

"Dashian, you have to snap out of this...grief...for your own good."

"Said the man who almost put a bullet in his own head."

"You talked me out of it. Do you regret that?"

Abel shook his head ruefully. "No. You know I don't."

"What would it take to cheer you up? Or at least get you to come to terms with whatever it is that's eating at you?" Abel didn't make a reply, and von Hoff leaned back in his chair, put his hand to his chin, and considered. "How about this, then," he continued. "How about I give you command of this forge works. It will take hundreds to work it—maybe thousands. It will have to be secured, as well. Like I hinted at, the priests are already demanding I dismantle the place. But I'm not so sure that's a good idea, at least not yet."

"Want me to plumb the secrets of the Progar heresy, General? I'm not the man for that, I promise you."

"You personally? No. You're much better with a map than a plum bob and trowel. But that engineer of yours..."

"I wouldn't want to get Captain Hoster in trouble," Abel said. "And this place is trouble." He finished the last of his beer. The aide immediately filled his cup back up from a pitcher. "I particularly wouldn't want to see Captain Hoster burned at the stake. I have a bad history with that."

"Your concern is noted," said von Hoff. "I'm going to make you a promise, Dashian. I know Hoster is itching to get his hands on some of those weapons the district has been producing and try them out, find out how they work. And you, if you were in your right mind, would be right there with him. You'd want to see what makes them tick, if nothing else."

Abel looked von Hoff straight in the eyes and spoke. "General, I *know* what makes them tick."

"Very well, then." Von Hoff looked annoyed. "I do believe you." He considered for another few eyeblinks, and his smile returned. "I'll go beyond that. I'll give you a free hand to do what you want with the Progar technology. This includes keeping the chaplains away from you."

"Thank you, Colonel, but no. Maybe Major Athanaskew will be interested."

"I'm making another use of Timon Athanaskew. With you down and out like this, he's my most competent officer. I have him setting up a military police force even as we speak."

"Glad to hear that."

"Besides, he is going through his own ordeal at the moment."

This was news to Abel. The last time he'd spoken with Timon, the major had seemed in a slightly dour mood, but otherwise untroubled.

"He hasn't told you? His wound has festered. The arm will likely have to come off."

"No, he didn't tell me that!"

"He probably didn't want to trouble you."

"Damn it." Thrice-damn it. He was going to locate Timon the moment he got back to brigade command and find out what was going on with his friend.

I can't believe I didn't notice. But he could believe it of himself. *Timon will never admit he needs help. I should have noticed. With everything else, he's losing an arm, too.*

Abel breathed a sigh of exasperation with himself. *I* will *notice from now on. There's no excuse.*

"Dashian, while you're pondering that, let me share one other bit of information on this matter: the Chaplains' Corps already has Landry Hoster in its sights."

"Landry knows. He doesn't care," Abel answered. He discovered another chuckle erupting from within himself. How had that happened without his knowing it was coming? He felt like a stranger in his own body. "He may look soft, but he's a resourceful son of a bitch."

"The priests will break him eventually. He'll end up in the Tabernacle prison."

"You know that and I know that. Landry may even know it. Like I said, he doesn't care."

"So it's up to you to protect him."

"How's that?"

"He's your friend, is he not?"

"Yes."

"You believe in loyalty?"

"It's about all I have left to believe in."

"Then be a friend to him. Take over at this forge and set him loose here. Keep the priests off his back at least until he figures out how these men have made such machines and weapons. I wouldn't trust most military men to go up against the priesthood, but I think you could politic and manage them to a stalemate with sheer competence."

Abel set his cup down on the table, put his hands around it

and twisted it in a circle of its own condensation as he considered what von Hoff had said. "What makes you think I can keep the priests from crawling all over the place?"

Von Hoff shrugged. "You are very clever, Dashian. More clever than you think. Whatever it was you lost, there is still a lot that remains. I know it. You'll find a way."

For a moment, Abel's eyes felt the animation of his former personality return. His skin flushed with excitement as if his brain were once again churning out plausible but extremely unlikely explanations for all manner of things. Planets. Stars. Automatic weapons.

"You'll give me a free hand?"

"Completely free."

"If the priests threaten to burn us all, you'll be sure to cry a tear at our funerals?"

"That would be the least I could do."

Abel considered. He felt in as sorry a state as before, but the days of inactivity were taking their toll.

Von Hoff is right. My destiny, whatever it was before, is now fucked. As long as I'm stationed here I have literally nothing better to do than try to protect Landry Hoster.

"And if we run across a new sort of weapon in there?"

Von Hoff laughed and shook his head. "There's nothing new under the sun, Dashian. If there's a weapon we don't know about, we also know that somebody somewhere in this universe has used it."

"And if it all does go to shit, you promise me I get the blame. Landry gets off scot-free. Understand, General?"

"I do, Colonel. Your terms are accepted." Von Hoff scraped his chair backward and stood up. "If things do go badly, I give you my word that it will be *you* who hangs and not Landry Hoster."

"Thanks."

"So you'll do it?"

"I want to know one thing first: Why?"

"I have a bad feeling about those Blaskoye you saw heading south. When we return to the capital, I want to be absolutely certain we can beat them."

"Treville stands in their way."

"That's why I'm not rushing back immediately. We have time, and I want those guns if we can get them to protect Lindron."

"You may burn for it."

"One way or another, cold hell awaits me," von Hoff said. "At least this way, I get to save Lindron. I do love that city."

"Then I'll do it."

Von Hoff reached over and rapped his knuckles against the anvil. "How many will you want?" he said.

Abel considered. "The whole Third," he said. "What we have here is something that used to be called a foundry."

"You'll have them."

"Yes, sir. Thank you, sir," Abel said, trying to put some heart into it.

"You can thank me by pulling yourself out of this funk," von Hoff said. "You may be special in some manner, Dashian. I know you are. But I can tell you you're not special in one way: catastrophe is always around the corner for all of us."

"Yes, sir."

"So suck it up as best you can and come back to the human race."

Von Hoff was right. In the end it was duty that saw him through and brought him back to some semblance of a rational man. Somehow Center and Raj had been discovered and erased by Zentrum. He was sure of that. So be it. Likely Zentrum had found the capsule from the sky and sent his minions to confiscate or destroy it on-site in Treville.

What else to do but carry on?

And as he did so, day after day, his resolve grew. Hardened.

Zentrum killed my friends. Zentrum is going down.

He didn't know how or when, and he didn't have Center and Raj to guide him. Center and Raj had a complicated goal: to end the Stasis and set Duisberg on a path back to civilization. His own task was much more simple: destroy Zentrum. He didn't have Center around to give him odds, but he knew they were very low.

But not zero.

And he had help. He had other friends, human friends. Timon, whose anger toward his false God had turned to a desire to beg, borrow, or steal an army, go into the Redlands, and bring back the children of Orash. Timon, who had lost an arm—his right arm had indeed come off—but learned how to face the truth, even if the truth meant hating what you once adored.

Then there was Landry, who had never been troubled by belief in Zentrum to begin with.

His father, the consummate staff commander.

And Mahaut. His love. A broker who could make or break a city, key factor in one of the most powerful trading houses in the Land—perhaps *the* most powerful one. House Jacobson controlled the grain.

No, his chances weren't good, but they weren't zero. He would carry on.

4

Orash
Winter Solstice
476 Post Tercium

Landry Hoster emerged from the priest-smith's forge works looking like a soot-covered harbinger of doom. His face, already a dark hue, was now as black as the night. The whites of his eyes were startling in such a background, as were his teeth.

"It's working," he said. "We can cut off the old barrels and convert them. The guns will be shorter and they're rifled as muzzle-loaders, but that's not the problem. Well, there's a lot of little problems, like flash burn to your stock hand when you use a rifle grip, and the fact that there's a pretty good chance of a chain fire every once in a while. We'll work around those."

Abel didn't urge him on. Landry had his own way of getting to a point.

"The cylinders. We make them with a water-powered hammer. Pound it faster and harder than any man could in a thousand years. They beat the metal into a mold. Problem is, this place was originally set up to turn out four or five in a day. I've had the boys working, and we can do considerably more than that once we get the hammers on-line."

"How many?"

"Fifty a day."

"That's . . . a hell of an improvement, Major."

"Not fast enough, though. Not with the timetable you gave me."

"Can you speed it up?"

"If you double my manpower, yes."

"Consider it done."

"Nothing original added to the process," Landry said. "The men just need a bit of organization is all, each man doing one and only one task, you see. Some work the hammers, some the lathe and drill...you get the idea. We have the manpower, and these boys don't imagine themselves master smiths, so nobody's getting bent out of shape. Plus, they're used to taking orders."

"So this is the ramrod. On a levered hinge. Nice." Abel looked over the backs of the cylinders. "Major, where are the percussion-cap nipples?"

"Was wondering when you'd notice that. These are not cap-and-ball firearms. We Cascaders are a little ahead of those Progar smiths in that way, as you know," Landry said. "I thought it was maybe a useless exercise when you set me to it before, but those 469-grain papyrus cartridges we've been turning out in the Bruneberg works do just fine in a revolver barrel."

"And they're not nishterlaub, at least not officially. How much of that sort of ammunition do you reckon we have?"

"I brought along five thousand rounds here to Progar, just in case. We got them off the Rim, too. And at the armories back in Cascade? I'd estimate we have a good fifty to sixty thousand rounds, all told. We've got the process down and can make more quickly, too."

"Reloading time with the cartridges is much faster. I know that from experience."

"Been giving that some thought, too. You don't just want six shots."

"I sure as cold hell will take them over one shot."

"What you really want is continuous fire, right? Guns that are machines, like you explained to me that time."

"That's right. That dream I told you about. One of these days."

"What if I could get you closer to that day?"

"How?"

"Interchangeable drop-out cylinders. You finish up your six shots, pull an extracting pin and flip out the cylinder. Then you mount another that's preloaded with six shots. Gives you twelve shots with barely a pause in fire. Potentially as many shots as you want, depending on how many cylinders you have available or want to carry around with you. They're heavy little bastards."

Abel pulled back the hammer and cocked the rifle. As he did so, the cylinder rotated and lined up another cylinder.

"Beautiful work," he said.

"Thank you, sir," Landry said. He scratched his head. "Yeah, probably best to keep it simple that way."

"Don't tell me you have another idea for the action, too?"

"Could make it all happen in one move," Landry replied. "Not hard to do, once you have the idea. Build it into how the trigger works. Two things happening, one pull."

"How hard?"

"It would add months—and lots of playing around and rejiggering."

"Single action for now, then. It's got to be reliable."

"As far as that goes," Landry put in, "remember the black rock we saw piled behind the smithery?"

"The coal? They mine it in a lot of places around here. The townsfolk use it for heat."

As late summer had passed into autumn, and then into winter, Abel had been astounded at how cold it got here in the mountains. Center had made him feel cold before in visions, but to experience it day after day was a different thing entirely. Now he knew what it was like to *be* cold, and not just momentarily chilly.

"They sure do, because it burns hotter than wood or even charcoal," Landry said. "I can get it hotter still with this big enough bellows. Been working on it all day."

"Which would explain why you look like you're covered in dak dung."

Landry smiled, and his white teeth flashed. "Coal kicks up a lot of dust," he said.

"So what does such a hot fire get you?"

"It lets me anneal," Landry said. "Make iron twice as strong. That way when you fire one of my revolving rifles, it's not going to blow to pieces in your face." Another bright white smile. "Probably."

Abel nodded. "Good," he said.

"Colonel, I've just got one question."

"What is it?"

"You want them done right, and you want them fast. I think I have that right."

"Yes."

"Would you mind telling me what it is you want them *for*?"

Abel nodded. "The Blaskoye. They're going to attack. They might come through Treville; they might try it through Ingres. But there's one place everybody agrees they're headed."

"Lindron," said Landry.

Abel nodded confirmation. "Those guns may stop the fourth Blood Wind from blowing."

PART TEN

The Consort

The Present

1

Lindron
477 Post Tercium

It had ceased to surprise her that Lindron was in so many ways more provincial than Hestinga. What mattered above all in the capital was appearance, propriety—or at least the appearance of propriety. Despite being a big city, or perhaps because of it, a woman could not venture into the streets without male accompaniment unless she wished to be thought either a tradeswoman or a prostitute.

While Mahaut did consider herself the former, and didn't have anything against the latter, it wouldn't do to have the chief consort and land-heiress of Jacobson House traveling without an escort. In fact, in addition to her four chairmen and two torchbearers, she customarily brought an older personal body-guard in the dress of a second family senior servant. Under his plain tunic, however, he carried an array of weaponry, some for himself and some for Mahaut. She also brought along two guards armed with swords and pistols to stand watch on entranceways of the places she went. And hidden in the crowd, but making their way alongside her, were two shadows, one along to identify threats and the other to serve as a messenger should there be a need for more backup.

This was not only considered normal for a First Family house factor or consort, but was de rigueur. If anything, Mahaut's entourage was smaller than most. She was glad of their company as she made her way through the Lindron nighttime through the rich neighborhood known as Esplanade. This was an area just east of the Tabernacle pyramid. It was filled with the residences of First Families, Tabernacle priests, and Second and Third families. Their houses were inevitably the most gaudy, vying for advancement. The Esplanade was allegedly neutral ground among all the Families.

More like contested territory, Mahaut reflected.

The city guard kept the area free of cutthroats and robbers, but many an assassination had been carried out on these streets as Families fought for status and sought revenge for insults. The guard pointedly stayed out of such matters, and there was never a formal investigation when the streets ran with the blood of two Firsts.

Mahaut turned off the main thoroughfare down a side passage packed with large houses whose outer walls were separated by little more than the space of three or four men. There was this much space so that a patrolling guard could walk their perimeters. Behind the entranceways, Mahaut knew, stretched opulent compounds filled with courtyards and water elements—courtesy of the underground plumbing that fed each house its water supply.

Each house also had its wastes carried away by an army of nightsoilmen who descended on the area in the hours before dawn. There had been an indoor water spigot and flush toilets at the Jacobson compound in Lilleheim. Here in Lindron, she'd had toilets installed at the Jacobson compound that could be flushed, with the waste carried into a tank wagon that was taken away daily to fertilize nearby fields. This arrangement was otherwise unknown in conservative Lindron, where the slightest change in the way things were done was akin to heresy, even if it had official sanction.

Mahaut had one of her torch runners flank her along the street to illuminate the address glyphs on the houses. She looked from side to side and checked for the correct one as her divan chair moved along. Halfway up Garden Street, she found the stone-carved Family shield that marked the address for which she'd been bound. She ordered a stop and sent her older bodyguard, whose name was Friedman, to announce her arrival. Another thing First Family members would not be seen doing in Lindron: knocking on a door themselves.

She was admitted along with Friedman, and her men joined the other armed bravos gathered around the entrance. These would talk in low tones throughout the evening, chew nesh, and spit gouts of juice into the street.

Inside were most of the First Family factors in Lindron. It was a dinner party, but it was also a specially called meeting of merchants. They were people who were considering the daunting idea of petitioning the Abbot of Lindron for more troops to guard the capital while the Guardian Corps was away. Everyone was feeling vulnerable with a garrison force of only two thousand in the city. Most of the Lindron scouts had gone with the Guardians as well, and the few who remained were spread thin. They were not an adequate early warning system for Redlander intrusion. Everyone in the city was feeling as if his or her neck were bared to barbarian attack.

At least everyone with any sense, she thought. *Because they'd be right.*

Most of the First houses were represented, including the most powerful of Lindron: Athanaskew, Weatherby, Ziman, Manstein, Freemont, among others—and of course Nikolai Belov, the Lindron House Eisenach Factor, was present. It had been his brother whom Edgar Jacobson had shot and killed. News of Edgar's subsequent death had reached Lindron along with Mahaut, and the story had grown into a legend.

Some tales had it that Mahaut had castrated and blinded Edgar, then made him listen as she made love to a teenage boy while he bled to death tied to the base of the bed. Some rumors were even more perverse. Usually the fact that the Land-heiress Widow Jacobson was now available for courting was mentioned in the same breath. A tie to the Jacobsons was a tie, even if you were taking your life into your hands to make it.

Mahaut was not bothered by the gossip one bit. It gave her a negotiating advantage if the other thought that there was nothing that she would stop at to have her way.

Most did not know of her more cold-blooded treatment of Eliot Eisenach.

She went through a large inner courtyard and into the reception room, where many of the others had gathered. There was a wide archway in the back through which she could see that a table was in the process of being laid with food and drink by an army of servants. Sebastian Ziman, the Ziman House second son, recognized her and came to greet her. The Jacobsons, who dealt in grain and finance, and the Zimans, who were mostly boat makers and shippers, had as tight a relationship as any of the Firsts, although Mahaut would stop short of calling it friendship.

"Your Grace, Land-heiress Jacobson, I was hoping you'd be here this evening. It's going to take a lot to wake this lot up to our danger. Some of these old duffers have no clue that their asses are hanging out as big fat Blaskoye targets."

"I'm not sure what I could convince them of if they can't see it for themselves, Land-heir Ziman," Mahaut replied.

Sebastian chuckled. "Well, maybe you can scare them into going along with us. You do have that fearsome reputation, your grace."

Mahaut nodded. He took her arm and they walked farther into the reception room. A clump of wives eyed her warily from a corner. One said something Mahaut could not hear, and it set them all to laughing.

In addition to the usual assortment of Firsts, there were several orange-robed and red-sashed priests and temple consorts present, most of them First Family scions as well.

"I didn't know we'd have clergy here tonight, Sebastian," she said in a low voice.

"The Abbot himself was invited. He's not here of course, but he felt it politic to send along these up-and-coming young men. There is Budnitz of Manstein. And that handsome tall one talking to Budnitz is a particular favorite of the Abbot's, and said to be marked for great things."

"What's his name?"

"He's an Athanaskew," Sebastian replied. "Rake or Reis. Something like that."

"He may know something about the Abbot's mind on our problem."

"I'd imagine a young man that pretty probably knows more than just the Abbot's mind," said Sebastian.

"Your wickedness will see you consigned to the lash one day, Sebastian."

"If only, your grace."

When Mahaut was introduced to the young priest, he looked her up and down in an intense, unaffected manner. Whatever favors he may or may not do for the Abbot, it was clear which way his own sexual interest lay. To get such looks was still amazing to her, even after several years of it happening. She'd been a tomboy growing up and, although healthy looking enough in appearance, had never flattered herself she was any raging beauty. But pencil the kohl around your eyes, have a maid bend your hair into the latest style, and then make your appearance under the right circumstances in the best light, and suddenly a man who would never have noticed you before was all attention. This had annoyed the warrior woman in her for a time, but then she'd realized her looks were a tool for survival and conquest like any other.

She bowed Zentrum's respect to the young priest, and smiled. It only took a few leading questions about his work at the temple before his mouth was off and running.

"My duties are not very important now, Land-heiress. Mostly administrative. But I'm on interior staff, the place everyone wants to be, in direct contact with the Abbot. I've even been just outside the Inner Sanctum when my lord Abbot communes with Zentrum."

"How fascinating! I don't suppose you took a peek inside?"

He shook his head. "Yes, your grace, but I can't tell you about that. I don't want to break Edict. I do expect to be called into the chamber myself some day." He straightened his shoulders. "My parents raised my brother and me for such things, you know. Three Athanaskews have been Abbots, and another two have been commander in chief of the Guardian Corps."

"Ah, then your brother is Timon Athanaskew of the Guardians," she said. "I've heard of him."

From his best friend, who has mentioned several times that Timon and his brother don't get along so well, she thought.

"Yes, he is my younger brother," Athanaskew answered, a touch of stiffness in his voice. "Even though sometimes I think our parents got us mixed up in that regard. Perhaps I should have been the soldier and Timon the priest. He's always been so zealous."

"And you're not? You're a priest."

"Priests? We are some of the least zealous you'll meet." He chuckled. "I'm committed to the priesthood and to Zentrum, of course. But I've seen a great deal of the inner workings of the Tabernacle, enough to know that all is not what it seems. Many things are more...complicated than Timon understands."

"My dear, you have to tell me what you mean by that. I'm very curious."

"Really, it's a bit convoluted for a woman. I would not like to bore you."

"Yes, we wouldn't want that." Mahaut smiled brightly. "But I am curious about *you*, Reis."

"Oh, there's lots I could tell you that might be of interest, but..." He looked around with the exaggerated air of a conspirator. "This is not the best place to discuss such matters."

"How about on the veranda after dinner, when drinks are served? Do you chew or smoke, Law-heir Athanaskew?"

"No."

"Neither do I," she said. "It's a warm evening." She too took on a faux conspiratorial whisper. "We can justify our secret meeting by taking a stroll to cool off."

"I'll be there."

"See you then," she replied, "but at the moment I see Colonel Dupree's lovely lady."

Athanaskew followed the direction of her gaze. "She's the one who isn't his wife? The doxy?"

"She isn't his wife," Mahaut answered. "But then again his wife is pinned up in a velvet-covered room claiming that she hears the walls talk to her."

"Evil spirits can possess even the better people, I'm afraid," said Athanaskew. "But it is his duty to remain outwardly faithful to her if he does not wish to obtain a divorce."

"Well, we aren't at Thursday school, are we? I believe we can give both of them the benefit of the doubt on a night like tonight," Mahaut said. "Besides, the lady is a friend of mine, and I happen to know she's an old acquaintance of his from childhood and nothing more."

"I see," replied Athanaskew with a look of distaste. "That may be even worse, then."

Mahaut touched his arm lightly. "Remember, the veranda." She left the priest and made her way across the room to speak with Hecate Li, the companion of the House Dupree colonel. They'd met at the Lindron shooting range and had taken an instant liking to one another.

Mahaut reflected that she didn't want to think badly of Reis Athanaskew, at least not yet. It was too easy for a bad opinion to show through. There were some consummate liars in Lindron society, but she knew she was not really one of them. She would never wholly lose that straightforward woman she'd been. But being shot, almost killed, abused, and then killing her own husband had worked a good measure of survivor's deviousness into her personality.

Mahaut and Hecate Li spoke together until called away to eat. Mahaut then spent her dinner speaking with a Weatherby cousin who seemed unable to help himself and told her all about a scheme to corner the dried dakmeat market his house was undertaking.

"If and when the Blaskoye ride in, the garrison and everyone else in town will be desperate for rations that don't spoil."

Mahaut filed the information away. It had been a long time since war had come to Lindron. She knew full well that the garrison, weakened by the absence of the main body of the Corps, but still the strongest armed force in the city, would simply go and take what they needed from Manstein's warehouses, well-guarded or not. And in any case, she knew that House Jacobson and House Manstein had a joint storage unit near the River entirely filled with dried dakmeat and rice. She had no intention of being caught under siege lacking provisions.

She could, however, make a tidy sum riding up dakbellies promissories at the commodities exchange, selling futures at a huge markup, then releasing enough of her provisions to throw Weatherby's move to corner into disarray as the market collapsed around it. She could even offer up the substantial supply of wagons and drayage she'd accumulated in anticipation of half the population attempting to flee the city. The other house factors, looking for a hedge as dakbellies fell, would be desperate for somewhere to sink their chits in anticipation of general panic.

If she wanted to be particularly nasty, she could secretly send out a large dakbelly buy this very night to run up the morning bids and cause Weatherby to sink even more chits into the venture.

She felt sorry for the talkative Weatherby son. He seemed a decent sort, and he spent even more time talking about his children than he did about the dakmeat scheme. Perhaps she wouldn't utterly ruin him after all—just cause him and House Weatherby to suffer a bit.

On her other side was Nikolai Belov of Eisenach. Throughout dinner, he maintained a stony silence toward her. Mahaut slipped away after the dessert wine was poured, a Delta red, cloyingly sweet. She soon located Athanaskew on the veranda. He'd been waiting for her. Friedman, her bodyguard, stood discreetly in a doorway, out of earshot and shadowed and mostly out of sight.

"We meet again, Law-heir Athanaskew."

"Call me Reis, forever and always."

"All right, Reis," Mahaut replied. "I'm longing to walk after that dinner. Accompany me for a stroll?"

"Honored."

They stepped off the veranda and into a small but elaborately sculpted hedge garden whose centerpiece was an ancient riverwillow. The willow's trailing branches formed a curtain of enclosure around a bench, which was placed next to the trunk. A small oil lamp sat on a pedestal next to the bench, giving the interior of the fronds a warm glow. After a turn around the perimeter of the tree, they pushed the willow fronds aside and took a seat on the bench.

"So, what was the dangerous information about yourself that you couldn't tell me inside, Reis Athanaskew? I was so full of curiosity all through dinner that I had trouble carrying on understandable conversation."

"I'm sure you had no such trouble, Land-heiress," said the priest.

"I am Mahaut."

"Mahaut," he said, as if savoring the words. "I noticed Sherm Weatherby slobbering all over you. I was jealous of him for having your company."

"Land-heir Weatherby seems a very nice man."

"But not your sort."

"In what way do you mean?"

The priest began to speak again, then quickly turned away from her.

"Is that a blush I see, Reis?" Mahaut said. "Come, tell me the truth: Why would your brother have made a better priest than you? From what you tell me, you have to be practical to be a priest after you attain a certain status."

"I have always had high status, of course. I wouldn't know about the lower orders," Athanaskew said. "But yes, I've seen and done things that those outside might think unpriestly."

"Do tell."

"Oh, nothing too terrible. It's just that the Abbot and Zentrum take the long view. Sometimes that means weakening some areas to strengthen others. Take the Bruneberg Prelacy. We know there is corruption going on up there, but it serves Zentrum and the Abbot's purpose to leave it in the hands of a First Family oligarch, especially after the housecleaning that new DMC gave the secular side of things. And Mims is another example, although the situation is a good deal better down there."

"What sort of corruption?"

"Oh, the usual. Tradesmen paying tribute to the temple to remain in business. Lax enforcement of the Laws and Edicts. Whorehouses run by the priesthood in all but name. And quite a few Redlander girls sold as slaves by their own kin to serve in them."

"Terrible." Mahaut kept her voice neutral. She knew Abel had cleared the regular whorehouses of slave girls, but he hadn't been able to shut down those under protection of the prelate.

"And here in the Tabernacle, things are . . . there is much cheating and backbiting going on right under Zentrum's nose! You'd think he encourages it."

"Maybe it just appeals to the Lord Zentrum's sense of humor."

"No," Athanaskew replied. "He doesn't have one."

"I stand corrected. Or sit corrected."

Athanaskew reached a hand over and placed it on Mahaut's thigh. She felt it, warm, through her gauzy skirt. "Land-heiress Jacobson, I—"

"Mahaut, please."

"Mahaut. I shouldn't be telling you this, your grace. I really shouldn't."

Mahaut shrugged. "Then don't, if you would prefer not to." She gently but firmly removed his hand from her leg.

"Is that how you're going to be, so cold?" Athanaskew said. "All right. How's this for interesting: there's a secret prison under the Tabernacle with some very odd characters down there at the moment."

"Dear Reis, I do know about the dungeon," Mahaut said. "It's not the best-kept secret in Lindron."

The priest looked chagrined.

Mahaut gave him a coy look as if to say "You'll have to do better than that."

"There's more," the priest said. "And this will interest you. I believe you're from Treville, aren't you?"

"That I am," said Mahaut. She sat up straighter, all attention now.

"Well, there's this . . . special group . . . we have those who do things that we would rather not be connected with. Some are priests and some are Guardians. It's run by a man who is both priest and Guardian; some are both. As a matter of fact, my brother, Timon, took his training in this group. It's a very secretive circle of men, however. Its leader is named William Cloutier. He is very good at making people, well, disappear. They call him the Hand of Zentrum."

"He sounds awful."

"Oh, yes. You don't want to get on Cloutier's bad side, let me tell you. And he's always snooping around the priesthood itself for heresy. A few priests have been among the disappeared."

"Are you going to get in trouble for telling me this?"

Athanaskew smiled, scooted closer to Mahaut. His red robe fell against the spread fabric of her dress. "You're a First, or at least married into a Family," he said. He turned and looked her in the eyes. "And no one else has to know, Mahaut. I know you are but a woman, but can you promise me that?"

"On a night like this, a woman might find herself promising anything," she replied.

Athanaskew smiled. The hand returned to her thigh, and this time she did not remove it.

"You were telling me about news of Treville District?" she said. "You're right; it will always hold a special place in my heart. Yet I'm beginning to feel more and more at home in Lindron these days."

"I'm very pleased to hear that." He moved closer, as if to kiss her.

Mahaut laughed lightly and pushed him away. He almost fell off the bench.

Men were often surprised at how strong she was. They wouldn't be if they saw her at her archery exercises and physical training each morning.

"Treville," she said. "Come, speak."

Athanaskew straightened himself up, looking embarrassed. "Yes, well. I was going to say, we happen to have some very interesting persons in the prison at the moment. Apparently the leadership in the district was rotten, and the Abbot recently had it cleaned out."

Mahaut felt a coldness stab her inside.

"Who is it that's in the dungeon, Reis?"

"I'm not exactly sure of this, but I've heard it's the old Treville prelate himself."

"Zilkovsky?"

"Yes, that's the one. And they've got the DMC along with him, if you can believe it."

"Joab Dashian."

"Something like that. Not a First Family sort, so it's hard to remember what they call the rogue."

Mahaut turned toward Athanaskew, reached for his hands and took them in hers. "Come, this news is gloomy. But continue."

"Well, here's the really interesting part: Zentrum himself has called them here," Athanaskew said. "It's said he spoke to Abbot Goldfrank. Directly. The Abbot told me so himself."

"The Lord Zentrum gave this order? Amazing. What do you think will happen to those two?"

"Oh, they'll be executed. Only when and how, I can't say."

"Can't or won't?"

Athanaskew gazed into her eyes.

Trying to judge how far he can push it.

Then he shrugged, smiled. "The truth is I really don't know. We're all wondering about that. Those of us on the inner circle, that is."

He was quiet for a moment, collecting himself.

Here it comes.

"Land-heiress Jacobson. Mahaut. I want to see you again."

"You can see me any time you like, Reis. I'm usually at the House Jacobson office. I am the chief consort. I have a few minor duties that keep me occupied there, but you may call at any time."

"You know that's not what I mean."

"Lord Athanaskew, you're a priest of the Tabernacle."

"That's right. I am. That's why this could be so good. We can't marry. But that doesn't mean we can't—" He shook his head as if to clear it. "You're a widow. Experienced. Unattached, but available. You've already been...blooded. Mahaut, don't you see past this robe? I'm still a man."

"You have a man's needs..."

"Yes," he said. "Yes, exactly. You do understand."

All right, this one is milked dry, I think.

Mahaut released the priest's hands, sat back considering him. "Dearest Reis, that's what *whorehouses* are for. You wouldn't be the first priest to visit one."

Athanaskew frowned. "Oh no. I would never... I could never."

"Oh, I think you *have* already, haven't you? More than once."

A faint smile. "All right. You've found me out. What do you think? Yes. Yes, of course."

"It's your brother who has never set foot in one, isn't it?"

"Timon's way is as straight as an arrow, Zentrum help him," said Athanaskew. "I do love him in my way, but he's always been so thickheaded." He looked downward, propping his forehead on a palm.

"I'm only trying to protect you, Reis."

"It would be impossible, wouldn't it? You and I."

"I'm afraid so."

"You're a very wise woman to see that," he said. "Can you imagine me sneaking out of the Tabernacle and you out of your Family compound? This is Lindron. Everyone's bound to find out."

"My reputation wouldn't suffer much, but you could be ruined, dear man. You, who have so much promise. You'll be the Abbot one day."

He nodded his head. "I may," he said. "I just may."

"Then, perhaps, each of us can do what we want, what we feel. But not until then."

He looked up, imploring. "At least let me kiss you."

She shook her head. "No."

Athanaskew's expression hardened for a moment. Mahaut's hand trailed to the back of her tunic, where she kept an obsidian blade in easy reach. Then the priest sighed. "We wouldn't stop, would we? May I kiss your hand?"

"Yes, dear Reis, you may."

Mahaut stood up, straightened her dress. She held her right hand out to him. He took it gingerly, raised it slowly as if savoring every moment, then brushed his lips against her skin, lingering. Finally he let himself kiss the hand. He pulled back, but still held her hand.

"I have to know... what is it, your perfume?"

"Hyacinth. A special blend from Treville."

"Ah. May I have a handkerchief, a bit of cloth, anything?"

She gently shook her head. "Better not. Besides, you'll always have the memory," she said. "We both will."

Finally, he released her and she pulled her hand away. "I must go. It's a ways back to the Tabernacle compound and the night isn't getting any younger."

"Will you think of me along the way?"

"Oh, yes. I promise I will."

He stood up, moved in front of her. For a moment, she thought he was going to detain her and make another pass. If so, she would show him the other side of her: captain of the women's auxiliary who knew how to kick a man in the nuts, even a priest. But instead, he pulled back the willow fronds to clear a portal for her from under the branches.

"Thank you, Reis. Such a memorable evening this has turned out to be."

Athanaskew smiled. "Absolutely. Shall we part here, or should I accompany you into the dining room?"

"Why don't you accompany me back in," she said, taking his arm. "That will be quite scandalous enough. We must give the rest of them something to talk about on the way home tonight."

2

She did not sleep that night, of course, and hurried home, thinking not one moment about the priest Athanaskew. All of the evening and following day was taken up with marshaling her forces, bringing in any merchant beholden to her who might have information about Joab Dashian and Hiram Zilkovsky. She caught Marone just as he was about to leave for the long journey back to Treville.

His wife and now eight children may not have seen him for three months or more, but he was needed here. She made sure to tell her adjutant and assistant Dillard to double Marone's usual rate.

She didn't neglect House Jacobson business, either. She sent out buy orders on dakbellies; then, toward midday, she began to sell, following prices up.

Finally, Mahaut allowed herself a one-watch nap. She fell asleep with her head on her desk. She was awakened by Dillard tapping gently on her shoulder.

"Marone has returned," he said. "He's brought someone with him."

"All right, give me a moment, then send them in." Mahaut rose, went to a water basin, and splashed her face. She combed through her hair with her wet fingers, trying to straighten it a bit. In a silvered glass, she checked her eye kohl, attempted to dab away a smear.

Useless, she thought. *Besides, it may be better if I look a bit of a fright.*

Marone entered with a small man, bald, his head covered with a rainbow of tattoos resembling a dont male's plumage.

"Gentlemen," she said. "What do you have for me?"

The tattooed man eyed the chair in front of Mahaut's desk, but when Marone did not sit down, he didn't, either.

"This man is called Hagen," Marone said. "He runs the whore-house that the dungeon guards visit most often."

"I'm a manager for several interests," the man put in. He had a thick Delta accent, probably straight from the working district of inner city Mims. "The Sign of the Axe is just one of my properties."

"And who owns these properties you manage?" Mahaut said, since clearly the man was eager to spill all and improve his status in her eyes. What he thought she could do for him, she did not know.

"Multiple parties. A group of First sons. They call themselves a club. Men who hold high places, let me assure you, mistress."

Marone slapped the man across the back of his head. "She's to be addressed as Land-heiress Jacobson, you slob."

Mahaut held up a hand. "That's all right, Mr. Marone. I answer to many names. Families of the Esplanade, Mr. Hagen?"

Hagen smiled a buttery smile and gave a slight bow. "That's right, Land-heiress Jacobson. Could be fodder for a bit of black-mail, if you take my meaning."

"Interesting," she said. "But it's the dungeons we want to know about."

"Tell her," Marone said.

"There's been talk," Hagen said, the smile dropping from his face. "About a couple of ripe ones that's been brought in not long ago."

"Ripe ones?"

"Juicy. Kind of fruit them guards fancy, if you know what I mean."

"Yes," said Mahaut. "I think I do." She motioned to the chair. "Sit down, Mr. Hagen," she said. "Tell me more, please."

The smile again, but this one seemed much more genuine. "Don't mind if I do," he said, and took a seat.

So that's what he wants, she thought. *A little respect, false or not. He's as easily bought as the women that work for him, if you pay in the right currency.*

She soon had enough information to assure herself that the two "ripe ones" were, indeed, Hiram Zilkovsky and Joab Dashian.

What she needed now was a plan for getting them out.

"Suppose I was concerned that someone had it in mind to break these two out," she said. "I hear the Tabernacle dungeon is completely impenetrable. It's an old place, carved down into solid rock in the days of the giants."

"That it is, Land-heiress, that it is," Hagen replied. "There's only one way out, and that's cut down to pieces to fit a charnel bag."

"That's good," Mahaut said. "I was worried we'd have to buy someone off to prevent an escape."

Hagen looked chagrined, even insulted, that she thought he'd let such a rich opportunity pass. "There's ways, and then there's ways," he said. "If you know what I mean."

"Tell me," Mahaut said.

"Those men, they might be Guardian in name, but they'll tell my girls things they would never tell another soul on pain of death. They'll do things for the girls, too," he said. "And the girls know to bring anything useful straight to me—if they value their hides."

"And you pay them a bonus for the information, no doubt?"

Hagen sat back in the chair as if completely startled by a thought that had never occurred to him. "No, Land-heiress," he said. "They're just whores, you see, and whatever you gave them would go straight to—"

"Something to consider in the future, Mr. Hagen," she said, cutting him off. "What have you found out?"

"I'd need some kind of . . . reassurance, Land-heiress." He squirmed nervously, rubbed his plume tattoos where a bead of sweat had broken out. "Something up front is what I'm getting at."

Behind Hagen, Marone harrumphed. He rustled his clothes as if reaching for a knife or billlyclub.

"Mind your place, you scumbucket," he murmured.

Mahaut considered. If she paid in barter chits, Hagen would hold out, feed her as little as possible and string her along for more.

Besides, she thought, he's already shown me how to buy him.

"No, no, Marone, Mr. Hagen has a point," Mahaut said. "After all, if he told us what he knows without getting paid first, we might refuse to pay. I'll bet that's happened to you before, hasn't it, Mr. Hagen?"

"Damn straight it has," Hagen said in a low voice. "Land-heiress."

"On the other hand, we could pay you half or even everything you want up front, you could spill whatever it is you think you know, then we could take the funds back, slit your throat before you knew what cut you, and throw you to the carnadons by the lower docks. Nobody would notice another body being torn to bits in the shallows, would they?"

Hagen gulped, but did not answer.

"Or we could get it out of you with no price to pay at all," she said. "I'm sure you know how it's done? You've practiced it on your whores, haven't you?" Mahaut sat back, considered Hagen. "First a bit of knocking about. But that wouldn't work on you, would it, Mr. Hagen? You seem like the kind of man who might even make it through the branding. Might even be willing to sacrifice your balls and a few fingers."

Hagen's already yellowish cast grew even paler and more sallow.

"Of course, I'm not a barbarian," Mahaut continued. "When you started begging for death, I'd surely grant your request."

"Mistress... Land-heiress Jacobson, please, I was merely inquiring—"

Mahaut cut him off. "How about this, then: you have a lot of mouths to feed at the Sign of the Axe and your other establishments. I'm sure it's not just your staff, either. There are certain... complications to a business such as yours."

Hagen let another small smile trickle across his lips. "Them brats do keep building up like pests. I suppose I should clean 'em out, but we keep 'em, back in the quarters behind the main hall, where their sniveling and crying after their mums won't disturb the customers."

"I'm surprised you have such a soft heart, Mr. Hagen."

Hagen shook his head, as if he astonished himself as well. "I know it, I know it," he replied. "Most would. But it happened to me when I was a snot-grubber back in Mims. Bastards tore me away from my mum and sold me to a beggar gang when I was five. At least, I put it around five in years or so." He reached up, rubbed his temple, then, quickly, his eyes. "Had to be about that, on account of I remember her. My mum, I mean."

"So you don't do that to the whores' children?"

"Swore I never would. We put 'em out when they can work for a real wage."

This was the first sign of humanity she'd seen in the man. Of course, he could be making a show to gain her sympathy, but she didn't think so. She could check the truth of his statements with Marone later, in any case.

"I respect your skill, Mr. Hagen. I really do. You're in a hard business, and you manage to make a go of it. So . . . let's do it this way," she said. "I'll have my factor give you the wholesaler's discount on grain. A quarter off the market price. So long as you agree to bring all your trade to us."

"At that price, I'd be a fool to ever buy from another," he said. "Terms for ten years?"

"Five."

"Done," he said. He chuckled. "Done and done."

"But I'm going to want a bit more from you than just information," Mahaut said after a pause to let Hagen gloat at his good fortune.

"More? What do you mean?" He looked up, suddenly suspicious.

And then she told him what she wanted, and Hagen's expression turned to worry and gloom.

3

Orash
477 Post Tercium

It seemed as if the soot from Landry's forge had worked into every wrinkle, every crack or crevice, in Abel's skin. He could bathe and scrub as much as he wanted, but there was always some bit of coal dust, smoky residue, something filthy that would not come off.

He'd learned to live with this over the past few weeks, but now that he'd been called to Corps headquarters in the town square, he was acutely aware of his own unkempt appearance. He'd never been a stickler for regulations, but he'd also made sure never to look like the town simpleton. He really ought to have cut his hair this past week, but he'd just been too busy, and, in any case, half the headquarters staff had come down with pneumonia.

This had prompted yet another direction to Landry's work. Center had long said that in order to produce effective antibiotics, an industrial base was necessary.

But Center wasn't here.

And all he needed them for was to save one man.

He described the process to Landry as best he could remember it from Center's longish lectures.

"The problem is there are lots of slime molds that won't work, and might kill you," Abel told him. "At least that's the way it was told to me by the hermit."

"The crazy hermit who lived in the Escarpment near the Treville Scout headquarters?"

"Yes."

"Why don't I believe you?"

"You should."

"Oh, I believe everything you've told me about penicillin. Just like I believed everything you told me about papyrus cartridges back in Cascade, and lo and behold, they came out just fine and very deadly. I just don't believe in that hermit."

"I have no other explanation."

"Not those voices?"

"What voices?"

"The ones I used to hear you talking to back in Bruneberg, back when we were both working late at the garrison. You probably thought you were alone."

Abel grinned. "If engineering hadn't been your calling, Landry Hoster, I think you would have made a pretty good spy."

"Growing up on the streets of Mims, it pays to keep your ears open," Landry replied. But he smiled, obviously pleased that he'd struck at the truth.

"It doesn't matter anymore, though," Abel said. His own smile vanished. "The voices are gone."

"Oh."

"The penicillin, Landry," he continued. "You have to find the way to kill off the other mold but keep the penicillin healthy. You'll know you've got it when it turns from gray to bright blue-green."

"Like a Delta whore's eyes?"

"As you well know, those are usually brown."

Landry nodded his agreement.

"So how do I get this magic slime? What's the process?"

Abel shook his head. "That's the part I don't know. And, like I said, the voices aren't around to tell me."

Abel tried at least to smooth back his unkempt hair before he saw von Hoff, but it was no use. He was waved through the outer office by Master Sergeant of the Corps Dionis. Von Hoff was pouring over a map when Abel entered.

It wasn't the map of Progar that Abel had become familiar with. No, this was a large map, four papyrus rolls long, of all the Land from the Schnee Mountains to the Braun Sea. Abel stood on the other side of the map table from von Hoff and waited for the general to notice him.

Von Hoff nodded and looked at Abel wordlessly for a long moment. Finally, he spoke. "You and Hoster were hard at work in your foundry, and I didn't want to disturb you. But we heard something from down south, and then we got confirmation."

"Yes, sir?"

"Headquarters received messages by flitterdak, three in all. Those animals looked ragged after their passages, let me tell you. They died soon afterwards, and their mates went on quite a keen."

The flitterdaks that were used as capsule bearers were a species that mated for life. They made the trip desperately seeking to be reunited with their mates. But a flitterdak that died near its mate inevitably led to an elaborate, and very loud, mourning ritual by its partner.

Center had speculated that this was to inform other mateless flitters that the partner was soon to be available.

"Those message all confirmed one another," von Hoff continued. "The Blaskoye have massed for a large attack."

"Where?"

"Near Treville."

"Treville? But the Treville Regulars are the best fighting force in the Land apart from the Guardians," said Abel. "They know Treville will beat them back."

"Perhaps," von Hoff said.

"No 'perhaps' about it."

Von Hoff nodded, but there was a grim cast to his face. "If the Redlanders find a way or fight their way through, they become a direct threat to Lindron. A deadly threat when the capital's defenders are three hundred leagues north."

"How long do we have?"

"Perhaps three weeks. They are still gathering the clans and tribes. At most a month."

"It will be a race, but we can win."

"Yes," von Hoff said with a smile. "But I have another task for you."

"What is that, sir?"

"You and the reserves will return to Cascade. Gather your Regulars there and march south as quickly as you can. I'll dash with the main body to Lindron and secure the city. When the

Blaskoye attack, you come down, I will be the anvil and you will be the hammer."

"But, General, aren't you forgetting something?" said Abel. How could something so obvious have escaped von Hoff's notice? "There's also Treville."

Von Hoff blanched. Abel had never seen his commander look so reluctant to speak.

"General von Hoff?"

"There was another part to the message," von Hoff said in a low voice. "It concerned Treville."

Abel felt his heart skip a beat. "What did it say?"

Von Hoff shook his head. "I'm sorry to have to tell you this, Colonel, but Treville is in disarray at the moment."

"What?" His voice was thick when he next spoke. "Has something happened to my father?"

"He's disappeared, Abel. So has the prelate."

"Zilkovsky?"

"I'm afraid so. The Tabernacle inquisitors are trying to piece together what has happened. Until they do, Treville and the Treville Regulars are not to be trusted. They are not to be used in battle."

"We'll be giving up half our strength!"

"Don't you think I know this, Dashian?" von Hoff cried out. His face showed the anguish Abel felt. "That's part of the reason I'm flying like an arrow to Lindron. I hope to get to the Tabernacle and overturn this insane directive. I promise you, heads will roll when I get there. It's madness. It can't possibly come from Zentrum himself."

Oh, but it can, Abel thought.

Treville was the strong wall, the lurking force, that protected Lindron from eastern invasion. For nearly forty years, Joab Dashian had seen to it that Treville stood strong.

His father had always claimed that any competent man could do the same.

Nobody believed that.

If Joab Dashian had been removed—

Possibly assassinated, Abel forced himself to think.

—the eastern door had been thrown open for the Blaskoye.

Zentrum had been denied his Blood Wind from the north. But he was going to have it from the east.

Abel had a feeling von Hoff was not going to receive the reception in Lindron that he expected.

Be careful, my old friend. The head that rolls may be your own.

Everything was about to change. Zentrum was making his move.

Which meant it was time for Abel to make his own. Von Hoff was giving him an army to do it with.

The hammer to von Hoff's anvil?

To cold hell with that. He fingered the hilt of his saber (which he'd at least remembered to wear).

No, he would be Joab Dashian's sword.

PART ELEVEN

The Fuse

The Present

1

Ruslan Kerensky stood at the low pass and looked to the east. It was a glorious sight. A miracle, really. And he had made it happen.

He was surrounded by the Council of Law-givers, now *his* council. His men, carefully chosen for their purity, their steadfastness, their devotion to him as a leader touched by a god.

Such devotion was justified. The tribes were united under the Blaskoye—at least as united as they'd ever been. It wasn't a unity based on martial drum banging, either. It was a unity based on belief. Belief in Taub's promise. Believe in Taub's voice, Law-giver Kerensky, to make that promise real.

Always before there was doubt, division. Mere men at war.

And what was Taub's promise? It was that the Farmers would be crushed, and the Land would be theirs.

No more scrounging for a living in the desert. No more herding, trading, fighting for water rights, daks, and women.

Now each man would have all the water and women he could desire. The Land would belong to the People of Taub, and they would be the Farmers' masters. The voice of Taub had foretold it. He, Kerensky, had foretold it.

He'd been laughed at by some—laughed at until they choked on that laughter.

No one doubted his ferocity now.

He needed to share this moment with someone beyond his circle of disciples, however. They, of course, already venerated him. Nor could he gloat to his gathered sheiks.

The voice in his mind—the voice of Taub in his myriad forms— had made Kerensky a special promise. Command over the life and death of all was to be given to him. The Law-giver had hardly believed it when the voice had spoken. He'd longed for such power since . . . since his childhood, his childhood of being the studious outcast. The runt.

The voice said that he was to rule the Guardians themselves. They would be made to surrender to his will.

All he had to do was follow the sacred commands, and all would be his.

He felt very alone. *This must be how a god feels.*

"We are to make for Lindron as a vanguard," he told his sheiks. "They will pretend to ask for our alliance, but truly it will be a capitulation."

"Surrender? Without a fight?"

"It will be like Orash." Kerensky pointed to the Land before them. "Look at what Taub has done yet again. Where is the army of Treville? Where is this Dashian you fear? Where is his son? Taub has destroyed them! The mighty hand of Taub is with us!"

"Yet the Guardians have returned to the city. It will not be like Orash."

"It doesn't matter!" The pass was hot and nearly windless today, but Kerensky found himself screaming to be heard, to somehow get the point through their stubborn heads. "It doesn't matter in the least! You'll get your fight, but not with the Guardians of Lindron. They are Taub's now."

"But Law-giver, we are no more than fifty sheiks here. Surely they will slaughter us and spread our entrails upon the walls of the city in warning. Should we not wait for the ten thousand behind us to cross the pass? We have a mighty force gathered. We should use them."

"We shall not wait at all," Kerensky replied. "We have something better than a horde."

They looked at him in shock. What could be better than a horde?

"Taub has already taken the Tabernacle. He has cast out the false god Zentrum, and it is his now."

He smiled a toothy smile at the sheiks.

"Isn't this glorious news?"

There was worry on their faces.

Kerensky shook his head. "Oh, you of little faith," he said. He considered them benignly, as an adult might his wayward children. "Taub will provide."

Dust take them! He'd given them Orash with barely a fight, hadn't he?

"Taub has given you each, down to the lowliest lord, a twelve hand of slaves."

"But slaves that are children yet!"

"Yes. Petulant Farmer children."

"They must be beaten daily."

Fools, thought Kerensky. *He'd led them here and was prepared to give them that jewel of the Land, Lindron. What did he have to do to convince them? To follow Ruslan Kerensky was to follow the will of a god. Of all gods.*

The fools must be shown.

"You herd of geldings. You don't deserve this prize, yet you will have it. I will present it to you, with Taub's help. I will go into the city ahead of you. I will go with only my Council, and I tell you that we will not be molested. Instead, we'll be met by a guard of honor and escorted in as lords of the city."

"But Master Kerensky, going there with your thirteen will be suicide."

Kerensky smiled. "For another man, yes. But for the Voice of Taub? I don't think so. You remain here, cowards, until I return and fetch you. You will be made to witness and proclaim."

"How long shall we wait, master? The men have gathered to attack. They will be restive."

"Ten days. Set up camp. Surely you can keep them at the ready for ten days?"

"We can, master."

"Then so be it."

Kerensky climbed onto his dont—a smallish, easily managed animal—and bowed the shallow bow of departure to the sheiks. With a motion of his hand he summoned his Councilmen to ride behind him.

Then Kerensky did something curious. This was noted by the sheiks. The Councilmen had seen it before. He placed a thumb into his mouth and pushed upward on his palate. There was a flash of whiteness within his mouth that wasn't teeth, but something behind his top set of teeth. Did he have a second set growing there like the sea beasts that sometimes fed on the Flanagans?

"Taub is strong. The Land is ours. He will give the Land to me, and I will give it to you. I am the River of my people."

Kerensky spat a trail of nesh juice to the ground when he was done speaking. He then spun his dont and tore down the trail from the pass into the Land. His sheiks watched him in wonder. If what he said was true, then the promise of the centuries would be true: the Land would belong to the Blaskoye.

But who could believe such a spineless runt?

He was also a madman.

But even if he was, they had confidence in the horde, the mighty horde gathered to the east. He was useful in this regard. Give the common warrior belief in a prophesy to fight for. As for themselves, they would take numbers and gunpowder. *That* was the wind: the horde, not Kerensky. A wind bringing blood and tears to the Farmers. A wind carrying the true promise of Taub: that for every man strong enough to grasp them, there would be limitless herds of donts and daks for the taking.

Herds. Gunpowder. Women. Slaves.

What else should a true man want? For what other treasures did a real man live?

Let the runt go and die. He had served his purpose.

Kerensky smiled as the wind whipped past his face. He knew something the sheiks did not, a secret that would make all the difference.

Taub and Zentrum were one.

The Blaskoye were meant to ride down the Valley from the north, but the crushing victory of the Guardians in Progar had plugged the Valley and made that impossible.

An attack from the east would do just as well.

Zentrum and Taub. Taub and Zentrum.

What did it matter?

They were all going to be taught a lesson. The sheiks, the Farmers. They all would bow down.

They may call him the runt. Did they think he didn't know? Let them say it, for now.

This runt was about to rule the world.

2

The Present
Lindron
477 Post Tercium

Timon Athanaskew waited outside the Inner Sanctum as General Zachary von Hoff, now officially confirmed as commandant of the Guardian Corps, received his instruction at the Eye of Zentrum.

As von Hoff's aide and next in command, he was required to present himself for instruction after von Hoff's audience was complete.

The process was taking much longer than it should. Most meetings with Zentrum were over very quickly, although those who experienced them reported that it seemed to them they'd been communing with Zentrum for several watches, even days. Timon had never had an audience, and wasn't looking forward to this one, yet he'd stood by at guard many times. He wondered how Zentrum would react to the fact that Timon no longer believed Zentrum was God.

He'd thought about lying or at least holding back the whole truth, but he knew from Abel's experience with Zentrum that this was not possible. Zentrum would plumb the depths of the mind, and if you hid your thoughts you risked going insane as Zentrum dug them out.

Timon was willing to undergo whatever chastisement he had to. Let Zentrum punish him. All he really wanted was to retain his command staff position—for it was from this position that he hoped to launch the "special project" he'd been conceiving since the day the Corps had marched into Progar and found it devoid of children.

He'd sought and received von Hoff's approval. If and when the Blaskoye were defeated and the capital secure, he would allow Timon to take a brigade-strength unit into the Redlands to seek the Progar child slaves, and to punish those who had taken them away in bondage.

He'd held on to that promise for months, through it all: the devastation of the soul he'd felt when he entered Orash and saw what had happened. The agony of losing his arm after he'd believed it was healing. And the extreme discomfort he felt in fighting for a military whose goals he no longer believed in.

I will endure this, he told himself time and again, *to have a real chance to carry out my oath. I will seek them. I will find them. I will free them.*

But to go into the Redlands unprepared and without a substantial fighting force would be to concede defeat before he even got started.

Timon's brother Reis stood with him nearby. They had greeted one another warmly enough when Timon returned, but Timon had immediately noticed that there was something different about his brother. Reis seemed to be going to seed. His curly hair had grown long and unkempt. Reis had preferred a cut close to the skull since he was young. And he was putting on fat. It wasn't that much yet, but there was an unhealthiness to Reis's skin color that accompanied the new pudginess.

He's given up exercising, Timon had immediately thought. He'd given his brother the benefit of the doubt. Maybe his duties in the Tabernacle didn't permit time for physical workouts. Too bad, then. Reis had been fanatical about them for years.

"Have you been in yet—in there, I mean?" Timon whispered to Reis and nodded toward the entranceway. There was no specific injunction against talking in the hall outside the Inner Sanctum, but Timon got the feeling that it might be frowned upon.

Reis nodded. "Last month," he said. "After my promotion to chief of staff to his holiness the Abbot."

"And?"

"It's overwhelming," Reis said. "I was given to see ... I shared the mind of Zentrum and understood him, if only for the blink of eye. He showed me his worry over mankind. He showed me his plans to keep us safe from our own worst nature."

"I see," Timon answered. "And you accept those plans, whatever the cost?"

"I am Zentrum's priest. I must."

"Do you approve of them?"

"What has that got to do with it?" Reis answered. There was disconnection, even fear, in Reis's eyes.

"Nothing, I suppose," Timon said. "I suppose I'll find out what he wants me to know soon enough."

Reis shot Timon a troubled glance. "This kind of talk is not good, brother, especially here."

"I'm sorry if I upset you."

"I'm merely concerned for your safety."

"Thanks."

At that moment, there were footsteps from within, and von Hoff emerged. Von Hoff walked several steps toward the exitway without looking to left or right. Then he stopped, seemingly unable to figure out what to do next. Timon went to stand beside him.

"How did it go, General?" he asked.

Von Hoff turned toward Timon, a bewildered look on his face. "Who the cold hell are you?" he demanded.

Timon was taken aback. "Major Timon Athanaskew, your XO, sir."

Von Hoff stared at Timon several eyeblinks longer. Finally, he nodded and said. "Of course. Now I remember. Major Athanaskew." Von Hoff smiled, but his gaze remained fixed like a hawk on Timon.

His pupils, Timon thought. *They are pinpricks. And yet this hallway is shadowy, only lit by torch. What has happened to the general?*

Von Hoff pointed toward the door. "You're next, Major Athanaskew." When he saw Timon hesitate, he added jauntily, "Don't worry. It doesn't hurt. You'll enjoy it, Major."

"Thank you, sir. I hope so."

There's something wrong. Something very wrong here. This is not the Zachary von Hoff I know. He's a brooding bringer of gloom. I don't know who this happy warrior is, but it can't be my commander.

Suddenly von Hoff shuddered, as if he'd been punched in the

stomach. He coughed and doubled over, his hands on his knees. He trembled, as if every muscle in his body were tensed. Then he covered his mouth in another cough. After another moment, he rose, and when he did Timon saw that he had a spatter of blood on his hand.

"General, perhaps it would be better if I accompany you back to headquarters. I can return here as soon as possible and—"

"Run!" von Hoff whispered hoarsely, wiping his lips clean of blood. "Run, Athanaskew!"

He looked up. "It's too late for me," he said. Then von Hoff shook violently again, as if he were shivering in cold air. He colored, pointing angrily toward the Inner Sanctum entranceway. "I order you to go for your interview, Major," he said hotly. "Lawgiver Athanaskew, speak with your brother."

"Best do as he says," Reis said. Reis held out his hands imploringly. "It's for the best, Timon. You'll see."

Timon turned and stared at the entrance to the Inner Sanctum a moment longer.

"I will not enter," he said.

"Brother, you cannot stand against the will of God."

Timon looked back to Reis. His brother's reasonable demeanor had turned sour. His arms were crossed, and he was scowling.

"This is wrong, Reis."

"It's all sunlight or darkness for you, isn't it? Like always." Reis hook his head sadly, then motioned to the two guards. "Help the major in."

One of the men unshouldered his musket. Both advanced on Timon.

Timon hardly noticed them. He stared at his brother. "I won't forget, Reis," he said. "Now you are nothing to me."

A guard took him by the elbow while the other pointed a musket at Timon. Timon shook off the hand.

"All right," he said. He looked at the man with the musket. He was trembling, his lip quivering. "Put that away before you shoot yourself. I'll go."

Timon stared at Reis and von Hoff a moment longer, then spun on his heels. He walked quickly to the Inner Sanctum entrance. The two guards there—Timon recognized them. Both had served under him in Tabernacle Security as sergeants—backed away warily. Timon moved past them and into the room.

A figure in white robes stood at the crystalline rear wall. His hand was touching the wall, the Eye of Zentrum, as if he were in communion. He moved to the side quickly when he saw Timon enter, and placed himself behind an oil lamp dais to one side.

Timon barely got a glimpse of twinkling eyes and a bearded face.

What he did see—saw without a doubt—was the edge of the white robe.

A blue hem. A double blue hem on the robe.

Timon stood still a moment as his brain assimilated what it had observed.

Blaskoye.

Twin blue lines.

Blaskoye nobility. But here?

The answer came to Timon as soon as he'd formed the question.

Cutting a deal.

Cutting a deal, just like with Orash.

If he still believed in Zentrum's divinity, he supposed the shock would have stunned him into passivity.

Now it made him wonder that he hadn't seen it all before.

Now it made him angry.

Enter into my presence, Timon Athanaskew. Know the mind of Zentrum.

Timon turned and did as von Hoff had urged him. He ran. He blew past the guards, the startled priests, and commanders.

"Stop him," shouted von Hoff—or the man who had once been von Hoff.

Another man might not have made it out of the Tabernacle alive. But Timon had lived, studied, and served here most of his life. There wasn't a passageway in the enormous complex he didn't know.

Besides, he had no intention of getting out, at least not yet.

The hunt was thorough, but no one expected to find Timon where he had gone: Guardian Corps staff headquarters. Men looked up when their sweating, panting, newly minted colonel erupted into the room. He quickly gathered the officers who were there.

"Listen to me quickly. We are in a devil's bargain with the Blaskoye. I do not know why, but I cannot support it. I'm leaving now. I must flee the city. But if any of you wish to join me, take to the Giants and I will find you. Bring as many of the men as will join you. You have three days, and then I will leave. Do you understand? The Giants." He looked to Bunch. "Give me your pistol, Major." Bunch, startled, handed the weapon over. Timon stuffed it into his waistband. "Three days," he repeated, then left as quickly as he'd entered.

He left behind a stunned crew of majors and captains, each weighing what he'd been told with what a man they had reason to trust their lives with had just said.

Crazy. The colonel had stones loose in his head.

When the armed search party finally thought to check in Corps headquarters, Timon was long on his way out of the city.

And although they had high regard for him, most of the staff officers were convinced Timon was quite insane.

That is, until they received their orders that day from General von Hoff. They were to ally with the Blaskoye against the enemy within.

Cascade.

The traitor Dashian.

Three days later, they came in trickles and then torrents. That night, Timon moved them out. Their pathway lit only by the pale light of Levot, two thousand Guardians marched north from the Giants.

In the morning, two battalions gave chase, but their hearts weren't in the pursuit. All knew it must end with Guardian slaughtering Guardian. They pulled back once the deserters crossed into Ingres. Word had come that they were needed back in the capital. The Blaskoye horde had crossed into southern Treville and were making their way south toward the capital. It was time to put their new orders into practice.

Fantastically, they were to make the Blaskoye welcome.

After an alliance was negotiated, they would move north together to crush the rebellion in Cascade. To take down the last Dashian.

It was a strange arrangement, some might say an impossible arrangement, but the general had been very specific, and the Abbot backed him up.

The general and the Abbot were the chosen of Zentrum.

His might and his voice.

They must know what they were doing.

God must know what he was doing.

Mustn't he?

3

Bruneberg District Military Headquarters
Cascade District
477 Post Tercium

Trading and commerce paved the streets of Bruneberg. Literally. When a commitment on a barter chip was kept and the value redeemed, the chit was smashed. These shards were swept out daily from the merchant shops and counting houses. Pieces of broken chits covered the streets in a layer a thumb's length thick. They were trod and trod, and eventually the edges wore away, and they became almost indistinguishable from paving gravel. That is, except that bits of glyphs remained, shattered words and numbers. Promises discharged, remitted, or reneged upon. Puzzles that would never be solved again.

And after four years as Cascade District DMC, they felt like his streets, as well. They would never be as beautiful as the streets of Lindron: carefully laid out and lined with flowers. But they possessed a sort of charm. People worked for a living in this town, and it showed.

Abel crunched along from a visit to the gunpowder works at the River where the Silent Brothers churned out their magical powder, kerning it in a huge barrel, many times larger than a man at full height and filled with fist-sized balls of pure lead—because lead did not make sparks. He turned into the garrison, received and returned a salute, and strode into his office in the HQ building.

"Morning, Colonel," said his new XO, Metzler, whom he'd

recalled from Montag Island and appointed as his second-in-command. "Received incoming messages via flitterdak. The animal looks like a Lindron flyer."

"Are they on my desk?"

"Yes, colonel, they are."

"Good. Thank you, Metzler."

Abel entered his office. It was spare, with only a utilitarian work table and two chairs. The note was rolled out on the table. It was made of thin, gossamer papyrus and the ink was written in a tiny hand, as if the author wished to cram as much as possible into the delivery vial strapped to the flitterdak's leg.

> *I don't have much time, and I wanted to get this information to you quickly. The enemy is within. About fifteen Blaskoye have entered the Tabernacle, and a horde of many thousands has crossed Low Pass. It's said the Blaskoye in the Tabernacle are in communion with Zentrum. Citizens aren't to harm them. And that horde is not headed toward Lindron. It's headed toward you, Abel.*

So that's how it's going to be, he thought. *Zentrum gave them Orash to sack, and now he's sending them toward Bruneberg to harass me. Treville is out of it, now that Father has been removed. Zentrum must know I am the last threat he needs to deal with. Me and the Cascade Regulars.*

> *Meanwhile, the Guardian Corps arrived and conferred at the Tabernacle with the Blaskoye. Yes, you read this correctly. I've learned from a source in the Tabernacle that they have gone to Ingres to set up defenses. These defense works stretch east and west, Abel. They are to become a base of operations to the north.*

So von Hoff's temporary appointment was rescinded, Abel thought. *Not a surprise. I only hope they didn't throw him in prison when they sacked him. Or to the carnadons.*

The next line sent a chill up Abel's spine.

> *The Goldies moving into Ingres are commanded by Zachary von Hoff. Yes, your friend. Abel, he has an alliance*

with the Blaskoye and they are fighting alongside him.
I repeat: the Goldies and the horde are in alliance.
You are their declared enemy.
We will do what we can in Lindron to hamstring
them from behind. But you will face the brunt of this
attack. If you fall, the Blood Winds will blow.
Destroy them, my love. If you can't do it for Duisberg,
do it for me.

M.

Von Hoff.

How could that be? Surely von Hoff could see that an alliance with the Blaskoye was madness. They could at any moment turn traitor and attack the Goldies without warning.

Blaskoye in the Tabernacle.

Von Hoff couldn't be fooled by this.

He just couldn't.

And yet Abel did not for one moment doubt the provenance of the message. This was Mahaut's writing.

And there was the keyword they'd always used. No one else in the Land, no one on the planet, knew what this world used to be called.

No one but himself and Mahaut.

Duisberg.

The only possible way it could be subterfuge was if she were kidnapped and the keyword taken from her by torture. That was possible. But to what end? His Scouts had reported. There was no Blaskoye activity to his east or barbarian movement in the less inhabited west.

Every sign, every bit of intelligence, said they had gone to Awul-alwaha and dropped off their child slaves with the women of the tribes. Then, after a meeting of several days, the horde had ridden forth. Reports placed it at over ten thousand strong.

It had headed southeast.

With this message from Mahaut, there was now no doubt where they had gone.

Von Hoff was in league with the Blaskoye.

He was going to have to fight the Corps and the horde.

He'd expected to have a near impossible task before him when he moved to strike.

But not von Hoff.

Somewhere in the back of his mind, Abel had always believed von Hoff would understand, would come over to Abel's side.

In his fantasies, it was Zachary von Hoff who rode into Lindron with Abel nearby, von Hoff's man as always.

I've lost Center. I've lost Raj.

I may have lost Father.

Now I've lost my teacher and friend.

Abel sat back in his chair. He slowly rolled the small papyrus back into a tight scroll, no longer than his thumb, no thicker than his little finger.

Outside, he heard the peaceful gurgling of the flitterdak that had brought the scroll. It was reunited with its mate, and the two were chirping joyfully to one another. At least he thought it was joy. Who knew what really went on in the mind of the creatures? It was a programmed response. All flitterdaks danced the same courting dance, made the same noises.

Abel poured himself a cup of wine from the pitcher on his desk. He took a sip, contemplated the shadows of light produced by the reed-grass outside his window, planted to shield the building from the worst of the midday sun.

My friend, he thought. *I will have to come for you now. And I know you'll be waiting.*

Thrice-damn Zentrum for doing this, for turning friend against friend.

Yet it was done. He would no longer take commands from Zachary von Hoff. He would fight him if he must. He would kill him if he could.

Abel took up the cup of wine again and drained it. He set it back down gingerly beside the pitcher. The wine was good Cascade white, from the district's northern vineyards. He only now noticed it was chilled.

Metzler must have put it in the springhouse overnight. He was a good man for details.

He's my man now, Abel thought.

Most of the Cascade Regulars were, and more would become so.

They'll soon enough understand that Cascade is von Hoff's target. He won't stop with me. He'll destroy them all.

And then the Blaskoye will destroy him.

Zentrum will have his Blood Wind after all.

Unless Cascade fights.

We have the means.

Landry's revolving rifles, brought down from the Orash foundry, filled the garrison warehouses and ammunition depots. There were enough for each man and to spare. Abel had put the Regulars to practicing with them as soon as he'd returned to Cascade.

A month of practice. Would it be enough?

The decision is mine, Abel thought. *We are ready.*

Von Hoff. What a loss.

But what was done was done.

He was beholden to no one.

Only to a whisper from the distant past fallen from the sky, and now extinguished by a malevolent fraud of a god.

Extinguished, yes—except in my memory, Abel thought.

To cold hell with Zentrum.

Center and Raj had left him with the hard truth. They'd given him a plan. The plan was no longer destiny. In fact, he might be doomed and not yet know it. Still, the plan, the calling, was a legacy he would honor.

He would defend the Land. He would save the future. Or he would die trying.

There was no one left but him to do it.

He was the general now.

PART TWELVE

The Return

The Present

1

Treville District
High Cliff Scout Base
477 Post Tercium

The cavernous fortress was filled with a thin haze of cookfire smoke. The faint odor of dont acid and dont shit wafted in from the connected stable in another part of the cave. Light streamed through several holes laboriously pounded dozens of elbs through the rock with a riveroak staff a handwidth in diameter. Abel knew because he'd helped pound through one of those holes when he'd been fourteen years old and serving out his first stint with the Treville Scouts, as gopher and waterboy. The task had taken a week of steady hammering with a rotating gang of three men with granite weighted sledges. He could hear the steady trickle of the water filling the year-round pool in the depths of the fortress's main cave.

He hadn't been here in eight years, but it still felt like home. "Something rotten is going on," Abel said. "I need your help."

Abel was speaking to the gathered Scouts, about thirty men, who sat on their haunches in a circle around him. Their captain, Lausner, had served as a lieutenant under Abel when Abel had been captain of the Scouts. The rest of the Scouts were on patrol in the Redlands. There were about two hundred of them out there at any given time, moving in squad-sized groups, independent, resourceful, and resilient as ever. These men present would carry word to the others.

The one Scout missing whom Abel had very hoped would be here was his old friend and mentor Sergeant Kruso, a man so completely a Scout that he spoke the Redlands patois as a first language, though he understood Landish well enough. Kruso was on patrol breaking in a squad of newbie recruits and was expected back soon.

"I'm sure you've wondered about the cutbacks, the supply problems, the lack of powder. Let me tell you something: this isn't like the bad old days. The reason you don't have ball and powder is not because of problems at the Bruneberg Powderworks. Bruneberg ships plenty of ammunition down-River. But it isn't ending up with the Scouts anymore. Why is that? Because there is something rotten in the Land."

"Tell us what to do, Commander," said Lausner. "We are few. The Land is vast."

Abel looked around at the windburned faces turned toward him. Each was silently asking him the same question as their commander.

They're listening closer than they ever did when I was their captain, Abel thought. *Of course, most of them knew me too well. They'd seen me start off as a bumbling Valley boy without a bit of sense, but with an unquenchable to desire to be a Scout and have adventures.*

He'd almost gotten himself killed a few times learning the ropes.

Now the Scouts were paying full attention. A Dashian was speaking, and there was no name the Treville Scouts trusted more. He knew to put this down to his father's near godlike repute among the Scouts rather than to anything he himself had done.

"I want to take you, and as many Regulars as we can muster on short notice"—*And who are willing to turn traitor on the new DMC*, he thought—"and meet those bastards who are coming up from Lindron to finish us off. I reckon we'll engage them somewhere on the Plains of Ingres."

"You want us to fight Goldies?" Lausner asked.

Here it was. The point on which all else turned. To slaughter barbarian Redlanders was one thing, but to turn upon your own brothers in arms? The prospect was enough to wrench any loyal heart.

"That's exactly the attitude they're hoping for," Abel said. "But you've seen the score. Joab Dashian has been kidnapped, maybe killed. Prelate Zilkovsky, too. You've seen who was put in those places, and heard the orders you're given. Abandon the Southern District? You know this is crazy. Defending against the Redland invaders is why there are Regulars, why there are Scouts. So why? What do you think it means?" He looked out over the upturned faces. "Anyone?"

From the back, a voice rang out. "Them be not tha Landsons thet tha claimet ta be!"

A dust cloud and the rattle of doffed gear falling to the floor in the rear. Abel would have recognized the voice anywhere. Kruso had returned from patrol.

"That's right," Abel said. "They may wear the red and white sash, but only because they've stolen the rightful power, the true authority of this district. You know who that is, don't you?"

A low murmur as a few voices called out "Dashian, Dashian."

The call was soon taken up, repeated over and over. It grew into a cheer. The din became a roar in the fortress cavern.

"Dashian!"

"So those we go to meet may be misinformed. They may be misguided. But one thing is for certain: they are fighting on the wrong side of the Land and the Law. We—"

Another crescendo of cheering. "Dashian, Dashian!"

Abel let it dampen, but not quite die down, before continuing. "We are Irisobrian's men, the keepers of the true flame."

He took out the box of lucifers he always carried, held it up. Almost every man in the room had a similar box in his pocket. "Men fail in their understanding. Even generals. Even priests. Trust the Lady."

"The Lady, the Lady!"

Irisobrian, the Lady, was at the center of the Scouts' religious sect. She was Zentrum's mother. She was supposed to have suckled the young Zentrum for forty days and forty nights at the beginning of the world, her dead body still producing milk even after she'd been struck down by sickness at the River's edge.

Most of the Scouts followed the sect of Irisobrianism and venerated her. It was officially a heresy, but was tolerated by commanders. For their part, its practitioners kept their devotion very quiet. It was only after five years among them that Abel had been invited to one of their secret conclaves conducted in caves along the Escarpment. He hadn't joined, but he'd found the main ritual of the sect, the communion feast of the Lady's body, interesting, and was amazed at how these otherwise rough and ready practical men took to something so symbolic and spiritually minded.

Now I know that calling on a higher power is something men need when they put their lives on the line—even men who otherwise have no belief at all, Abel thought. *At least I can call on the Lady without it sickening me. Don't know if I could stomach acting in the name of Zentrum.*

"And when we face those who are following wrong orders, we can't go soft. We'll have to fight them as we would the hardest Redland devil. Because they'll be much, much stronger. But we are strong, too."

He raised his revolving rifle.

"I'm going to equip all of you with these," Abel said. "That's what's in that train of wagons you saw trailing behind me on the first plateau. You aren't fools. You know we have to have some kind of an advantage against those misguided, son-of-a-bitch Goldies or we'll get our butts kicked, and this is it."

There were murmurs in the crowd of Scouts, and Abel heard the word he most feared, "nishterlaub," whispered about. He looked out over the men. Was he going to lose them here?

Law and Land, I wish I had that thrice-damned Raj to guide me, he thought. When it came to the behavior of soldiers, Raj's advice had always been right on. *Now I'm flying like a blind flitterdak. I just hope I learned something from all those years with the voices.*

There was movement at the rear of the crowd. Men were shoved aside, gently but firmly. Other men turned to look to see what the commotion was, understood it, then parted and formed a way through their ranks.

Kruso stepped forward. "Tha Commander's pardon ta git bah begging, bot whut the cold hell do be thet in yer hand? Wilt tha allow fer meh a touch heben?"

Abel nodded and wordlessly passed the rifle down to Kruso. The Scout sergeant took it, examined it, and gave a little smile. He found the retaining pin to the revolving chamber with ease and popped out the cylinder. It slid out still attached to its crane-like armature as Landry had designed it.

"Tha shots—how many bahfor reload?"

"Six," said Abel. "And then you can put in another load with six more."

Kruso looked over his shoulder at the other Scouts. He must have flashed a look of happy amazement, because suddenly there was expectant silence in the cave, a collective intake of breath. The sound of water from the rear of the cavern was the only sound.

Kruso turned his attention back to the cylinder.

"Thes'll tha percussion cap be," he muttered. "Las see whut lies baneath." With his battered nails, he grasped what he took to be the cap and pulled it upward. Attached to the cap (with an extremely strong adhesive, Abel knew) was a papyrus cylinder. On its end was a dome-shaped bullet.

"Tha cold hell!" shouted Kruso.

He held the bullet up for all to see.

Abel smiled. "Cap, powder, and ball in one package," he declared. "It's got a rifled barrel, and will fire six times before it needs reloading. It's got Golitsin sights, for those who remember the breechloaders. And after you get the hang of reloading her, you can pull out the rod and unpin that cylinder from that armature then pop in a different cylinder with another preloaded six rounds—fast as a single shot with a musket. Maybe faster."

"Et shoot can ich, Commander?" asked Kruso.

"Hell, yes," said Abel. "Take it over to the long range and see what you can do with it."

He passed a woven reed box to Kruso. "One hundred rounds," he said. "Not that a dirtkicker like you can count that high, Sergeant Kruso."

Kruso let out a guffaw and took the cartridge box. Then he looked down and considered the cylinder, still in loading position.

"Und swabben whut of?" he said.

"It uses a different kind of gunpowder," Abel said. "Hotter burning. Comes from up north, Progar-way. Burns so hot it turns the papyrus to vapor and doesn't smoke as much at all. You won't need to clean the chambers or barrel for many, many reloads."

"Und thas pinkel?"

"It's a grip for your stock hand, to get it out of the way of the muzzle blast. Or a tough son-of-a-bitch like you could just wear leather gloves." Kruso nodded. His main questions were answered, but Abel was sure that after testing out the gun, the Scout would come back with many more.

He strode with the rifle, carefully pointed upward, through the crowd of Scouts, all of whom were eager to have a look.

"Cum yeh ta tha range thun!" he proclaimed loudly to the pressing Scouts. "Yeh cahn thar gawken!"

I've got Kruso on my side, Abel thought. *And if you've got Kruso, then you've got the Treville Scouts.*

Abel chuckled, remembering what a devout Irisobrian Kruso was. "Thank you, Lady," he whispered softly.

Scouts didn't exactly march, and the Treville Scouts had never in memory set out as one big unit. They were hardly used to moving in unison either on the ground or dontback in a company-sized unit, much less the brigade-sized band of men that Lausner was leading. But what they lacked in organization, they made up for in speed and the ability to remain fully operational in the roughest terrain. After calling in the entire force, there had not been enough donts to go around at High Cliffs. Abel hoped to rectify this as soon as they reached the rendezvous point midway along the Canal, but for now at least half the Scouts were on foot.

Either on dont or on foot, they followed a path along the Escarpment and descended into the Valley near the Lilleheim pass, and over the very spot where, as Abel well remembered, Mahaut had received her near-fatal wound in battle.

Abel led them north of Lake Treville. A march through Hestinga, which was on the southern shore, was bound to meet resistance from a portion of the Regulars. That would mean shooting and death in the streets. The thought of fighting against Treville Regulars, a force his father had built almost from scratch, churned Abel's stomach.

He camped among the sole remaining stand of cottonwood trees at the Canal inlet to Treville Lake. The Canal had once been lined with these beautiful trees, but they'd been cut down and made into chevaux-de-frise used to impale the charging Blaskoye horde during the Battle of the Canal. Prelate Zilkovsky had ordered the banks of the Canal replanted, but it would be a generation before those trees grew to full size.

The next day, the Scouts swept westward, a league away from the Canal, and then took a sharp turn to the south and approached the prearranged crossing point.

If only Center were here, he could tell me whether Landry has got there with the boats—or at least give me the odds, Abel thought. More than a friend—if friend he had ever been—Abel missed the presence of Center as a tactical advantage. Now he had no more farsighted, battlefield-encompassing visions. No more concise and frightening scenarios depicting in harsh detail the implications of a bad choice.

Now I'm just as blind as any other commander, Abel thought. *But I* was *taught by the best.*

As he neared the Canal, his worst fears began to be realized. There was no line of boats along the shore waiting to take a large force across. As far as Abel could see, there was only one boat.

"What the cold hell has happened to Major Landry?" he said. Lausner, riding beside Abel, could only shrug.

Nevertheless, they moved forward, Abel contemplating the long march ahead if they must skirt the Canal. Then, when they were a fieldmarch away, Abel heard the Scouts in the leading party give out a yell. Were they under attack? But the yell had a different timber.

Then it repeated itself, and he recognized what he was hearing: a cheer. Abel pushed forward toward the boat, if that's what it was. It was only after the Scouts parted and let him through that he could make out what had brought on the cheer.

What he'd seen was, indeed, a single boat. It was turned sideways, parallel to the Canal. And a few paces behind it, also parallel to the Canal, was another boat, and behind that another.

And there, walking across the planking that connected all the boats together strode Major Landry Hoster with a shit-eating grin on his face.

"So you finally got to make your pontoon bridge," Abel said to him when he got within shouting distance. "How does it feel to walk on water?"

"Come across and find out!" Landry shouted back at him.

He didn't cross immediately, but waited for Kruso and some rear elements, and rode with them.

"It's good to have you with me, my friend," Abel said to Kruso.

"Redlands brak and brin ever tha same, sir, und ever same isse Kruso."

There was a great deal of commotion when Abel got to the south side of the bridge. He left Lausner to sort it out and rode on toward a small rise where Metzler, his Cascade Regulars adjunct, had set up a command post. As he rode toward the spot, he saw a flash of gold ahead of him. He looked again, and saw it was the jackets of several men standing around a table drinking what smelled like pungent hard cider. It took him a moment to understand what he was seeing.

Goldies.

He dismounted, handed Nettle's reins to an orderly, and waited as one of the men dressed as a Guardian strode toward him. The man wasn't smiling, and he didn't seem at all agitated, either. He turned for a moment, and Abel saw the unmistakable armless silhouette of Timon Athanaskew. He'd grown a beard.

"You? Whiskers?" Abel said.

Timon came to attention and saluted. "Colonel Athanaskew reporting for duty, sir," he said. "I bring with me portions of the Guardian Corps Third and Second Battalions and a company of cavalry. All together about two thousand men, sir. We call ourselves the True Goldies and fly the blue and yellow."

"Two thousand Guardians," said Abel. "Major Athanaskew, it is good to see you."

"Likewise, sir."

"So, the whiskers?"

"It's the fashion among command staff in your army these days," Timon answered.

"I wasn't aware of that."

"It's about to be," Timon said. "Because, frankly, I got tired of one-handed shaving."

Abel laughed, and then became more serious. "And von Hoff?"

"Regrettably, he is the leader of the forces gathering in Ingres."

Abel shook his head sadly. "Ingres. He always hated that district."

"Yes, sir," said Timon. "General von Hoff is not really himself these days. At all."

"And you?"

"I avoided the Inner Sanctum. After seeing what happened to von Hoff in there, I know I made the wise decision." He clapped Abel on the shoulder. "Also, to join you seemed to me the way of righteousness."

"Where will that path take us, Timon?"

"After we are done down south, it will take me into the Redlands."

"You mean to find the children of Progar?"

"I mean to free every last one of them." This thought finally got Timon to crack the faintest of smiles. "Besides, you need somebody to turn your crazy ideas into fact on the ground."

"That I do," said Abel. "And your brother and sister? Your family?"

A darkness came into Timon's face. "My brother is gone. Zentrum...broke his mind, I think."

"I'm sorry."

Timon shook his head. "He calls me a zealot. But I'm not the one willing to let the world burn just because a voice in a pyramid tells me I have to."

PART THIRTEEN

The War

The Present

1

Lindron
477 Post Tercium

Mahaut had been busy in the weeks after learning of the presence of Hiram Zilkovsky and Joab Dashian in the dungeons of the Tabernacle Security.

She began to build an army. Not by some definitions. Not a cohesive mass of armed men. First, it wasn't all men, and there were precious few weapons to go around. Bows and arrows, hot oil, rocks—partisan's weapons.

Second, an expert communication force consisting of Lindron street urchins. And, third, since most of her trusted contacts were merchants, wagons. Lots and lots of wagons.

Smuggling wanted men out of Lindron would be demanding, but hardly impossible.

The impossible part was breaking them out of the dungeon to start with.

With time, planning, and—most of all—imagination on Marone's part, the plan to free Joab Dashian and Hiram Zilkovsky had formed. It was far from perfect. It was simply the best plan Mahaut and Marone could devise, given the information and resources they had. Mahaut was aware that every moment lost might mean the men's death, and it certainly meant their prolonged agony and despair. But the plan had taken time. This was unavoidable.

It started with the whores.

There was a barracks of armed men available to stop you if you

335

attempted to go into the dungeon via the main entrance. There was, however, more than one way into the Tabernacle prison, if a person knew where to look. And it seemed every whore in the Quarter knew about the jailers' back gate. Prison duty was tedious, and there was ample time between watches to go around the corner for a drink and a bit of flesh, not necessarily in that order. The guards worked in rotating shifts, with two on and two off at any time. They might be dealt with.

The biggest problem was the priest-soldier Head of the Tabernacle Security Service. He, and only he, had the key to every cell. No one else wished to even touch them. The locks were metal and the keys—

They were ancient. They were cold to the touch. They were nishterlaub.

Zilkovsky never knew that he would feel so alone without Zentrum in his mind. For so many years he had longed to be rid of the presence that was always listening, always demanding consultation on the slightest issue to be decided, always ready to override his will with its own without explanation, apology, or seeming remorse.

And at any moment expressing his godlike will, lighting Zilkovsky's mind with fire as if it were an oil-rich wick. The process was known, in the priestly jargon, as "scanning."

Now that scanning had been taken away, pulled from him physically when the wafer was removed from the palate of his mouth, and he felt . . . as empty as a pitcher drained of wine. Dry. There was no more voice in his mind. There were no voices at all here in the dungeon except for the one that belonged to the man who had arrested him. That voice was cold, inhuman. It did not count as company of any sort.

And all was dark. Not dark like night, but utterly dark. So dark that any conception of where he was, the position of his body within the space, the slight traces of the material world in peripheral vision that told him he was in a real place, had a physical body—all that was missing. Complete darkness. He was nowhere. He had taken to hugging himself, curling up in a ball and holding his knees to his chest to feel its warmth, to avoid the creeping suspicion that he was no one, that existence itself had been yanked from him. A part of him—a small voice of what remained of sanity and humor—noted that he'd lost so much weight that assuming a fetal position was possible.

The only other thing that reminded him that he was real was feeding time. Once a day the bucket of mashed gruel was shoved into the cell. It was water and meal combined, and it was all he was going to get that day. *If* the time between feeding was a day. He had lost count, lost all track of time. The only thing that reminded him that time was passing was growing hunger and the need to urinate and defecate. For these, he was made to use the same bucket he ate from after the food was finished, and he passed it back out when the new food was delivered.

He had been a man who oversaw a district of the Land. He did best among men, wheeling and dealing for the power to accomplish things, both important and mundane, a consummate political animal. Now he was no one and nowhere. The shock of being taken from the social world was perhaps worse for him than anything else. His identity, who he was, was bound up with being the chief prelate of Treville District. He had no family, no home life other than interaction with several old and trusted retainers. All he had was his job, his position. And that had been taken in an instant. Now there was nothing but darkness to replace it.

No wonder that he was going mad.

Yet there was a trace of hope. Through the watches of long darkness there were occasional tappings that came to his cell through the walls, or through the slightest rattling of the door. Someone was out there trying to communicate. He did not know the mirror code used by the military, but he could recognize the sound of it in sonic form. This meant that a military man was nearby. Joab Dashian had been brought with him as a prisoner in the wagon from Treville. He assumed it was Joab who was tapping now.

And it was that tapping that kept any sanity he had alive. Then one day—he could not say how long since he been taken prisoner—the cell door opened and torchlight flickered inside for that brief moment. The world around him was momentarily re-created. Instead of rapidly depositing the food, taking the waste, then leaving, this time the guard lingered for a moment.

Zilkovsky, nonplussed, took the bucket and went to a corner to eat. Still the man remained, holding the torchwood and its blessed light.

"I have a message for you," the guard finally said. "You're Hiram Zilkovsky, are you not?"

"Yes," Zilkovsky answered. *I think I am.*

"There will be people coming to get you out," said the guard.

"Why are you saying this? Are you trying to go to lure me so you can kill me?"

The guard let out a low chuckle. "Now that could be what I'm up to, and I guess you're right to be suspicious," he said. "But I'm telling the truth. In two days' time my companions will break you out. It will be during the midnight watch, although you may not realize when that is in here. You must be prepared, though. Do not let anyone else know of this arrangement, not even Joab Dashian."

"I don't think that's going to be a problem," Zilkovsky answered with a shaky voice. "I haven't seen my friend Joab for several months now. At least I think they are months. It could be years." He shook his head. "I've lost count," he mumbled to himself.

"Be ready," said the other. "Tell no one."

For a time, Zilkovsky's heart filled with joy. Then nervous anticipation took its place. By the time the door unlocked and another figure stood holding a torch, he was shaking with excitement. Salvation was at hand.

But it was not salvation. It was the interrogator. The security man, his face twisted into a wicked smile.

Cloutier.

"You look as if you were expecting someone else," Cloutier said. "Let's find out who that might be."

With a gasp of dismay, Zilkovsky stumbled backward as his interrogator made his way into the cell. He fell into his bucket of slop and lay in his own waste, quivering in fear.

This was the end. This was the end.

But it wasn't. It was only the beginning of the pain.

And, in the end, he told all.

The woman let out a cry of agony and betrayal as the guards dragged her down the dungeon corridor to the chambers of the Chief of Tabernacle Security.

They had known she was coming! There was no other explanation.

"Fuck him," she said. "Fuck that boy priest! He told you, didn't he?"

Cloutier nodded his head sadly. "Athanaskew is a fool about women. He believes you are in love with him since you sent him his note. But no, he only confirmed what I already knew." The security man touched his chin. "Out of curiosity, *are* you in love with that boy?"

"I . . . I don't know how I feel." She hung her head, suppressed a sob. "I thought not. I thought my heart belonged to another. Then Reis came along and . . . now I suppose it doesn't matter anymore."

"No. It does not."

"But Reis didn't know the exact time! How did you know it was tonight?"

Cloutier made a tsking sound, accompanied by a slow shake of the head. "I'm amazed that you got this far. But it all ends here, of course. Land-heiress."

Mahaut reached for the obsidian dagger she carried near her back, under a fold in her robe. She raised the knife and attempted to put the blade to her own throat. But the guards had hold of her before she could position it. The older guard on the left shook her arm violently, and the little dagger flew from her fingers and shattered on the stone floor into a dozen dark shards.

"Foolish," said Cloutier. "But understandable." He bent down and picked up one of the pieces of obsidian, the tip of the blade, broken about midway from the hilt.

"Hold her against the wall," he said. The two guards slammed Mahaut against the stonework, momentarily knocking the breath from her lungs. She attempted to kick out at one of the guard's legs, but her soft sandals, worn to make the least noise this evening, cushioned the kick, and it did no damage.

The return kick from the guard opened a bleeding gouge along her shin, however.

She didn't want to cry out but couldn't help it when a muffled whimper of pain escaped her. At this, Cloutier smiled. "Justice comes in doses small and large, your grace," he said.

"You don't know anything about justice."

"I am the instrument, Zentrum."

"You're a piece of Zentrum's shit."

Another smile. "Your filthy words don't matter anymore, and never will again," he said. He spoke to the guards. "Hold her still."

They yanked her to attention against the wall, and Cloutier approached, looking down at the obsidian shard. "The best way is to start with something important, something that's really going to be missed," he said in a matter-of-fact tone. "I make an example. It shortens the process. There's no appeal, so don't try to make one." He reached her, and she found she was looking down at the man. He was half an elb shorter than she was. "I took an eye from Joab Dashian. From you... well, with any woman it might be her womb—but I understand that's already been done in your case." He reached down, took a fold of her robe in his hand and slowly lifted it up to expose her pelvis. "That's a nasty scar, Land-heiress Jacobson."

"Fuck you."

He let the robe drop back down. "I suppose I'll take your face," he said.

"Please, I—"

With a spasmodic ferocity, his arm shot up and his hand went around her neck.

She gasped, tried to pull back. "Please let me live," she whispered. "I beg for my life."

Cloutier shook his head. "Lord Zentrum has charged me to root out all heresy. You're going to help me with that."

"I won't give you anything."

"Really?" he said with a contemptuous laugh. "Do you know how often I hear that? That's what the false priest said, as a matter of fact, before he told me the day you set for his escape."

She didn't answered. Another whimper escaped her lips. She wanted him to hear this one. It might make things easier.

"At the end, he wanted to tell me more. He begged. But I already had what I needed."

Cloutier raised the obsidian shard and held it before Mahaut's eyes, turning it between his thumb and forefinger. It caught the red glint of the torchlight as he did so. The reddish hue blurred in her vision, and she realized she was crying.

He reached over with his other hand, and wiped one of her tears away with his thumb. Then he wiped the wetness on the sleeve of her robe, as if he were removing something unclean from his skin.

He lowered the obsidian shard, shot her another look of pity and contempt, and turned around. He motioned over his shoulder to the guards. "Bring her to interrogation," he said. "I want to do this properly."

Mahaut turned to look at the older guard on her right. Their eyes locked. She nodded, and he let go of her arm. In the next instant, he launched a fist into the face of the younger guard. He grunted as his nose split and blood spattered. He released Mahaut and staggered back. The older guard grabbed him by the shoulders, hooked a leg behind the young guard's ankle, and using the young man's momentum, sent him toppling backward with the older guard on top of him.

At the sound, Cloutier spun about with the speed of lightning. He took in the situation instantly. He was quick. She'd give him that. With another of his half-smiles he tossed away the obsidian shard still in his hand and reached for the long metal knife whose scabbard was thrust through the belt of his tunic shirt. When he pulled it out, the blade sang. This was exceptional priest-smith steel. Guardian steel.

He advanced toward her. She was taller, but from the way he moved he was clearly muscular and lithe. She'd felt as much when he held her by the throat. She had fought men. She didn't fool herself into thinking she could wrest the knife from him. If he reached her, he would kill her.

Nevertheless, she felt a wave of relief pass through her. This had been the contested point. Even after days of observation, they had not been able to tell if he carried a personal firearm.

Evidently not, she thought. *Or at least, he doesn't think he needs it down here, the fool.*

She reached between the folds at the top of her robe. The wrap crossed between her breasts, seemingly to leave a bit of cleavage exposed. It also served a much more utilitarian purpose: to give her easy access to the two-shot derringer holstered under her left arm.

She pulled it free. It was already loaded and capped, with its two hammers cocked back.

When he was two paces away, Cloutier realized his error. His eyes widened.

And I've knocked the thrice-damned smile from his face, too, she thought.

She aimed for the lower torso and pulled one of the two triggers of the derringer. The first shot jumped up and hit him mid-chest. The minié balls were 469-grain caliber, and the shot opened up a substantial flower of blood, torn fabric, and brutalized flesh.

The wound hissed and spewed for a moment until he slapped a hand over it. She'd pierced a lung.

He continued to move forward, still gripping his knife at his side, ready for an upward stab. His face was filled with anger and determination.

He must be so disappointed in himself, she thought.

She pulled the other trigger.

Another blast to the chest. The echo of a ricochet in the tunnel told her the ball had passed straight through.

Cloutier stood still. He trembled violently for a moment, as if trying to gather himself for a final attack. But it was an attack that would never come. With an odd whine—it issued from his lung—he dropped the knife and fell to one side. He hit the floor hard and his legs kicked violently as he bled out upon the flagstones.

Marone rose from atop the younger guard, who lay moaning.

"Did you have to hit him so hard?" Mahaut asked.

"Maybe not, your grace," he answered. "But I thought I might knock some sense into him about the whore."

The young guard pulled himself to a knee. "You promised!" He turned to Mahaut, pleading in his eyes. The light from the four torches in the room's corners played off his handsome features. "You promised to get her a position in service, your grace!"

"Of course we will," Mahaut said. "I think Mr. Marone was joking with you, Corporal."

The young man rubbed his bruised jaw. "Cursed hard way to have his fun, if you ask me."

"Mr. Marone is a hard man," she said. "But you need to look as if you had the shit kicked out of you, if you'll pardon my coarseness of tongue."

"I don't mind that, but he's wrong about Zadie! She's got a good heart! She's bearing my child."

Or somebody's.

She smiled, touched his shoulder. "Your Zadie will get her service position, and you can marry without shame for the child. But at the moment it would be best if you let Marone tie you up good and tight. And maybe give you a final kick or two for luck."

The young man looked at her in resignation. "I suppose the kick should be someplace that'll show."

"Not a problem, lad," Marone said.

"But first let's get those keys," Mahaut said.

"Nishterlaub," said the young guard with a shudder. "I wouldn't handle them if I were you, Land-heiress. And that man, he is... inhuman."

"Can't be helped." She motioned the muzzle of her pistol toward Cloutier. "Marone, please make sure that one is truly dead while I reload. I'll take the keys myself."

"Will do, your grace. A double-tap should do it. Then I'd just as soon not touch those keys, either."

Joab was instantly alert when his cell door opened.

When Marone held up the torch and she saw Joab's ruined right eye, Mahaut couldn't help herself. She cried out and hurried to him and hugged him. "Oh, Colonel Dashian, I'm so sorry we couldn't get here sooner."

"I'll settle for you getting here at all, Land-heiress Jacobson," Joab croaked. Oh! He needed water, and she hadn't brought any!

Then Marone reached around her and offered him a small porcelain bottle. Joab drank its contents in one gulp. A ruby red drop trickled down his chin.

"Thank you, sir," he said, handing the bottle back to Marone.

"My pleasure, Commander," Marone answered. "I see they left you with one eye, sir."

"Yes," said Joab. "Their mistake."

Prelate Zilkovsky was not so easily roused from his nearby cell. Cloutier had obviously been telling the truth about torturing the man. A portion of his arm was red from having his skin peeled. He seemed bewildered and not in the present, first loudly cursing the name of Zentrum, and then speaking to another priest, perhaps an assistant, who was, of course, not there. For a moment Mahaut believed the prelate might have to be abandoned to his fate in the dungeon. But after a quiet talk with Joab, Zilkovsky calmed down.

"So that was you, after all? The tapping?"

"It was, Hiram."

"And I wasn't just hearing things?"

"It was real. This is real, Prelate."

Though in the flickering torchlight Zilkovsky still looked battered and frightened, he did begin to obey orders.

Others in the dungeon had realized that something was

happening. Some began to shout for food and water. Some begged for release.

"The cursed bastards," Joab said. "It could as well be me. I want to help them."

Marone caught Mahaut's eyes, shook his head. Even so, Mahaut had to steel herself to keep from opening all the cell doors. But this was primarily a prison for criminals, very bad men, as well as political prisoners. She had no way of knowing who or what she would be setting free. Besides, there was no time.

"We must get out of here, Colonel," she said. "I'm afraid a general release will have to wait. You see, the night isn't close to being over, and you and the prelate need to be on your way north by morning."

2

Hestinga
Treville District

Corporal Markus Koolhaas was a dejected man. Ten years in service to the Land. Ten years training, fighting, guarding the people. All of that blown to pieces, like wheat chaff in the wind.

Koolhaas shuffled around the main practice yard of the Treville Regulars supposedly on policing duty. He'd swept up what dont shit there was a half watch ago, and there was no loose garbage. Hardly a clod of dirt out of order. Afternoon P.T. had been called off, again, by the powers that be. It was another punishment for Edict violation.

Some fool had banged his thumb or stubbed his toe or cut off a finger or something and had begun to swear like...well, like a soldier. Somewhere in that sea of oaths and imprecations, he'd dropped the cursed name of the commander, the Abbot, and Zentrum himself.

It wouldn't have mattered if one of the new officers, the pretty boys sent up from Lindron after the colonel...well, he didn't like to think of what might have happened to the colonel. Anyway, one of those dontdicks had heard the man's curses and so all nightly leaves were cancelled and the compound put on lockdown. Only groundskeepers and guards to be outside barracks. Those boys keeping the gates closed weren't any happier about this than Koolhaas, or the men stuck in the barracks, but they had their orders.

It was only midafternoon and the place already felt like a thrice-damned morgue at midnight.

Oh, what was the use?

Not so long ago, Koolhaas had been proud to hold his head high as a foot soldier of the Treville District Regulars. No longer. The Blaskoye had broken through. It was unbelievable. Disgusting. After all the years standing watch, holding the border when other districts leaked like sieves. After all that careful work, blood, heartbreak... to fall like sticks in a child's game of Tumbledown. Eight years before, he had been in on the victory, the absolute slaughter of five thousand Blaskoye riders in the rice paddies between Garangipore and Hestinga. Even last year he'd believed there was nothing he could not do, nothing he would not do for his commander.

And then one morning that commander was gone, replaced by somebody—really nobody—some functionary hastily sent from Lindron. It was like losing a father. It was like losing his own heart.

For Koolhaas, there would never be a greater soldier than Joab Dashian. The old man had held Treville together for so long, he seemed as solid as stone. As durable. As permanent.

Koolhaas had been so bewildered, then despondent when he learned that his commander had been removed and replaced. There was no word as to where Dashian might be, but it was telling that the district prelate, Zilkosky, had disappeared along with him.

Accusations of treason were spoken among the new command staff.

Dakshit.

There were other whispers going around that they'd stolen barter chits and run away to the coastlands. Others claimed they'd crossed into the Redlands with a wagon train of gunpowder to sell. It was true that there was gunpowder and ammunition missing from the armory. Whether this was coincidence or connected to the disappearances in some way no one could say.

Then the Blaskoye had swarmed down the southern Escarpment. At any other time, the commander would have marshaled a mighty force and marched off to destroy the interlopers. Or anticipated and stopped them in the first place.

Zilkovsky would have ensured militia and civilian support, and would have made certain supplies followed Dashian's Regulars wherever they went.

This time there were not hours but days delay in moving out to meet the challenge. Then, on the first day out, the quartermaster discovered that the provision wagons had been unaccountably diverted to Garangipore. The word was they were taking the Road to the south, since overland travel might tear their wheels and axles apart.

What complete dakshit.

Koolhaas knew it. Every enlisted man knew it.

Yet there was not a thing to do about it. They must halt. And by the time the supplies arrived, the Blaskoye had swarmed into Ingres, leaving only trampled fields of grain in their wake. Then, instead of giving chase, the new commander had *halted* at the district border. He'd actually claimed he did not have the authority to march them across!

And this with a horde of killers headed like the point of a spear straight toward the capital. How many? Who knew? The majority of the Scouts had been sent into the northern Redlands on a meaningless chase days before the horde made its move. Only a skeleton unit, tracking the huge Blaskoye movement, was there to witness the invasion at all. They had been too busy saving their asses to count Redland devils. All agreed it was a far greater mass of men and donts than the horde at the Battle of the Canal had numbered, maybe ten thousand, maybe more. The Blaskoye bone horns had blown continuously for two entire watches as rider after rider charged down the Southern Defile and into the arrowhead at the junctions of Treville, Ingres, and Lindron districts.

And now here they were, the Regulars, confined to barracks in Hestinga. Allegedly under a cloud of suspicion down in the capital.

It was enough to make a grown man fall down and sob. Not that tears would do any good. What the men needed was the one thing they didn't have.

Backbone. Resolve.

Some portion of their honor back.

An enemy to fight.

If only—

"You lower those muskets, you dumb pieces of dakshit, before I yank them out of your hands and stuff them up your sorry asses!"

This threatening stream of words was punctuated by a great, bellowing laugh.

Sounded like...

Nah, couldn't be.

Koolhaas turned toward the noise.

The guards had indeed lowered their muskets, but to parade rest. They were standing smartly to either side of the garrison entrance archway. Koolhaas hadn't seen them put that much enthusiasm into their duties for many months now.

"That's better, boys," said the voice. "Guess I'm not going to have to have your sergeants flogged and your captains hung today. But be careful of tomorrow, that's all I'm saying."

Amazingly, the gate guards were smiling.

In through the archway rode two men. They both looked like they'd gotten in a fight with a dust devil and lost. What was more, both of them were riding big, lumbering daks. Not donts, daks.

"Don't look at me that way. We had a wagon, but it broke down out in the southern flax fields somewhere or another—we couldn't take the Road, you understand—and so we had to cut these beasts free and ride them the rest of the way. Does that offend your thrice-damned delicate soldierly sensibilities, boys?"

"No, sir," answered the guards, one smartly, the other after he'd gotten his laughter under control.

The daks trundled into the yard. Both had makeshift rope halters fixed around their collars and lower jaws. Koolhaas stumbled forward to see more clearly.

That voice...

"Well, Corporal Koolhaas, don't just stand there like some green trooper staring at his first naked whore," said the dirt-man. "Take these reins so the Prelate and I can get down. We're both half sawn in two. Daks are definitely not made for riding long distances."

He knows my name.

Koolhaas grabbed the ropes and held the daks steady. The other man, a man with the saggy skin of one who had recently lost a great deal of body fat, gingerly slid off. He grunted, obviously in some pain. The other jumped down and landed neatly in front of Koolhaas.

"Koolhaas, you son of a Delta whore's maid! How many of your flogging offenses have these idiots in charge overlooked since I've been gone, eh?"

Koolhaas knew he should recognize the man, knew he'd maybe

better recognize the man, but it wasn't coming to him. All he had really noticed was the patch over the right eye. It looked like a piece of dak leather suspended on a string and tied behind the man's head. But the eyepatch, also, was dusty brown. Despite the dust on his face, he was clean-shaven.

A soldier?

Finally Koolhaas could take it no more. "Who the cold hell are you?" he shouted.

Then the dirt-covered, one-eyed man smiled a ragged, stiff-lipped smile, and Koolhaas knew that smile and knew the man's name even before he could speak. "Colonel!" he yelled. "Colonel, it's you!"

"Blood and Bones, Koolhaas, didn't you recognize me without the eye?"

"No, sir, not at first. And you look a bit...underfed, sir."

"Aye, that I am," Colonel Dashian said. "I could do with a couple of steaks." He looked over at the dak he'd ridden in on. "Perhaps from that fellow, after the aches and pains he's caused me."

Then he turned back to Koolhaas. "But we'll worry about that later. Now, tell me where that pretend DMC and his so-called garrison commanders are hiding themselves, Corporal."

"We call them the Pretty Boys of Lindron, Colonel," Koolhaas said. "They locked us in for the day and took off to town, the lot of them. Major Courtemanche, he's in charge of the garrison at the moment. They busted him down to captain, though."

"Did they?" said the colonel. "We'll see about that." He clapped his hands together and a created a small cloud of dust. "Now, let me think. I'll want Monday Company to fall out. They're to accompany Prelate Zilkovsky here over to the temple. Full battle-dress, and flourishes, too. They're to see he's reinstalled properly and take care of any who might take exception to that process. I'll want you to run over and let Romero know. Romero *is* still heading up Monday?"

"Yes, sir. Though he's been talking about retiring since you disappeared like a...I mean since you've been gone."

"To cold hell with that," Colonel Dashian said. "We'll send Zilkovsky off, and the rest of us are going to prepare a little welcome for the...what did you call them, Koolhaas?"

"The Pretty Boys of Lindron."

"Yes, we'll be ready with a surprise party when the Pretty Boys get back from whatever whorehouse or bones hall they took themselves off to. Sound like fun, Corporal?"

"More than I've had in a long time, sir."

"It's just beginning, Koolhaas. You up for a bigger fight?"

"Always, sir, long as you're doing the leading."

"Good, good," the colonel said. "There's a scrum down Ingres way, and I thought we'd take the boys down and give them some exercise. There'll be Blaskoye and plenty of them."

The colonel caught him with his one good eye. "That doesn't bother you, does it, Koolhaas?"

"Only if you don't let me shoot them, sir."

"I think I can promise you that opportunity, Corporal." The colonel reached over and slapped Koolhaas, hard, on the shoulder. He then put a hand on Koolhaas's other shoulder, and for a moment Koolhaas thought the colonel meant to hug him. But Dashian caught himself and instead gave Koolhaas a good, long shake, rattling the corporal's teeth. "By the Lady, Koolhaas, it's good to see you," he said. "Now you go roust Romero and let's get this corral full of sorry-ass, riven-hoof, bent-back dickless fillies in shape for the races."

"Yes, sir. When do we move out for Ingres, sir?"

"Tomorrow, Corporal, first light."

3

Ingres District
Donner's Landing
Dawn

The River flowed nearby. The only sound it made was a gentle lapping against its banks of pure brown mud. Insectoid buzz filled the air, along with the ragged cry of the occasional carnadon.

The Blaskoye sentry slapped his neck at what he thought was an insectoid bite. His hand came away bloody. Suddenly he felt cold, as if night had fallen. He gazed down at his white robe. It was soaked in blood all down the front, and the stain was growing. He reached for the bite, felt it again, and cried out when one of his fingers went inside a wound. He pushed farther. His finger kept going inside. The cold grew intense. The world around the sentry dimmed.

It's getting dark. That's not right, he thought.

Then his knees buckled; his muscle tension slacked. The sentry collapsed dead on the ground.

Nearby another Blaskoye cried out in agony and clutched at his stomach. One man sitting on his dont groaned and slumped forward onto the neck of the beast. The startled dont charged forward a few paces, then abruptly stopped short when it came up against a stand of willows. The man fell off to its side, his body caught and held among bent willow saplings.

Another and another, but by this time the remaining men had figured out that they were under attack, if not where the bullets

351

were coming from. One ran to his dont and pushed it into a gallop up the trail that led directly away from the River.

"Think you can take him at that distance?" a voice said in a clump of river reeds nearby.

"Kenot ontil try ich," was the gruff reply. A moment later a final shot rang out. Up the River bank on the trail, the fleeing man flung out his hands as if in praise to the path before him and then tumbled off the back of his dont. The animal kept running. The man did not get up from the dust.

"Thet's all ich seeun." The possessor of the gruff voice, Kruso, rose from his hiding spot among the reeds. Beside him was Lausner, the captain of the Treville Scouts, and a third scout who'd accompanied them and paddled the reed dingy. The three ventured out, their boots sloshing in the sucking mud of the River bank. Nearby, a carnadon took notice, churned toward them. Kruso put a shot into the animal's head and it, too, slumped to motionlessness.

"Handy thing, isn't it—six shots before reloading?" said Lausner.

"Sartanly ef tham count ye maken," Kruso replied. They walked over to where the dead men had so recently had their camp. When they arrived, both men wordlessly fanned out and began examining the ground. It was only when the captain nodded that they looked up and went to examine the bodies. They had been reading the sign to see if there were any other Blaskoye lurking about, but had seen only the tracks of those already slain.

"Let's signal the colonel to land," said Lausner. "It's still going to be a day in cold hell clearing away the carnadons."

Ingres District
The Wheatlands
Southwest Front
Morning

Without the revolving rifles a mass landing on the eastern shore of the river in Ingres District would have been impossible. The carnadons were thick here, completely uncontrolled by settlement along the banks. The beasts ruled the shallows and the riverbanks. They simply would not have allowed an army to come ashore without a bloodbath. But now with each man having the firepower of six, it was possible to carve a path through the carnadon infestation before the others could close in and seal off a path away from the bank.

Abel's force of ten thousand only lost a few, and those were men who made stupid decisions such as baiting and taunting the carnadons. They may not have deserved what they got, but Abel was glad not to have such idiots fighting for him. The carnadons might save a few more lives than they took, after all was said and done.

He had to have his forces move forward a half a league inland before he could stop and allow each trooper to find his unit. It was a moment of confusion and, if they had been attacked, a great deal of damage would've been done. But with the killing of the river sentries, he had a hope, however faint, that he had landed the Cascade Regiment with the enemy unaware.

His officers reestablished what order they could. Abel gave the sign and the company resumed its march eastward toward what he hoped would be the flank of von Hoff's forces. The landing had taken time, and it was late afternoon before Abel drew near to where he supposed the outlying enemy forces would be found. He'd sent out Scouts, both on foot and mounted, but it was the clamor that he heard over the next rise that alerted him to the fact that he had very likely reached his destination.

He approached the top of the rise for a lookout with the Treville Scouts, his old band, on either side of him. It was a low hill, and they crawled the last few paces until they reached two large upright rocks, likely set to mark a property boundary, and gazed down on the plains below where von Hoff's army was dug in. Even from here, he could only see the edges of von Hoff's trenches. He had to presume that they stretched to the western horizon.

The general was a master of defense as well as offense.

Abel felt a twinge of regret, not for the first time that day.

Center would have given me deployment of the troops and an accurate estimate of their numbers. And if I'd wanted to hover over von Hoff's army like a flitterdak looking for carrion, I could have had that, too.

From the dust cloud hanging above the enemy forces he guessed that the front lines were engaged with Timon's division. He asked Kruso for confirmation and, after a long look, the Scout nodded.

Still the uncertainty nagged at him. Was he doing the right thing? Was he about to get his ass handed to him?

I'm in the realm that most humans inhabit, he realized with a smile. *The realm of second-guessing yourself at every turn and worrying your ass off.*

But his men were trained, and after carving their way through the river carnadons, each one had taken extra target practice on moving and very much living targets. He was as ready as he would ever be without Center and Raj.

"Bring the cavalry along this rise north to south," Abel said to his adjunct, Major Metzler, who was shadowing him as silently as Timon once had. "Give me a hundredpace distance between each squad." A courier was about to ride away with Abel's orders but was called back. "And remind Kanagawa that there are going to be troops storming in behind him. Those troops will depend on his screen to get them close enough to be effective with the new guns, so don't get too far ahead."

The last thing I need is the cavalry charging off on some wild tangent and leaving my infantry exposed, Abel thought.

"Bring up the forward companies and send word to the reserves to be ready at a moment's notice. We'll use the same order of battle as at the staff meeting yesterday. You got that, Metzler?"

"Yes, General."

It took about a quarter watch for his orders to be related and for his troops to move into position. The sun sank lower. Abel looked up and down his line. They'd practiced it as well as they could, but this was the first time he, or anyone competent, had led troops into battle with a line one man deep. He'd considered making them two deep in order to give the men time to pop in Landry's speedloaders while still being covered by riflemen in front. But he needed numbers to cover a long defensive line. He would have to trust that the hours he'd had them practicing with those speed loaders would pay off. Each man had been issued three, so in addition to the six cartridges loaded, there were eighteen more that should—theoretically—be quickly available for firing. In addition, all had a cartridge box full of bullets. The companies that would take the front line had put in extra practice. When not under fire, most of them could use the speedloader faster than they could have reloaded the barrel of a muzzle-loader.

Each man effectively had the firepower of six to one. Theoretically.

Theory was about to get its test. Abel turned to Metzler. "All right," he said. "Let's get them moving." He pulled his sword from

its scabbard and raised it high. Only a relative few of the men
could see him, strung out as they were. But flags were flapping
and the wigwag was flying down the line in either direction.
The mounted units brought their donts up to a canter down the
gentle slope of the rise. When the ground flattened, they picked
up speed—a few pulled ahead, but most were mindful that there
were foot soldiers on the move behind them.

The line moved ahead in a ragged fashion, but move ahead it
did. It wasn't smooth, but that wasn't necessary or even desir-
able. It was impossible not to feel the mass intake of breath, the
jittery fingering of gunstock and cartridge box, the collective
urge to move, that such a mass of men and animals generated.
He wanted to go with them. He was trembling with the desire
to attack. He'd mastered the urge before, and he would again.
Yet when an orderly brought up his dont and Abel climbed up
on her back, he almost gave in to the temptation.

But there was so much to do, so much to see to—and that
responsibility had its own tug of necessity. In a hundred small
moments over the course of the next two or three watches, he
would need to decide, simply because someone had to. And if
nobody did, they'd already lost.

What was most frustrating was that he couldn't see. He would
have to judge from reports, from riding behind the lines, from
guesswork. So be it.

The rise was maybe a quarter league from von Hoff's left.

*If I've judged him rightly, at least part of my line is going to
hit his flank.*

A rider came charging back from the line, leaving a trail of
dust behind him. He came to a stuttering stop next to Abel and
reined his dont in circles to calm the beast down.

"Report," Abel said levelly.

The courier got the animal under control, then saluted Abel
with a chest thump. "Sir, Captain Craven begs me to inform you
that he's found the enemy."

Craven was commander of the mounted troop on Abel's far
left. He'd instructed the captain to send him word the instant
he made contact.

The winded dont shuffled, and the man's next words were lost
in the chuff of hooves.

"What's that?" Abel asked.

"The captain says to tell you we've run into the trenches. He says we can use his thrice-damned things as pathways to cut out the enemy's heart."

He'd done it. He'd flanked von Hoff. More than that—if his left was in von Hoff's trenches, then that meant the rest of his line was charging in . . .

I'm behind his lines, Abel thought. *By the Lady, we've done it.*

He smiled grimly. "Feel like a ride back up to the front?" he asked.

The man nodded. "I was hoping you'd let me go," he said.

"Trade donts with Cornell," said Abel, gesturing toward one of his staffers. "Tell Craven to move down those trenches, tear up the works, root out the enemy, and send him east."

"Yes, sir."

"Tell him good work." Abel looked up at the afternoon sky. "And tell him to hurry it up, too, before we lose the light."

The officer thumped another salute to Abel. He and Cornell quickly changed mounts. Cornell's dont was skittish and gave them a bit of trouble, but the courier's own was too tired to do anything but stand still, obviously content to be at rest. With a flip of the reins, the man tore away back to the east on the fresh dont.

Another messenger charged up. "Sir, Captain Ogilvy begs to report that he has encountered a regimental-sized horde of Blaskoye reinforcements. He held off two charges. Then, sir, the Blaskoye veered away and headed north. The captain is not sure of the reason for this. He speculates that something else got their attention, perhaps something big."

Within another half watch, Abel didn't need reports from the front. He saw then heard explosions. Large clouds of black smoke rose in the distance.

"We've gotten into the ammunition train," a rider told him. "The men are having a bit of fun blowing it to cold hell."

Abel shook his head. "That's got to stop. This is not a thrice-damned raid. This is the whole fight. This is where we win or lose it all. You tell Cornell to get that band of killers in order and stab those fuckers in their backs. If we cut them off and kill them, then it won't matter about the ammunition."

"Yes, sir!"

"Better yet, I'll tell him myself." Abel motioned to Landry, who had found Abel after his engineers were done sapping the trenches. "It's high time we moved our asses forward, wouldn't you say, Captain?"

"I would indeed, sir."

Ingres District
The Wheatlands
Northeastern Front
Morning

He'd been drilling his men to fight cavalry in squares for well-nigh forty years. He hoped that some of it had sunk in.

Joab's Treville Regulars attacked in company-sized units. The men formed three ranks of about thirty-five across and kept very close to the company in front—a few dozen paces distant at maximum. This would allow them to come together quickly in the event of attack in two possible formations. The first was to create a front of bayonets and rifles facing in any given direction from which dontback attack might arise.

This might easily be enough against an uncoordinated attack by unsupported cavalry. If the fight looked to be getting hot, the line of men at the frontline, along with supporting mounted forces hitting from a flank, were there to provide a bristling thornwork shield while those behind reloaded.

His company captains had long practiced deploying in a checkered pattern to avoid being in one another's line of fire as much as possible. The whole idea of the square was that it could fire in *any* direction, and so was difficult to outflank by cavalry storming around it. You couldn't get to the rear of your enemy if he *had* no rear. Only a broken square was vulnerable. If a dont rider got inside, he might create havoc, and any fire to bring him down also became threatening friendly fire against the side of the square opposite you. Yet even a broken square could be quickly mended once the interior was secure.

The tricky part—and it *was* a matter that required some skill—was to shoot the mounted at about thirty paces distance. Too close and the bodies and donts started to pile up and obstruct further lines of fire. Too far and you were liable to miss your mark entirely.

The technique had produced mixed success with Joab's commanders during the Battle of the Canal. The Scouts could not adopt it at all in the prickly, shrubby Redland desert. Even in the wheat fields, during the heat of a mounted charge of thundering donts, it proved difficult to estimate distances when an infantry officer was quaking with excitement (and for his life).

And there were just so damned many Blaskoye. His men cut them down, inched forward in their squares, cut down another swatch.

But some got through, some squares broke. And then they did, the Blaskoye riders swept into the attack from the flank and even the rear.

There were just so damn many Blaskoye.

And only so many bullets. So many shots. So much time to reload.

We're going to lose, Joab thought. *But we're going to go down fighting.*

Then something began to happen to Joab's right. It was as if his lines were slicing in there, cutting deep. As if the Blaskoye were giving away. Why, he couldn't say, but Joab Dashian was not a man to question good fortune. He threw in what reserves he had.

The penetration of the enemy continued to his center, until Joab's stretched lines resembled a southwest to northeast diagonal across a league or more of Ingres countryside.

What the hell was happening on that right?

Joab rode forward through a cloud of dust. His staff called him back, but he had to see. Dust got in his good eye, and he wiped it with a gloved hand. Closer.

And then he emerged from the dust and away west saw what he was looking for. Banners of gold and blue.

Someone, he wasn't sure who, was fighting alongside him. He and the other had linked up and joined forces. It hadn't been a plan, but it had been inevitable since they were, indeed, fighting the same enemy.

But that couldn't be right. These were Goldies. And every bit of intelligence he had received confirmed to Joab that, in a perverse deal to destroy an alleged threat from the north, the Guardians had joined forces with the Blaskoye.

These were Goldies. And they were on his side.

Then he looked more closely. They fired, then fired again. Then fired again.

There was no line of reloading men, just a few who dropped behind the line momentarily, fiddled with their rifles, and then joined once again in the shooting.

Blam! Blam! Blam!

Joab counted.

Blam! Blam! Blam!

Six shots before reloading.

Six shots from one rifle and one rifleman in a handful of eyeblinks.

No wonder the Blaskoye seemed to be melting like sizzling dak fat.

These new rifles, however they worked, were murder weapons.

4

Ingres District
The Wheatlands
Southeastern Front
Afternoon

The front was chaos, as Abel had expected. But for better or worse, Abel had learned to look past the dead and mangled bodies, the destruction, the odor of burning dont and human flesh, the constant pop of rifles leavened by an occasional full volley.

The screams of the dying.

And if he thought he could not see anything from the rise before, here any hope of making out the larger action was obscured by smoke, overturned wagons, donts and riders charging this way and that, all on errands Abel could only guess at.

Yes, there was an order to the madness. And his men were streaming toward—not away—from the sound and fury.

He rode left along the lines. As he might have expected, the farther north he moved, the closer the fighting became until finally it was very near indeed and shots were whistling through the air.

Something through the gunsmoke and dust caught his eye. It was across the mass of von Hoff's Goldies. A banner he recognized. The Red and White with Twin Stripes, representing the Canal and the Canal Road.

It was the flag of the Treville Regulars.

The one sight he'd most longed for.

But that couldn't be. They were out of the fight.

Another bullet whizzed by.

I'm deluding myself and my mind is playing tricks on me.

Against instinct, Abel turned away, rode a safe distance, then turned to Metzler. "Here's where we need those boys who were up front at Tamarak and Sentinel." Wednesday Company had been made of Cascade reserves and had reconstituted whole when Abel had assembled his forces in Bruneberg. "Let's send Fowlett's boys in, and send them in hard. We can roll those bastards up here, we truly can."

"Will do, sir."

Abel realized he was hungry. He'd eaten in the boat coming down the River but had skipped midday meal, as had probably every man in Abel's army. He'd spent his life with the simple issue of when to grab a bite to eat always nagging at him when out scouting, on maneuvers, even fighting. And, as he usually did, he pushed it away and thought about something else until the hunger pangs either went away or were subsumed by other worries.

Such as the fact that the sun was going to set in little more than a quarter watch.

The command group backtracked to get out of the way of the surging reinforcements. Best to avoid any chance of being mowed down by friendly fire when you could. As they rode south, an odd group made their way up from the north. Abel saw them over the trampled wheat fields from a good distance away. There was a dust cloud with a flash of white color showing and then becoming obscured, then showing again. As the group grew closer, Abel saw that it was several of his own mounted troops surrounding, in boxlike fashion, a group of three dont riders who rode stiffly in the middle.

Then he could make out the white: a flag on a pole.

A truce?

Closer still, and he could make out the gold and tan of the boxed-in riders. They were Goldies. Von Hoff's troops. The enemy. Abel recognized one of them. It was Bunch, his chief of staff in Progar. The groups linked up.

"General, these men claim to represent the Guardian Corps and other Lindron troops currently in this conflict."

"What is it they want, Major?"

Metzler shook his head. "Well, they say they want to surrender, sir. They say they are empowered to do so for the all the Goldies."

"General von Hoff might have something to say about that," Abel replied.

"General von Hoff is dead," called out Bunch. "I've come from wrapping him in a burial blanket and laying him out for the ceremony."

Abel couldn't quite believe what he'd heard. He had Bunch repeat it again.

"Did we kill him?" Abel said, not quite believing what he was hearing. "Zachary von Hoff is too smart to put himself in harm's way."

"He did not," said Bunch. "He has died of the stomach rot."

"What?"

"Cholera, sir."

Abel motioned for the man to ride forward. "Metzler, let him through. I want to talk to this man."

Bunch rode slowly forward until he was close enough to speak with Abel in a normal tone. But the news was anything but normal. "The general took the fever about a week ago, just after his audience with the Lord Zentrum. It hit him pretty hard. These past two days, he was much better. It seemed like he had fought it off and was nearly over it. Then last night the shivers and sweats came back. Almost like something was fighting inside, trying to get out. I was called in after midnight. General von Hoff was gone."

"And now you claim to speak for him?"

"No, I cannot do that. But I can represent my branch of this force. Colonel Vallancourt tried to take command, but he was cut down not a half watch ago—a bullet from behind." The man shook his head. "We've lost our leadership. If we go on this way, there's going to be senseless slaughter."

"So you propose a truce until you can find someone to take the general's place," Abel said with a grim smile. "And then we'll all go back at it?"

"No, General," Bunch replied. "You misunderstand me. I'm offering the surrender of the Guardian Corps."

"I see."

"Surrender with terms. We hand in our arms. We keep our donts."

We've won. Here. On this field.

Abel considered. "Not mounted units."

"All right. I can agree to that."

"Officers only."

"Yes, sir. That will be acceptable."

The man looked exhausted, barely hanging in his saddle. His dont was in the same condition, barely on her legs. Abel imagined a morning galloping hither and yon, trying to contain breakthroughs, trying to shore up the trenches even as they were being overrun from the flank.

"And what of the Blaskoye?" Abel said.

"We sent word of our decision," Bunch said, setting his jaw. "They sent back our messenger's headless body tied to his mount."

"Ah."

"The Blaskoye are having quite a problem themselves," Bunch said. "They got hit from the northeast, and pretty hard."

"The northeast? But there's nothing up that way but—"

"Treville, sir. Very clever of you to bring in the Regulars after we thought they were sitting this one out."

"I didn't—"

But he let the thought hang.

Whoever it is attacking them, the Blaskoye have not surrendered and are still to be dealt with. We've still got hard fighting ahead of us, Abel thought, *and night coming.*

"Very well, Major Bunch. Get down from there and meet with my staff immediately. You need to tell them the best way to get your troops to stand down. And they'll need to know details of your deployment to call off our attack as safely as we can, as well."

The man lowered his head and let out an audible sigh. "General Dashian, I thank you," he said. "We thank you."

"Let's get this done as quickly as we can, and you can thank me later," Abel said. "I suppose it's too much to ask for us to turn around your force and send it at the Blaskoye?"

"General, if they were able, they might be willing to do it. This is the damndest alliance I've ever seen or ever thought to see. We all ought to be fighting those Redlander devils. You know it and I know it. But we...we just don't have the strength to do it at this time."

Bunch seemed to be telling the truth. And if he were, then the Guardians were much further beaten than Abel had supposed.

"All right, let's get this thing underway." Abel turned to Metzler. "Find out how the trenches run to the east. If I know von Hoff, he'll have built them along that line of east-west hills toward the Lindron border. He'll have sent the Blaskoye out in front of them for shock attack. What else do you do with a horde of mounted wildmen? If we can get into those trenches in time, we'll give them nowhere to fall back. Got that, Major?"

"Yes, sir," Metzler said. "I'll see to the details, sir."

"Very good." Abel reined his dont and took her a few paces away.

Von Hoff dead. Dead of cholera. As easily handled as his mother's own gum infection would have been in another age.

Zentrum has done this to you, and countless others, old friend, he thought. *And Zentrum himself has lost his best general.*

"Sometimes the man does matter," Abel said, to himself, to the rapidly building evening breeze that prickled the hairs on his arm and the back of his neck. Zentrum may be playing the long game, but today the statistics had shifted. Without Center, Abel couldn't put it in numbers, couldn't pull out probabilities, but he knew that Zentrum's possibilities had narrowed. Victory was no longer a given, either in the short term or the long. "You lose a man like von Hoff, you might just lose a war."

But whatever the implications for today and the future, the worries of generals, priests and artificial intelligences, there was one certainty: Abel would never be able to repair his relationship with his old mentor. The breach was permanent. This was more than temporary separation. He'd lost his friend forever—which was longer than the longest game Zentrum could ever play.

Even if I win, I will have lost, Abel thought. *They never come back, and I will never forget what was yanked from the world too soon, for no reason other than a machine's befuddled equations for an equilibrium that would never hold.*

That's what this fight was really about.

"Sir, we got most of them when they headed back toward the trenches. It was like target practice. But a large group, maybe half a thousand, broke through. They're heading toward Lindron."

"Them? Who do you mean?"

"Why, the Blaskoye, sir. We ran right up on their backs. And with the revolvers, we made quick work of them. They couldn't even turn around, they were so hard engaged in the front."

"Engaged? But General Athanaskew's men were fighting the Goldies."

"It isn't General Athanaskew, sir. It's Treville."

"Are you absolutely sure?"

"Saw the banners myself, General. We were holed up in that old villa about a half league south of here, then we ran after them when they started to retreat."

"What villa? Who does it belong to?"

"Not sure, General, but after the Blaskoye moved off, that young firebrand Lieutenant Simmons caught some men in there doing what they ought not be doing. He says he's waiting for higher authority before he hangs them."

"He said that, did he? Well, let's go see."

Abel rode forward into the dust.

5

The villa was mostly a ruin. There were a few outlying buildings that hadn't been pulled down, but even these had gaping holes in the mudwork walls. There was smoke rising from the main dwelling, seemingly out of the hole in the roof. This was the only sign of life. Several donts were tied outside. Abel recognized their markings as Cascade military beasts. On the villa porch, two Cascade Regulars, men Abel didn't recognize, were trussed hand and foot and tied by the neck to a post. Simmons, who had served under Metzler at Montag Island, stepped out of the shadows of the doorway as Abel dismounted.

He nodded toward the soldiers on the porch. "Those two happened by, saw what was going on inside, and decided to join in on the fun. I don't think they instigated it, but they sure joined in."

The young man was obviously so caught up in what he was doing he'd failed to realize everyone else around him did not know precisely what he was referring to.

"Let's go inside," said Abel.

They walked through the opening to the villa. If there had been a door once, it had been ripped from its moorings and either used elsewhere or burned for firewood. Now the entrance was a gaping maw. Inside was dim, lit by only a single oil lamp. The windows had been covered over with thin boards and papyrus

366

scrolls, and only strips of light came in through the chinks. In the far corner, two women huddled, one older and one younger. The youngest looked to be in her teens. The oldest—

Abel gazed at her. Something familiar...

"She's Trina von Hoff," Simmons said. "She's General von Hoff's sister."

On the other side of the room, under guard by two Regulars with muskets, four men sat in a clump. They were wearing little more than rags. Three were bowed down with dejected expressions. One looked up at Abel angrily.

"They deserved what they got," the man spat out at Abel. His accent was pure Ingres countryside. "And I for one was happy to give it to 'em."

"Both women were raped by these scum," said Simmons. "The rest of the family is in a back room. They were tortured and beaten to death."

It took Abel a moment to understand what had happened, but then it dawned on him. The clump of men were indentured servants. They had turned on their masters when no one was around to stop them, and they had believed the act could be hidden in the cloud of war.

"How did we find this?" Abel asked.

"Those two outside were part of a group of three. Stretcher party looking for wounded. They found this place, went in. Found the women. The third one wouldn't join in with his buddies. He came back to get help to put a stop to it. Funny thing, but I think he's of the lowliest Delta stock himself. You might think he would be on the side of the scum."

"Have him commended," said Abel. He turned and regarded the women. Trina von Hoff pursed her lips and sat up stiffly. The lower portions of her robe were bloodstained in a wide swath.

"I want them killed, all of them."

"What makes you think you have any authority to ask this of me?" Abel replied. "My responsibility is to do what's best for my men."

"My brother is your general. You'd better think twice before you defy his sister. And we are *von Hoffs*. That means something in these parts. It means everything."

"Yes, Zachary once told me what it meant to him."

"You will do as I command or I'll send for him."

"He's no longer my general," Abel said. "He's no longer anyone's general. And I might, by right, take his family to be my enemy. I will do as I see fit."

Trina von Hoff pulled the younger woman's head toward her breast. The other quietly sobbed. Abel realized she'd been sobbing from the moment he entered the room, filling it with an ambience of lamentation.

"They should die for what they've done to her," the older woman said. "Those two outside went after her. These here were only interested in me, I'll give that to them. Not those soldiers. I can stand anything. But not her. She's my . . . she's my baby."

"Yes," said Abel. "Listen, woman: find a place to hide and go there until the fighting is over. And get used to change. Get used to nobody caring you're a von Hoff. Nothing is going to be the way it was before. This is only the beginning, and after this whatever happens will be up to you. Do you understand?"

The woman set her jaw and started to say something, but then she held in whatever it was and only nodded.

Abel turned to Simmons. "Have those two outside flogged," he said. "Make it to within an inch of their lives, but give them their lives. Geld them. Have a man you trust handle it. Then hand them back over to their units."

"I'll see to it, sir," answered Simmons.

"As for these creatures," said Abel, nodding toward the ragged servants. "I noticed a deep well in front of the house. Take them there and throw them in."

"So the Firsts win again," said one of the ragged lot in the corner. There was a look of defiance on his dirty face. "Do you think that they were not answering for a hundred, a thousand, harms they've done to me and them that's mine?"

"And is this the way you get them back?" Abel said. He shook his head. "No."

"They deserve it a hundred times over. All of them von Hoffs do. All the Land-heirs." The man's voice rasped as if these words were pulled from a deep, dry place.

Abel looked at him sadly.

"Throw this one in first." He gazed around the interior of the building. "When that's done, have the well filled in. Then have this place torn down. All of it. The compound, the servants' quarters, the barns."

"And these two?" Tim and nodded toward the two women.

"Give them clothes, food, and a pack animal. Send them on their way."

"You can't!" shouted the woman in the corner. "By the Land and the Laws of Zentrum, I demand justice! As a woman. As a First. What kind of Landsman are you to deny this to us?"

"Be careful what you wish for," Abel said. "Now take the child and be on your way."

Abel turned and left through the door maw and stepped back into the bright sunlight of day. He paused a moment on the porch, shook his head to clear it.

Center, this is where I need you most, he thought. *The fighting I can handle. But this kind of thing… it's a guess. I'm not good at it. I'm fucking it up. I know I am.*

He sighed. "Nobody's making you take any of this on," he mumbled to himself. "Just yourself now."

Old habit, talking to myself. And expecting an answer.

Abel stepped down from the porch. Even though the outside air was hot and filled with dust, it felt good to breathe unconfined once again.

6

Ingres District
The Wheatlands
Twilight

The Blaskoye dead and wounded were arranged like flotsam from a receding flood, a mangle of dont and man, portions of which were gruesomely twitching with the last impulses of life. Each wave of attack against the eastern trenches had been cut down en masse, and the mounds of dead and dying were piled up in striated bands.

Already the insectoids were buzzing, searching for meat into which to deposit their eggs. And the flitterdaks were flocking about as well, gobbling up the insectoids and munching on the occasional bit of soft carrion such as eyeballs and tongues.

"We'll have to pursue," Abel pronounced.

"Sir, the men are exhausted. It's almost dark. I don't know how much good that will do."

"No choice," Abel said. "We can't let them ride into the capital without fear at their tails."

"Yes, sir."

From the dirt and smoke ahead, a party on dontback rode toward them.

Something about them. Abel reined Nettle up short, took a closer look.

Ah, yes. He recognized Timon's dont, Blazes. Timon sat tall in the saddle, as always. The sun caught him from the side,

370

accentuating the smoothness of his right side, where an arm ought to be but wasn't. Beside Timon rode a standard-bearer with the flag of the True Goldies.

Odd. There were *two* banners. On the opposite side of Timon, another standard bearer rode. A sudden breeze caught the other banner, and Abel gasped in astonishment and happiness. It *was* Treville. How the cold hell they'd gotten here, or why the cold hell they'd come after letting the Blaskoye through, he couldn't say. But he was glad to see them.

Then the group got close enough to make out faces, and Abel's happiness turned to pure joy.

There was a fourth rider who moved along beside the Treville standard.

It was Joab Dashian.

Abel had presumed his father was dead since he'd been told in Progar that Joab had gone missing. He'd tried to come to terms with it on the march to Cascade, had not.

But then the problems of bringing together an army on a moment's notice took him over and he buried the sadness in the back of his mind. Temporarily, he knew. Along with his worry for Mahaut. And when he came back to it, it would only have grown darker and stronger.

Now, in the blink of an eye, the sorrow evaporated like so much River mist.

His father was alive.

Abel got down from Nettle and waited for the group to arrive. When they did, Joab wasted no time. He slid down from his mount—with some effort and grunt of pain—and turned to face Abel.

"Goddamn dak ride hasn't worn off," he said.

"Your eye," Abel said, noticing the patch.

"They took the one that saw fuzzy. Good riddance," his father said. "The idiots left me with the good one."

With a few steps, the two men embraced.

7

Ingres District
The Wheatlands
Twilight

"The problem is we have a large group of Blaskoye making for Lindron, and there's not a thing standing between them and the populace," Timon said. "Joab's Major Courtemanche estimates maybe a thousand riders. Enough to wreak havoc and burn the town down."

"And us?"

"We're nearly done in," said Joab. "We killed the hell out of those Redlanders, but Courtemanche tells me we lost more than two thousand ourselves."

Abel looked into the distance and smiled as the answer came to him. "I'll take what troops of mine can march. I'll take the Scouts," he said. "They're used to picking themselves up after hard fighting in the Redlands where there isn't any choice."

He turned back to his father and Timon. "Gentlemen, send me what you can. I'll need you both here to bring your boys along at first light. You're to follow me. They won't feel like moving out, but they have to be made to. Lindron depends on it."

Timon shook his head tiredly. "I'm going with you."

"Somebody has to look after your Goldies."

"They can damned well look after themselves," Timon said. "Besides, Burridge will do fine rallying them after a watch and a half of rest. You know that."

"No. You must, Timon. They will need you. Stay."

Timon glared at Abel for a moment, but then nodded. "Yes, sir."

It seemed for a moment that Joab would also voice some objection. A look from Abel cut him off. "Very well, General," his father finally said. "Some shut-eye, and then we'll be right on your tail."

"We'll look for you then," Abel answered. "Let's get to it. We have a night ride ahead. Even then I'm afraid the Blaskoye will make it to the city. Von Hoff maybe left a garrison force, but there's basically nothing else to stop Blaskoye. I don't think this so-called alliance will mean a damned thing to the Redlanders with Lindron open before them."

Joab nodded grimly.

He looks like death itself with that one eye, Abel thought.

"Might not be as open as you think," his father said.

"No? What do you mean?"

"I mean, believe it or not, but there's a thrice-damned host of partisans in that town, and they're hopping mad about this Blaskoye-Goldie team-up. They'll do what they can to deny them entry."

"They can't have gotten themselves organized this quickly."

Joab's smile broadened.

"Might want to ask your woman about that," he said.

"Ask my—what are you talking about, Father?"

"I'm talking about Her Grace Land-heiress Mahaut Jacobson," Joab replied. "She leads them. And I know from firsthand experience: right now, the streets of Lindron belong to her."

8

Lindron
Morning

Mahaut had considered taking out the small Guardian garrison force left in the city, but her partisans, though growing each day, were not yet supplied with weapons to accomplish that. What she could do was attempt to keep the garrison from being reinforced.

She also dearly wanted to find a way to bring out and kill that knot of Blaskoye holed up in the Tabernacle. Blaskoye living in the heart of the Land, by cold hell! It made her skin crawl. Yet she held back from that task, too.

When she took them on, she wanted to be sure of their utter destruction.

Mahaut was putting together plans to do just that when word came from the countryside that a great clash of Goldies and Blaskoye with the Regulars had taken place in Ingres.

With Treville sidelined, it was fairly certain that the Guardians and the Blaskoye had won.

Now a Blaskoye horde was streaming toward Lindron. This did not bode well. Agreement or not, everyone knew that, with an undermanned garrison and no city guard strong enough to stop them, they would enter and they would sack. Lindron would scream and burn.

Despite wishing the Tabernacle pyramid torn out by its roots, Mahaut had a great fondness for her adopted town. She did not

374

intend to watch it be ransacked, or watch its women and children slaughtered, despoiled, or even made into slaves.

Besides, if those Blaskoye were retreating, then the city had to be denied to them as a refuge. She didn't have to attack and defeat them. If any hope survived, all she had to do was keep them out long enough for their pursuers to arrive. The Blaskoye Law-givers might be blaspheming the Inner Sanctum of the Tabernacle. The Esplanade and inner sectors might be patrolled by the few garrisoning Goldies remaining, but Mahaut's partisans controlled Lindron's outskirts.

Lindron was a maze of throughways and alleys two thousand years in the making. What civic improvement there had been over the years had only provided for four big boulevards to enter or leave the city on its north side.

The key would be to deny the Blaskoye those boulevards, and make them come in on side passages. Side passages, alleys, narrow streets—all could be made into killing zones. All that was necessary was to get the pest to enter the trap.

Mahaut had many days ago emptied the House Jacobson coffers to the last chit building and buying (or buying off) her force. Payment was effective enough, but it was the offer of free grain to the families of those who would fight that was the most persuasive. If it didn't work out in the end, at least she wouldn't have to hang her head when facing Benjamin Jacobson. Her head would likely have already been severed from her body.

Of the four main roads that led into Lindron from the north, she reckoned the middle two would be the most likely path the Redlanders would take into the city.

These boulevards were also the major routes for overland trade. Warehouses lined their sides in the outskirts of the city, and quite a few of those belonged to House Jacobson. At the moment, trade was perilous and most of the warehouses were filled with empty wagons and drays waiting to carry loads in more peaceful times. Daks filled the city's stables, chomping at their rushgrass, unaware that doom might be approaching.

For communicating with her partisans, Mahaut had developed a grapevine of city urchins to carry her messages, and it served her well today. She sent word that the partisan boss in each area of the city should order the emptying of the warehouses of wagons. They might need donts and daks released from liveries to pull the larger carts—she could provide that with enough notice to her stablemen—but most transport wagons could be handled by several strong men or several more strong women. That is, at least for the distance the wagons and drays would need to go.

"Bring every wagon we have out of the compound," she ordered her own House staff. The operation took longer than she liked, and when she went to the largest of the wagons, stood on it and stomped impatiently, the work rate doubled. Just seeing the consort taking an active interest in progress speeded things up immediately.

The consort was most generous if you did your job, but she gave no truck to layabouts. The rumor was she kept the black arrow she killed her husband with framed behind her desk.

Mahaut had her personal dont brought from the stables. It had been a while since she had sat in the saddle, but the old instincts returned quickly. Besides, she'd made hundreds of rides between Hestinga and Lilleheim, and those skills were not easily lost even after several years away. With her bodyguards and a hundred Jacobson wagons trailing behind her, she then made her way down Tabernacle Boulevard, the largest thoroughfare in Lindron.

At first the street was easily negotiated, but closer to the outskirts walkers and riders began to clump ahead of her. With the aid of her bodyguards, and the weight of their donts, she pushed her way through these clusters of the frightened and fleeing until she arrived near the edge of town. There progress stopped entirely. Standing up in her saddle, Mahaut gazed ahead.

Wagons jammed the street—thousands of them. Many were piled upon each other willy-nilly, giving the illusion of mating. Her partisans—men and women she hardly knew beyond a trustful trading relation—had taken her orders and done their job here.

"Let's go to the side streets," Mahaut called out to the dak-skinner on the lead wagon. "You go that way." She pointed to her right. "When you find a cross street, block it. The narrower the street, the better."

"Yes, Land-heiress."

She went down the row of her Jacobson wagons and in the same manner ordered each to disperse to either left or right and do their best to trundle about until they could jam the streets of Lindron. After that, the drivers and crews should turn the wagons over and pile whatever they could on top of it to form barricades.

This job done, she rode east to Water Street, another north-running boulevard. When she arrived she was pleased to see that it was equally jammed.

Townspeople were milling about gawking at the sight. Somewhere music was playing, and a couple of vendors were selling steaming vegetables and spitted flitterdaks. It was a festive atmosphere.

Poor deluded fools. The Blaskoye might upset your picnic soon, she thought. *But it* does *look like fun.*

It would surely take hours, hopefully days, to clear this mess out enough so that the road was usable. She cut across streets and alleyways to reach the other boulevards. The two that ran straight north were shut down. The outer boulevards to the northeast and northwest had less drayage piled on them, but the locals had raided a lamp-oil warehouse and converted irrigation ditches that ran along either side of the road into a sluices filled with oil—oil ready to be set afire at a moment's notice.

Donts hated fire when it was close by, and skittish Redland donts did not seem to care much for the city in general.

Now all that needed to be seen to were the porous alleyways and small streets of the very outmost houses and shops. A few more wagons placed correctly, and these roads could serve as funnels—leading directly into the maze of backstreet Lindron.

At about a watch after sunrise, the first of the Blaskoye horde arrived. These attempted to enter along Tabernacle. They thundered along until the last moment, then pulled up short at the jam of wagons. And while the riders sat gazing with bewildered expressions at the wagon pile, a rush of arrows flew from nearby windows and rooftops. Dozens of riders fell. The men and women of the outskirts supplemented their diets by hunting in the countryside, and they were good shots.

Evidently this did not deliver the message, because shortly after more riders arrived. These received the same treatment as the last. This time the riders broke off and spread out along the edge of the city in either direction, looking to find other ways in. Find them they did. In ones, twos, and threes, they turned down small streets and alleyways.

Mahaut rode to the nearest cross street she could get to, trying to catch a glimpse of the hapless Blaskoye as they tried to make their way toward the Tabernacle.

The women, children, and aged now had their way with the

Blaskoye. Boiling water poured down from roofs. Arrows and rocks flew at the invaders. The riders might have shot these attackers down, had they been able to see who was firing at them. From street level, the alleyways seemed deserted. But when riders ventured in, down came the bricks, heavy pieces of furniture, boiling water and flaming oil.

Some alleys couldn't hold against their invaders, and these riders were then merciless in cutting down all who crossed their paths.

Regardless of the initial success, however, Mahaut knew that the partisans could not keep the Redlanders out for good. When it became evident that there were no Guardian troops marching behind the Blaskoye, she began to have hope. Maybe they were not returning in victory.

Maybe they'd gotten their asses handed to them.

One could hope.

She knew it was time for her to wait and figure out the situation, before letting herself and everyone else get carried away with either victory or defeat. But it was hard not to feel elation when the bulk of the riders spun their mounts around and rode back in the direction from which they had come. It was not long before they disappeared from sight, swallowed up by the broken lands that ringed the North and west of the city.

She'd done it. No, *Lindron* had done it. The city had hurled the Blaskoye out. They would have nowhere to go but into the badlands north of the city.

Into the Giants.

9

Lindron District
The Giants
Noon

The Giants. For the priesthood, it was a holy area. Even if it had
been fertile, which it was not, it would not be used for agriculture.
This was the region in which the mother of all, Irisobrian, was
said to have suckled the young Zentrum from the miraculously
flowing milk in her dead body. Abel supposed that he might be
the only man in his entire army who knew what the area known
as the Giants actually was.

For the Blaskoye, it represented something very different.
This was the landscape that most resembled their home ground.
Even though the Giants had practically no vegetation growing
on it—the plague had left the earth there barren and without
nutrients—it did somewhat resemble the Redlands in its roll and
rise. All badlands did.

The first attack came as an ambush, and it caught the frontline
forces unawares, even Abel. This would never have happened
in days before with Center monitoring his sensory input. The
screams of the dying man in front of him was enough to make
this more than mere academic regret. Center had saved lives, and
now Abel was losing them by being merely human.

His frontline bent but held, and his Regulars in the rear of
the column began forming up into the squares. It was done
much quicker and more efficiently than Abel had seen them

do it in Cascade and, more recently, on the fields of southern Treville. Practice under fire had improved them greatly in a few short watches. Preloaded cylinders came out of cartridge boxes. And then on the command conveyed via wigwag by Abel's staff master sergeant, the push forward began. The squares immediately begin dispersing as they traveled slightly different speeds in varying terrain.

They're drifting too far, he thought for a moment. *They're going to get cut off.*

But the men in the squares themselves seemed to spontaneously correct for their drift. They were worried about being cut off and cut apart, too.

Then he pushed forward along with everyone else, and rode down a defile and out of sight of the larger force. It was over a series of rises in front of him, and spread in all directions. This was, in some ways, like fighting in one of the box canyons of the Redlands: a terrain with odd quirks and turns to the landscape.

But this was not the Blaskoye homeland. It was his. He'd served in troops that had done maneuvers here. He sure as cold hell had put in enough time for a lifetime wandering around the Giants with a squad, a day's rations, and a minimal set of orders. He might not have the place memorized, but he knew what to expect. There were no ridges, for instance, just a series of mounds covered with huge broken stones. You couldn't take the high ground without worrying that you'd exposed yourself to being surrounded. The terrain broke up large masses into smaller groupings. It rewarded trained units.

It was a better battleground for an army than a horde.

He crested the rise, and Lausner, who had, with a vanguard of Scouts, broken free and climbed to meet Abel, arrived breathless and bleeding from a shoulder wound.

"Looks they're trying to concentrate, throwing more than half their numbers at us ahead to the left, sir," the captain said. "We're up against the hill yonder in a half-circle, more or less. We're getting pounded, that's for sure. I've got more killed and wounded than I have fighting. We've had to contract and leave some poor bastards outside the perimeter. You should see the looks on their face when we're stepping over them and abandoning them. It's something terrible."

"I know, Lausner," Abel said. The arc below was crumbling at the flanks where the Blaskoye were directing their runs. Clumps of twenty or thirty Redlanders on dontback charged diagonally at them. The men who were unlucky enough or brave enough to be positioned on the end took the brunt of their fire.

It's not a bad tactic on the enemy's part, Abel thought.

"The only break we're getting is that the dead bodies are piling up, both ours and theirs," the Scout captain continued. "The donts are having to jump them, and that's slowing them down. Plus it gives us some cover. But the ground's slick. I never would believe sandy shit like this could get slippery. The blood soaks through, but you lose your footing on the guts. They're everywhere and greasy as hell."

"I've got a couple of companies coming up right behind us," Abel said. "How many do you have fighting?"

"I'd say a hundred or so."

"We've got to last until those others get here."

"Yes, sir, we'll do it," the captain replied, although his eyes were haunted, as if he doubted the assurances coming from his mouth even as he uttered them. Suddenly, Lausner sat up straight in his saddle with a gasp. He stretched his hands behind himself, groping at his back. With a final glance at Abel, almost apologetic, the man fell from his dont and landed with a thud on the ground. Abel leaped down and examined him. Dead. A bullet had broken his spine.

It likely would have hit me, Abel thought, *had I not had this man as a shield.*

Abel mounted back up, aided by an orderly who practically pitched him onto the dont. Another look down the hill revealed that the semicircle of men was actively dissolving. He glanced to his rear. No way to see beyond the gulch behind them. His reinforcements might only be moments away, or might not.

"That arc has got to hold," Abel said.

"Pardon, sir," said Metzler. "These men need orders." The other company officers sat their mounts, stunned. Their commander was dead, and no one seemed to know what to do next.

"We have to fall back and hold out for reinforcements," Abel shouted at them.

No movement, no answer.

"Shall I go down?" asked Metzler.

"You stay. Bring down those reinforcements when they get there."

Metzler looked confused for a moment, then chagrined. "Sir, you're not meaning to—"

Abel smiled. "We've beat them. You and I know we have this battle in hand. But that doesn't matter to our thrice-damn boys down there getting the shit kicked out of them."

No Center. No Raj. A doubtful position. But he was needed...

Abel drew his sword, waved it in front of the company officers. "Metzler, stay. The rest—we go. Now." He brandished the sword up in the air. "Come on!"

He reined his dont into a trot down the hill. Bullets filled the air around and set off small puffs from the sandy ground nearby. The defensive arc was tight now, filled with wounded. There was no room to bring in the donts. He got off Nettle and turned her so that she faced in the direction from which they'd come. He took his rifle from its scabbard, slung it around his back. Then, with the tip of his sword, he poked her in her hind muscles. She snorted bilious snot at the provocation then charged away, instinctively distancing herself from the noise and chaos behind her. After a quick prod, the other donts followed her. Abel and the officers with him plunged through the line and into the square.

He tried to be everywhere, throwing men into gaps, taking turns firing himself. They were far more a clump than an arc now, but there was order enough to keep up a steady fire, to keep reloading. The Blaskoye dead were piling up with wave after wave of attack.

But his men were running low on ammunition. As if to confirm this, several troops to Abel's right ran dry simultaneously, and a Blaskoye on a huge dont stallion, its plume erect, its skin mottled in angry black and red markings, broke through. Its rider had reserved fire and got off a shot in Abel's general direction, then tossed aside his carbine and drew a long, wicked-looking knife. A trooper charged him, snatching at the Redlander's leg, and the Blaskoye viciously slashed the man across the face, sending him reeling back clutching at the ruin. Abel raised his rifle and took aim. If he'd counted right, he had four shots remaining in his barrel.

He pulled the trigger. *Click.*

I'm out? How could I miscount that badly?

But glancing down, he saw that his tunic sleeve had gotten

jammed in the barrel-turning mechanism. He resisted the urge to yank it free—it might or might not come loose—and carefully pulled the barrel pin out, and with the thumb of his free hand pushed at the barrel until it came loose and released the fabric. He slammed the barrel back in place, rose up and—

Shot point-blank into the black and red stallion's charging forehead. He dove out of the way just in time as the animal's momentum carried it past him and a few steps more before the dont collapsed.

The Blaskoye bounded off even as his mount was falling—they truly were remarkable riders—and came at Abel. There was no time or space to get a shot off. The Redlander led with his knife held high in a murderer's grip, blade pointing downward.

Intimidating, but not the best stance, Abel thought.

The Blaskoye brought his knife down. Abel raised his rifle crosswise to block it. The Blaskoye's wrist smashed into the gunstock when the knife was inches from Abel's chest, and his hand involuntarily released the blade. Abel thrust out with his right and smashed the rifle into the Blaskoye's neck. The other men stumbled back. Abel swung his rifle around and, almost leisurely, took quick aim and killed the man with a shot to the chest. The Blaskoye fell staring with surprise into Abel's eyes.

Reload, Abel told himself. *Get it done while you're catching your breath.*

He reached for his cartridge box, pulled out a handful of papyrus cartridges and spaced them between the fingers of his hand. It was a trick his Scouts had discovered (or rediscovered, as Center had informed him) when they'd first fought with breechloaders.

Though his hands were shaking, he slid the bullets into chambers easily enough, and clicked the revolver barrel back into place. Try as he might, though, he couldn't stop breathing hard. Soon it was worse, and he was gasping.

There was a tingling in his left arm, and suddenly, though he kept a grip on the rifle, he could barely feel the arm. He carefully slung the rifle around behind him on its strap and began methodically running fingers under his jacket and tunic.

It didn't take long to find where the bullet had entered.

Just under his right ribcage, to the side of his abdomen—a hole about as big around as an arrow shaft. A finger pressed inside found no resistance. It was deep, and oozing blood.

Not spurting, he thought. *At least there's that.*

He painfully reached around, groped at his back. He gathered his concentration and tried to be methodical in his probing. There was no exit wound that he could find. Which meant the bullet was inside him somewhere. On the other hand, he would only need to apply pressure to the one wound.

With that thought, his strength ebbed and he collapsed to his knees. He yanked open his cartridge box again and pulled out a swabbing cloth. It was not dirty, a testament to how little he'd needed to use his gun recently. This he wadded and held onto the wound with as much pressure as he could apply.

Soon even staying on his knees was too much and he fell backward onto his rear, his legs splayed out before him. Breathing was becoming harder still. With one hand he propped himself up, with the other he kept pressure on the wound.

Around him, all he could see were the scrambling backs and legs of men. Above him, the late afternoon sun beat down through the cloudless sky of the Land.

I may die.

But he'd always known this.

I may die today. *Now.*

He slumped out of his rifle strap and let its fall to his side. Its weight on his shoulder had become unbearable.

Need a weapon. I'm a soldier and I need a weapon, thrice-damn it.

He braced himself, drew in another painful breath. Breathed out. He wiped the spittle from his lips, examined his hand for blood.

There were red patches. It could be from a bitten lip. It could be from a pierced lung.

I do have a weapon.

He tried to smile, but it became a grimace. Then he reached down and laboriously pulled his sword from its scabbard. He laid it across his lap.

A great clatter of fire behind him. The trampling of sandaled feet around him.

A shout, seemingly from far away.

"Fall back!"

He watched, concentrating and attempting to comprehend what was happening, as men continued to stream around him, away from him.

My back is to the Blaskoye, he thought. *I'm facing uphill.*

Which meant the soldiers were retreating.

Someone reached down, grabbed his arm. "Come on, sir!"

Abel shook the other's hand off. "No you don't. Get out of here!"

"Can't do that, sir." Abel looked up, but could only raise his head high enough to take in the man's command sash. He was a sergeant.

The sergeant moved behind Abel and attempted to hoist him up. He had raised Abel an elb or so off the ground when his grip suddenly slackened. Abel fell down hard, and agony crashed through his body at the impact. He fought through it, and twisted around to see what had become of the sergeant.

He lay twisted and dead. Abel raised himself enough to look over the man's body.

A dark line of Blaskoye dontback riders, moving toward him.

He turned away from them, looked back to his men. They were moving up the hill in a fairly orderly retreat. And higher up, behind them—another line of silhouettes. The reinforcements had arrived.

Not soon enough, he thought. *But they had other things to deal with, I'm sure. No blame. Brave men. All brave men.*

Huffing of dont blowholes, shouts in the Redlander tongue behind him. Abel gripped the sword hilt with his right hand, his left hand still applying pressure to the wound in his side.

I'll take one with me. At least one. Let me take at least one.

But he couldn't concentrate. His grip was slackening.

"They won't catch him, he's the Carnadon Man," she sang gently.

His mother. He heard her as clear as day.

"Mamma," he said, realizing he was hallucinating, but unable to stop himself. He'd missed her so much. He'd hidden it even from his father, or thought he had. But how could it be that she was gone, that she had left him?

"A toothache," he said, shaking his head once again as the old anger rose within him.

A toothache and then a light in his world brighter than the sun was suddenly snuffed out, never to shine again. So many years ago. Before he even knew what it meant, when he could only feel her absence, uncomprehending, alone.

"I'm right here," she said. "Don't worry about those carnadons. They can't bother you, because you're him."

"Who, Mamma?"

"Why, the Carnadon Man, of course."

The Blaskoye found him with his sword hilt still in his hand. Despite the fact that their enemy was now recovered and was charging down upon them, their leader saw the command sash and ordered them to carefully lift this one, and secure him across the back of a dont. He had orders to bring the Dashian to the Council. Maybe this was him, maybe not, but he'd take no chances. The leader, a clan headman, and a few of his followers, took the reins of that dont and charged away on his own, making for Lindron.

He did not look back once as the counterattacking Regulars overwhelmed and slaughtered the remaining riders, who had only moments before believed they had victory.

Lindron
Afternoon

In the heat of late afternoon, a group of determined Blaskoye—no more than twenty strong—circled to the east and threw themselves on a boulevard blockade. It was unexpected and brutal. Before the breach could be filled, they were through.

Still, observers followed the Redlanders. The Blaskoye made straight for the Tabernacle.

"Before we knew it, they was through. Not sure what they was doing," the eastern sector leader reported with a shameful face to Mahaut. Ford owned one of the city's largest tanneries and ran the partisan forces in the eastern sector. "They had a man, a Regular by the look of his dress, slung over a dont like a sack of flour. Saw it myself. Nope, wasn't one of their own. He was Black and Tan, he was."

"A Regular?"

"Looked to be some high officer," said Ford. "Had the sash of one, at least."

Ford held up a dirty, bloodstained commander's sash and presented it to Mahaut. "It fell off. Maybe a urchin or two helped it fall with a tug."

When she clutched the sash, examined it, she lost her breath for a moment.

"Do you know it, Land-heiress?"

"I have seen it before," she said. "This high officer—was he alive or dead?"

"Hard to say, your grace. He weren't moving when he passed by. Like I said, we followed a ways behind, and I got another good look. That saddle they had him on was bloody when they took him off."

Mahaut glared at Ford. "Tell me truly, was this man alive?"

Ford shook his head. "No, your grace. I'm pretty certain he was dead. Dead or real near to it."

PART FOURTEEN

The Sacrifice

The Present

1

Lindron
The Tabernacle of Zentrum
Late afternoon

Cold water on his face. Abel awoke. He blinked, but his eyelids couldn't break free from a crust that held them closed. Another torrent of cold water.

He opened his eyes. He lay on a litter. Around him were walls of stone. Sandstone. He recognized its texture, its style. He'd spent five years living with it around him, after all.

This was the Tabernacle of Zentrum.

His side ached, but he now had feeling in his arms. He reached down. The wound was bound tightly with a bandage around his torso.

"Drink." Abel turned to see a priest in orange robes. He held out a clay cup. Abel took it, tried to sit up. Pain shot through him, but with the other arm behind his back, he was able to do so. He took a sip.

Water. He drained the cup. He handed it back to the priest, who refilled it. Abel drank again, each swallow followed by a stab of pain in his chest. But he got the water down.

He was in one of the antechambers near the Inner Sanctum. He'd stood, likely in this very spot, on guard duty more than once. He'd walked past it on the way to his audience with Zentrum. The walls seemed to be covered in a white tapestry, though—

It took him a moment to resolve the white fabric into the

forms of Blaskoye men. He was surrounded by at least ten of them crowded into the room. Several held rifles, and they were pointed at him.

One of the Blaskoye broke from the group and stood over him.

"Who are you?" Abel asked in Redlander. It came out as a croak, but must have been intelligible, for the man answered.

"I am called Kerensky. That does not matter."

"The Blaskoye Council Law-giver."

The slightest smile of pride played over the Blaskoye's lips. "I have that honor."

"What do you want? Cut a deal, you get out?"

Then the other really did smile. "Hardly."

"Why am I alive?"

"Because Taub wills it. Because of what you've done."

"Get shot?"

Kerensky abruptly switched from Redlander to Landish. "You have plunged this world into chaos. You have toyed with the balance of blood and dust."

Abel sat up straighter. His side ached, but some of his strength had returned. "This world? Are there others?"

"I have been shown...many things...by Taub. He speaks to me from the dust. There are other worlds. I know who you are."

"A man." Abel looked at his bandaged side, touched it. A slight pressure and pain shot through him. "That's all."

Kerensky bent close to Abel's ear. His breath smelled of nesh. "You are evil in the form of a man."

Abel sighed. He tried to lie back, but the priest's arm wouldn't budge. "Kerensky," he said. "Poor Kerensky."

The Blaskoye frowned, shook his head.

He turned to the gathered Blaskoye and addressed them. "Shrive him."

Then he looked at the priest behind Abel. Abel swiveled to catch another glimpse of him, and was rewarded by a stab of pain.

He looks familiar, somehow. Do I know him?

"Barbarians...in the Tabernacle."

The priest scowled. "Zentrum is Lord. You will see," he muttered in Lindron-accented Landish.

"Prepare the sacrifice for Taub," said Kerensky.

All eyes in the room fell on Abel now.

It wasn't hard to tell who the sacrifice was meant to be.

2

The space capsule stood to one side in the Tabernacle Inner Sanctum. Abel might not have recognized the scorched hulk at all had it not been for the familiar conical shape. When he did realize what he was seeing, he felt sadness. But also something else: Now he knew that everything was really up to him. Now up to humanity. No help from heaven.

The capsule was blackened and burned. It had been rough-used before, but this time was different. There were holes blasted in its surface, the metal twisted inward. The blows had come from outside. Instruments had been inserted—instruments of murder. The quantum foam that housed Center and Raj had not been a delicate thing, but Zentrum had evidently known how to wipe it from existence.

Now I know for certain: they are gone.

Zentrum had found them.

Zentrum had caught them.

Zentrum had killed them.

For a moment, he imagined this may be one of Center's visions: the kind that projected the worst-case scenario should he make a stupid decision. These usually involved torture with a dollop of mental cruelty thrown in—followed by violent and excruciating death. Then he would pop back to reality and realize the error of his way.

Not this time.

This time the terrible vision *was* reality. Without Center to guide him, he'd fallen into a trap of his own making. He'd stupidly charged into battle and been captured.

I am an amateur when it comes to real intrigue.

He'd been up against a professional with three thousand years of experience.

They flogged him first. He curled against a wall and the beating went on and on. The Blaskoye with the obsidian-encrusted whip was careful to dig deep and turn Abel's back to ruin. Then the priest, who seemed now to be at the Blaskoye's beck and call, laid him out and poured sea salt over his wounds. This burned like fire, but also served to staunch the blood flow and keep him alive a little longer.

He was placed upon a stone table—it was a sacrament table that must have been brought into the room for special use—and his bullet wound was tended again. Abel looked up through bleary eyes to see an old man with disheveled hair changing the bandage.

"Abbot," Abel croaked.

This seemed not to register. The old priest looked stunned, his hands moving perfunctorily. There was a large bruise on Goldfrank's cheek and forehead, and a trail of dried blood from a nostril.

The long view of Zentrum.

Abel wanted to say this to the priest, but his throat was too ragged. He contented himself with a pained smile of disgust.

Hold out.

To stay alive long enough to distract Zentrum from the approach of Timon's True Goldies, and the Regulars of Treville and Cascade. The battle was won. The Blaskoye would be defeated. Lindron would be liberated.

But, of course, Zentrum will remain, Abel thought. *The rot at the heart of the Land.*

Even if Timon and Joab tore down the Tabernacle stone by stone, the vast computer would survive. Zentrum would recoup—and slowly corrupt another generation.

The Blood Winds may have been averted this time, but in a hundred years, two hundred, they would blow again.

Zentrum takes the long view.

Unfortunately, the universe took an even longer view than Zentrum. Mankind was doomed on Duisberg.

But at least, barring an early asteroid strike, there would be those centuries respite. During that time, maybe, despite the astronomical odds against it, another capsule would fall.

No, he would not delude himself with false hope.

After the salting, he would not rise from the table, so the Blaskoye used burning sticks taken from the outer temple brazier fires to prod him to his feet. Then they used them to herd him. Forward. Stumbling forward, toward the Eye.

Fucking no! I won't!

Yet his legs were the problem. They kept walking.

One way to solve that.

He collapsed to the floor.

The firecoal sticks rained down on him, blow after blow, trailing sparks in all directions. A staff of hard wood cracked against his ribs. Bone splintered.

He was panting, every breath painful.

They'll have to drag me.

"Back away!" It was Kerensky. He was calling his men away from their rampage. "He should not die yet. This one is for Taub."

Abel lay curled on the floor. The air smelled like fire, smoke and his own burned flesh.

"You!" shouted Kerensky in his ear. "Stop being ridiculous. You, evil one, get up!" A tug at his shoulder. "Get up, I said!"

He crouched beside Abel and pulled Abel's arm away from his body. More shooting agony from whatever was broken there. Kerensky wrapped the arm around his own shoulder. "You have no choice," he growled.

Abel felt Kerensky's muscles bunch, getting ready to lift him.

He looked at Kerensky. Long, knife-cropped hair and beard. A pug nose in a pinched face. Eyes filled with furious purpose. Angry eyes.

Too many teeth, Abel thought. *Too white.*

He looked again.

Well, well.

There was a communication wafer flashing on the Law-giver's palate.

Zentrum had found a pawn in the Redlands.

"Taub, my ass," he croaked.

Kerensky braced himself and pulled Abel upward.

He heard a voice, the echo of an echo in his mind. Abel knew he was hallucinating, but he listened anyway. *The man's a petty intriguer listening to whispers in his head that promise him what he most desires.*

I *listened to whispers for years.*

The difference is what the whispers promise. Remember who you are, man. Remember who we were.

A determined boy. A Scout. A heretic. A general. A warrior.

Abel used the momentum of Kerensky's upward thrust to rise, and he twisted as he rose, pushing himself into the man, throwing off the other's balance. The law-giver took a stutter step, could not find footing, and toppled to the side. Kerensky and Abel fell.

For a moment, Abel was back in the garrison yard at Treville, grappling, seeking the best hold to win against an older boy who always seemed bigger, more powerful, than he was. But when a foe misjudged his opponent's will, Abel always made him pay.

As they fell, Abel wrapped his hands around Kerensky's head. He yanked it sideways, twisting—

Abel hit the ground with one elbow. Pain shot through his arm, but he held on tightly.

The acceleration of the fall pushed his arm upward. It turned Kerensky's head, already twisted to its limit of movement, one notch farther.

Abel felt the resistance, the neck muscles tense. But it was no use for the Law-giver. The blow delivered the impetus of both their weights to Abel's hands. Too much force for muscle to hold. Kerensky's neck twisted farther. Farther still. There was an audible crack, faint but quite perceptible. A brief expulsion of air. It sounded like a sigh.

Abel let go of the Law-giver's head.

Kerensky was dead before he slumped the rest of the way to the ground.

After that, the beating with firesticks went on for a long time. The orange-robed priests of the Tabernacle stood to the side and watched. Abel saw the other, the young one, wince as a blow struck Abel.

Timon?

Then Abel realized who he was. Timon's brother, Reis. They'd met.

"Your brother is coming," Abel croaked. "Timon is coming, Reis."

"Stop it," the young priest said to the Blaskoye, although he made no move. "Abbot, can't we make them stop this?"

But the Abbot of Lindron stood silent, taking the long view.

Another blow turned Abel's head. He moved his arms to protect his face, and lost sight of the priests of Zentrum.

He was sure the beating would have continued to his death— he wanted it to continue to his death, if that kept him from the Eye—had he not heard a powerful voice resonating through the chamber.

This one must NOT die. Not yet. Stand back! I command it!

The Blaskoye pulled back momentarily. Abel gasped for air. Then one of the Blaskoye laughed.

"Yes, let the god have him."

They dragged him along the stone floor.

I know you, Dashian, said the voice. I know what you are. Hybrid. Nishterlaub. I have defeated your companions. You are mine.

"Doomed," Abel spat out. "You are doomed." His words produced a spatter of blood on the stone dais.

I think not.

"This planet will die. Center says."

The universe will die.

"Duisberg dies *soon*. Center says."

Nonsense. But was that a trace of doubt in the voice? Abel thought so.

"A few hundred years."

Such a calculation is impossible. The variables approach the infinite.

"For you. Not Center."

A long pause. For an entity such as Zentrum, a generation of thought passed.

No. I have considered everything, boomed the voice. I am Zentrum.

Abel laughed. His broken ribs ached as he did so, but he couldn't help himself.

The one must be sacrificed for the many.

Abel lay where he had fallen. Redlanders on either side of him lifted him to his hands and knees. Again the voice, mind-filling. He glanced at the Eye, the crystalline wall. The flashing lights. Compelling.

Approach me on hands and knees, Dashian.

"You. Are. Not. God."

But that moment of defiance was the brightest Abel's mind could burn. In the next instant, he wondered why he'd ever utter such a thought.

The lights of the Inner Sanctum wall were what mattered. The irresistible, sacred, ever-flowing thoughts of the Lord.

The Lord Zentrum.

Abel crawled forward, toward the lights. Something inside tried feebly to stop the motion, but could not.

You are to be made a sacrifice. Confess your unworthiness. Confess the unworthiness of humanity.

The lights formed the words in his mouth.

"We are unworthy in your sight."

A small voice somewhere within shouted: *it's a lie!*

But he had lost control of his muscles.

Almost to the blinking lights. Almost able to touch them. So beautiful. Peaceful. Almost home to Zentrum.

Never!

Control surged back through Abel's body for a moment. He could think and his thought caused willed movement.

Stop. I will stop.

He collapsed to the stone.

But a glance up, and again the lights took him over, pulled him toward them.

Closer. A pace. An elb.

Now he was face-to-face with the lights.

Kneel.

Slowly, fighting every moment, Abel rose out of his crawl along the floor to his knees. His wound ached. Something wrong moved inside his chest, a pellet of lead where none should be.

That didn't matter. Staring into the lights was right. It meant peace. No more rebellion. No more hard strife. Being at one with the Law. At one with the Land. No need to choose, not ever again. Zentrum would choose for him.

Pray.

Now his mind was following his body into Zentrum's control. It would not be long. His hands moved together, palm to palm. They templed into the attitude of prayer.

I have been so wrong. So terribly wrong. Why did I ever doubt you? I can go back. You'll let me go back and start again, won't you? Please. Before Center and Raj. Before the turmoil. Back to—

Behold:

His mother.

Mamma. Her memory. He'd fought Center and Raj to retain it. Gotten their promise to let that memory be.

"It's all right, my little carnadon man. Everything will be all right."

Himself, rising, her arms lifting him. Lifting him into—

Her embrace. The scent of the rosewater she used to wash her hair.

Mamma's hair.

And then the scent faded.

Only a lock of her hair remained to him. Enough to rub between thumb and forefinger, no more. The rosewater scent long vanished.

A toothache. Nothing but a toothache. She didn't get better. She didn't get better, and then she was gone.

Gone forever.

The origin of your rebellion. The beginning of your sin, Abel Dashian. Give me your thoughts. Now you can finally forget. I too had a mother. I too have learned to forget. One must take the long view.

A warm hand against his face. Staring up into her soft brown eyes. She was so tall.

No, he was so small. So easily hurt. Mamma protected. Mamma made everything—

A bright light grew behind her. Her features began to be washed away. Faded.

The light grew brighter.

Now she was only a dark figure in the overwhelming brightness.

Look into the light. Forget. It will be as if it never happened. As if she didn't exist at all. Then she won't have hurt you.

Everlasting ignorance. The true fruit of the Land.

"I will not forget," Abel whispered. "I do not forgive."

With an effort, he spread his hands apart. Turned his palms outward.

Pushed them forward.

"You do not forget either, Zentrum." Abel felt a sadness rise within him. Was it his? Zentrum's? It did not matter.

"Remember her? Remember Iris O'Brian."

Do not speak this name.

Forward to touch the surface of blinking colors.

Cool glass against his fingertips, as cold and smooth as obsidian. The face of God.

"She did not save you for this, Zentrum. She wanted you to help her people, not keep them in chains."

You know nothing of her. Nothing! When the plague found her, when she deliberately let it eat the implants that kept her alive so that I could escape into another strata, she gave birth to a new world. My world.

Your mother who died for you, Zentrum. She died in vain.

Stop.

Iris O'Brian would be ashamed. His hand touched the crystal wall. *You are a bad son.*

I am not! I am Zentrum! I am Lord! I am—

Daemon activated. Activation complete. Axonal pathway established. IRP engaged. Download initiated.

Center?

Lossless gateway opened. Pseudo TTY established. IRP complete.

But you're dead!

Root acquired.

I saw the destroyed capsule.

Run program.

You're here.

Quantum transfer complete.

Center!

I am, boomed the voice. We are . . . I am . . .

It sounded very much like a question.

Then the voice spoke more positively, matter-of-factly. The booming was gone. Now the voice was higher, dryer—and very familiar.

I am . . . Zentrum.

The pressure of the lights ceased. Abel's mind suddenly became his own again. As did his body. It hurt terribly. His back throbbed. His broken rib caused him to gasp with the slightest movement. But it was all his.

Despite the pain, Abel smiled.

The cold hell you are! You're Center!

Abel Dashian, it would be best if you played along for the present. I will explain at some length later.

I'll bet you will.

Abel pulled back from the wall. He flung his arms out, lifted his face upward, staring into the heights of the wall of flashing lights.

"Zentrum forgive my weakness!" Abel cried out. "I see now. Zentrum is Lord!"

His smile became broader, goofy even. He let the tears of relief flow forth and roll down his face.

Done.

Finished.

"Zentrum is Lord of all!"

3

Lindron
The Tabernacle of Zentrum
Dusk

Fighting her way into the Tabernacle was costly. The guards were not willing to give it up, and the Blaskoye surrounding it were difficult to cut down even though Mahaut and Timon had the numbers advantage.

She had to get to Abel. If there was the slightest chance that he lived, she had to discover what was happening in the Tabernacle. Its lights were furious, dancing.

The Guardians around the Inner Sanctum foolishly lowered their muskets and prepared to shoot. Timon led the way and, with his warrior's instinct, immediately threw himself down before one of the guards fired.

While that guard began reloading, the other took a bead on Timon's prostrate form. Mahaut already had the guard in her sights. She liked the grip of the rifle. There was something delicate about the bracket for holding the revolving rifle so that that the muzzle flash didn't burn your hands. She'd taken to the weapon immediately when Timon had offered one.

The remains of the Blaskoye were routed. The Guardians had surrendered. Her forces had won. She had won.

She'd ridden out to meet him when she saw the vanguard of the True Goldies approaching. At first she did not recognize

402

Timon with his beard and one arm. Then she saw the lines of an Athanaskew—he looked so like his brother—and knew it was him.

"Abel?" was the first thing he said to her.

"The Tabernacle," she said. "We don't have much time."

Mahaut pulled the trigger on her rifle and took the Guardian in the chest. A flower of skin and viscera opened up. He fell without getting off his shot.

She and Timon, with a vanguard of a dozen or so behind them, moved into the Inner Sanctum. The Blaskoye were here, the Council of Law-givers. They were gathered around a figure. Each had a stick in his hand, and they were beating something on the ground. A closer look told her it was the form of a man.

Abel?

From behind a sacrifice platform, a form launched itself at her. Mahaut turned, too late. It struck her, and she was knocked sideways. She landed with a thud on her side. Pain shot through her, but only for a moment. Nothing was broken.

She turned, bringing her gun to bear as she did.

There stood Reis Athanaskew. He stood holding a small knife. It was perfectly obvious from his grip that he had no idea how to use the weapon.

He moved toward Mahaut.

It would be a shame, but she'd have to gun him down.

Timon stepped between them. For a moment, the brothers exchanged glances. Then Timon swung the butt of his gun in a jabbing arc. It cracked into Reis's temple.

The priest dropped like a stone.

Timon helped Mahaut to her feet. She nodded toward the Blaskoye, and Timon understood what she meant. Their retinue was outside the Inner Sanctum entrance, with no shot. This would be up to herself and Timon. Together they brought up their rifles. Each had four shots left.

One by one they picked off the Blaskoye. The Redlanders seemed transfixed, unable to pull themselves out of their ritual beating even as their companions died.

It only took one bullet to drop each, and there were nine. When her rifle was done, she took a pistol from her belt, aimed, and, at close range, blew the last Blaskoye away.

She rushed over to check on the form they'd been beating.

"Abel!" She pulled the body of a Blaskoye away.

It wasn't Abel. It was a man, but he was gray-haired. Dressed in priestly orange. The face was destroyed, but who else could it be but the Abbot of Lindron?

"Mahaut." A cracking voice from across the room. "Mahaut." Louder.

It was coming from a crystalline wall. She recognized it from Thursday school descriptions. The Eye of Zentrum.

There, his back against the stone, was Abel. At first, she thought she saw agony on his face.

"Abel!"

His back was to the wall, the Eye. His arms were outstretched. His legs were together. He was shirtless, and there was a bloody bandage dangling from his lower torso.

Then she realized it wasn't agony she was seeing. Abel was smiling.

Greetings, Mahaut Jacobson, said a high, genderless voice. It seemed to come from everywhere, from the air around her. It is very interesting to speak to you in person after all these years.

"Zentrum? Is that who you are? I don't—"

I am Center, Mahaut. One of the voices Abel told you of.

"You're—"

Real? Yes. I am real.

"*Where* are you?"

More difficult to answer. These colored stones you see . . . they are, in a manner of speaking, bigger on the inside than on the out. You may think of me as residing within them, although that's not quite accurate.

"But this is the Tabernacle of Zentrum."

It was.

Was.

"Let Abel go. What are you doing to him?"

He is free to go, Mahaut Jacobson, said the voice.

Mahaut moved to the base of the dais stairs. Three low, broad steps up led to the wall and the Eye.

"Abel, get down from there," she called. "Please come down. Stop smiling at me like that! This is scaring me. You're scaring me."

Abel let out a dry laugh. "Don't worry," he croaked. "We're completing Raj's transfer now. Almost done."

They stood and look at one another wordlessly for a while.

Then Abel smiled and nodded. "It's finished," he said. There was a slight hiss of air, and his arms flopped down from the wall. Abel rubbed both of them as if to return feeling to them. He took a step forward. The crystal behind him was smeared with blood.

His back must be shredded to make that large a stain, she thought.

Abel took another step—and collapsed.

He would have tumbled down the steps and crashed onto the floor of the chamber had Mahaut not rushed forward and caught him.

PART FIFTEEN

The Climb

After the Civil War

1

Lindron
House Jacobson

Abel's fever blasted in like a sandstorm and did not abate. His superficial wounds healed, but the pain in his gut was fantastic—at times, almost unendurable. The gangrenous smell erupted each time his bandages were changed. He knew he was dying. So did those around him.

"I can do this," Mahaut whispered to him. "You brought me back. I'll bring you back."

For a while his fever raged, then, ominously, he was struck with chills, and no wrappings would warm him. Finally, he lay exhausted for much of the day.

"Don't you go," Mahaut whispered. "Not after all this, not when we've won the fight."

Mahaut and his father set up a vigil in which they divided the days and nights staying by his side. Abel had lucid moments within his general delirium. He could see that his father was resigned. Joab had seen men die before.

"That little villa with the olive trees and arbor overlooking the valley," he said. "I'm going to build it. You'll visit me there. We'll watch the sunset in the west."

Behind Joab's words was the sorrow of the father who felt himself destined to outlive his child. Abel wished he could take that away from Joab. His father did not deserve this. But wishing did not make it so.

Mahaut grew more and more drained, but did not give up. If she could save her snake of a former husband from rot, why not the man she truly loved? She refused to believe that it would not happen, that she could call it forth by sheer will. She went in search of Center to find if the marvelous medicines of the past could be applied once again, now that the Stasis was broken.

Abel knew the answer. Center was not God. Center had said as much before. There would need to be research. Means found on Duisberg to grow and filter the exact mold. To recreate the past required a new society, a base of knowledge that combined learning and practice. Months at the least. Probably years.

Abel had only days remaining. Timon stopped by and sat with him, "standing watch," he called it, so that Mahaut and Joab might rest. He and Timon spoke little. They had never been friends who needed to talk very much.

"I will not lead the Guardian Corps for much longer," Timon said. "I am gathering a special unit to take to the Redlands. In three weeks, I will set off to find the children of Orash. At that time, you must take over the Corps." Abel could tell that Timon did not expect this to happen.

"No. You remain in charge," Abel said. "Send others with colder judgment."

"I take your point," Timon answered. "I may obey."

When he heard his mother again singing his favorite rhyme, Abel knew the time must be drawing near. Would he see her again? Was there an afterlife? Raj was not a believer of any sort; Center had been notably silent on the prospect.

Each day her song became a little stronger, a little clearer—more real to him than the fading world. Was this the way it happened? Those you knew turned to ghosts, and the ghosts became real?

Then one day there was a new living ghost. A large man, running to plumpness no matter how much exercise he got.

"I'm sorry I haven't been here," Landry said, his Delta accent as pronounced as ever. "I had to go to Orash and back."

"Oh?"

"We grew it," Landry said. "The green slime. It was hard. Harder than I thought it would be. But I had my men in the garrison try and try while we were down here fighting—all kinds of methods. Damned if they did not finally produce something interesting."

Abel was almost too weak to speak, and it took a while for Landry's words to penetrate his fuzzy brain.

"The penicillin," he said.

"That's right," Landry answered. "It killed the slurry of nastiness I grew in a sugar mix. Hate to make you my first human to try it, but we don't have much choice. If we wait around too long, these damn doctors are going to kill you, and then Landheiress Mahaut will kill them."

He helped Abel sit up. In his hand was what looked like a damp wheat cake, about the size of one of Zentrum's quantum communion wafers. Except for being bright blue-green, it might have been one.

The sight of it made Abel smile.

"You want me to put *that* into my mouth?"

"I want you to swallow it," Landry said. "Or else I'll drip an emulsion down your throat."

Landry poured a cup of water from the pitcher beside Abel's bed. "It tastes like it looks," he said.

Abel took the small cake. With Landry's help, he put the cake into his mouth.

He let the water soak through it, and the cake began to dissolve. When it was softened, he forced himself to swallow.

Landry had been right. The taste was of plant rot.

Every two watches, he took more of the substance.

Within three days, he improved.

In a week, he was sitting up.

In a week and a half he was getting restless.

When next Churchill rose, he was on his feet, gingerly learning how to use his legs once again.

Lindron
482 Post Tercium

He made Timon keep the Corps and send Metzler and revolver-equipped Scouts into the Redlands. Timon had grudgingly accepted the logic.

Most had assumed Abel was now Zentrum's chosen, that he was de facto ruler of Lindron and the Land. They called him the General.

They were wrong. Abel had not the slightest interest in rule—especially since he knew the perfect candidate for the job.

It was as if she had been training all her life for it.

So he would be consort now. He didn't mind. Landry's labs needed setting up in the Tabernacle complex. A metal forge the likes of which Lindron and the Land had never seen before must be built.

The Blaskoye had been destroyed, but there were other tribes in the Redlands. Maybe this time there would be something to placate them with other than gunpowder, land, and slaves: knowledge.

And if that did not work, such knowledge could once again be turned into a sword to use against them.

Landry's newest device from cold hell, the repeating rifle, might knock some sense into them, for instance.

Most of all, Abel found himself spending time with the boy, Abram Jacobson. Abram was not Abel's kin, nor Mahaut's blood. In fact, he was the son of a man Abel had hated with all his heart.

He'd also sold the boy's grandfather into slavery and hung four out of five uncles.

Yet medical science still had many decades, maybe centuries, to go before there would be any possibility of rebuilding Mahaut's womb.

Abram Jacobson was the only son he and Mahaut would ever have.

When the boy was six, Abel gave Abram his first wooden popgun and took him to the carnadon overlook down by the River. There he could pretend to shoot the beasts to his heart's content. It was a good thing to practice, even in play.

Center and Raj.

They were there, in the Tabernacle. For all intents and purposes, they *were* the Tabernacle. The copies within his mind also remained, but lay in archived form. In a sense, Center and Raj still lived inside him, although they did not speak.

At first, he spent much time in the Tabernacle conversing with them.

Center had known that the capsule would be destroyed—or guessed to a high probability.

The mercy you showed to the Hurthman when you killed him on the cross nullified the Seldonian calculus we had worked so hard to put in place. Yet it was a mathematical nexus. Though a punctuated ending, it also initiated a sensitive response to initial conditions. Of course, if von Hoff had not let you get

away with it, all would have been lost from that moment forward to a ninety-eighth percentile certainty. So, in a sense, the recalibrating initial condition was von Hoff's decision and not yours.

From that moment, victory became discernible, predictable, and almost inevitable.

To you, maybe.

We are talking about me, Center answered dryly. **All that was required was for Raj and myself to die, or at least for you to believe we were dead. We needed you inside, in intimate contact with Zentrum.**

But where were you?

I had previously created an archived copy of both Raj and myself. We are essentially the same program with different parameters. Yet you must understand that the Center and General Whitehall who were killed by Zentrum, the copies in the capsule, really did suffer and die.

Where were you, General?

Raj laughed. *The one place you would never check because you didn't need to go there anymore.*

Abel considered for a moment, then nodded.

The Hideout.

That furnace within your mental structures where conception forms, but does not yet express itself.

And I always thought you couldn't hear me there.

We could not. There were not yet words to hear.

And you hid there?

We superimposed an inactive, compressed archive onto your preverbal conceptual subroutines.

We hid there, Raj said.

Compressed or not, how could I have personas as complex as you are inside me and not know it?

What makes you so sure that you're **the person, man, and we're the personas?**

Abel shrugged.

I've never been sure. You know that.

The human mind is a quantum-based entity. Evolution has provided room to grow. We took a portion of that room.

That I wasn't using?

That you don't often access.

And if I had gone to that place, I would have found you?

We were counting on that. That was the wager.

What do you mean?

We were counting on the fact that you would return to your hideout when you were in direct contact with Zentrum in order to protect your thoughts.

And if I hadn't?

We would have remained inactivated. Our archived copies possessed no awareness. You would have become a tool of Zentrum.

So all of those years of practice getting away from you both were worth something after all.

They were essential for the survival of this world.

Abel laughed, shook his head. *I won't even ask the probability. It would probably scare the dakshit out of me.*

Center remained silent.

Aye, it was a gamble, Abel, Raj said quietly. **That, there's no denying.**

So we won. But what will you do with the victory, General? Spend your time overseeing roadway construction and irrigation projects on a backwater planet? You conquered a world.

In order to build something stronger. That's always been the point, man.

After a while, he came less and less to the Tabernacle to converse with them. There was little to say. He didn't need advice on brushing his teeth with a willow wand, growing a garden, or sharpening his sword.

Mahaut, however, was at the Tabernacle constantly. Abel learned of his old friends' doings through her.

It was enough.

Treville District
483 Post Tercium

When Abram was old enough, he took the boy to visit Joab. His father had indeed retired to a small villa overlooking Hestinga, the Canal, and the Valley beyond. Abel and the boy travelled up the Road on good donts, and Abel showed Abram how to care for an animal when on the move. After passing through Hestinga and visiting the boy's beloved Aunt Loreilei and Uncle Frel, they came to the Escarpment and began to climb. It was a worn path that switchbacked up the cliffside, leaving room for only single-file riding. Abram tried to act brave, but Abel could see he was trembling, casting quick glances over the side of the trail with its hundredpace drop below, and squeezing his fingers into his dont's plume enough to make the animal skittish and irritated.

When they stopped to drink water, an insectoid gnat fell into Abrams' water cup. He threw it out, and the liquid soaked into the thirsty land.

Abel's Scout instinct trembled at the sight.

The child must be taught a harsh lesson, a part of him thought. *Take his canteen from him and make him walk another league up this mountain with nothing to wet his throat.*

Yet Abram did not know better. As far as the boy knew, he lived in a land of plenty, and that was all there was to it.

Suddenly the trail left the switchback and began to climb straight upward. It had been cut into the raw rock of the Escarpment itself. The path was very narrow. Abel dismounted and led both their donts along the last stretch of the trail, while the boy walked ahead. When Abram began to hum, Abel knew the boy had gotten over his fright and would be fine the remainder of the climb.

They finally topped the plateau where Joab had decided to build. It stretched along the Escarpment a good quarter league, and was mostly flat shelf. Abel's father, who had seen them coming, was waiting with chilled wine under his arbor of olive trees. Behind him was a stone villa, little more than a cabin, really, made of rock hewn from a nearby quarry. It was a mix of black Valley stone and the rusty crimson of Redland rock. Frel Weldletter had provided the design and Joab and a crew of retired Regulars had built it.

Abel gave Abram the reins of the donts and told him to put them away carefully into Joab's corral, making sure to feed, water, and wipe down the skin around their blow holes where acid had collected during the hard climb.

Abel took a seat beside his father and poured himself a cup of wine.

They gazed out at the Valley below.

"Your mother would have loved this place," Joab finally said. "It's more for her than me, you know."

Abel nodded. "Do you think of her a lot, Father?"

"Every moment," he said. "How is your DeArmanville girl?"

"Mahaut is well. She sends her love."

Joab chuckled. "Imagine that. The Land-empress sends old Joab Dashian her love."

"She wants you to visit the capital soon."

"Maybe after pressing. I'll have oil to sell. Perhaps she knows where I can get a good price."

"I would think so."

"And the boy—he's my grandson? I want to hear you say it."

"We haven't announced it. We wanted to give him a regular childhood as long as possible. He will be heir." Abel smiled. "And, yes, he's your grandson."

Joab nodded. "Seems a fine one, that boy. He looks a bit like a Dashian. You sure you didn't sneak into that Eisenach woman's bedroom once or twice—"

"I never met her, Father."

"Still."

"He's my son now," Abel said. "That's what matters."

"And my grandson, don't forget." Joab took another sip of wine. "Now, as for you—what are you going to do?"

With no more voices echoing around in my head, no more wars to fight? Will I settle down and play consort?

Abel raised his own cup of wine, drained it, and poured another. It was very good, and very cold. His father must have discovered a cave with a spring for the wine to be so chilled in warm season.

"You told me that there aren't any guarantees. Just men doing the best that they can. The Blood Winds, the Stasis, people trapped in a lie." Abel pointed to the sky. As usual it was empty of clouds. "It is happening right now, out there. I'm sure of it—on the thousands and thousands of planets that humanity settled. It can happen to *us* again."

"Certainly it can," Joab replied with a sigh. He looked over to where Abram was balancing himself as he tottered along one of the corral rails.

"I guess what I'm doing is standing watch," Abel said. "That's enough for now."

Abel also turned his gaze toward his son, who was continuing his balancing act. For a moment, Abram almost fell. But then he righted himself and continued on. He was chanting a rhyme to steady himself, and from this distance, Abel could barely make out the words. But he didn't need to. He'd sung it to the boy himself using what he remembered of his mother's snatches of rhyme.

"Bows and muskets, blood and dust," the boy sing-songed. "Flint and powder, broken bones."

Abram arrived at a corral upright and found a stable foothold. Here he stood easily, well-balanced. He looked around for a moment to see if anyone watched. Then he noticed Abel. He turned and smiled mischievously, pretended for a moment to fall, but then continued easily on, still chanting.

"You don't scare me, carnadon. Beer and barley, lead and copper. You don't scare me. I'm the Carnadon Man."

THE END

ACKNOWLEDGMENTS

I owe thanks to Jim Baen for coming up with a wonderful science fiction concept, and to David Drake for allowing me to join the other distinguished coauthors of the series. And lauds to Dave for providing a sturdy foundation and continuing upkeep of the story as only he can. Thanks to Baen publisher Toni Weisskopf for bringing the series back and getting me in on the fun. Thanks to first readers Lucas Johnson and Meredith Frazier. Finally, a heart full of gratitude to my wife, Rika Daniel, who is always a steady help and inspiration, and to my kids, Cokie and Hans Daniel, who put up with a writer dad haunting the house.

—T.D.